DARKRIDGE HOLLOW

NICKY SHEARSBY

SRL Publishing Ltd
London
www.srlpublishing.co.uk

First published worldwide by SRL Publishing in 2024

ISBN: 978-1915-073-30-3

1 3 5 7 9 10 8 6 4 2

A CIP catalogue record for this book is available from the British Library

SRL Publishing is a Climate Positive publisher offsetting more carbon emissions than it emits.

Day One

1

I didn't know it, but today was set to trigger a catastrophe I couldn't foresee, a pivotal moment spiralling us towards disaster. It was bad enough I was lost, although in fairness I'd been lost for months, psychically, emotionally—my recently deceased wife the pitiful reason for such a sorry state of affairs. I no longer knew where I was going or what I was doing, the idea of finding a small, isolated town in Midwest America, seemingly impossible. A crumpled piece of scented paper sat in my hand, inconsequential directions scribbled hurriedly, my wife's handwriting fading rapidly. I needed to relax. After all, nothing good ever came from stress.

I glanced to my right, exasperated by my daughter's continued huffing and head shaking, my inability to keep us en-route ensuring I was unable to think straight. It didn't matter. To my sulky adolescent daughter, the details of today's journey were irrelevant. She'd already deduced with confirmed defiance and folded arms that, at *some* point, we would get to our destination. How I achieved that end was entirely *my* problem. The poor kid didn't need to know I lived every day on a knife-edge, my existence questionable, and I didn't want her to look at me with sympathies she couldn't sustain. Georgina was suffering enough, her grief ensuring she'd be stuck in limbo for the rest of her life, the drunk driver responsible for sideswiping our existence, wholly unaware what his actions had started. It was unfortunate a lack of direction had now rendered me obsolete in the eyes of my young charge, *my* grief making everything worse, this day threatening to join the chaos that had become my life. I hoped she would one day forgive me for losing her mum, losing my way something I couldn't have helped.

Of course, today's task sounded simpler in theory than it was in reality to achieve. The steering wheel of this rental vehicle was on the wrong side of the car, the wrong side of the *road* alien to my thinking. I was stuck in this blisteringly hot, confined space with a hormonal twelve-year-old and I didn't assume things could get much worse. The continued grunted sighs emanating from my right ensured no matter what I did, this day was never going to end well.

'Where *are* we?' Georgina was staring out of the window, her headphones over her ears, her innocent question incapable of reclaiming any logic I assumed I possessed.

'Somewhere.' I was convinced I could retrace my steps, eventually, go back a few miles, take a different route. *Oh, the irony.* Of course, if the sat nav continued to misbehave, I didn't stand a chance. I doubted the thing knew *where* to direct me, the image on the screen oddly placing us in the middle of a field. It didn't matter. It was my fault we were lost—a bad workman and all that.

'Somewhere?'

'Yes. *Somewhere.* We always have to be somewhere, Georgie, it's the law of physics.' I was stressed, failing to dislodge my irritation, my daughter failing to distract this moment with anything of value. The map I'd earlier purchased wasn't helping, these roads unfamiliar, navigation left to a young girl who could barely read them. It might have been funny had my stress levels been less heightened. Yet, my child innocently believed the shapes printed on the oversized, awkwardly folded paper in her possession were nothing more than haphazard doodles she couldn't understand the logic of. She couldn't appreciate how *anyone* could make sense of directions drawn on a flat surface, her inability to transfer what she was looking at on paper into the real world frustrating us both.

It didn't help that the monotone electronic voice in the background barely contributed. I couldn't turn it off. We'd be driving *forever* if I did. I didn't mean to snap at the poor kid. I was supposed to be the grown-up, the one in control. I wasn't about to share my failing emotions with my daughter, of course, *control* something I hadn't experienced for some time. Besides, we'd never travelled this far beyond familiarity before. Arguments were inevitable.

'Sorry,' I breathed, reaching a free hand across the central console to rub my daughter's exasperated shoulder blade. 'I'm just hot.' I wanted to bring our moment back on track, apologise, offer a smile she might appreciate, any meaningful words of no real relevance right then. She'd kept me functioning more than she could comprehend, the last few months leaving me a fragment of the man I once was. It was a shame she didn't know.

'Oh, and I'm *not?'* Georgina sighed sarcastically, tugging her headphones around her neck, allowing the muted noise she classed as music to filter into the car.

Her long dark hair was pulled into a high ponytail, her torn, baggy trousers and skull-laden vest top failing miserably to showcase the bright personality my young charge usually possessed. I assumed her continually changing appearance was a coping mechanism—an attempt to protect her identity in a world where she could be anyone, do anything. She needed to find her voice, her way. I knew how she felt. I glanced at my flush-cheeked girl, today's outfit an eclectic blend of two styles she couldn't decide upon. Was it Goth or Punk? PunkGoth, Poth? Gunk?

'*What?*' Georgina had turned her attention to me, the passing farmland of no interest, brow furrowed, her deep blue eyes piercing the side of my flustered head. I was grinning. I couldn't help it. It was unfortunate my expression had no real emotion attached to it aside from temporary amusement I couldn't subdue.

'Your mum would have been proud of the young woman you're becoming,' I chided, nudging her playfully on the arm, trying to concentrate on the road and failing. I almost burst into tears with the magnitude of my own words, a sudden sting behind my sinuses forcing me to take a lungful of air.

'Come on, Dad. Stop it.'

'Stop what?'

'You don't have to do that.'

'Do *what?*' I hoped she couldn't see the tears perched in my incessantly saddened eyes, the wobble in my throat undeniable. I didn't want her to assume me weak, and I couldn't afford to break down in front of her. But it was true. Anna *would* have been proud to see her little girl experimenting with new styles, growing up—the make-up and clothing she'd taken from her mother's wardrobe keeping her busy. Anna wouldn't have minded, and I wasn't planning on clearing out her belongings any time soon. They still smelled of the woman we missed more than either of us had yet accepted, the scented paper in my hand testimony to a painful realisation that we'd be clinging to our memories forever.

'You don't have to bring Mum into every conversation we have. I'm hardly about to forget who she was.' Her map-reading attempts were now forgotten, ruffled paper discarded on the dashboard.

Georgina may have been right, but I couldn't help it. She was twelve, forced to grow up without the mum who adored every hair on her head, every freckle on her cheeks memorized in detail. I was trying to keep Anna's memory alive and ensure Georgina never forgot how loved she was. How loved she will *always* be. I took a breath, swallowing thoughts I couldn't afford to share.

'Sorry.'

'And stop saying *sorry*. It's hardly *your* fault.' Georgina pulled her headphones over her ears again, irritated by words I couldn't help expressing, slumping deep into the passenger seat. She folded her arms across her chest, tantrum in full swing.

I took a breath and held it. It wasn't my fault but I couldn't help feeling guilty. It wasn't fair that her mum had died unexpectedly, leaving her young child to placate *me* in the process, *her* emotions left out in the cold. It wasn't fair neither of us knew how to deal with our pain, my hormonal child having far more excuses for unchecked agitation than I did. I had no genuine idea how to deal with this. It was embarrassing. I was still coming to terms with the fact I'd never see my wife again—our lives cut painfully short by an event no one saw coming. And now, to make matters worse, we were travelling across America, attempting to locate the town where Anna was born, a place we'd talked about visiting for years. *Nothing* about this was right.

'I *do* wish Mum was here, though,' Georgina muttered, willing at least to share some of my emotions, some of my burden. My child didn't look at me. She didn't need to. I patted her arm with a sigh of my own before turning my attention to a journey I never expected we would take without Anna. Still, we were here now, nothing to be done about that.

'I do, too,' I found myself replying, more to myself than to Georgina. I couldn't allow her to see my true emotions, my head in a murky place I was scarcely able to acknowledge. It wasn't something I'd anticipated sharing with anyone, especially my twelve-year-old. She didn't need to know how I dealt with my grief when the silence of the night became too much, nothing to do but battle hidden demons that lingered in the shadows of a once loving home. Anna hadn't yet been dead six months, our entire world slipping into slow motion without her infectious laughter—that fateful day one I will *never* forget.

I glanced to my right. Georgina had either fallen asleep or was ignoring me, avoiding having to deal with her deluded dad who barely found the time in his day to breathe let alone provide his growing girl with the support she desperately needed. I could do nothing about that, unfortunately. I was trying my best. Yet, it seemed my best wasn't good enough, my lapse in parental ability creating havoc I didn't know where to place, my lack of navigational skills ensuring I'd been driving for two hours in the *wrong* direction. I had no concept of nearby towns or how I would ever find my way back from the private isolation I'd unavoidably slipped into. I could understand my child's annoyance. She deserved better.

It would have been apparent to any onlooker that I wasn't coping with my grief, yet I wholly believed myself incapable of raising a child alone. What the hell did I know of such things? It was unfortunate I had no one on which to unload my suffering, no one to share my pain, so was left to my own devices, left to deal with whatever my brain cast into the ether. I couldn't burden Georgina with that shit. She had enough of her own to deal with. The truth was, I wasn't ready for a life without Anna, wasn't willing to accept a reality no one could change. I was bordering sanity, skirting the abyss, this day just another in a long, drawn-out battle with a ticking clock and abandoned promises. I despised the fact my time with Anna was nothing now but a terrifyingly brief moment in my tainted life, memories that would fade over time, lost to the confinement of ageing photographs.

I tapped the sat nav, no longer convinced the thing worked. Where *were* we? I didn't have a clue what I was doing, that truth becoming my life now, today no exception. I was driving along a U.S. highway, everything a hazy blur, my allocated map reader bored by the concept of watching for road signs and clues to our destination, my exhausted child far happier absorbed in music unfit for human consumption than observing me.

Darkridge Hollow was located somewhere between Cincinnati and Columbus, yet beyond that, I knew nothing. The old town had long succumbed to troublesome times, according to Anna, with most of its residents moving away decades ago. Many horror films were filmed here, apparently, many a true-life horror story to be told. Or so my wife had said. She often regaled me with tales of ghost towns and forgotten locations peppering the state of Ohio, the concept oddly mocking my decision to come here. I couldn't tell Georgina. I didn't need the taunted sarcasm or sideways glances. I was out of my depth, out of my mind to believe I could board a plane on a whim and see where we ended up, my vulnerable child lagging behind an apparent adventure I claimed we'd have; emotions I had no genuine idea how to appease left to their sorry devices.

'Are we *still* lost?' Georgina's query came from nowhere. She hadn't bothered opening her eyes, the idea of acknowledging her poor old dad unimportant, her metaphoric question of no real relevance to anything.

'We're not *lost,* just slightly diverted.' Who was I kidding? The roads stretched on for miles, no end in sight, one horizon extending to the next, few bends or turns to keep me alert. Junctions crept up on me without warning, veering off towards isolated farms that dotted the landscape. The entire place was beautiful yet alien to my brain, the wrong side of the road indifferent to my driving. My map was telling me one thing but logic was telling me something else.

'Remind me again *why* we came here, Dad?' Georgina sighed, shuffling in her seat. I felt sorry for her. At that precise moment, I assumed *anything* would have been better than my company, the last six months testimony to the fact I was barely present, barely functioning—just a terrible dad in the making. Poor kid.

'Your mum would have wanted us to see her hometown and track down her family.' It was true, I'm sure. Anna spoke fondly of her beloved Ohio and a childhood that sounded idyllic, yet I was troubled to admit she rarely spoke of her family. I didn't need to share that with Georgina. Was I right in assuming my wife would appreciate me telling them she was no longer with us? I presumed they would *want* to know.

'Yeah, Christmas and birthdays have been *great* fun,' my daughter scoffed, peering sarcastically through a fringe of thick, ruffled hair.

'Less of the sarcasm please, young lady.' Georgina was right, of course, but I couldn't confirm it. Although my wife shared many compelling stories of her life in America, it was troubling that we *never* heard from her family, never spoke of them, never spoke *to* them. Georgina never received Christmas or birthday cards, the occasional phone call or text message seemingly too much to ask. They didn't even know Anna and I were married, hadn't been told of our pending nuptials, had *not* been invited. Whenever I mentioned them, Anna would become moody and uncooperative and I learned not to push it. I always believed she would talk to me in her own time. It was unfortunate she could never now do that, something in the back of my mind nagging me. I couldn't tell what. It didn't matter. It was too late now anyway.

'I'm hot.' Georgina released an exaggerated sigh that threatened to take the air out of this car once and for all, removing us both from a world that had become impossibly strange and stark. Maybe she would be doing us a favour? She'd certainly be doing *me* one.

'There's a drink in the cooler on the back seat. I guess you Americans call it *soda?*' I adopted the strongest U.S. accent I could muster. I could *do* American when the moment called for it. I wanted to impress.

'Actually, in Ohio, it's called pop.' Georgina rolled her eyes again, nothing more to say about that.

'*Pop?* The same as in England.' Who knew? Apparently, I was way overthinking *that.* I smiled anyway. She was sounding more like her mother every day.

'I want an ice cream.'

I glanced at my child, cheeks flush, hair glued to her forehead in places where she'd leant sideways against the headrest for too long, flustered, bored. Despite attempting to act grown-up when the occasion called for it, times like these reminded me she was still just a child, still my baby girl. It *was* hot in here. She was right about that, the air-conditioning yet another thing in this annoying vehicle that didn't work.

'See if you can find a petrol station on that map.' I nodded towards the hastily folded sheet now lying mockingly across the dashboard.

'It's called a *gas* station, Dad.'

'Gas. Petrol. Whatever. Are we anywhere near one?' I resisted the urge to scoff, half expecting her to adopt the accent permanently, her mother's influence complete. Anna would no doubt be chuckling somewhere, watching her every move, watching *mine.*

'How am I supposed to know *where* we are?' Georgina sat upright, tugging her headphones around her neck again, raising exasperated hands towards passing fields and farmland, everything beyond the windows blurred, nothing of interest to placate my preoccupied pre-teen.

'I think we just passed mile 142, according to that blue sign.' I glanced in my rearview mirror, no time to double-check.

'What blue sign?'

'Does *anything* on the map look like mile 142?' I was flustered, my backside numb, my bones aching with continued stress.

'No.'

We both sighed at the same time.

It didn't matter. This was the United States of America. We would find salvation eventually, my body numbed by a continued sedentary position that should never be thrust upon anyone. This car was slowly entombing us, sending us sprawling towards something we couldn't have appreciated. It was probably just as well I couldn't see the future. Nothing good ever came from overthinking that shit.

2

Georgina's unnecessary sighs of frustration created irritation I didn't know where to place. I could no longer decipher reality from hyped emotions, my current lapse in cognitive function nothing more than unrequired misinformation left unchecked for too long. When I spotted a sign with the word "GAS" printed in large white letters, it provoked an impromptu yell for joy that almost gave the poor kid a heart attack. I either displayed exaggerated enthusiasm or screamed my head off. The day was slipping by with a vengeance and I didn't assume my young charge would appreciate the latter. I didn't want to drag her down with me, my mental health of no genuine relevance to anyone.

'Jesus Christ, Dad,' she muttered, shaking her head. I ignored her tone, her sarcasm, merely grateful for the respite I wasn't convinced I'd find inside this car. My belly churned unrelenting nausea that had nothing to do with the hunger I'd ignored for a while. I could barely stomach food anyway. Everything tasted like *shit*. We were desperate to use the facilities, Georgina's continued jigging up and down ensuring I needed to get out before I passed out or jumped out, whichever came first, this day already too much.

I took the next junction, glad to have found an escape, the highway services a welcome relief, a welcome sight. Georgina practically fell out of the car, unable to get the door open fast enough. Her legs ached – apparently – the groaning she proclaimed into the afternoon haze somewhat amusing. She was *twelve.* There literally was no hope for the girl. I filled the tank with fuel whilst being told expressively to use the term "gas" so I'd fit in better with the locals, my use of the word "highway" at least offering a molecule of passing satisfaction. I rolled my eyes. I could have done without the lecture. My head was pounding enough as it was.

The *gas* station attendant seemed as despondent as Georgina, his single-syllable grunts and head shakes reminding me my developing child would be going through a similar moody stage for some time to come. *Brilliant.* The kid didn't look much older than twenty, his facial hair more fuzz than beard, his attire more skater boy than professional service assistant. The badge on his t-shirt confirmed his name was Troy. I paid for my fuel, bought two oversized ice creams and left young Troy nestled behind the protection of his oversized counter. Mobile video games were more important to his day anyway, his uninterested, strained mutterings adding nothing to my dejected mood. I shook my head, the attitudes of teenagers never failing to annoy me.

Georgina was making the most of the afternoon sun, lying on the grass next to the car, arms across her face, peering skyward. She looked innocent and, for a moment, it stopped me in my tracks. I was anticipating another unrewarding conversation—further grunts of frustration. Yet, thankfully, words were unrequired once my daughter saw the ice creams, the squeal of delight released – by accident, of course – firmly noted by those around us. A few people smiled, noticing the elevated excitement on the face of my delighted child, this simple joy enough to turn her back into the sweet kid I miss so much.

Georgina didn't notice, too busy staring open-mouthed

at the colossal offering in my grip, temporarily happy to turn her attention to the real world and the dad in much need of appeasement. We sat on the grass verge, this moment one I wasn't about to forget. It didn't matter. I could taste nothing of value, my taste buds unwilling to allow such simple pleasures. I was grateful for the time we were given, my daughter giddy with the volume of sugar I was allowing her to consume, against my better judgment, against rational logic. I couldn't overthink the overhyped moment she'd be having in an hour's time.

I closed my eyes, visualising the roll of her mother's, and the shake of her flabbergasted head as she drilled metaphoric holes into the back of mine with her all-knowing stare. It was, however, comforting to see our child tucking into a rich layer of vanilla and rainbow sprinkles, my little girl still a baby in so many ways, still clinging to childhood. Either that or it was wishful thinking on my part. Whatever it was, I was happy for this moment, a contented dad. Time was slipping by so fast she'd be grown up with kids of her own if I wasn't mindful to appreciate this time whilst I still could. I leant on my elbows, staring skyward, happy to allow Georgina her overindulgence, no rush to get back into that overbearing car, no rush to reconnect with my failing emotions. Our bellies were full and our bladders were empty. Right then, all was good in our small, tainted world.

Georgina wasn't my biological child and I never openly confirmed that truth unless asked. Despite the fact I was a black man married to a white woman, I maintained the possibility that mix-raced kids didn't always inherit *every* gene, her hair dark enough for me to pretend that she was mine until someone pointed out the *obvious.* Yet, I loved that little girl more than I could ever express. She was *my* daughter in every way that mattered, needing me now more than I probably understood. I was the only dad she'd ever known, the only one she'd ever need, our lives in England meaning more than I could *ever* tell my sulky stepdaughter. She knew no other world than the one I'd created for her, my over-protectiveness knowing no bounds, our life in London, precious. She'd come into my life in the pouring rain, ready formed and cradled in Anna's arms, just seventeen months old—that wild winter afternoon one I'll never forget.

I didn't know which of us this journey was for, the very idea built on a promise made by a mother who could never now fulfil her deepest desires. Yet, despite having never met Anna's family, they deserved to know what had happened. After all, Georgina had grandparents she'd never met—aunts, uncles, cousins. My wife's unexpected removal from our lives had left so much unsaid, so much unresolved. It was uncomfortable to admit, painful even. I was driving on the wrong side of the road, struggling with oncoming traffic and only avoiding several collisions because of angry words and frustrated horns. *Everything* felt wrong—this entire place overwhelming, my surroundings far more consuming than I'd anticipated. I was out of my depth and I didn't like it.

Several exhausted families in weary station wagons ambled around us, discussing their journeys, their plans. Crying kids, barking dogs, dads with agendas and mums with headaches—big ideas, big dreams, this colossal country able to appease them all. I turned to see a young couple excitedly discussing their trip. I wouldn't have noticed them had I not recognised the accent, Scottish, their broad, rich vocals reminding me of the tiny island I'd left behind. I expressed a fond hello as they walked by, just an excited duo taking a well-earned break.

'English?' The guy stopped and held a broad hand towards me as if he couldn't believe he'd travelled so far to find a familiar accent aimed his way.

'Scottish?' I joked back, shaking his sweaty palm whilst

Georgina rolled uninterested eyes into the air. With sugar in her system, my pre-teen had returned with a vengeance. *Perfect.*

'You guys on holiday?' he queried, sliding a massive backpack from his shoulders to the ground, his rosy cheeks engulfing my paler versions, his broad Glaswegian accent strong. 'I didnae expect to find a fellow Brit out here.'

'Visiting family,' I confirmed, embarrassed I didn't know who such people were. I hadn't even seen a photograph of them. It didn't matter. This guy didn't need to know the details.

'With ye wee lassie?' He nodded towards Georgina who was leaning backwards across the car bonnet, face pointed into the sky, eyes squinting. A section of dark hair was sandwiched beneath her nose and upper lip, no participation offered as she watched distant clouds float by.

'I am indeed,' I confirmed proudly, knowing Georgina probably didn't care. She was ignoring me, avoiding this conversation, her dad of no immediate importance. I tilted my head, contemplating the muddled young thing in front of me and wondering what was going through her impressionable mind.

'My wife and I are touring the country, East to West,' the guy laughed, assuming I needed to know. He pointed to a woman in her mid-twenties, digging a torn map from the side pocket of her rucksack, unconcerned her husband had struck up a conversation with me. 'We got wed last week, so we're kinda on our honeymoon.' He was grinning, glad to be enjoying precious time with his new wife.

'Congratulations,' I replied, pleased to have been given something to think of other than myself. I *was* pleased for them, really I was, yet my thoughts drifted again to Anna, to *our* honeymoon. It felt so long ago. 'I don't suppose you know a place called Darkridge Hollow?' I needed to change the subject before I said something I'd regret. I was being unkind, I know, but I was hot, lost, and in the company of an annoying adolescent. Surely I could be forgiven?

'Dinnae ken.' The guy shrugged, offering me a blank smile. He didn't know and he probably didn't care. I could appreciate that.

I nodded, offering a brief smile and shrug of my own.

'The name's Mac, by the way,' he confirmed. 'And that fine wee filly over there is my wife, Morag.' He pointed a finger across the car park, a grin spread ear to ear. I remembered the feeling of being so much in love that nothing else existed. It wasn't ideal for me to ponder such memories. It wasn't Mac's fault.

'Josh,' I replied. 'And that sulky thing over there is my daughter, Georgie.' Georgina's exaggerated sigh was all the confirmation I needed as to the state of her mood for the rest of the day. It never fails to amaze me how she manages to hear every word I say when I *don't* need her direct attention.

'Nice to meet ye, Josh,' Mac concluded as he picked his rucksack from the ground. 'You too, Georgie,' he called over to my sulky, sugar-infused girl. She ignored him, of course. Too busy fiddling with her hair.

'Enjoy your holiday, Mac.'

'Aye. You too.'

Mac stepped away, returning much-needed attention to his newly acquired wife. A pang of sadness shot into my chest at the idea I would never again embrace Anna like *that*.

'Finished?' Georgina's snippy vocals reconnected us in a single dispassionate query. At least I still had something of utmost value that belonged to my wife. *Her child.*

'Have *you?*' I glanced towards her now empty ice cream container. She smiled, and for a split second, my kind, carefree young daughter returned. It was fleeting, of course, but I was happy to take whatever I could.

Our brief respite had at least given me a chance to check

the map again, retrace our steps and see where I'd gone wrong. These alien roads all looked similar to my sense of navigation, any ability to find my way missing from this trip *and* my existence. I appreciated why Georgina was finding it difficult to focus on anything I added to the equation. I didn't blame her at all.

***

Darkridge Hollow *was* difficult to find on the map, the place not so much a thriving town than a selection of forgotten streets whose existence no longer warranted valid attention. Blink and you'd miss it, according to Anna. The turn-off would be indicated by three agricultural silos towering from the landscape—the narrow lane running alongside the road almost impossible to see unless you knew where to look. It explained my uncooperative navigator sitting once more in the car, waiting for me to do something interesting.

'Are we *still* lost?' Georgina called sarcastically through the open window.

'No. I think we're good.' I wasn't convinced, yet I didn't want her to know this. The poor thing looked exhausted. I was still half-watching Mac and Morag enjoying their not-so-private moment, still half-wishing the last six months had been nothing more than a nightmare I'd wake up from soon.

Georgina's breath smelled of sugar and vanilla, her lips and chin coated with melted ice cream now drying in places. She didn't know. It was adorable. I wanted to lean into the car and kiss the top of her head, exactly how I used to—wet a finger, wipe her chin, exactly how her mum used to. Instead I handed her a tissue, pointing a wayward finger towards her cream-infused face as she looked at me with unseeing eyes. She wouldn't have appreciated the attention anyway, deeming such an action disgusting, *embarrassing,* my child no longer a willing participant in parental affection.

'It'll be a miracle if we *ever* get to Darkridge Hollow the way you're going,' she muttered, wiping her sticky mouth across a sleeve, ignoring the tissue in her hand, stabbing remnants of melted confectionery with a wooden spoon.

Although still only twelve and a month away from her thirteenth birthday, I could firmly see snippets of *teenager* seeping into her daily behaviour, the occasional sarcastic response. As a single dad, I didn't know how to deal with it, hormones something her mother should have appeased. Still, here we were, just the two of us, nothing to be done about that. We needed to make the best of a terrible situation. I climbed into the car, recounting directions I probably wouldn't sustain, imposing images of farm buildings doing nothing for my failing sense of deliberation.

Georgina looked hot again and just as flustered as me. I was still scanning the map, attempting to regain my bearings, the gas station attendee of no real help to *anyone.* His grunts of disinterest matched my child's, his attitude identical. We drove back onto the highway, our windows down, the afternoon traffic building steadily along with the incoming sugar rush I'd anticipated. I concluded I needed to continue south a little longer, that we would find Darkridge Hollow before nightfall, a hotel surely available *somewhere.* My child could then find sleep that had avoided us both for months. She looked as if she needed it.

We drove a few more miles, the continued straight road of route seventy-one hell-bent on driving me – excuse the pun – around the bend. When I eventually spotted those elusive grain silos in the distance, I couldn't help wondering if was imagining them. I slowed down, passing a battered green sign that displayed the words "Darkridge Hollow – 15", the turning upon us before I could think. Georgina sprang upright in her seat as I released a sharp "yes", the look she gave me matching the unimpressive manoeuvre I was about to make as I guided the car into the nearside lane. I was keen to leave this unrelenting road behind us, nothing more, yet that sign made me nervous. I had no idea why. I knew nothing about the place aside from what my wife had told me and had no reason to fear it. Whether it was anxiety over meeting Anna's family or something else, I couldn't tell, but whatever it was niggled my thoughts. The location seemed deliberately hidden, as if they didn't want tourists accidentally happening upon the place, unwanted, uninvited.

It had begun to rain and the afternoon heat produced a lingering haze that elevated my stress levels. I still had no genuine idea where I was going, merely grateful to have spotted at least *one* sign telling me Darkridge Hollow wasn't a figment of my imagination brought about by memories of my dead wife. A low mist had descended steadily across the road, changing my perception, changing the view. It created demonic shapes in my mind, my thoughts once again left to their own devices, my daughter collateral damage to it all.

The sun was to blame, of course, peeking through thickened clouds to blind me, droplets of rain and flickering reflections doing nothing for my failing sense of direction. I squinted, straining to see beyond unhelpful windscreen washers that smeared dust and sludge in front of me, forcing me to slow down. Under normal circumstances, I might have enjoyed the journey. This place was quite beautiful with its isolated farms and whitewashed properties littering the surrounding landscape.

'I'm bored,' Georgina muttered, folding her arms in misplaced defiance. She began fiddling with the radio, her mobile phone no longer holding her interest, the fading scenery no longer holding her attention.

I took a breath. 'I can't help that. We can't be far away now, though.' I wasn't sure which of us I was trying to convince. I couldn't overthink the fact the closer we drove, the denser the mist became. The country lanes were now heavily laden with a low-lying fog, bringing forward every horror movie I could think of. I was trying to maintain concentration, failing, Georgina's consistent fiddling with the radio adding to my heightened irritation.

'Georgie, will you please *stop* doing that? It's hard enough to navigate by myself as it is.'

My child scoffed, offering me a sideways glare that, had I been looking directly at her, would have no doubt made things worse. Yet, I was accustomed to her forever-changing mood, her perpetual frustration, such a simple response momentarily easing my mood. It made me want to laugh. I glanced casually towards my child, a smirk already threatening to soften my features and ease my stress. This trip was meant to be bringing us closer together, not create unwanted arguments we'd laugh about later.

I opened my mouth to speak, but as usual my inability to drive in a straight line was ready to mock me. A loud pop jolted me violently into reality as both front tyres exploded, sending the car into a spin. I didn't see it coming, nothing ahead confirming the danger, nothing of our surroundings visible, my lapse in concentration to blame. Georgina screamed. I panicked. Yet, no matter what I did, the car was fighting back, the steering no longer in my control, the emergency break I applied making everything worse. I held my breath as the car veered towards the grass verge, spinning several times before rolling aggressively onto its roof, our possessions flying into the air along with our measly bodies. My daughter's small frame crumpled like paper, the ground beneath unforgiving.

I held my breath, this moment occurring too fast for my mind to keep up, yet painfully slow, as if time was deliberately suspending me in limbo for the hell of it. I tried to move but couldn't, the world tipped at a violent angle, the car protesting angrily amidst the tangled overgrowth of an incoming ditch. What the hell was *that?*

I attempted to turn my head but pain shot through my neck into my back, my arms set at an awkward, unnatural angle. All I could think of was Georgina, the screaming car wilfully silencing her terrified reaction. Was she wearing her seatbelt? *Was she okay?* When I opened my mouth to ask, hot sticky blood filled my cheeks, choking any futile attempts to reclaim control. I wasn't ready for the world to slip into a void, removing me from this moment, this agony, Georgina left to her own devices. Yet it did so anyway, darkness enveloping everything, taking me along for a terrifying joyride I wasn't about to escape.

3

When I opened my eyes the first thing that struck me was the smell of fuel and distinct burning leaving a throbbing sensation in my windpipe. The world was tipped upside down, my brain unwilling to cooperate with my immediate surroundings and for a moment I couldn't understand where I was. I turned to my right, expecting to see my injured daughter, no concept of what had happened aside from a brief incident I was failing to acknowledge. I wanted her to complain about my inept driving abilities, shout at me, roll her eyes. I needed to hear her voice, her sarcasm. I hoped to *Christ* she was okay.

'Georgie?' I croaked. My throat was a tightened knot, blood clogging my lungs, overthrowing any sanity I possessed. I blinked, yet from this angle, I was struggling to locate my bearings, let alone my child. My head was aching, my body set in an awkward position that jolted sharp pain along my spine as I cranked my neck sideways. No matter what I did, I couldn't see her, nothing of that mop of dark hair readily able to appease my increasing dread.

A stupid idea shot into my mind that she'd been thrown from the tumbling wreckage, her open window mocking my current position, my thoughts left to race unchecked. I fumbled to unclip my seatbelt, panic setting in, my actions sending my body plummeting into the roof of the car. Where the *hell* was my child? I kicked the driver's door violently with an outreaching foot, searching for signs of Georgina's mismatched outfit with my outstretched hands. All I needed was a simple glimpse of her brash appearance. Her loose-fitting trousers often dragged along the ground as she walked, the things too long, her bright red trainers out of place here.

'Georgie?' I called out again, louder this time, my lungs not ready to acknowledge reality, my brain unwilling to acknowledge *anything*. I assumed she'd scrambled free of the wreckage and was sitting on the grass, dealing with her own wounds whilst waiting for me to wake up and join her in the real world. *If only things could be so simple.* I anticipated frustrated grunts of annoyance, irritated sighs, hoping one glimpse of her bemused face would appease mine.

I slid my aching body from the car, the ground cool against my back, not a comfort, the rain fresh, still falling. I had no time to assess any damage to either myself or the vehicle, the thing now only fit for the scrap heap by the looks of it. It was a fitting analogy to my pathetic existence. It didn't matter. I clambered to my feet, glancing around for signs of life, desperate for Georgina to answer me and confirm she was okay.

'Georgie?' I yelled into the mist. Nothing. *Jesus Christ.*

I raced into the road, scanning my location, needing a sign, *just one,* that by some impossible miracle, she'd crawled to safety. I had visions of her lying on the ground, unconscious or worse, one look all I needed to confirm my increasing fears. As it was, misty rainwater had now fused with the thickening fog, ensuring I could see less than ten feet ahead. I didn't care about my injuries, too busy thinking of Georgina's—even when my foot twisted aggressively beneath me, sending me sprawling to the ground. Pain shot into my ankle but I didn't care. I was panicking, this day threatening to dislodge my brain once and for all, leaving me a convulsing wreck on some forgotten piece of ground. It would have been a fitting conclusion to the last six months, my life already in the gutter, this car now ready to join the chaos.

'Georgie!' I screamed into the void, towards an alien environment, amid an alienated country I wholly wished I'd avoided. Even the sound of Georgina's name felt wrong. Darkridge Hollow was still some miles ahead, as was salvation I now questioned we'd find. I was limping. I didn't care. The only thing I could do was check repeatedly for signs of life, visions of Georgina's lifeless body something I didn't need in my head. I was a madman possessed, nothing of this situation real, no rational logic to conduce any fitting end to this day.

***

When an old truck trundled along the road towards me, I almost didn't notice. It appeared from the mist, damaged, demonic, aged beyond acceptance, the landscape hell-bent on removing all traces of civilization, nature claiming back everything around me. Its rusted, copper tinge loomed into view, coming to a halt some feet away, struggling windscreen wipers disguising a foggy image at the wheel. When a woman in a pale blue raincoat jumped from the driver's seat and rushed towards my crumpled body, I barely acknowledged her. My devastated mind was in pieces, this moment a fitting end to it all.

'My goodness, are you okay?' she yelled, her rich Ohioan accent something I'd become unaccustomed to since Anna's death, her concerned vocals foreign to my ears.

'I can't find my daughter!' I yelled back, no idea what I expected the poor woman to do about *that,* my only aim to placate my savage emotions with the swift appearance of my despondent twelve-year-old. I fully expected her to race from the fog into my outstretched embrace—my searing agony concluded by an innocent gesture I desperately needed. I glanced towards the trees, the damaged car, then the stranger in front of me. 'We had an accident. I can't find her.' My words sounded unhinged, stupid. I couldn't believe such things were leaving my mouth. *Where in God's name was she?*

The woman was already by my side, a warm hand on my shoulder. 'Your *daughter?*' she asked, as if questioning my words, querying my logic. By the look on her face, she assumed my ramblings ridiculous, my desperate persona at odds with a truth she hadn't yet confirmed.

I glared at her, unable to see much beyond consuming thoughts of Georgina that left me cold. She couldn't have *disappeared.* She *wouldn't* have left my side. If anything, she would have tried to wake me up. I visualised her slapping my cheeks, rattling my bones, frantically trying to locate a signal on a phone that never left her possession. She was a good kid despite hormones neither of us knew how to process. She wouldn't have run off, even had she deemed help a necessary consideration, my unconscious body a potential moment of horror I genuinely didn't want to think about. Flagging down a passing car would have been far more conducive, logical. Nothing else made sense.

'It's okay. Slow down and tell me *exactly* what happened.' The woman was speaking calmly, stroking my trembling shoulder with a bony hand, her attempts to ease my rising panic failing, her words emerging slightly patronising, if I'm honest.

I wasn't sure what *had* happened. One moment I was driving, minding my own business, trying not to yell at my daughter. The next, I was waking up in a ditch.

'I'm not sure,' I breathed. My head was pounding, a trickle of blood creeping along my eyebrow, threatening to blind me where I stood. I was searching my surroundings, trying to pinpoint Georgina's tiny frame set amidst the dense fog behind me. Everything about this moment was wrong.

'Why don'tcha take a seat in my truck? Catch your breath.' The woman was trying to be nice, of course, attempting to help me in what she believed was the aftermath of an unforeseen car accident, these roads unfamiliar, my presence unnatural. 'You're English?' she queried.

I nodded. Was that *relevant*? Was she not listening to what I was saying? I needed to find Georgina. Anything else was unnecessary.

'Please, *help* me find my daughter?' I was begging. It was pathetic, a tear already forming, unhinged thoughts left to wander. It wasn't ideal. I jerked my shoulder away from my would-be helper and pushed away my stray tear, retracing unsteady steps along the road. The only thing I needed was to understand where she'd gone.

'Georgina?' I yelled, her full name only ever used when she was in trouble, this day threatening to become one of those momentous occasions. Surely she would have tried to pull me from the car, if she could, wake me up—the vehicle now threatening to erupt into flames. A flicker of orange had sprung from the bonnet, spilling black smoke into the hazy air, choking my surroundings, threatening to choke me.

Undeterred, I stepped forward and yanked open the upended rear passenger door, despite protests from a woman whose mission was simply to offer a helping hand. A sudden rush of heat came from nowhere, sending me reeling towards the embankment, the car holding the potential to explode, taking me along with it. I couldn't tell if it was a lack of air conditioning, lack of air, or the encroaching fire that had caused such heat. Whatever it was, I should have taken it as a sign of things to come—the way this day was heading.

'Ope! Be careful,' the troubled voice behind me struggled to maintain composure. 'You're hurt.' It didn't matter. I didn't give a *shit* about myself. I hadn't heard anyone say "ope" for a while. Not since the last time I'd heard my wife's voice. It wasn't ideal.

'I *need* to find my daughter,' I screamed again, yelling at her now, my impatience and desperation apparent. Anna would have been mortified. Of all the things my brain chose to focus on, it was the face of my wife I saw clearly, her furious features set in sheer panic, prepared to seal my fate in knowing the most valuable thing she'd left me with was now lost to the ravages of this isolated location. *Jesus Christ.*

'This ain't helpin' none. Come into town with me. We can call the cops. Getcha car sorted.' The woman was trying to help, believed she *was* helping, yet nothing she could do or say was about to placate my rising trepidation.

'Where is she?' I spluttered, practically bursting into tears in front of this stranger, ready to spit snot and salty water into her face, the poor woman as much in the dark as I was. It wasn't her fault.

She shook her head, something in her complacent tone I wasn't expecting to see. Was it disbelief, or *pity?*

'Where's Georgie?' I was sobbing now, my yells reduced to muttered confusion, my trembling hands pressed over my reddened face. I couldn't help it. My child's name emerged almost incomprehensible, my ramblings aimed blindly towards the trees. A light breeze snatched my words skyward, my tightened throat rendering such utterings useless. I must have looked pathetic.

'Please,' the woman pleaded. 'You *need* help.' She paused before adding, 'I'm sorry to say it, but I think you might be mistaken.'

I spun around, staring at this stranger as if she had turned into an alien, no logic to her words, her relaxed mannerisms unbefitting of this moment. 'About *what?*' What on earth was she talking about? She didn't know me but surely she would be as frantic as I was? Concerned. Why wasn't she helping me search?

She sighed, her head as weighed down by emotion as mine, rain soaking into her flame red hair, weighing that down too, this moment becoming heavier by the second. 'You're *alone*, sir,' she confirmed slowly, needing me to understand the truth of my unhinged predicament, appreciate the declaration she was expressing. 'I hate to be the one to say it, but *nobody* was in the car when you crashed.'

I let out an automatic laugh, the gesture erupting sarcastically, her comment ridiculous. 'I already told you. My *daughter* was in the car.' I couldn't have said it any clearer. What did *she* know? Who the hell was she, anyway?

She shook her head, expelling rainwater from the ends of sodden tresses. Frizz was not a good look for the woman. 'I'm sorry, butcha ain't thinkin' straight.'

'What on earth are you talking about?' I stared at her, she stared at me, her sympathies wavering, patience waning. I couldn't read any emotion behind her dark eyes as she blinked away rainwater in the gloom.

She pointed along the road, back towards the direction I'd driven, that single moment seemingly so long ago now. 'I saw you. A few miles back at the gas station. Talkin' to some Scottish guy and askin' Troy for directions into Darkridge Hollow.' She sighed, offering a smile that looked more like a grimace.

I wrinkled my brow, forcing her to continue.

'I'm sorry. I didn't mean to pry. It's just that we don't get many visitors around these parts.' She held her hands aloft, hoping I wouldn't take offence to such an innocent confirmation. Did she *know* Troy? I staggered backwards, unable to comprehend what I was hearing. 'But I'm pretty sure you didn't have a child with you.' She was looking at me now as if the blow to my head had triggered a memory lapse, my brain recalling things incorrectly. *What the hell?*

'*What?*' I was glaring at her. I couldn't help it. My face was set in a tight knot, my mouth agape. I no longer held the capacity to string a sentence together.

'I said, you did *not* have a child with you,' she repeated calmly, ensuring she spoke slowly whilst continually shaking her head. She needed me to understand the clarity of her words, my head injury an overriding factor she assumed needed dealing with, immediately. She glanced towards the ground, her raincoat doing nothing to keep her dry, the rain heavier now, threatening to drown us where we stood. 'I'm real sorry.'

I was staring at an unfamiliar face, unconvinced I was hearing anything of value. The world was spinning, threatening to spin me out of control. I couldn't speak. Just because I was black and Georgina was white, didn't mean she could make assumptions about my family. *How dare she?*

'I just noticed you askin' for directions to Darkridge Hollow. It's my home town,' she confirmed with a shrug as if I needed clarification of why she'd been listening to a private conversation, sticking her nose where it wasn't wanted.

I shook my head. 'No,' I spluttered, 'you're mistaken. My daughter was next to the car. I bought her an ice cream. Long hair, attitude, thinks she's twenty bloody years old already.' Just talking about her made me feel sick. I really needed to give her a hug.

'Nope.' It was now the stranger's turn to shake her head. 'I'm afraid you're mistaken. There was no one with you. Of that, I'm certain.' She glanced at my injuries, my twisted ankle, wounded head and torn clothing something she wasn't about to ignore as readily as I was. I didn't care about any of that. I couldn't, even if I wanted to. 'Why don't

I drive us back into town, getcha dry, somethin' to drink. You need help for those injuries.' She appeared sympathetic, concerned, the tiny smile she offered entirely missing its mark. 'I live just a few miles back-'

'No!' I yelled, nothing the poor woman could say able to make a difference to the way I felt. 'You have this all wrong. My daughter's name is Georgina. She is twelve years old. She has long dark hair and a little mole on her right cheek, a scar on her leg from where she fell off her bike last summer and a large birthmark on her shoulder that she hates.' I patted my shoulder, practically giving myself the very hug I was desperate to give my child, unconcerned by blood trickling down my cheek, rainwater turning it a sludgy pink. I was convinced the wound was just a scratch anyway, unimportant, heightened adrenaline to blame for my current appearance. None of it mattered. Georgina claimed her birthmark made her ugly. I thought it was the most beautiful part about her. So did Anna. I almost threw up.

The woman continued to stare at me, sympathetic yet unhearing, unwilling to accept a truth she evidently believed was wrong. I hadn't even asked her name. I didn't care.

'Come with me, *please,*' she insisted, holding a hand towards mine she assumed I would take without question. I didn't. Instead, I hobbled along the road towards a car now smouldering in the rain, the engine fire thankfully no longer an immediate threat. I stumbled into the ditch and yanked open the boot, indifferent to danger, my only intention to prove I wasn't losing my mind. My child was *real.* And, more importantly, she needed me. God knows what she must be dealing with, alone, out there somewhere, lost.

I scrambled around on my hands and knees, trying to locate belongings that Georgina never went far without—a suitcase covered in Mickey Mouse stickers, a hand-knotted macramé bag she made a couple of years ago, weighed down now by several key rings hanging from the handles. We'd planned a trip to Disney World one day, our ready-made family complete. The fact we never made it beyond the outskirts of London mocked everything I now assumed I stood for. I fully understood the need to cling onto possessions that made my daughter feel close to her mother, the reason she spoke rarely of her, my wife's passing too recent, too raw. The sadness I saw lingering in her young eyes every day had become something I could barely live with. Maybe that's why we'd been arguing so much recently.

I stumbled around the embankment, searching, desperate, unable to accept what I didn't want to acknowledge, hoping they were on the roadside somewhere, undamaged, the ditch too rich with vegetation for me to see *anything* clearly. I clambered deeper inside the wreckage, arms flaying, mind spinning, my only intention to prove to this stranger I wasn't a complete idiot as I lifted an old blanket no doubt left by a previous customer, putting on my old leather jacket to stave off a sudden rush of cold. Despite tossing several unwanted items around the space, my efforts to locate her possessions remained as illusive as finding Georgina. *Where the hell were they?* I glanced around, assuming they must have been thrown from the car during the crash, no logic to confirm they could have been tossed from a closed boot.

What the hell?

I dived across the upturned seats, tugging open the glove compartment, the lingering fire of no concern to me. I pulled out my passport, searching frantically for Georgina's, yet I couldn't find it. SHIT! No. *No!* How could this be possible? *Where was it?* I staggered back onto the road clutching my own as if it was a death sentence ready to claim me, the grim reaper leaping from the nearest tree.

'Whatcha lookin' for?' the woman called out.

I didn't respond. Georgina's headphones were gone, as was her mobile phone and that bloody ice cream tub she'd earlier discarded in the door panel despite my complaining, telling her to put it in a bin. It had threatened in the heat to spill sticky vanilla onto the leather interior of a car I'd be expected to pay the excess for if she damaged. I ignored the irony of that concept.

I dragged the cooler frantically onto the roadside, now containing nothing but a few crushed sandwiches and a half-peeled orange. Where I'd purchased two large bottles of Doctor Pepper, only one remained. *Bloody hell.* Georgina had all kinds in there. Twinkies, bars of chocolate I was making her save for later, a large bag of gummy bears, doughnuts.

I stood in the road scratching my head, nothing else for me to do that made sense. 'Sir?' the woman queried, my back still to her. I turned around, confusion evident.

'What happened to my daughter?' I spat, my words almost failing to make it out of my mouth.

The woman shook her head, a solemn expression I didn't appreciate. 'I don't think you *have* a daughter,' she confirmed, her chilling words biting into my brain, the cool rain freezing me to the spot. Did she assume me concussed? Potential amnesia resulting from injuries I didn't yet know I'd sustained? I swallowed, reaching a damp hand into my back pocket, pulling out my wallet, trembling fingers prodding, unfeeling, this moment surreal.

I always kept photographs of Georgina and her mother in my wallet, including one of our wedding day. Anna looked stunning that day. It was a memory I'd never forget, my photographs all I had left of the woman I would adore forever. It was all the proof I needed to verify I wasn't insane, confirming to this stranger that it was, in fact, *she* who was mistaken, not me. I flicked through several thin leather pockets, allowing my driver's license, credit cards, gym membership and several used cinema and train tickets to fall to the sodden ground around me. What the *hell?* My photographs were *gone.* Georgina as a baby. Anna and Georgina together in the park. *Our wedding photo!*

'Lemme help!' I was being spoken to as if I'd lost my mind, the rain pelting down now, drenching us, mocking me, rooting me to the spot. The woman didn't seem to notice. Neither did I.

'Please tell me what's going on?' I whispered, slumping to the crumbling tarmac, my knees collapsing with the magnitude of this impossible moment. I wasn't going mad. My daughter was missing, as was everything she had brought on this godforsaken trip. Where were my photographs? And, more importantly, *where the hell was Georgina?*

4

I knelt on crumpled knees, the sodden road uncomfortably unwelcome, unsure what to do or how to feel. The pouring rain did nothing for the pain, my mind along for the ride, prevailing panic erupting violently as my world collapsed around me. Without warning, Darkridge Hollow had become a dark, hollow grave I'd slipped face first into. It was a fitting analogy, my head a violent, twisted knot of earthworms burrowing into the inner recesses of my brain, choking my thoughts, mocking my actions. I could see nothing beyond my agony, unconcerned for the welfare of the stranger who only wanted to help, incessant rain threatening to compound me to a hell I already knew well.

The woman had caught me at a bad time, a terrible time made worse by this unfathomable day, my usual upbeat personality gone from any reality I might have deemed normal. It didn't matter. Georgina wouldn't leave the car and abandon me. I'd taught her better than that. She would have dialled the emergency services, her mobile phone permanently welded to her hand, her young thumbs set in twisted compaction. There would have been no hesitation on my child's part to do what was needed to help her injured dad at such a desperate time.

'Mister?' My newly acquired companion was beginning to sound stressed, despondent, almost as confused now as me. She was probably getting a chill standing in the rain, nothing about me suggesting I was worth falling ill over. 'You can't stay out here all day,' she protested, my unheeded absence steadily threatening to devour us both.

She was right, of course, I couldn't. Yet, I didn't know what else to do. I didn't want to acknowledge rational logic, her words unwelcome, my mind unsure how to respond. I didn't need anyone's consideration or misaimed comments, no matter how thoughtful they were, nothing able to bring me back from the abyss. I scooped several discarded items from the loosened gravel and stuffed them back in my wallet, getting to my feet, my legs along for an excruciating ride. My missing photographs had created a far deeper hole in my rational thinking than anything else could, nothing the torrential rain had done to cause such a violent reaction to my immediate surroundings.

'I *need* to call the police,' I confirmed sharply, panic giving way to logic, my brain finally flicking a switch. *Thank Christ for that!* I pulled my mobile from my back pocket, resisting an urge to throw the thing into the surrounding overgrowth when it refused to turn on, my index finger numbed by unsubstantiated determination. I stood in the wet, heart pounding, my throat twisting with volatile rejection I wasn't convinced wouldn't kill me—kill us *both.*

A thought leapt into my brain that maybe Georgina's phone had suffered a similar fate, my terrified girl unable to do anything other than follow her trembling feet in some vague hope she would eventually find help. After all, we were only a few miles from our destination, a few miles from reality. It was the *only* logical conclusion I could reach. I glanced along the road, the entire environment peppered with patchy mist, no clear vision provided that might ease my troubled, rapidly accelerating mind. Maybe she'd flagged a passing car, hitched a ride, already dry and warm somewhere. Safe.

I clung to the idea I was overthinking all this, yet it didn't explain why she would have taken her belongings with her—even that damned ice cream tub and unopened bottle of pop. Those things would have been of little importance to my child, the last thing on her mind, her unwillingness to tidy her room mocking any idea of locating a *dustbin.* I couldn't understand why she would drag her suitcase along the road, knowing her dad was unconscious and bleeding in a slow-burning vehicle behind her. She'd be too panicked and desperate to give a shit. She'd made me carry the thing twenty feet from the airport trolley to the car, disinterested in my elevated heart rate, on her phone as usual—complaining about the exhaustion I'd thrust upon her. None of this made sense.

'I have a telephone back at my house if that'll help,' the woman called out. She glanced at my useless mobile phone before heading towards her truck. She probably wanted to get out of the rain and away from me, my unhinged ranting no more important to her day than this unexpected moment. She was done waiting for me. I could understand why. 'What's your name?' she called back, her truck door open, a foot already on the ledge.

'Josh,' I replied, unsure what else I was meant to do.

'Well, it's pretty darn good to meetcha, Josh.' She offered me a smile I didn't return. 'I'm Megan.'

I had no choice but to follow, heed her commands, climb into her vehicle. I wasn't ready to head away from this heinous location, my child out there somewhere, alone, probably as terrified as me. I could only hope she was with the police already, warm, dry, enjoying a much-needed drink, a sugary snack, a friendly chat. I assumed they were already on their way. Yet, consistent panic kept me on the edge of chaos, my blood pulsating so violently I could barely see straight. I had no concept of how long I was unconscious, the day waning fast—my mobile phone and rental car unable to offer assistance that might have calmed my unfettered emotions. The vehicle was still smouldering in the haze. I had no idea where my phone charger was.

We drove away from the side of the road, the silence unbearable, my own ageing suitcase isolated in the back of Megan's truck. It slid pathetically from side to side, mocking me, annoying Megan—nothing of Georgina's possessions left to confirm she even existed. I didn't care about the car and I dared not think too long about those recent months Georgina and I had become virtual strangers, my child left to suffer alone, her failing dad rotting in a private hell of his own.

Megan chatted freely as we drove into Darkridge Hollow, her tone purposefully casual and calm—too calm. I assumed she wanted to steer my focus from the inevitable and keep my spirits aloft. She was failing. To add to my disappointment, this small town was not how I'd imagined, my thoughts left to run wild, vivid images swirling inside a torrid skull I couldn't willingly expel. I assumed Anna's taunts were nothing but banter, set to annoy me because she knew how to press my buttons, knew how much I despised horror stories. Now I didn't know what to think. She couldn't have known I'd be taking this trip without her, without *Georgina,* already deep inside a horror story of my own. We passed a sign. It was battered in places by weather and age, rust streaming down a metal plate from screws barely holding it in place.

Welcome to
DARKRIDGE HOLLOW
Home of America's best-grown corn crops
If we don't grow it, it ain't worth eatin'

I took a breath. Small towns in Ohio often lay claim to

fame of some kind, Darkridge Hollow's turn to prevail over the corn industry, it seemed. The town was once a thriving corn farming community – according to Anna – many awards given to the proud farmers who'd kept the funds coming in and the place profitable. Now, run-down properties sat on either side of the road, dilapidated trucks slumped in forgotten driveways along with overgrown, weed-ridden spaces that would never again be mistaken for gardens.

'D'ya have someplace to crash?' Megan asked then. She'd been instigating most of the conversation, our time together one-sided. I didn't care. Right then, I doubted anything would appease my abysmal emotions, this dismal day unforgiving. I glanced her way, taking a sharp breath, my lungs filling with a poison that would have passed for air had I been able to breathe.

'No. I was hoping to find a hotel or a B&B somewhere.' It was ironically meant to be part of our plan, part of the fun. We were heading into the unknown, just the two of us. Father and daughter, a great adventure.

Megan laughed. It wasn't appreciated. 'You'll be lucky to find a hotel around these parts.' Her smile slipped as she noticed me staring at her with narrowed eyes, her flushed features confirming she shouldn't make light of my current situation, my own set-in grim noncompliance. I was in no mood for chitchat, no tolerance for *fake* reassurance.

She was trying to be nice, of course, turning her attention to how she liked England. She wanted to visit my country one day, her limited travels confined to a neighbouring town, unfortunately. I wasn't listening. Too busy watching the road for potential signs of my wayward girl, her red trainers strikingly bright and alien against this dank, unhinged backdrop.

'I have a room goin' beggin', if that'll help?' she added flatly, realising I wasn't in the mood for much else, nothing about her tone confirming she actually *meant* her suggestion.

Under normal circumstances, I might have been grateful. But the last thing on my mind was the inconvenience of where I was going to spend the night. I didn't care if I had to camp out on this very roadside, no passing stranger immune to my indignant wrath. I doubted I'd sleep much anyway. The last thing either of us needed was complications adding to this already impossible day. What I *did* need was the nearest police station. I'd managed to convince myself Georgina would be with the police by now, waiting to be brought back to our location, back to the dad she'd left unconscious in a ditch. She *had* to be with the police. I couldn't allow any other concept to roam my tainted mind.

'If you could just drop me off at the nearest police station, I'll be forever grateful,' I muttered. I was staring out of the windows, my hands pressed against glass already thick with condensation from our damp clothing and hot breath. I was practically begging, my legs jolting violently with the magnitude of this surreal moment. I honestly thought I was going to be sick.

Megan swallowed, offering an unsavoury sigh, something she hadn't yet confirmed ready now to make a demonic appearance. 'I'm afraid this is a small town, Josh. The nearest police department is quite a few minutes away. It might be easier if we head to my place and I can call 'em from there. You look exhausted.'

I glared towards a face I couldn't read, her eyes cold, like stone, nothing of my suffering important to this stranger. Exactly how many *minutes* were we talking? Ohioans don't refer to distance in miles. To them, everything is measured in minutes. I guess they assume their time is more precious than distance. I could appreciate that. Yet, how far had my child been forced to walk? Was she still out there, *still walking,* regretting her rushed decision and wondering if I was okay? Thoughts of psychotic strangers with meat hooks in their basements and murder on their minds sprang wildly into mine, the sudden urge to get out of this truck leaping from nowhere. The idea of my child in the hands of some would-be serial killer was exactly the type of thing I didn't need in my head.

'I need some air,' I managed to stutter, vomit and bile rising to the back of a throat I was unable to control. The last thing I needed was to be violently sick over this poor woman's seat. She *was* trying to help me. The poor sod didn't need that kind of gratitude aimed her way. 'Pull over.' It wasn't a request.

Noting my urgency and my pale complexion, Megan swerved her ageing truck to the side of the road, allowing me to swing the creaking door wide, my trembling, uncooperative legs falling to the dirt below. I closed my eyes, recalling how Georgina had responded similarly to an overheating rental car, my brusque amusement coming back to haunt me. How on *earth* had everything gone so horribly wrong?

Megan jumped from the driver's side and raced swiftly to where I was now crouched on all fours, my face a slurry of reddened veins that threatened to burst open at any second. She placed her hand in the middle of my back and rubbed firmly.

It was a simple action, meant out of innocent concern. Yet it was something Anna used to do, my wife's reassuring vocals jumping once more into my head. No matter which of us was sick, Anna knew what to do. Now such an action didn't help, only aiding to tip me further towards a black hole I was barely keeping myself from the edge of. It brought the last ten years of my life to the surface, the fact we'd been unable to have more children, *not* her fault. Georgina became the light of her life during several frantic months of failed IVF treatments—that beautiful girl *always* the light of mine. I couldn't lose Anna's child too. Her *only* child. *Our child.*

Something snapped inside me and I slumped forward and sobbed, my stomach wrenching its contents into the street. My brain wasn't sure what it wanted to do first—vomit into the dirt or obliterate every savage emotion I possessed. I can confirm ice cream is nowhere near as tolerable the second time around.

'Shush, you're fine,' Megan soothed. 'You're fine.' She handed me a handkerchief from her pocket. It was cream cotton, hand-embroidered, the initials M.E. sitting neatly in one corner along with a tiny pink heart. I almost didn't want to soil it. It barely looked used. I'm sure Anna had something similar.

'I'm all right, really,' I confirmed, brushing away her outstretched hand, such kindness unrequired, unappreciated. I wasn't all right. Nothing about this was all right. I wiped my tears on the back of my hand, sludgy rainwater blending with salty acid and vomit that threatened to burn my face and remove my putrid existence from this world once and for all. It was nothing but a rancid confirmation I was of no relevance, no real importance. I'm sure she had far better things to do than pander to my miserable, depleted corpse.

Megan looked no older than Anna. Her auburn hair was tied roughly at the nape of her neck, most of it falling freely into clouded eyes, wet now, stuck to her face in places, her freckled cheeks and pale skin reminding me of Georgina. *Brilliant.* The last thing I needed was yet another bloody analogy, *everyone* reminding me of Anna during those early painful days and weeks of unmitigated grief.

'I appreciate your help,' I offered. It was true. 'But I *have* to get to the police.' There wasn't room in my head for anything else, no other reality for me to acknowledge. 'I don't expect you to drive me.' She'd done more than enough as it was. 'Where can I get a taxi?' I was already on my feet, on my toes, sludgy vomit trickling freely towards the nearest drain, rainwater attempting to wash away all traces of my suffering. It still had bits of peanut in it from an earlier sweet indulgence along with other things I couldn't remember eating, a vile taste of stomach acid peppering the insides of my flustered cheeks.

Megan laughed again then, making me scoff. How dare she make light of my situation? None of this was *funny.*

'Cabs don't run from Darkridge Hollow, Josh,' she confirmed, glancing around, oblivious to the pained look I was giving her.

The entire place looked sinister in the pale afternoon haze. Either that or my brain was creating a reality that didn't exist, ready to turn Darkridge Hollow into something it didn't need to be. I honestly had no idea why Anna loved the place so much. Maybe it looked better on a sunny day. Maybe the town had declined since she was last here, my wife unable to confirm such a truth for herself. *Maybe* my current state of mind was inventing nonsense for the sheer hell of it. None of it mattered. I couldn't care less about fond memories held for a town slowly turning to shit. I assumed once I found Georgina, we would leave, everything always appearing better in the cold light of a rational day.

'Then will you drive me to the police station? I'll pay you, of course.' I pulled my wallet from my pocket, those missing photographs the only things I could see, ghosts of my past haunting every frantic movement. I tugged several dollar bills from a large flap, handing the whole lot to my newly acquired acquaintance, hands trembling, nothing left of Joshua Raymond that would have made much sense to anyone.

Megan waved a hand towards me. 'Your cash ain't what I need,' she replied sharply, shaking her head dismissively. What *did* she need? She turned, pointing along the street.

'My house is down there. You should come with. I'll call the cops. It's the least I can do.'

I honestly didn't see I had a choice. I nodded, climbing back into Megan's truck, the rain thankfully dissipating, a brighter sky threatening to emerge behind slow parting clouds. I was desperately hoping Georgina would come waltzing around the next corner and ease my suffering with her light hearted manner and unconcerned smile. My heart was pumping so fast I seriously wondered if it was preparing for a heart attack. I needed relief from this impossible moment, this day—the last six months too much.

Megan's truck spluttered into motion, trundling forward, the engine unwilling to respond. She turned left onto an uneven dirt track, the thing hardly passing for a driveway, more dilapidated farm lane than anything else. Deep tyre marks were carved into the well-worn ground, weeds and long grasses left to grow wild in the centre.

Why was I here? Anna's fondness for her childhood home town seemed terrifyingly misplaced. I had considered mentioning that my wife was born here, although *now* wasn't the right time. Megan probably wouldn't care. She didn't seem concerned for my missing child, my dead wife just another stranger she didn't need in her day. She might not even remember Anna's family anyway, most of the town seemingly abandoned long ago. *Just like me.*

5

Megan's truck came to a shaky halt, jolting my brain into stark reality, the lining of my stomach scarcely intact. The only thing my mind permitted was that Georgina wouldn't know how to find me. I took a breath. If first appearances were anything to go by, it was probably advantageous the property lay hidden, this location not a welcoming space by any stretch of the imagination. Mangled branches of several large oak trees were sandwiched on either side of the property, converged by years of neglect and misuse, fingers of degradation clawing towards the street. Nearby fields were left to their own devices, the crops long dead, nothing remaining but crumbling grey spears jutting from dusty clay ground. Everything had rotted away, inhabited only by brave animals who'd set up home amid the deterioration—field mice, rats, snakes.

'Here we are then,' Megan stated, a little too brightly for this occasion. We were outside an ageing building that looked like a forgotten timber shack, no better cared for than an old garden shed. It could do with a clean, a lick of paint, several windows hanging unsteadily in their frames, the surrounding grounds sadly forgotten. I was surprised it was still standing. Yet, who was I to judge? Megan didn't seem concerned by the state of the place she called home.

I climbed out of the truck, only wanting to use the telephone and plug in my mobile phone – if I could find my charger – potentially bringing this day to a satisfying conclusion. I didn't mean to appear ungrateful, yet she did not hold the power to ease my cluttered mind. I was convinced if Georgina *had* been able to use her phone, she would have left a text message for me, confirming where she was. The fact I was unable to retrieve it wasn't my fault, my mobile phone mocking me with its looming silence. An innocent message could relieve my unfettered thoughts, put everything into much-needed perspective—tell me the truth of what had happened on the roadside. Surely there was a simple explanation, a simple conclusion.

'I appreciate your help,' I muttered as I headed unsteadily towards Megan's property, the smiling stranger next to me far too calm for my liking. I'd drummed it into Georgina to *never* get into a stranger's car, no matter how friendly they appear. Now, here *I* was, about to enter a property better suited to the set of a horror film, in the middle of a forgotten town, the pouring rain only adding to the stifling atmosphere, the woman by my side a potential *axe murderer*. It was ironic, uncomfortable, and I was overthinking the impossible. Yet, how was I expected to react? The *only* rational motivation keeping me going was the concept of finding my daughter, and soon.

'I'm happy to help,' Megan confirmed as she swung open a creaking porch door, allowing me to step inside. Staleness lingered in the air. It smelled *old.* I concluded it would be the building, nothing more, the property remembering far better days. I glanced towards Megan, unkind thoughts hovering longer than intended. I was beyond stressed, and it was still raining.

The property was fairly dark inside, the windows laden with dust that clung to net curtains hanging from forgotten frames. I glanced around in search of Megan's telephone, a connection to civilization the *only* thing I required. I tried not to concern myself with the woman's apparent housekeeping failures. It didn't matter. It was none of my business how she chose to live. I'd hardly been on top of things recently, either.

Megan handed me a towel. Despite a few spots of mildew that clung to the edges, it smelled clean. 'Get dry. You'll help no one if you catch your death,' she confirmed, wrapping another around her head. *Catch my death?* At that moment, I would have welcomed it.

I ignored my silent emotions as I set about drying my afro, annoyed I'd left it to grow longer in recent months, a barbershop unrequired in my current mindset. I was momentarily grateful for the warm aroma of lilac flowers that wafted up my nose. It was a distraction. A good one. Anna loved Lilac.

'Feelin' better?' Megan asked dismissively, unaware of the thoughts I couldn't help having. I refrained from responding. She disappeared into the kitchen, the condemned look on my face ignored, her bare feet padding haplessly across sticky lino. Her raincoat hung from a peg in the hallway, water dripping freely onto a dated tiled floor, a low hum in the background setting my teeth on edge. It would be a boiler no doubt, nothing more. Either that, or it was my brain, finally ready to explode. I slipped off my jacket and boots, leaving my footwear on a mat by the front door, clutching my jacket because I didn't know what else to do with it.

There is something about entering a stranger's home that unnerves me. I don't know why. Maybe it's the thought of other people's smells—their pets, the food they eat, the fragrance they wear. It wasn't ideal, yet because of this ridiculous concept, I found the proximity of this building overwhelming. The walls seemed too close together, the cluttered interior to blame. I didn't know what I should do with the damp towel in my grasp, my dated leather jacket already heavy in my arms.

'Come on, Josh. Lemme fetcha a drink,' she suggested, yelling from a kitchen I wasn't yet familiar with.

'Just the use of your phone, if you don't mind?' I confirmed, hoping I wouldn't have to keep asking, wondering why she wasn't concerned by my continued query. It was the only motivation driving me forward, driving me insane.

Megan didn't respond, instead busied herself running mugs under a tap before pouring coffee into both from a steaming glass jug. As I stepped into the kitchen she handed me a large mug of dark substance, not about to take no for an answer.

'Drink that,' she stated flatly, holding the mug towards me as if I was a child who needed placating. 'It'll calm you down.'

I didn't want to calm down. I wanted to call the police. I wanted them to instigate a search, *immediately*, before I launched into a full-blown panic attack and did something I'd regret. I took the drink, anyway, not wanting to appear rude. My mother had raised me better than that.

'Thank you,' I confirmed, taking a sip of hot liquid, not caring that it burned the back of my throat. I was beyond feeling a damned thing, my body now numb from the neck down. My hands were shaking. I tried not to notice.

Megan was looking at me as if assessing my damaged demeanour, uncertain what lay behind the frantic, awkward malingerer in her kitchen. She reached forward, taking back her towel before tossing it across the back of a kitchen chair with a sigh. I hadn't realised I'd smeared blood onto it, a pale pink smudge mocking me, my injuries more concerning to Megan than they were to me.

'Lemme take a look at that head of yours.'

'I'm okay, honestly. It's my daughter I'm concerned for.'

Megan didn't share my apprehension, or my urgency, instead offered a blank smile I couldn't read. 'I think you might've hit your head harder than you realize, Josh.' She stepped forward, raising a steady hand towards my forehead whilst pressing the other firmly across my temple. It was an innocent gesture. Done out of innocent concern. Yet, I automatically stepped backwards, uncomfortable with such close proximity. I didn't know this woman and I didn't need the attention she was readily providing.

She laughed again. She *actually* had the nerve to laugh, in my face, tilting her head to one side as if I'd done something ridiculously amusing.

'Jeez, I won't bite,' she sniggered, shaking her head before retrieving a first aid box from a nearby cupboard she set down on the kitchen table next to me. 'It'll get infected if I don't clean it up.' I still had no idea how bad my injuries were, my headache unimportant to the magnitude of this moment. I didn't give a shit how I looked, *or* how I felt. I automatically stepped away, causing Megan to place chastising hands on her hips. She looked exactly like Georgina when she's about to tell me off. 'D'ya *want* more problems addin' to your day?'

No. Of course I didn't. I shook my head.

'Good. Then sit down and lemme take a look at that head.' She pulled out a chair, requesting I sit down or suffer the consequences, her chastising words concluded. I did as instructed, draping my unwanted jacket across the backrest, hoping I wouldn't receive a telling off for that, too. I still needed to use the telephone.

'Where *is* your phone?' I was glancing around, darting my eyes every which way, my head continually being pulled towards Megan's awaiting hands. She smelled of violet and honey and something else reminding me of Anna. I couldn't tell what.

Megan was busy dabbing my bloodied head with a

damp cloth. 'It's in the hallway,' she chided. 'But it ain't goin' nowhere right now.' Under normal circumstances, I might have found the attention soothing, Megan's warm cloth oddly inviting to my awkward senses. As it was, Megan held no power to soothe any part of me, psychically or otherwise. The telephone may not have been going anywhere, but my daughter had. I wanted to understand her complacency. 'Tell me, Josh. What brings you to Darkridge?' Megan was trying to be nice, of course. It wasn't helpful.

I sighed. The reason for my visit was no longer important, no longer relevant. 'We were *meant* to be locating some of my daughter's family,' I confirmed solemnly as my head was continually prodded by a piece of damp cotton. I'd given up looking for the phone.

'Family?' Megan queried, unconcerned, too busy retrieving fresh water for my cuts, rinsing her cloth under a hot tap, enjoying her brief, motherly moment.

'My wife comes from Darkridge Hollow,' I confirmed, nothing about *that* truth holding the power to calm my emotions. 'My daughter, Georgina, and I were passing through in the hope we could meet them.' I didn't tell her the real reason. It was none of Megan's business.

'Well, I've lived here my whole life. Maybe I know them.' Megan was still smiling, her cheeks flush with potential excitement making her look bizarre. It was unnerving. I didn't want her asking about my wife, her current whereabouts something I didn't have the strength to explain. I doubted Megan could help anyway. 'What're their names?' she added.

I honestly didn't have a clue. I only knew Anna's maiden name. It wasn't ideal. I was embarrassed to acknowledge we'd rarely spoken of them during the entire decade we'd shared together.

'Ellis,' I confirmed, the word emerging little better than

a strained mutter. I was impressed I remembered.

Megan hovered for a moment as if trying to recall the name, yet judging by the blank expression she was giving me, was failing miserably. 'Ellis, Ellis? Mm. I'm not sure. I vaguely remember a family who lived around here once. They *might've* been called Ellis. A funny lot they were, though. But they left this town a decade ago.' She laughed again, unconcerned by the look of frustration I gave her.

This conversation wasn't helping. 'Sorry, I just *need* to call the police.' I motioned to my feet, needing to bring this moment back to reality, back on track, not anticipating Megan would pull me onto the chair so forcefully, the sigh she offered not expected, not appreciated. I wasn't about to beg, yet I was growing increasingly impatient and intolerant of a situation I had no current control over.

Megan shook her head, something in her tone telling me she wasn't used to people demanding her attention, her time. I got the impression she only usually dealt with locals, dead animals, *anything* that might not talk back.

'*I'll* do that.' She threw her bloodstained cloth into the bowl, the water swirling, turning pink. She wiped her hands on my discarded towel before retreating into the hallway, leaving me alone in her kitchen, too much on my mind and not enough action happening to keep me satisfied. Yet, without her help I wasn't certain where I'd be right now. Probably still standing in the rain, drowning my thoughts, the rainwater steadily drowning *me.*

Megan's wasn't a modern kitchen by anyone's standards, the place a throwback to the 1970s, vintage retro no match for the reality of decades-old untouched décor. You couldn't fake what this property had, a staleness that lingered in the air, uncomfortable, unwelcome. The room was covered in cheap Formica, from the rapidly degrading heat-damaged worktops with scorch marks where pans had sat too long, to the wipe-clean cupboard doors no one had wiped clean for a while. Mismatched metal-legged chairs had rusted where they stood, leaving behind orange rings that dotted the floor. Bakelite appliances sat abandoned, a thick layer of grime coating every surface. Trailing wires were left exposed and dangerous, nothing of the location inviting. The colour should have been deep orange and cream, yet hints of burnt brown now freckled the peeling lino, the cream more a sludgy beige, the orange tinged with streaks of faded yellow due to years of unrelenting sunlight and neglect. There was a clock in the background, its low tick faint, probably in another equally forgotten room of the property.

I had no choice but to sit and listen to a one-sided conversation behind me, the police finally on the end of a telephone. *Thank Christ for that.* I took a sip of coffee, sitting upright, momentarily grateful for Megan's calming words, the drink in my hands oddly appealing. I didn't delude myself that if *I* had called them, I would have screamed into the phone, desperate, demonic, creating far more panic than was necessary. I would have looked wholly deranged to these strangers who, because of today's events, would never now know the *real* Joshua Raymond.

'Yes indeed, sir.' Megan's soothing vocals and upbeat words eased my emotions for the first time since we'd met. 'There's been an accident out on Hillborne Avenue. Yep, I have the gentleman here with me right now. Yes, sir. No, sir.' A laugh. 'His name? Josh. Sorry, he didn't tell me his surname. He claims he lost his daughter. Says she was in the car at the time. Absolutely. Yes. Yes, sir. Sure. Thank you.'

She hung up and came back into the kitchen, not even bothering to look my way as she busied herself tidying the mess she'd created attending my wounds. She slung her bloodstained towel across her shoulder as if, like me, it was of no relevance to her day. I glared at her, something missing from this moment.

'What did they say?' I was already on my feet. The only thing I needed was confirmation that someone was coming. *And soon.* I'd happily wait in the street if I had to, walk back to the wreckage on foot. I glanced beyond the windows, wondering if the rain had stopped. It didn't matter.

'They said they'd send someone along.' Megan wasn't concerned. Instead, she ran warm water over a dinner plate, tilting the thing on its side to dry on a draining board already brimming with cobweb-covered crockery.

I sighed, my relief audible. 'Did they confirm if anyone has *seen* Georgina?' Someone must have seen her by now. *Surely!*

Megan shook her head. 'D'ya want somethin' to eat?' She was avoiding this conversation, avoiding the conflict. I could appreciate why. There was nothing more she could do, nothing else but to offer whatever assistance she could to the stranger in her kitchen while we waited for help she probably needed more than I did. From her point of view, she'd gone above and beyond, helping a stranger in need, a man she didn't even know still hovering in her private space. She was taking a huge risk asking me to come here, helping me at all. It wasn't her fault she hadn't directly *seen* Georgina.

Food, of course, was the last thing I needed. My stomach was a tight knot that kept me borderline nauseous, my toes curling with continued panic I had nowhere to place. I didn't need to add anything edible to the equation. I wouldn't keep anything down, anyway. Even the coffee I'd only moments earlier consumed was beginning to churn.

'Did they say how long they were going to be?' I was wringing my hands together, nothing else to do with them, the things otherwise left to dangle by my sides, hapless, awkward. My lips were dry, my throat narrowing with the deranged sound of my own pathetically weakened voice.

'You don't need to go worryin' 'bout that. They'll send

someone along soon enough. Right now, you need to concentrate on your injuries.'

But that was the problem. I did worry. I reached up and touched my head. My ankle was still throbbing, my bloodied head now joining the confusion, becoming more painful by the second. It was *irrelevant.* My t-shirt was torn in places, ready for the dustbin, my jeans ripped at the knee. I'd only just noticed. Blood was beginning to dry, a sludgy blend of angry pink set against a dark grey background. It didn't matter. It matched the colour of my skin. Malignant. Desolate. *Dead.*

'I'm okay.' My cuts didn't feel too bad. I deduced the adrenaline in my bloodstream was responsible for ensuring my injuries looked worse than they were. I couldn't feel a thing beyond my emotions anyway, my mind too busy creating drama elsewhere. 'Maybe I should go outside and check along the road.' I was mumbling. I didn't care. Georgina couldn't have gone far. Surely she wouldn't *keep* walking. I could barely get her to walk the length of our house to the kitchen table for dinner. I motioned to stand, ready to thank Megan and leave. She'd helped all she could. I was grateful. I couldn't ask anything more and I didn't want to take up her valuable time.

'Not a chance,' Megan snapped, the woman not about to be challenged in her own home, not about to let me leave without just cause. I assumed it was because she didn't want the guilt of responsibility if anything happened. 'Sit down and drink your coffee before it gets cold. I already *told* you. The police are on their way.'

I didn't want to sit down and I didn't want to drink any more coffee. Neither did I intend to hover in a stranger's kitchen longer than necessary. My child was out there somewhere, walking the streets, alone, potentially hurt, or *worse.* I couldn't think of anything beyond finding her, telling her off and giving her the biggest hug she'd ever had in her life. I hoped to *Christ* she was okay. I clambered to my feet, my single intention to step outside and get some air.

I have no idea if it was the strong coffee, the stress of the day or the overwhelming heat, but I began to feel a little off, my throat tightening, my lungs struggling. It stopped me in my tracks, taking me by surprise.

'I need air,' I gasped, my body threatening to expose my rapidly increasing fear to the stranger in the room, the unanticipated loss of Georgina something I hadn't expected. I turned around, needing to get outside and take a well-needed break from my frustratingly rancid thoughts, my body not enjoying the stress it was constantly under.

'Ope! My goodness, Josh, what's wrong?' Megan was already racing towards me. It was the second time today she'd done so, her hands outstretched, ready to steady me before I fell and added more potential damage to this impossible day. I stared at her, nothing of what I was seeing logical, the woman now a hazy blend of three forms converging violently, blurred, surreal, words I could barely understand leaving her mouth. 'Are you okay?'

I was sick of hearing the question. *No, Megan, I am not okay. How on earth can any of this be okay?* I shook my head, grabbing the collar of my ruined t-shirt, heat rising to my cheeks, my legs no longer willing to hold me upright. I staggered sideways but tripped, my feet reluctant to hold me steady. The room began to spin, the lightness in my head unexpected.

I can't remember passing out, wasn't expecting the floor to come up to meet me, this moment shockingly distressing. I hoped the police would hurry up. My body was unwilling to cope with the nonsense my brain was thrusting upon it. I found myself flat on my back staring towards a grease-stained ceiling, Megan standing over me. She was speaking, but I could no longer understand a word she was saying.

6

I awoke to a dark, colourless room and a thin sliver of silver that filtered through a set of closed curtains. I blinked, struggling to recognise where I was and what had happened—unable to understand why I was on someone else's bed, on my back, this dank-smelling bedroom odd and uncomfortable. The surrounding darkness sinisterly threw shapes against an unfamiliar backdrop, the far wall a pained expression of my deepest fears. It was a simple floral pattern, nothing more, yet it forged demonic impressions that worsened the fragility of my failing mind, making everything ten times more malignant than they were. Everything about this room confused my senses. I couldn't tell why, yet I sat upright abruptly, sending a sharp pain through my head.

Someone had removed my t-shirt. Anna had bought that t-shirt. It didn't matter. It was beyond saving. Like *me.* I assumed it was Megan's aberrant way of helping, having now dressed my wounds, wiping away all traces of blood from my body. A bandage was wrapped around my ankle, a dressing covering my injured forehead. It was a shame my jeans still bore testimony to the day, with dirt and torn patches highlighting an event I no longer wanted in my head.

I glanced around, no rational concept of how it had

turned dark so quickly, my body throbbing, all traces of the earlier adrenaline firmly wearing off. I didn't know how long I'd been here, my apparent respite unrewarded in the darkness. For a moment, I almost forgot about the incident in Megan's kitchen and the impossible stresses of the day. I lifted myself from a lumpy mattress that protested angrily beneath my weight. *Hours* must have passed. Surely the police would be here by now. Why hadn't she woken me?

My ankle was still aching but it was only a sprain, nothing important, nothing that would prevent me from finding my child this day. I'd run into the night, barefoot if needed, shirtless, breathless. I was already out of my mind. Everything else was irrelevant. I took a mistimed breath, unable to understand how I'd fallen asleep so readily, the idea of passing out not something I wanted to address. The last thing I remembered was looking up at Megan from her kitchen floor, the room spinning, my head wilfully creating demonic images from ideas that didn't exist.

I assumed my wounds were superficial, nothing requiring urgent medical attention, the strong coffee in my system to blame for a lapse in concentration, my judgment impaired by stress. I wasn't convinced I'd either passed out *or* fallen asleep. Falling asleep was *never* going to be an option, passing out entirely illogical. Yet, maybe I'd hit my head harder than I realised. Maybe Megan was right about me. An idea shot into my mind that by avoiding my emotions I'd unintentionally made things worse. It wasn't comforting.

A muffled conversation outside the window caught my attention, bringing me back to a reality I was wholly unconvinced existed. Thin walls and ageing windows allowed me to eavesdrop, this room no protection to its oddly sleeping inhabitant. The building was made of timber, nothing more, most of it threatening to collapse beneath a heavy weight of neglect and misuse. It wouldn't take much to punch through this brittle wall if I had to, the thing no doubt riddled with woodworm and degradation, the drywall no longer as dry as it should be. I hobbled over to the window, barely able to make out the crux of their conversation, muted words needing no more emphasis than the attention I was ready to give. I peeled open the curtains, allowing dust motes to swirl frantically around the wallpaper behind me. I couldn't get over the fact someone had deliberately pasted it to a wall they assumed looked appealing, though it probably looked better in the daylight.

'Has she told him yet?' A man was asking. I could barely make out his words, practically holding my breath in anticipation. *Told me what?*

'Not yet. She's got him held up inside. But she's playin' with fire if you ask me,' another responded.

'Did'ya find anythin' out there?'

'Nope. Nothin'. Just a trail of blood leadin' from his car to the woods.'

Oh my God!

Of all the rational explanations as to where Georgina might have gone, being taken by a wild animal wasn't one that immediately popped into my mind. Now I could think of nothing else, no other logical explanation available—the idea of my child being savaged to death by a vicious animal rendering me incapable of rational thought. I staggered sideways, my legs needing something solid to lean against, finding only groaning floorboards and the edge of an unyielding bed frame.

I swung back the curtains as far as they would go, almost tearing them from their dated hangings, pulling hard against the rotting sash window to open it. I needed to provide a valid point of view whilst explaining my unfathomed, unrelenting position. I tugged firmly yet it wouldn't budge, nothing I did able to dislodge the sliders, years of paint and misuse sealing the frame in place. *Jesus*

Christ.

'Hey!?' I called through thin glass to the ground below, my tone unhinged, my voice unbalanced. I thumped the panel, ensuring I was heard. I'd break the thing if I had to.

The men turned and looked my way. They didn't speak, didn't acknowledge me, their faces expressing something *I* now didn't want to acknowledge. They almost looked pleased. What the *hell* was going on?

'Have you found my daughter?' I screamed, the closed window no match for my rising temper, my heated breath fogging the glass, obscuring my view. I was furious I'd left the car, Georgina potentially a mere few feet away. She could have been lying savaged in that ditch, bleeding to death, out of sight beneath decades of twisted plant growth, her body already out of time. Had I *missed* her? The thought wasn't worth thinking about. It was too terrible. Yet, there was nothing else on my mind, nothing to do but churn unresolved events around my unstable head.

The two men continued to glare at me, their whispering kept purposefully muted, unwilling to share further thoughts with the stranger in their midst, their conversation no longer private. I barely caught the words 'hold onto him' before they disappeared around the side of the property.

'Hey!' I yelled again, my closed fists ready to punch the brittle glass into the overgrowth below, causing more trouble I didn't need in my day.

I stumbled around the bed, the moonlight of no real help—that bloody wallpaper too intense. I needed to locate the door and a light switch, yet I found only damp uneven walls and a rug I tripped over in my haste. When I eventually found the door handle, I was mortified to discover it wouldn't budge. The door was either locked, or my strength had finally left me, six months more than enough time to see me on the brink of no return.

I tugged the knob, twisting it haphazardly, rotating

violently, rattling, laughing at my inability to think straight. Had they locked me in? *Why would they lock me in?* And, more importantly, where were the police? Questions I had no logical answers to swarmed my unsettled brain like sharks ready to attack, my shouts and disgruntled banging going unheeded for several frantic moments.

My panic lasted a few seconds, no longer, yet this day seemed never-ending, set on a timeless loop of torment from which I feared I might never emerge. When the bedroom door opened, Megan strode casually into the room, her hair dried and styled now, a change of clothing making me question everything. It was obvious my presence was of no genuine concern as she flicked the very light switch that had evaded me, plunging the space into soft focus. She did not look impressed.

'Josh, what on earth is wrong?' she asked calmly as if she honestly couldn't understand the ruckus, my continued banging and yelling unappreciated, my actions irreproachable.

'Why don't you tell *me*?' I returned her ridiculous question with my own. The only thing I required was a rational explanation, fresh air, *Georgina.* I was, after all, a rational human being. Or, at least, I used to be.

Megan sighed, folding defiant arms across her chest. 'Your head injury was a little more serious than we realised, so we putcha to bed to sleep it off for a few hours.' She was shaking her head as if I was mad. Maybe I was.

I automatically touched my forehead. I was sweating. I hadn't noticed, the dressing on my head coming loose, dislodging my senses. *We?* I assumed she meant those men outside. It made sense, of course, that she would have wanted me to lie down, a darkened room potentially helpful, that unexpected kitchen incident more than willing to convince this woman I wasn't a well man. She wasn't wrong.

'But why lock the door?' I couldn't understand the logic of *that* action. 'What did you think I'd do?' I glared at her before realising my question was as stupid as my appearance, no immediate reply required that would have made sense anyway. She didn't know me, didn't know *what* I was capable of—had no idea what I'd been through.

'This is a small town surrounded by miles of open countryside. I didn't wantcha wakin' up and wanderin' off. Heaven knows whatcha might have gotten yourself into.' Her words made sense, of course, yet nothing about this day seemed logical.

'Where are the police?' I needed to refamiliarise myself with normality and relocate rational thinking. What *time* was it?

'You gotta remember, Josh, that in small towns, the cops work on different time scales-'

'Don't give me that crap,' I cut in, no more lies needed today. I wasn't a total idiot and I was done being palmed off. 'My child is *missing*.' Surely that made this a priority? Time was of the essence.

Just then one of the men I'd seen outside loomed from the darkened hallway, his face as featureless as Megan's. He pressed two large hands over her shoulders and squeezed.

'Speakin' of which, we need to verify a few things, if you don't mind, Josh,' he asked, staring at me as if he assumed I wasn't right in the head.

'Who are *you*?' It was none of my business. *I* was the one who'd readily invaded their lives, *their* home. It didn't matter who he was. He wasn't important. I just wanted to get out of this room. Out of this house.

'Never mind,' he stated plainly, a blank expression set across his even plainer face. Thick stubble blended into what was left of the hair on his head, the entire thing shaved to disguise an obvious bald patch, his skull oddly shaped and poised for a fight. I quickly nicknamed him "stubble guy", suppressing a sudden urge to scoff. 'You claim someone else was with you. Is that true?'

I stared blankly at strangers I'd met that very day, people who knew nothing about me, my reasons for this trip or my child, the familiar face of my daughter the only thing I needed. That word again. *Claimed.* I'd claimed nothing but the facts.

'Yes,' I spluttered sullenly, attempting to remain neutral yet failing miserably. 'My *daughter*. I've already explained all this.' Why was I continually repeating myself to these god-awful people? I didn't mean to sound insensitive. They were probably very nice under normal circumstances.

'Butcha were *alone* out on the road when we found you. Correct?'

We? What the hell did he mean by that? 'Yes!' I didn't mean to yell. It was unintentional, unwanted, entirely unrequited. I was frustrated. I didn't mean to behave so infuriated. 'Because when I woke up she was *gone*.' I couldn't have said that any clearer. Why were they looking at me like *that?* What was I missing?

'Josh, your clothes were covered in blood.' Stubble Guy was speaking slowly as if I was a child who needed a simple explanation. Either that or he thought I was a simpleton who needed childlike communication.

I know. I'm not stupid. I glanced down, remembering my semi-naked state, no shirt, no shoes, my bandaged foot, my bandaged head reaching conclusions I didn't need. I automatically folded my arms across my nipples. I don't know why. Naked flesh has never bothered me, especially my own. I don't have a beer gut or pigeon tits. If anything, I hadn't been eating well lately, the upside of that unavoidable tragedy meant I'd lost weight. I looked oddly better than I had in a while, slimmer, leaner. I'd never been athletically built, yet it was a shame Anna could no longer see the improvements. It is ironic what neglect can ultimately do to the human body.

'I think I hit my head,' I confirmed, staring at a woman who'd willingly helped me only hours earlier, who'd driven me to this house, poured me coffee, cleaned my wounds. She'd been *nice*. She'd even called the police on my behalf because I was too fraught with emotion to do it myself. Why wasn't Megan confirming this? I wasn't the enemy here. I wasn't the bad guy.

'There was a lotta blood on your shirt, Josh, includin' some that trailed from the car to the woods.' Stubble Guy took a deep breath, glancing at the back of Megan's head as if he wasn't sure if his next words would be well met. 'Far more blood than would've come from the cut on your head alone.'

My mind lunged again, causing my heart to miss several beats. I knew what he was getting at and I didn't like it, my mind already a sludgy mix that had nowhere to go. I recalled what I'd heard outside the window.

'You think a *wild animal* did this?' I honestly didn't want the answer, didn't need the confirmation. He was continually calling me Josh as if we were old friends. I had no clue *who* he was. I didn't give a shit.

Megan glanced towards the disgruntled male behind her, something in her tone confirming they'd discussed this in my absence, in detail. 'We don't know, Josh,' she sighed. 'We only have your word thatcha not-' she paused, unable to finish her sentence.

'That I'm not *what?*'

'Coverin' somethin' up.' Stubble Guy was speaking again yet I could no longer understand a word he was saying. None of them were able to look at me now.

'I beg your pardon?' I glared towards a void that had opened up between us, a cavernous drop that threatened acrophobia. 'Cover *what* up?' What the hell was he trying to say? I glanced towards strangers whose tones held no comfort, trying not to lose my balance, trying not to scream. Nothing of what I was hearing made a shred of sense, nothing of what I was seeing, familiar.

'Thatcha didn't hurt somebody,' Megan muttered.

'*Hurt* somebody? Who on earth would I hurt?' I glared at them, their words irrational. 'You think I hurt my *own* child?' The idea was ludicrous. I honestly couldn't believe what I was hearing. Believing a wild animal had dragged my child into the woods was one thing. This was on a different level entirely.

Megan continued her so-called evaluation, my desperate response of no interest. 'As I said, we don't *know* what happened. You might've accidentally hurt-'

'What the hell are you talking about?' I was screaming now. It wasn't ideal. 'I'll *tell* you what happened. Georgina and I were driving into Darkridge Hollow when my front tyres blew out and I ended up parking the goddamned car in a ditch.' I refrained from adding, "upside-down". It was irrelevant. I didn't need the reminder, thoughts of a screaming engine and my screaming daughter too vivid. 'I came round to find my twelve-year-old daughter missing. *Missing!*' I repeated firmly, in case she'd missed it the first time. 'I need to speak with the police. *Now.*' It wasn't a request.

'So you claim.' Stubble Guy was sticking his nose in again, putting words where they didn't belong, setting a tone I didn't appreciate.

'It's alright, Tommy,' Megan stepped in, touching his arm.

'I claim?' I shook my head, unable to take this in. That bloody word was beginning to annoy me. I glared at Megan. 'You *saw* the car, saw the state of me.' I was pleading with her to explain what had happened to this demonic creature by her side who assumed he had all the answers. At least I knew the guy's name. I had no idea where the other one

was. Hopefully to get the police promised some time ago. I would willingly explain everything when they arrived. *Anything* would be better than this.

'You were standin' in the road, covered in blood that wasn't your own, actin' deranged,' Tommy concluded.

I shook my head. This idiot was beginning to piss me off. Deranged? *I'll give him deranged in a minute.*

'I wasn't acting *anything*. I was freaking out about where my child had gone.' I still was. Why were none of these people helping me look for her? Why had *I* suddenly become a target? 'Where are the police?' The concept was laughable. I was frustrated, my stress increasing with every passing second I was forced to explain events I had no control over.

'Don't worry, they're comin'.' I was told firmly. I didn't believe them. I had no idea what they were expecting me to do about the impossible situation I'd unwittingly found myself in, nothing I could do about *anything*. It wasn't my fault I'd crashed the car, damaged tyres something I couldn't have foreseen.

As if in response to my untethered aggression, stubble guy – sorry – *Tommy* stepped forward, stepping into the room, the second male I'd seen outside suddenly appearing behind him. A silent communication ensued as in tandem they motioned towards me, grabbing my shoulders, gripping my arms. I was nothing but their prisoner, potentially dangerous, my immediate incarceration required for the protection of all.

'What the *hell* are you doing?' I screamed, kicking out wildly. It was two on one, their bulk easily able to secure mine, a general lack of food and enthusiasm for life ensuring my psychical and emotional strength were ultimately failing.

I wasn't expecting the intrusion into my personal space, wasn't ready for such a violation thrust upon me. They forced me towards the bed, tethering my wrists and ankles with rope to a bedframe that creaked beneath our incoming weight. I glared at Megan, screaming profanities, still ranting, the woman looking at me as if *I* was the problem. This room was about to become my prison cell, this building rotting my already rotted brain matter to mush.

Megan stepped forward and forced a needle into my veins, although what she'd injected me with, I was yet to appreciate. I couldn't stop her. I honestly thought they were going to kill me. I'm sure my screams would have invited external assistance eventually if Tommy hadn't hit me across the cheek to shut me up. I might have sounded like a *girl*. I no longer believed Megan a willing adversary. I no longer knew *what* she was.

'If you're innocent, ya'll have nothin' to worry 'bout,' she confirmed. 'But we can't have strangers showin' up, covered in someone else's blood, claimin' all sorts, no explanation for none of it. When the cops arrive, you can explain what happened out on the road.'

'*Nothing* happened!' I was beyond angry, my kicking legs limited to knees that jolted up and down against the force of thick ropes, springs that buckled and groaned beneath my weight. My statement was incorrect. *Plenty* had happened. I just couldn't begin to comprehend what.

7

I was abandoned, this room nothing more than an amalgamation of shadows and whispers that emanated from the darkness. Each breath alienated reality, every noise a demonic presence I unashamedly believed were *actual* supernatural beings left to supervise my movements. They hid in the corners of the room and the pattern of that goddamned wallpaper, laughing, waiting.

I lay on my back unable to shake the ridiculous idea Megan had *drugged* my coffee and was therefore the reason I'd woken up in this room in the first place. *Jesus.* It would explain a lot. Yet, I shrugged off my stupid consideration before it had time to take root, unable to comprehend such an illogical course of action. I'd done nothing to warrant that kind of attention, nothing about my behaviour ensnaring Megan's unmitigated wrath. I couldn't imagine she'd do something like *that*.

As it was, manic strangers now formed an existence I hadn't envisioned when I got off the plane this morning. Why did it feel so long ago? I'd inappropriately assumed driving through Midwest America would be fun, an adventure, Georgina knowing little of other cultures, other countries. It was a shame that wondrous trip now only existed in my imagination, this journey futile, unrequired. I was in a locked room, tied to a bed, my own devices something I didn't want to be left with a moment longer than necessary.

'Hey?' I yelled towards the unfriendly darkness, my words reaching nothing but stagnant air. 'You can't do this. I need to find my daughter.' I had no idea how long I'd succumbed to further unconsciousness, more hours passing—these restraints ensuring my continued compliance, this moment as crazy as this day. 'What are you doing to find my *daughter?*' I called out, rattling the bed, straining ropes against fragile limbs that bruised easily under duress.

'You wanna be gagged?' I heard a muffled grunt behind the closed door. *Tommy.* No, of course I didn't want *that*. Having bound hands and feet was bad enough. Being gagged as well may finish me off entirely, leaving me dead in a stranger's house, suffocating alone with no one to confirm my existence. I fell silent, heavy thoughts threatening to encroach the very air I breathed and smother me where I lay.

A few seconds passed before dull footsteps headed away from the door, whispered voices too softly spoken for my strained ears to acknowledge. *Jesus Christ.* Surely this was a stupid dream? I'd be waking up soon. Maybe I'd fallen asleep at the service station, on the grass, Georgina busy enjoying her ice cream whilst happily *ignoring* me. I'd be okay in a minute, this impossible instant nothing but fading visions I'd gladly dissipate into the afternoon air. I closed my eyes, trying and failing to force myself out of this unhinged timeline. Something had gone wrong. I hoped it wasn't my brain.

Whatever it was, there was no way I could lie in the dark, accepting a fate I had no intention of becoming a depleted part of, hoping someone would step in and fix this. I was an average bloke from South East London, nobody special, a freelance digital artist who worked from home, not Samuel L Jackson. I twisted my body every which way, my restraints unrelenting, my mind unyielding. I tugged my wrists, the things tied above my head, the groaning headboard unforgiving. Every movement sliced through the silence, showcasing my struggle with each laboured breath I took, every twitching muscle enough to send *them* running. I had visions of the door being flung open, of being hit over the head with something heavy, ensuring my *permanent* silence, no way for me to help my vulnerable daughter then.

I spent several frantic minutes twisting my wrist in an attempt to grab a section of the bed frame behind me, desperate to take back some of the control that had been cruelly removed. The frame was solid pine yet not well maintained, *thankfully*, and I was able to slide a strip of decorative wood within my grasp. I took a breath, almost unwilling to believe this old piece of furniture might help in my *literal* hour of need. I motioned the spindle back and forth, trying not to raise unwanted attention, unrequired suspicion. I pulled and tugged, every movement taking forever, inching the splintering pine from its rotting frame.

Seconds passed slower than seemed psychically possible, time ready to seal my fate, seal me into this unwitting tomb, every wisp of air dragged painfully from my already failing lungs. When I heard something snap, I couldn't assume it wasn't my bones. I wiggled my wrist, overwhelmed when the spindle came away in my grasp, painful air escaping my throat like shards of glass. I honestly hadn't expected to pull it off, anticipating the consequences, my pathetic attempts observed churlishly by those outside this room. I expected the door to burst open, my escape attempt foiled. Instead I took in a deep breath and held it, a muffled television in the background keeping my jailers entertained elsewhere, masking my movements in the darkness above.

With no time to think and little thought for

repercussions, I shook my hand free, the rope untangling easily. I reached for the other, my fingernails tearing with the effort of untying a knot that momentarily felt like lead. It took forever, this restraint not as forgiving as the last. I anticipated failure, yet after a few frantic moments of wondering what the hell I was doing, chastising my stupidity and failed parental ability, I was free. Both wrists were aching, matching my throbbing ankle, but it didn't matter. I sat upright, hearing nothing beyond the television and muffled giggles aimed towards thankfully unassuming ears below.

I untied my ankles, mindful to lift myself slowly from the mattress, every movement emphasised, every spring mocking this impossible interjection. I sidestepped several creaking floorboards, reaching the window, the twenty-foot drop to the dirt below unimportant, my fragile bones unable to oppose my mission. I just needed to get it open, my stealthy attempts more "bumbling wreck" than "SAS assassin". I was no James Bond, that's for sure.

The window was an old-fashioned sash, single pane, no doubt draughty in winter, decades of paint welding it shut and probably the only thing keeping the outside world at bay. I couldn't turn on the light, the ill-fitting doorframe ready to showcase such stupidity and highlight the madman who'd escaped his tethers. I thought about my boots still by Megan's front door, the rest of my belongings in a suitcase somewhere, probably still in the back of her truck. It didn't matter. Nothing mattered other than getting out of here, preferably in one piece, *alive*. The alternative was unimaginable.

I crept around on tiptoes, my bare feet thankfully muffled against the ageing floor, trembling fingertips reaching brail-like along each surface. When I spotted a crowbar glistening in the gloom, I had to look twice, the thing propped against a chest of drawers, *waiting*. For what,

I couldn't say, yet unless someone was planning my ultimate downfall, I didn't assume its presence was necessary. Whatever the reason, I was grateful. I had a weapon now if nothing else.

I held my breath and wedged the flat end under the window frame, forcing layers of paint to blister and flake onto the floor, the splintering sound too much for my deranged mind to contend with. I needed to leverage the thing from its clogged seal, inching it open wide enough for me to slide my body awkwardly onto the window ledge. It didn't matter my legs would be dangling mid-air behind me. I held my breath, waiting for the moment when my actions would be discovered, the crowbar firm in my grasp. *What the hell was I doing?*

My ankle was still smarting in places, my bandage still fresh, any fall liable to ensure it snapped completely. I almost changed my mind, convinced I couldn't cope with more pain today. Yet, staying in that room wasn't an option either. It was too late to turn back, no way for me to accept whatever fate Megan and those men might have in store for me tonight. I held my breath as I dropped my weapon to the ground outside, expecting a clatter, shocked to hear only a low thud. I lowered myself downwards, my dangling feet trembling, the weight of my body unexpectedly encumbered. It was fitting, the way this day was turning, my body confirmation of how my mind had fared over the last few hours, the last few months set for an ultimate conclusion. I was in limbo, reality wholly ready to hit me where it hurt.

I took a breath and dropped, those precious seconds freefalling to the ground more terrifying than I anticipated. I landed hard, my knees taking most of the impact as my legs bucked beneath me. *Bloody hell.* Yet, I had no time to check for fresh injuries or register the pain. I clambered to my feet and ran, nothing else to do, my throbbing ankle joined now by a twisted knee, the incoming limp not something I had time to acknowledge. The ground was thankfully softened by the recent rain, overgrown in places, thick grassy weeds aiding my escape, as if whispering in the darkness, helping my cause. I left the crowbar where it landed, unwanted, unrequired. I couldn't have known that getting into Megan's truck would result in *this,* my continued warnings about "stranger danger" to Georgina coming back to bite me on the backside.

***

I was unprepared for the darkness or how black the sky would be without street lamps to guide me. I was accustomed to a brightly lit city, visibility a given, even during the dead of night when the only creatures on the prowl were foxes and drunks. This place couldn't have been more different. Distant stars lay hidden behind thickened clouds, heavy rain still lingering. It helped, of course, that in the pitch black no one could see me, yet neither could I see a damned thing, my desperation and bare feet made all the more infuriating by dying crops in damaged fields I didn't notice until it was too late, stumbling around like a fool, wild animals that saw me long before I saw them, odd sounds that left me genuinely afraid for my life.

I was relieved when pinpricked lights from nearby properties trickled across the damp pavement, the edge of Megan's property a place I was glad to have left behind. Yet, all I could think about was Georgina, alone somewhere, probably as terrified as her stupid dad and just as lost and confused. I couldn't think about what wild animals might have done to her as I crept along those empty streets, my bare feet catching loose stones and shards of glass sending fresh pain into my body. I had no idea where I going other than to locate a friendly face, the idea that I was *safe,* something I couldn't quite accept.

In a city, you can disappear, hide in plain sight, locate salvation via the protection of late-night cafés and bars, the police never far away. Yet this was a small town, its inhabitants potentially as worrisome as Megan. It sent a cold shudder down my spine. How many local residents knew the woman? How many liked her? Would they assume *me* the liar? At this rate, I'd probably disappear, too. I wasn't stupid. I'd seen movies about apparent tight-knit communities, heard stories from Anna. Megan undoubtedly knew *everyone* in this town, one whiff of my whereabouts sending them directly to my unwitting location under the pretence of help that would see me dead by daylight. I couldn't take the chance. What the hell was I thinking, escaping with no *actual* plan? It didn't matter. I couldn't allow raw emotion to cloud my judgment, or unfounded hindrance to foil my impossible mission.

I ventured further into Darkridge Hollow, this place more sinister by night than I ever assumed it could be during the day. The entire location was peppered with forgotten roads that intersected every so often, shops that barely remembered the last time they'd seen an open door, dilapidated buildings unfit for purpose, their owners no doubt long departed before sanity departed them. It reminded me of something. I couldn't tell what. "The Walking Dead" perhaps? I fully expected a group of zombies to greet me around every corner, every noise I made too intense. After all, the *black guy* always got killed first on TV. As it was, the only things that met me were cats and rats that scurried away when they saw my approach, debris blowing in the breeze.

I wished I had a map. I glanced down. And a pair of *shoes.* If I knew where the nearest police station was, that would be helpful, too. I checked my pockets, my wallet and mobile long gone. I wanted to laugh. The irony of my predicament wasn't lost on my failing brain, yet I couldn't understand why Megan had turned on me so readily, so cruelly. She had offered help, seemed *nice.*

I kept low against the road's edge, close to the grass verge and open countryside beyond. A fertile landscape awaited me now, housing a vast array of wildlife, all the creatures of the world awakening to the call of the evening, threatening to swallow me whole. I glanced around, the darkness engulfing my senses, my exposure to nature and lack of clothing to blame for my rapidly declining mood. A distinct call of crickets and the pad of bare feet on damp gravel kept me on constant alert, this night so dark, so terrifyingly real. I honestly didn't assume I'd make it out alive. I glanced towards the trees, nothing but rustling leaves to unsettle my nerves, demonic shapes racing freely through my turbulent mind.

I fully expected to be caught, each passing vehicle sending me diving for cover amidst the questionable safety of the tree line. I assumed they would be out looking for me by now, every noise a potential danger, every movement a threat. I walked until I reached the edge of town, nowhere else to go, exhausted yet grateful for the freedom this blackened night afforded. I was glad to be out of that place, away from locked rooms and troubled minds, my unyielding stupidity obvious.

When a police car drove past, I almost hid from view. *Oh, the irony.* My brain didn't immediately register what was happening, the vehicle almost driving into the night before I saw it. I panicked, unable to do anything but dive into its path, no time to consider I might be killed in the process, no reason to assume being run over would make this day any worse. The car came to a shuddering halt, the officer behind the wheel assuming I was either drunk, out to cause trouble, or both.

'What the *hell* are you doin'?' he yelled, his deep voice a welcome intrusion to my evening. He was out of his car before I could react, already reaching for his gun. Under normal circumstances, such an act would have scarred me for life, yet because of the evening's events, I was too relieved to care. It didn't matter if the guy had me face down in the dirt with my hands behind my back, a heavy boot pressed against my spine. Anything would have been an improvement to the last few hours.

I grinned, allowing a laugh that, to this poor sod might have looked unhinged. I was losing my mind, I may as well look the part. My jeans were still coated in blood, my body injured, no shirt or shoes to confirm I hadn't either escaped from somewhere or *killed* someone. I couldn't deny the possibility of either, Georgina's potential death something I should have prevented. I had nothing to my name, no identity, no possessions, my brain as tattered and bruised as my body. Yet the sight of that young officer had me grinning as if the gun he was holding was nothing but a child's water pistol. He could have shot me on the spot and I would have kept on smiling. I had found the police. *Honestly,* right at that moment, I couldn't be happier.

8

I was standing in a darkened street in the middle of a dilapidated town, barefoot, broken and unhinged. It wasn't how I'd planned to spend my first day in the States and I was still trying to assess how I'd got to this point, still assuming I had control. After seeing I was no threat and lowering his gun, the police officer gave me a blanket from the boot of his car that I took without question, settling me into the back seat of his vehicle with a disconcerting nod. When he spoke into his radio, I was too stressed to listen, the explanation he gave, wholly inconsequential. It didn't matter what he thought of me. *I* wasn't important.

The way he looked at me at least provided hope I was in capable hands, finally safe. I should have been grateful for small mercies, despite believing me some kind of vagabond, no doubt from an unforgiving background, probably mentally ill. It didn't matter. His authority rose over everything; his badge, his gun—even the way he stood should have calmed my shredded nerves. As it was, my body was numbed by several hours of torture that came in the form of patterned wallpaper, flying fists, and harsh words. It twisted reality into Georgina's frightening features along with torment from strangers who assumed keeping me inside a locked room was acceptable.

'Have they *found* her?' It was the first thing I asked, my

only consideration, my mind no longer willing to form rational conclusions.

'Who we talkin' 'bout?' The officer glanced at my thin body, weakened arms clutching my recently acquired blanket as if my life depended on its limited protection. I was barely able to dissipate any assumption this guy had of my failing composure, my torn clothes, wild eyes.

'My daughter.' I could hardly appreciate the magnitude of my words. I was out of breath, out of my mind. I had no idea how to explain the several hours that had passed since Georgina's unfathomed disappearance.

'You'd better start from the beginnin',' the police officer instructed as he climbed into the car, ready to make our way through the blackened streets towards deliverance I hoped wasn't far away.

'There was an accident.'

'What kinda accident?'

The kind where I lost my child. I closed my eyes, needing to catch my thoughts, my breath, nothing of this day intact. 'I need to find her.' I was mumbling, my throat a tightened knot of elastic bands

'Your daughter?'

'*Yes!* I just told you.' I was angry, impatient, glaring out of the window for a sign, anything that might explain my child's absence, disgruntled that the only thing staring back was my pathetic, hollow reflection. I was furious with this officer for not grasping my failing words or appreciating my urgency. It wasn't his fault, of course. Yet, after the way Megan had turned on me, I needed to know I was in the validated company of those out searching for my vulnerable child. 'Her name's Georgina. She's missing. Please. I just need to know the police are out there looking.'

'I thought you said there was an *accident?*'

I nodded. 'And when I woke up, my child was gone.'

The police officer narrowed his eyes, not convinced I

was giving him the whole story.

'Please, just radio it in. Check that a search has already begun.' I couldn't imagine that no one had yet started looking. 'Her name is Georgina Raymond. She's twelve.' I leaned forward, the metal grid separating us too encumbered, rigid, my mind a treacherous place in which to exist. 'Please,' I was begging, digging my fingertips through the grate, attempting to provoke a rational, helpful reply. It wasn't ideal and it didn't help. But I was desperate, terrified. Surely this guy could understand that.

'Can you sit back a little for me, please,' he instructed firmly, something in his tone I didn't like. What the hell did he think I was going to do from back here? Apart from have a full-blown panic attack, potential heart failure. More shit he'd have to deal with.

'But my daughter is *missing*,' I repeated. I just wanted to be heard.

'And ya'll be given the opportunity to explain it all in due course.'

The officer lifted a radio from its cradle, ready to ask a distant voice the very question I wasn't convinced I wanted the answer to. He looked at me as if he honestly didn't know what to make of me, as if he'd never seen someone like me before. I could already feel the bruising on my face and wrists. It probably made me appear the type of person who willingly got into fights. I didn't. I just bruised easily. Always had.

'Darkridge Hollow ain't exactly the place for tourists.' His throwaway comment was true enough. It wasn't a place I'd have willingly visited—no brochure in existence capable of highlighting any area of this unwelcoming town I'd want to experience twice.

'Does visiting family count?' I mumbled, more to myself than the man in my company, my head hanging low, bitter words spilt mutedly into my lap, unheard over unrelenting radio chatter that filled the car. I closed my eyes, wishing I were elsewhere, desperate for answers and terrified I wouldn't cope with what I might discover. I wasn't expecting good news. The officer turned his attention to his radio, my presence of no concern. I couldn't bring myself to listen. Coming here was a mistake.

'Whatcha doin' out here by yourself anyway?' he asked eventually when the chattering radio returned no confirmation. He looked relaxed, this night just another in a long line of many. It didn't help.

'Just passing through,' I grunted, not wishing to get into details right then. It didn't matter that I had raced into the night, afraid for my life, only here to find Georgina's family, a family I'd obsessed over because of my dead wife. Now I no longer cared if I found them or not, didn't care if I *ever* saw Darkridge Hollow again. All I needed was confirmation they were looking for my child, put me out of my misery and tell me the *truth*. Yet, I couldn't assume Georgina was the only missing person they were forced to deal with, mine not the only case being investigated. It wasn't comforting to assume missing kids were something they deemed a normal, daily occurrence. I couldn't help worrying they'd already found her and were merely sparing me the agony of verifying she was dead until they could confirm the tragedy in person.

We drove the rest of the way in silence, the officer no longer willing to partake in a conversation with the madman in his company, his radio less than conclusive. I wasn't convinced Georgina would have headed in this direction. I was struggling to maintain the idea she was *alive*. These ailing roads narrowed sporadically, no pavements to keep her tiny frame safe from passing vehicles or rabid animals, few nearby buildings to find sanctuary. Something terrible had happened. I could feel it.

The idea churned my belly to sludge as I sat in the

backseat of the police car, powerless and afraid. There was nothing to do but clutch an icy blanket around my trembling shoulders, my mind wandering to places I didn't want to follow. Megan was right. The nearest police station was several miles away, a place called Abbotts View looming into soft focus as we pulled into a brightly lit car park.

In contrast to Darkridge Hollow with its black outlook matching a perpetually blackened sky, Abbotts View was peppered with an artificial glow, a warm tinge making the puddles left by the earlier rainstorm dance in the breeze. It looked as if the people who lived here at least cared about the place they called home. The car door opened and I was helped to my feet. I was limping, shoeless. I looked like a decrepit old man. No wonder Megan had already forged a sinister idea of what she assumed I'd done, my bloodied t-shirt no doubt kept as *evidence*. I needed to set the record straight, and fast, confirm Georgina's disappearance was being dealt with. I needed to *find her*. It was all I could think about.

'Is this the guy you picked up?' An officer behind a large desk barely looked up as we entered a double-fronted building highlighting several unsmiling people within. The blanket I'd been clutching was becoming a burden, weighing me down. I looked as if I'd escaped from somewhere. *Oh, the irony.* Yet I was grateful to be inside a building with light fittings that didn't hang from dusty, damaged wires, a fire hazard waiting to happen—people around me who at least appeared *sane*.

'Yep. Found him by the side of the road,' my chaperone pitched in, eager to transfer me to someone else, no longer appreciative of my company. 'Thought it best I bring him in. He seemed a little…' He glanced sideways at my bare feet, adding 'troubled,' with a sigh.

I narrowed my eyes, unappreciative of the tone he'd

acquired, unable to confirm his response wasn't a racist reaction. 'My name is Joshua Raymond,' I stated, clear enough so these officers wouldn't assume me mentally incapable of responding. I needed a t-shirt, a pair of shoes—my *daughter*. I glanced towards a badge pinned to the shirt of the guy behind the desk, the words Deputy Chief McDonald, Police Dept. Ohio, printed on its face, the officer by my side, State Trooper Robert Bailey. 'Earlier today you received a phone call from a resident in Darkridge Hollow.' I couldn't help choking out my words. I wasn't sure I wanted visions of Megan in my head right then. It didn't matter.

'Is that right?' Deputy Chief McDonald didn't appear troubled by the idea, his response laid back.

'Yes.' I wasn't asking, I was stating a fact. 'Her name is Megan.' I had no idea what her surname was. It was unimportant until now. 'She reported a young girl missing. She's my daughter.'

'Megan's your daughter?'

I blinked, shaking my head. '*No.* Megan's the woman who helped me.' I was glaring frantically at a face reddened by stress and an overreliance on fast food. Constant nausea sat in the back of my throat, yet it was from nothing I'd eaten, Megan's strong coffee unable to dislodge the cancerous thoughts devouring my every movement, the drugs in my system not a comfort.

'I'm real sorry to hear that, son,' Deputy Chief McDonald smiled, although I wasn't convinced he meant it. *So was I.* 'Lemme go check.' He headed off somewhere, his urgency not forthcoming, several strangers staring at me as if I was the problem. He returned a moment later, a dismissive look on his face and a cup of coffee in his hand. He took a swig, seemingly unconcerned by my urgency. 'I'm afraid there's been no missin' person reports filed today or any other this week, come to think of it.' He laughed, sounding pleased by the confirmation.

I glared at the deputy, then at Officer Bailey still by my side. Neither appeared concerned. 'No. That can't be true. A woman called *Megan* called you this afternoon. I should know, I sat in her kitchen drinking coffee whilst she made the call directly.'

Deputy Chief McDonald shook his head, his eyes darting up and down, taking in my unkempt appearance, my trembling legs, bare feet. I didn't appreciate his tone, couldn't assume his attitude wasn't due to the colour of my skin, the way I was dressed ensuring an unfettered conclusion. 'Sorry, but there ain't been no report 'bout a missin' child today. *I should know*. I've been on duty all day.' I couldn't breathe. The only thing I caught from that statement was that *nobody* was looking for Georgina.

'Are you serious?'

'Serious as a heart attack.'

Jesus Christ. 'Can you check again?' I was confused, ready to either vomit or pass out, whichever came first. What the hell was happening?

'Just hold your horses there, boy. I can check again, but it ain't gonna change the outcome.'

I leant against the countertop for support I knew I wouldn't find, hoping someone would tell me this was all just a bad dream.

'D'ya wanna file a missin' person report?'

What kind of stupid question was that? 'Yes, of course I do,' I stammered. 'I need you to *find* her. We had a car accident this afternoon on the way into Darkridge Hollow. When I woke up, the car was in a ditch and Georgina was gone.' I could barely breathe, could scarcely get my words out straight.

'Okay, no need to get excited.' The deputy raised a disinterested hand towards me.

Excited? Was this guy serious?

'I assumed the police were already looking for my child, on their way into Darkridge Hollow to question me and search the area. Now you're telling me that *nothing* has yet been *filed?*' I couldn't take this in. 'Who took the phone call?' Why the hell hadn't the police taken Megan's call seriously? I tried to think back to *precisely* what she'd said but I was panicking, nothing of value willing to engage my rapidly deteriorating brain matter. I was no longer convinced by *anything* Megan had done. Anything could have happened to Georgina by now. She could be dead.

'What's your child's name, please?'

'*Georgina!*' I yelled, causing several people to glare at me. How many more times did I need to say it?

'Her *full* name.' Deputy Chief McDonald was unnervingly calm, yet I could tell he was unimpressed by my outburst. He was chewing something. I hoped it choked him.

'Georgina...Charlotte...Raymond.' I stated slowly so the idiot could write it down before he forgot again. Did he need me to spell it for him, too? 'She's twelve years old. Has long, dark hair. Last seen wearing red trainers, dark grey baggy trousers and a purple t-shirt with some kind of logo on it.' I was too stressed to remember the exact motive on her t-shirt or to adequately explain the silver decorative panels that ran down the outside of each trouser leg. I didn't know if she had her mobile phone with her, her headphones *or* her belongings, the rental car still lying in the ditch where I'd left it—everything my daughter had with her seemingly vanishing into thin air.

The police took as much detail as they could and I verified the whereabouts of the abandoned rental car, providing a detailed description of Megan, the help she'd initially given now feeling more like an unwanted moment in time I would never get back. I didn't tell them about being inside a locked room, tied to a bed, drugged up and forced to jump out of a window. I hoped they wouldn't instigate a drug test. I didn't know what they would find in my bloodstream. They wouldn't appreciate the unfathomable reasons why three strangers believed me capable of hurting someone, restraints and locked doors not yet substantiated. I didn't need that kind of attention, fingers pointing in the wrong direction. The clock was ticking.

'When was the last time you saw your daughter, Mr. Raymond?'

I had no idea. I didn't know how long I was unconscious or what had happened to my child during those moments I could never explain. Hours could have passed, or minutes. I closed my eyes, thinking back.

'It had just gone three when I last checked.' Moments before we headed back onto the highway, in fact, the day so different then to how it was ending now. I'd give anything to go back, argue with Georgina some more. Buy her another ice cream.

The officer looked at me briefly before checking the clock on the wall behind him. It was a few minutes before midnight. 'Okay, so around nine hours?'

I nodded. Nine hours was too long. Georgina wouldn't survive with no money, no food, no way of knowing where the hell she was. I thought the worst.

The two officers gave each other a brief look, equally knowing what nine hours meant for a missing child. Time was crucial, vital, every second passed was a second too long. The deputy looked at me, his face momentarily softening, willing to finally take me seriously. I should have been grateful.

'Why didn'tcha report her missin' this afternoon, after the crash?'

'I *did*. I mean, Megan did.'

'And, how d'ya know this Megan?'

'I don't really know her at all.' That was the problem. 'She lives in Darkridge Hollow. Found me by the side of the road. *Helped me.*' The world was spinning. I couldn't think straight. I no longer understood *what* Megan had done. It certainly wasn't help.

'And what've you been doin' since this afternoon?'

It was a simple question, of course, asked out of simple concern. He looked me up and down, no doubt troubled by the condition I was in, the bruising on my cheek from Tommy's earlier punch already angrily forming. How the hell did I respond to that?

'I was waiting for the police.'

'At Megan's house.'

'Yes.'

'All this time?'

'Yes.'

'Because you thought she'd already called us?'

'Yes!'

The guy took a deep breath. I didn't want to acknowledge why. 'And you've done *nothin'* since then? Nothin' *stupid?'* He was glaring at my bare feet, emphasising the word "stupid" as if he already believed I had.

'No!' I narrowed my eyes. *Stupid?* This whole day was stupid.

'D'ya have a picture of your child, Mr. Raymond?'

I reached for my wallet before remembering it was gone. I had nothing to show them, Megan oddly taking everything of value from me in a single unwitting action. Georgina was *twelve.* I hadn't yet allowed her to open a social media account. She was too young, too vulnerable, potential grooming and online bullying too real. Now I wished I'd been less protective. It might have offered the protection she needed, a simple photograph of her something I desperately needed. I couldn't imagine that because I was *black* my child was deemed unimportant, couldn't now confirm *she* wasn't, her photograph something I couldn't share. I shook my head.

'And d'ya have an address for Megan?'

I stared into space. No. I didn't have that either. I had no idea where she lived or how to navigate back to the house. 'Not exactly,' I responded, trying and failing to retrace my steps. It didn't help I'd barely escaped my captives, racing into the night towards potential doom, my bare feet sore and savaged by the unrelenting ground I'd been forced to cover.

I was able to recall the dirt track that led from the main road, vaguely remembering it was set along a street called Hillborne Avenue, overgrown trees arching carelessly into each other, twisted and forgotten. There was a sign, *I think*, but it was faded now, letters once painted onto a piece of whitewashed wood erased by the relentless passing of time. It was pitch black when I'd left, my feet pointing me as far away as I could get. The last thing on my mind was retracing my steps, going *back*. Yet, the town wasn't huge, wasn't special. I could probably find it, at a push. It didn't help that these people were looking at me as if I was covering for something far darker and more sinister than I'd willingly expressed—watching each other now as if *I* was the one telling lies.

Deputy Chief McDonald shifted position, staring at my filthy feet for the umpteenth time. It was annoying. I didn't want to know what he was thinking. I could barely bring myself to look at him.

'I know it looks odd. But I've had the day from *hell*.' It was true. All I needed was rational consideration, a sane conversation. 'I can probably *take* you to the house.' In truth, going back to that place was the last thing I wanted. Yet with the police by my side, Megan and her goons couldn't do anything stupid. Besides, she still had my belongings. I damned well wanted them back.

Day Two

9

It didn't take a huge stretch of the imagination to appreciate the police weren't familiar with the concept of urgency. My indulgent demands seemed too much for them, their time needed elsewhere. I was failing to understand *why* they were acting so casual, their consistent throwaway attitude already wearing thin. They had a job to do. I damned well expected them to do it. Since my arrival, I'd lost my daughter, my belongings, my *mind*, rapidly losing track now of how long I'd been forced to endure the confining walls of this overbearing building. Several times I almost left, leaving them to it, wondering why I was sitting around doing *nothing*. Yet the idea of authoritative control kept me sipping weak tea into the early hours, watching, waiting.

They took a statement, of course, the description I provided written on log sheets for later assessment. I wanted to explain what Megan had done, the locked room I still couldn't get out of my mind, rope burns I couldn't hide. Yet where would I begin? How could I explain *that* without securing my own fate in the process? I left my third cup of tea to go cold, calling my father from a pay phone along a corridor, forced to reverse the charges because I had no money to pay for the call. It wasn't ideal. We hadn't been close for years, his home in Spain far removed from everything I knew, my current reality included. My African upbringing was something I'd always been proud of, mostly because of my mother. It was a shame he didn't know, the man hardly possessing the ability to connect with his only son.

'Josh, what the hell are you doing calling this early in the morning?' My dad's gruff voice filtered down the phone, an unfamiliar operator ensuring he almost refused to speak to me, several annoying moments passing before I heard his familiar tone.

'Sorry, Dad,' I cut in. 'I couldn't think of anyone else to call.' It was true. I hoped he wouldn't take offence, his frustration apparent. My father usually needed at least two cups of strong tea in his system before he could hold a conversation, especially with me. It had just turned two o'clock in the morning here, eight o'clock in Spain. He would be out of bed by now—awake, alert.

'What's wrong? Why are you reversing the charges? Do you think I'm made of money?'

My dad always spoke to me as if he didn't want to, as if he didn't need the stress that came in the form of his only son. I took an unsteady breath, unsure how to broach the subject, the reason for my unfounded morning phone call still lingering.

'It's Georgina.' I was biting my lip, no words capable of describing my turmoil.

'Christ, what's wrong with her *now?*'

I didn't appreciate his dismissive tone. 'Don't be like that,' I muttered, unsure how I was going to tell him what *had* happened. My father never accepted Georgina, never acknowledged her as his granddaughter. He always proclaimed he wasn't a racist, didn't *care* that I'd married a white girl, my mother merely unable to deal well with the unfortunate truth that Anna couldn't have more children. It added to the shit show that had become my life, the reason I barely spoke to my father now.

'So, what are you calling *me* for?' I could tell he was busy, as always, making tea, my call something he didn't need in his day. There was an intake of breath and something that sounded as if he'd dropped a spoon.

'Georgie's missing.' I could barely bring myself to think about it. I was only calling him to hear a familiar voice and gain support I wasn't sure where else to find it. He was thousands of miles away. What could *he* do from Spain?

'What?' Another clatter. 'How the hell did you lose a twelve-year-old?' My dad's sarcastic chortle sounded as if he was finding this funny, private musing left unchecked. *Was he laughing at me?* I honestly didn't think the man was grasping the reality of the situation. 'Where are you?' he asked, oblivious to my emotions, a low grunt leaving his mouth as he bent to retrieve his dropped items. I thought I heard a snippet of concern in his voice, though it was probably my imagination.

I glanced around. Where the hell did I start? 'I'm in Ohio, Dad.' I took a breath.

'Oh, for Christ's sake, Josh.' There was an uncomfortable pause.

'I knew you'd think me crazy if I told you where I was going.'

My dad scoffed. I visualised the veins popping at the side of his skull, his lips pursed, blue. 'Crazy? You've been acting *crazy* for a while, so that hardly matters, does it? Ever since…' He trailed off, unable to finish his sentence, unable to conclude his unkind comment. We both knew what he wanted to say. *Ever since Anna died.* It wasn't an issue to make light of.

'Calm down,' I spat, trying to defuse the situation and failing. He didn't need to make this about him. 'I came to see if I could find Anna's family.'

'Christ, not that bloody obsession again?' My father had aptly called Anna's family an "obsession" in front of

Georgina once. I still had visions of my sobbing child, could still hear her voice to this very day. "Why doesn't Grandpa like me, Daddy?"

I took a breath, biting my lip, wishing that for once in his life, he would shut up and listen. My father and I never had a stable relationship, yet it was declining in a way I was no longer comfortable constraining. Since Anna's passing, things had taken a sinister turn and I had no idea how to deal with it. I wasn't confident he didn't blame me for her death, although he may as well. He blamed me for everything else.

'Firstly, you lose your wife in a tragic accident and fail to let me know for weeks,' he ranted, oblivious to my current situation or state of mind. *It wasn't weeks, just a couple of days. I was in shock. Grieving.* 'You've become obsessed with people you've never met, your job is hanging by a thread, and I dread to think what the *hell* you thought you were doing, taking off without a word to anyone. And now you say Georgina is *missing?*' He took an audible breath that made me want to scream, his accusations hanging in the air.

I felt a pang of anger at my dad for his harsh words, my grief consuming me in a way he couldn't understand. *Accident?* How the hell could he call a "drunk driver" an accident? He was right about the rest, though. My job was tied to Anna and a life that no longer existed, my so-called *obsession* emerging because of a wife I'd never see again. My parents hadn't been close for years, splitting up several times when I was young and only getting back together because of *me.* The man knew nothing of my sorrow. He barely knew anything of love. My mother was clinging to life by a thread, her dementia taking all memories of hate and betrayal that my father was forced to live with daily. It was exhausting.

'I'm sorry,' I replied. 'I didn't have time to think. I just grabbed Georgie and got on a plane.' I took a breath that hurt my chest. 'She's been missing since yesterday.' It wasn't a truth I wanted to accept.

More silence.

'Dad, did you hear what I said?' I scoffed loudly, almost choking on my words.

'I heard you.' There was a further pause that felt like a cavern had opened up between us. 'So, where *exactly* are you?'

'At the police station.' I glanced around, wanting to say more than I was comfortable expressing, needing to make sense of the shit I was dealing with. I positioned my face towards the wall, speaking into my hand. 'There's something odd going on, but I'm not sure how to explain it.'

'Odd, how?'

'I have no idea.' I honestly couldn't understand the lack of priority provided, my daughter no priority at all. And the way they looked at each other—that didn't seem *normal.*

My father tutted.

'Why are you tutting?' I felt ten years old again.

'Because you're making no sense. You never make sense. You're like your mother. Do you know she's worried about you?'

I hated the way he threw Mum into every conversation we had, a blatant attempt to make me feel guilty for things I had no control over. My mother had been an alcoholic for years, her subsequent mental decline ensuring she barely knew what day it was. Mum wouldn't have questioned my whereabouts, wouldn't have noticed. The truth was, my father had no other way of communicating with me, anger his only means of escape, his move to Spain no escape at all, in the end. I needed to get off the phone. This wasn't helping.

'Say hello to her for me. Give her my love.' I needed to end the call before I went insane and did something I'd regret.

'When are you going home?'

'When I find my daughter.'

No reply.

'Dad?'

I could hear his breath, his lungs struggling for air.

'I don't mean to get onto you, Josh,' my father's voice had found a calmer intonation, ensuring I refrained from hanging up, my trembling hand hovering.

'I know.' He could have fooled me.

'But this is *so* typical of you.' He paused again, taking a sharp breath. 'You do *exactly* what you want, when you want, and you never think of the feelings of others in the process.'

Was he speaking about Georgina now, my mother, or *himself*? I'd spent my entire life thinking of everyone else, putting everyone before me, the majority of my childhood ensuring I'd looked after him because Mum was rarely in a fit state to do it herself. I was only sticking with my current job because the money was just about good enough to pay rent on a property that Anna loved far more than I did, the upside being that I got to work from home. Everything I'd achieved up to this point had revolved around what everyone else thought I should be doing. Christ, I was only here *now* because I wanted to do the right thing by people I didn't know. Things needed to change.

'Tell Mum I said hi,' I no longer wanted to continue this conversation. I was on the verge of breaking down. I didn't need my dad to see *that*.

'You can tell her yourself when you finally make an appearance.'

Sarcasm. *Perfect.* Just what I needed. 'Goodbye, Dad.' I offered no more words, nothing left to say, too angry to care *what* he thought.

I hung up before he was able to provide further snippets

of supposed wisdom, suppressing an overwhelming urge to scream, punch the wall or the nearest police officer, whichever came first. I was shocked by his continued ability to make me feel angry and small, despite thousands of miles and an entire ocean between us. Georgina meant nothing to him. *I meant nothing to him.* I was steadily losing everything, including the ability to think straight. If I'd known that was going to be the last time we'd ever speak, I might have thought of something better and more profound to say. Yet, as it was, he'd left me with profanities on my lips and frustration that had nowhere to go.

'Family trouble?' Deputy Chief McDonald called from the safety of his desk. I didn't answer. I didn't assume he'd appreciate my response.

***

I sat in the station for a further three frustrating hours, lost in thought, reaching for my missing wallet several times for comfort I couldn't locate, finding nothing but my skinny backside and ill-fitting jeans. I was given a police-issue t-shirt that was too big and a pair of lace-up trainers that my hands struggled to tie. I could hear Georgina in my head. *In Ohio, Dad, they use the term 'gym shoes' or 'training shoes', not sneakers. Jeez, get with the programme.* I could see her rolling her eyes skyward, tutting. Christ, I really missed that kid.

I stared at a stranger's face in a cold bathroom mirror, the man I knew well offering a reflection I no longer understood. My eyes had sunken into my skull, the white of my eyes unseeing, my cheekbones as hollow as the very town I could barely bring myself to think of. There was a bruise across my cheekbone from a punch I'd been unable to block, a wound on my forehead from a crash I'd been unable to foresee, and purple marks around my wrists and ankles from ropes I'd struggled to untie.

I peeled the dressing from my forehead and unwrapped the bandage from my foot, the thing filthy now, tossing both into a nearby waste bin. I needed to remove all traces of the *so-called* help Megan had provided. It was nothing but false assistance anyway, false kindness. She'd probably done it to wind me up, Darkridge Hollow a place that appreciated no other entertainment than what passing strangers could provide. I pushed my feet into footwear that had seen better days, shakily tying frayed shoelaces, thinking of Georgina's recently acquired bright red pair that she barely removed. I wanted my clothes back, my old boots far more comfortable. I was losing more of my identity with every painful second I remained here. What more could these people take from me?

It had gone six o'clock in the morning when I was finally dispatched to Megan's property, accompanied by two state police officers who made it abundantly clear they didn't appreciate the intrusion to their daily routine. They had guns and attitudes and *I* didn't like *their* company, but it was protection I could scarcely do without. There was something about their attitudes that didn't sit right with me, something in their eyes I couldn't appreciate. I didn't know what. Probably the fact that I was a black man in a predominantly white community.

Up until this point, I'd had very little dealings with the police, knew nothing of the law, despite stereotypes assuming otherwise, yet I was confident this wasn't how things worked. Missing children are met with urgency, necessity, limited time available to get them back in one piece, alive. Georgina's disappearance barely seemed to register with these people. I honestly couldn't understand why. We drove into Darkridge Hollow, continued chatter on the radio something I didn't find comforting. Every sound skyrocketed my thoughts into overdrive, each voice expected to confirm the location of a dead girl, found God knows where, in God knows what condition. I didn't need my imagination niggling away at me.

It took some doing, retracing steps I'd taken in a blind panic, every property the same as the last, overgrown, forgotten. The chalky dawn light shone onto ageing façades and discarded vehicles in abandoned driveways. No wonder most had left this community. Eventually, I recognised the driveway that led to Megan's house, that unreadable sign pinned to a gnarled oak tree denoting the location, no less inviting by daylight than it was in the dark. I didn't want to go back, didn't know what I'd find, yet I couldn't tell these strangers, of course, or adequately explain my fears. They wouldn't understand. Judging by their faces, they probably wouldn't *care.*

A hazy panel of light filtered through the car window, highlighting my lifeless body to anyone unfortunate enough to notice. The resulting reflection allowed my skin to blend into the dark stains on the seats, ensuring I was as lost to this world as I felt. It hadn't yet been twenty-four hours, but without Georgina in my world, it could have been a year. A piercing police siren jolted me out of my pensive thinking, forcing me back to a reality I didn't want to acknowledge. I took a breath as Megan's property loomed into view. This wasn't going to be a good day either.

10

Going back to Megan's property wasn't something I ever expected to do, yet we trundled along her forgotten dirt track anyway, featureless faces aimed steadfast in my direction. I held my breath, wishing I could be anywhere but here. I couldn't tell anyone the reasons for my anxiety, forced to suppress a hidden fear neither of my chaperoning police officers would appreciate. The only thing I could do was sit and wait, struggling with the concept of patience, no choice but to absorb their nonsense. I was nothing more to these people than an unwanted corpse, of no real relevance to *anyone.* I swallowed. I didn't need further unpleasantness. Not today. I'd had enough of that shit to last a lifetime.

Distorted voices emerged mockingly from the confines of the overbearing vehicle, adding confusion to my failing composure. Car doors slammed, followed by footsteps that hit the gravel with ill-founded purpose, the boots of the ill-fated officers they belonged to unaware of the quivering wreck behind them. I had nowhere to go, nowhere to escape, the outcome of this morning affording nothing good.

I closed my eyes. The sunlight was already threatening to burn the back of my retina and remove me from this world, leaving behind a body that held no relevance to a human being at all. Nobody needed to deal with *that.* A putrid stench of rotting food wafted across my nostrils, Megan's unattended bins adding nothing good to this moment, my mind creating drama that didn't exist. I hadn't eaten since yesterday. It was a trivial thing to notice. After all, what did I need of food when my daughter's life hung in the balance? I wiped sweat from my brow, rubbing it across a t-shirt sleeve that didn't belong to me, forcing down a sudden urge to vomit.

'Anyone home?' State Trooper Robert Bailey (Bob) drummed a clenched fist against Megan's front door, this place too quiet and imposing for my liking, the distraction unwelcome. His colleague, State Trooper James Montgomery (Jimbo) stood by the car, next to my listless corpse, silently watching my every move. He didn't say a word, didn't need to, but it was obvious he didn't trust me by the way he continually moved watchful eyes across my shrivelled posture. I returned his glare, the feeling *entirely* mutual.

I assumed Megan was still in bed—a flustered night spent searching for me returning no results. I wondered how long they'd spent looking before giving up, giving me up to the prevailing night, abandoning their mission and leaving me to the unknown. Maybe they assumed I wouldn't last long. It didn't bear thinking about what might have happened if they'd found me before the police did. I glanced towards the very window I'd jumped from only hours earlier. Could Megan see me standing in her driveway, waiting for the attention she probably didn't want to give?

Eventually the front door creaked open and Megan appeared, blurry-eyed, in her bathrobe, looking to the outside world as innocent as I'd originally assumed her to be. Yet, looking at her now, my earlier presumptions were entirely misplaced. I no longer knew what to think of the woman.

'Is there a problem, officer?' she asked, her quiet tone no longer holding my respect. After what had happened yesterday, I didn't now see Megan as an ally, a potential friend in the making.

'I'm real sorry to disturb you ma'am, but we have a gentleman here who claims you can shed some light on a small issue we need clearin' up.' He was speaking as if the matter of my daughter's disappearance was nothing more than a lost dog he needed to deal with swiftly so he could get on with his day in peace—more important matters to be addressed, better use of his time to be had. He pointed a finger my way. I was standing by his vehicle, struggling to remain upright, no better than a homeless man with my unshaven appearance and unkempt hair. My newly acquired trainers mocked me, ill-suiting my ill-mannered frame, the things as unwanted as I was. It didn't matter.

'He claims you called the cops yesterday afternoon to report his kid missin'.' Officer Bailey was oblivious to my existence, my needs. I may as well not have been in attendance. That word again. *Claimed.*

Megan shot a cold look towards him as if she'd learned a terrible truth that genuinely troubled her. 'Ope! My goodness, I'm real sorry to hear that,' she proclaimed, clasping a hand to her throat. I hated her tone, the way she brushed a stray strand of hair from her face with the other. 'However, I've never seen this gentleman before in my life, officer. I'm afraid I can't help.'

What? What the hell? I stepped forward, my face contorting, my only intention to uncover *why* she would tell such outrageous lies. What was this woman's problem? I assumed my recent incarceration would have something to do with her silence but I wasn't expecting to be dismissed so swiftly, so intentionally.

'Don'tcha recognise him at all?' Bailey queried again. He was looking at me as if I was a piece of shit he'd scraped off his shoe. They *all* were. Why did I feel so invisible?

Megan looked my way as if trying to assess an impossible situation, glaring straight through me, seeing nothing of the Joshua Raymond she'd rescued from the roadside. 'No, I'm afraid I don't recall *ever* havin' met him before. Did somethin' happen to his daughter, you say?'

Bailey licked his lips, frustration apparent. 'So you didn't help after an incident out on Hillborne Avenue?'

'No. Gosh, I'm pretty darn sure I'd have remembered that.' Megan laughed. She *actually* laughed. What a bitch!

'What the hell are you talking about?' I yelled. I couldn't help it. I began walking towards her, no other intention than to extract the truth.

Both officers stepped forward, stepping in front of me, palms outstretched, guns ready, unappreciative of the chaos they assumed I was about to provoke.

'You *know* who I am. You *helped* me.' I didn't mean to come across as hostile or unfriendly. I left out the part about being locked in a darkened room, tied to a creaking bed and unexpectedly punched in the face. Neither of us needed *that* reminder. It wasn't *help* she'd offered me.

'I'm real sorry for what seems to have happened, but I'm afraid you're mistaken. We've *never* met. I don't know you.' Megan was staring at me as if she had no genuine idea who I was. I almost believed her, believing this entire thing was nothing more than my crazed, overactive imagination. Was this a ridiculous dream I was unable to wake up from? Was I in a coma? *Was I dead?* Maybe I was in a hospital bed, Georgina by my side, holding my hand, unable to wake me up, our car accident far more serious than I realised.

'Can you confirm your name *is* Megan?' Bailey asked calmly, his tone light, oddly upbeat. He was talking as if he simply needed to clear up a few things before he could leave the poor woman in peace. I wanted to throttle the stupid bitch where she stood.

'It sure is.' Megan nodded, folding delicate arms across her chest. She looked confused. How fitting.

'Well, this gentleman *was* able to confirm that, ma'am.'

I stood upright, folding my trembling arms across my chest. *Finally, someone willing to see sense!* I almost smiled, wondering how she was going to get out of *that*. I bit down on my bottom lip in anticipation.

'My goodness, why, everyone in town knows my name,' she laughed, waving a nonchalant finger my way. 'He could've asked *anyone* around these parts who I am.' Megan had the nerve to shake her head as if *I* were crazy, rolling disinterested eyes into the morning air.

'*You* called the police. *You* cleaned me up and made me a cup of coffee,' I yelled in defiance. I was beginning to sound desperate. It wasn't a good look. I didn't add that she'd also locked me up, drugged me, treated me like *shit*.

'I'm afraid my old telephone hasn't worked for years.' Megan glanced over her shoulder, embarrassed by a truth she probably never expected to share so early in the morning. 'But you're more than welcome to take a look around, if you like.' Megan moved to one side as if anticipating they would need to check, collaborate her story, prove me wrong.

'That won't be necessary, ma'am,' Bailey confirmed with a dismissive wave of his hand.

I couldn't believe what I was hearing. If she hadn't called the police, then what the hell *did* she do? And why did she pretend to be speaking to them in the first place? Why did she lock me up? Were her intentions to help at all? Was this just some sick, twisted joke? I thought about her dilapidated bedroom, that dated kitchen. Why weren't the police willing to look around? Nothing made a shred of sense.

'What on earth is going on, Megan?' I yelled. I was beyond furious.

'There's no need for animosity,' Bailey stepped in, stepping ahead of me, preventing me from getting too close to a woman everyone assumed innocent of any wrongdoing. I glared at him. What in God's name did he think I was going to do? 'Sorry to have bothered you, ma'am.' He nodded an apologetic head towards Megan who offered him a conformational smile of her own. What the hell?

'No. Wait. Please.' I pleaded, unconcerned by their attitude or the guns in their possession. 'This isn't right. Megan *helped* me.' I turned to her again, her featureless face dispirited. She was already heading back inside the house. 'Why are you lying?' It was a simple question. I honestly only needed a simple answer. She hadn't helped at *all.*

Megan turned around, leaning towards Officer Bailey, whispering something into his ear that I couldn't hear from my halted position. He nodded, glancing my way as if in full understanding of words I couldn't hear.

'What?' I asked, still sounding as unhinged as I felt, still trembling, still contemplating being sick.

Megan pulled her nightgown tightly around her body. 'Y'all have a good day now,' she concluded as she motioned back inside the house, closing her creaking porch door firmly behind her. I had no idea where *stubble guy* was. I didn't want to know. She'd probably deny his existence, too.

'What did she say?' I asked as Bailey placed his Stetson on his head and walked disinterestedly past me towards the car, fully satisfied he'd done his job well. He didn't respond. 'She still has my belongings.' It was true. The police merely needed to take a look around to verify I wasn't lying about that. Her truck was parked to the side of the property, no doubt still containing my suitcase, my boots still behind her closed front door. I considered racing onto the porch to batter it down but was stopped by Bailey whose hand was already hovering over an unclipped holster.

'I'm not going to *hurt* her,' I confirmed, my brow now so tight I felt I might pass out. 'I just want to know why she's telling lies.'

'Why would she lie?' he asked calmly, unapologetically ready to deal with anything I might decide to do, his tone far darker than I appreciated. *I had no idea.* 'Just so you know, Josh, we're the ones calling the shots around here.' He opened the car door for me.

'Can I at least take you back to the car?' I needed them to appreciate I wasn't the one going mad. I was desperate, frantic. It would still be in the ditch, all the evidence they needed. Despicable visions flooded my head of Georgina taken to God knows where by God know what—traces of blood still where I'd left it. I almost threw up. I couldn't allow messed-up thoughts like that in my head.

Bailey nodded, his begrudged tone infuriating. I could tell he wanted to be anywhere in the world but with me. I knew precisely how he felt. He took a lasting glance towards Megan's property before ushering me into his vehicle, his time needed elsewhere, his morning already waning. We proceeded past decaying cornfields that flanked either side of the car, past trees still desperate to break free from each other in the breeze.

I turned to see a net curtain twitch in an upstairs window. It wasn't comforting. I couldn't understand why Megan had acted so brutally, so coldly. Why had she *lied?* Maybe she assumed I'd already told the police about the locked door, the unwarranted punch to my jaw, the ropes I could still feel around my wrists like a noose around my goddamned throat. Those drugs in my system were still potentially making me see things that weren't there. Maybe she didn't want that kind of attention brought to her day, didn't need the stress. To be honest, neither did I, the very questions such a declaration would have provoked, something I didn't need to deal with right then. Megan was safe. For now.

***

The drive out of town sent shivers along my spine, the memory of driving wilfully into this god-awful place, too much to recall. We'd been too busy arguing to notice much else, a simple break something we hoped would ease our grief-stricken hearts for a few days. We needed the respite, wanting to learn more about the woman we adored more than life. Or, at least, *I did.*

'What did Megan say to you?' I did not expect an answer, yet I asked anyway. I was in the back seat, my existence of no concern, my emotions of little importance.

I was given a dismissive glare, an incurious shrug. 'Just that someone fittin' your description was seen by a neighbour yesterday afternoon hovering' along the roadside, claimin' to have lost his way.' Bailey glanced towards my feet, the things no longer exposing my inadequacies. 'Apparently, some guy was standin' barefoot in the rain ravin' 'bout ghosts n' shit.' He was chewing a piece of gum, his throwaway words matching his throwaway attitude. He was looking at me exactly how he had when we first met, last night's car ride still uncomfortable.

I furrowed my brow. *Ghosts?* What the hell? 'No. That isn't what happened.' I swallowed, unable to appreciate the lies that seemed to leave Megan's lips so readily. She was making me sound *deranged.* Maybe that was the point.

Bailey shrugged, turning his attention to his colleague. He didn't care.

I glared out of the window, nothing else for me to do, nothing of our surroundings familiar until I recognised the stretch of road I'd stood along only yesterday, feint tyre marks still where I'd unavoidably put them.

'Here!' I yelled, stabbing a frantic finger out of the car window. The police car came to a steady halt and I was allowed out of the back seat, fresh air reluctantly given, no better than a criminal who'd bought his capturers to the location of a sinister burial ground.

'Where're we supposed to be lookin'?' Bailey was scanning the road, tracing frustrated eyes across the overgrowth and into trees that didn't look as if they'd been disturbed for years. It didn't take a genius to appreciate they assumed *I* was the one telling lies, this location untouched by humanity for a long time.

I raced along the road, manic, deluded, searching for a rental car that wouldn't be difficult to spot, hunting for debris, clues. I'd left it the wrong way up for starters, its roof hidden by the dampened ground, its body crushed, fire damaged, upended tyres easy to see in the surrounding overgrowth. It may have been in a ditch, but the carnage it had caused wouldn't have disappeared overnight.

Nothing. *Shit.*

'Maybe it was further along the road?' I queried, questioning myself, confused, my brain a random pattern of uncertainty I no longer trusted.

'There's *nothin'* out here,' Bailey confirmed flatly, his depleted tone nothing more than a collection of irritated tut's and guttural sounds I found almost as frustrating as he was finding *me.*

Where the hell was the car?

'Have the police removed it already?' I was frantically searching, failing miserably. Maybe they collected it during the time I was sitting in the station, waiting for a miracle, hoping for the impossible?

'Not that I know of.' Bailey shook his head.

'Then where the *hell* is it?' How could an entire vehicle disappear? How could Georgina?

'Listen, wise-ass. I don't know whatcha game is, but this is a quiet town and we don't like outsiders creatin' drama for our local folk. I suggest you go home, go back to where you came from and leave the good people of this community alone.' The man who had spoken so tenderly to Megan only moments ago, who'd calmly wrapped a blanket around my shoulders the night before, was glaring at me now as if my time wasn't worth his, that my missing daughter was little more than a tale I'd invented to piss him off. *Go back to where I came from? Seriously?*

'I'm telling the truth.' I reached for my wallet, the thing still missing, nothing of my identity intact. What the hell was Megan trying to do to me?

'D'ya know what gets my goat?'

I shook my head.

'Dime a dozen punks like *you*.' He looked me up and down. 'I suggest you stop playin' games, stop wastin' our time.' It was obvious Megan had said more than I was being told. *Was I being warned?*

It was Officer Montgomery's turn now to speak, the continued glare he gave me confirming his colleague's stern warning. 'If we see you round these parts again, you'll find yourself enjoyin' the inside of a jail cell. Am I makin' myself clear?' He glared at me as if I was nothing more than a troubled teenager he didn't need in his day. He'd probably seen his fair share. With my dirty jeans, borrowed trainers and ranting, I could understand why, the colour of my skin no doubt adding to his hatred.

'Can you at least give me a lift back into town?' I muttered. I needed to locate a phone and speak to someone other than my dad, potentially a higher authority who might *actually* be willing to help. I didn't see the point in making things worse by providing further unwanted bravado. It was obvious these people were never going to offer any genuine assistance.

I was on my own.

11

I was too stressed to recall the journey into town, the back of this police car no longer offering the protection I'd initially convinced myself I needed. My daughter was out there somewhere, alone, frightened. It wasn't a pleasant feeling. I was ejected onto the side of the road, told expressively if I knew what was good for me, I'd get on the first plane out of there and never return. I needed to "toe the line", they said. They didn't for one second "buy my shit".

I didn't like the way they looked at me, their expressions a telling reminder I was nothing more than an unwanted outsider whose words were not about to be taken seriously. I appreciated many isolated towns didn't like outsiders, yet there had to be more to this than I understood. Anna used to joke about such things. Most didn't like *each other,* she claimed—gay people, black people, *women.* But I struggled to conclude it was my skin tone they didn't like, dismissive responses to missing children unheard of, these people detached for reasons I was yet to understand.

Something wasn't right. Those officers assumed I hadn't noticed the eye contact they gave each other when they thought I wasn't looking, unspoken conversations shared in the oblivion of several sideways glances. I couldn't question it. My ill-fated presence was incapable of obtaining the truth about *anything.* Whatever it was, I didn't like it.

I walked around in circles until fresh rain prickled my skin, jolting me out of my self-depleting self-pity, the unwanted appearance of yet another rainstorm adding further frustration to my day. I sheltered in an alleyway, unable to think straight, seeking solace behind a row of bins that smelled of rotting meat and death. I must have looked a troubling sight with my pale skin, sunken eyes and blackened veins visible beneath clothing that wasn't mine. It was as if death was waiting for me in the darkness, smiling, watching. I hoped no one would notice me quivering and trembling like the inhuman freak I was now convinced I was. I wondered what Anna would say if she could see me sitting alone in a backstreet alley, afraid for my demise whilst oddly welcoming the swift relief of death. The way I felt right then, I wouldn't have the strength to defend myself against the Grim Reaper I'd metaphorically morphed in the shadows behind me.

I was entrenched in a terrifying world of my own, my living corpse on display for the rats who could see me far better than I could see them, my existence wrapped only in the concept of finding Georgina. If it weren't for such a desperation to find my child, I might have given up there and then, six months of depression long enough to see my willing departure from this world, antidepressants resulting in nothing but frustration I no longer wanted to endure.

Since Anna's death, I'd kept myself busy, not wanting to think of much beyond getting from day to day, her loss a pivotal moment in my life, changing my existence, my personality. I'd gone from carefree dad to moody, psychotic, if not slightly *questionable* human being. In the process, Georgina had become an unfounded casualty of my prolonged suffering. That alleyway now consumed me as if I'd been placed into a straitjacket and left dangling by my feet, my pitiful corpse nothing but a marionette puppet some unseen entity was amusing itself within the solace of a forgotten corner of a world I barely understood.

Constant nausea lingered in the back of my throat, events happening too fast for my overloaded brain to contend with. In my current condition, looking the way I did, any passing police officer could have shot me dead and easily legitimised their actions. To everyone else, I must have appeared untethered, steadily unravelling, a crazed idiot who needed urgent mental evaluation. After all, none of my recent endeavours were backed up by tangible evidence that my daughter *existed.* The police didn't even have a photograph of the poor kid to go on, nothing to confirm she was real. Where would they start looking? This entire trip was devouring me in a way I hadn't imagined, couldn't imagine, no longer convinced I wanted the answers to the questions racing around my severely damaged brain.

I wanted to scream. I couldn't care less what happened to me, but there was no way I could leave this place without my child. Everything here reminded me of Anna and a home far away—a scent of lilac that hung in the air, distant laughter. It was obvious I was never going to recover from the unremitting grief that burned my brain, my current predicament too much. I didn't know how much longer I could hold it together.

A stack of rotting pallets barely kept the rain off but at least afforded me a place in which to contemplate my pathetic predicament. Nothing about this trip had gone to plan, nothing much left of my mind to consolidate stability. Once the rain had abated, I forced my aching body into those hollow streets, my attention focused on every young girl who walked by, the potential sight of Georgina's mop of long hair the only thing keeping me going when I had nothing left to give. I felt as if my eyes were about to pop out of my head, my gaze shifting from left to right, probably appearing bewildered to those unfortunate enough to witness my approach. Yet, I *needed* to find her. Nothing else mattered.

Along with the rainstorm that had – despite my best efforts – left my body as dampened as my mood, the new morning brought a fresh insight into the town's disowned appearance. A solitary shopkeeper carelessly dragged wooden boxes into the roadside, fresh vegetables, fresh bread, and newspapers sharing news of no real relevance to the people here. His face was a telling expression that this day was, for him, no better than the last, his life no different to those neighbours willing to share this tragic space.

The occasional vehicle bustled past, old trucks with equally ageing owners, nothing of a missing child on the lips of those strangers today, nothing of my child's disappearance meaning anything to *anyone.* A few people muttered half-hearted acknowledgements. Others bowed their heads. I was a foreigner in their midst, of no relevance, none of them concerned who I was.

I needed to speak to Megan and find out why she'd lied. Of course, I couldn't head directly back to that old property without backup, or, at the very least, a backup plan. I wasn't stupid. I'd already found myself in her spare room, tied up, drugged, my mind in knots along with bound hands and feet I'd been lucky to untether. I couldn't assume it wouldn't happen again if I were foolish enough to wander onto her property unprepared, my wits anything but with me, my stomach a tightened mess of twitching muscles I couldn't settle. Instead, I ambled around, hijacking several strangers, my question always the same.

Had they seen a young girl with bright red gym shoes, long hair, bad attitude?

Yet, their replies were always the same too, a shake of a head, a step in the other direction. Why wouldn't they *help* me? Why didn't they *care?* I was running out time, running short of options.

'Excuse me,' I called to the shopkeeper. The guy was lining up trays of produce outside his dilapidated shop window, proud of his achievements, even if no one else noticed.

'Can I help ya?' He stood up straight, arching his back, his ageing hands covered in dirt and dust, his fingernails looking as if they hadn't seen hot water for some time.

'Have you seen a young girl with bright red gym shoes?' I asked for the umpteenth time. I sounded unhinged, I know, my words emerging as if my voice didn't belong to me, nothing but a strangled squawk that ricocheted violently inside my head. 'We had an accident. I can't find her.' The entire thing was messed up, this town hiding secrets I didn't yet wish to acknowledge.

'Jeez, I'm real sorry to hear that,' he breathed, genuinely sounding troubled by the concept. It was something, at least. 'But I'm afraid I ain't seen too many folk around this mornin', apart from old Martha across the street.' He pointed to an old woman currently brushing wet leaves into the gutter, her attention set on me rather than what she was doing. It was still early, the town still waking, those I'd already encountered too busy with their own depleted lives to care about mine. I stared at the shopkeeper, his glowing cheeks flushed by the effort needed to scratch a meagre living from the life he probably hadn't meant to create.

'Why don'tcha come inside for a moment? Ya look as if ya could use a strong coffee.' The old man rubbed his filthy hands across the front of his dungarees, obviously noticing my increasing panic and not wishing to add to my desperation.

I nodded, unable to recall the last time I'd *eaten* anything either, the tea I'd earlier consumed still sticking to the back of my throat in clumps, remnants of vanilla ice cream still churning my gut to shit. Stress always had a nasty side effect of making food taste bitter, my stomach launching unwanted contents into the toilet bowl with ease. I wouldn't have kept food down anyway. Not that he'd offered.

'I'm Peter, by the way,' he stated, offering a semi-clean hand that I shook begrudgingly, not wishing to appear rude, the guy only being polite. We headed inside his shop, the floorboards aged and dusty, a distinct scent of orange and eucalyptus reminding me of my grandmother.

Peter ushered me into a tiny space behind his storefront, tucked away from the stale smell of sawdust and unwanted vegetation that littered the heavy air. A couple of dated armchairs sat to one side, a log-burning stove set inside a crumbling brick fireplace, a creaking floor and a rug. It was warm and inviting, with plants on the windowsill that barely clung to life, cushions on the chairs, a small coffee table beneath an even smaller window, and long forgotten trophies stacked on a broken shelf. Farming awards, from what I could tell, silver metallic ears of corn protruding from stained wooden bases gathering dust in the gloom. I thought about Megan's decayed cornfields and the "welcome sign" that led into Darkridge Hollow, suppressing a saddened sigh for a town my wife once spoke so fondly of.

'We don't get too many folk around here,' he offered, handing me a cup of black coffee that came from nowhere. 'What brings y'all the way out here?'

Family. A ghost. Memories I didn't have the right to acknowledge.

'My wife was born here,' I found myself admitting instead, the entire concept alien in my head now, Megan's nonsensical whispers of ghosts and barefooted strangers still dominating my thoughts.

'She didn't marry a local boy then?' Peter was laughing, my accent something he probably didn't hear often, found amusing, my skin tone confirming his statement. He probably found *me* amusing.

'No,' I sighed, needing no jokes made at my expense today.

'And your daughter?'

I glanced up, unseeing, my body numbed by the mention of her. 'When I woke up, she was gone.' I still couldn't accept it. Couldn't believe it.

Peter looked at me as if he wanted to say something, yet refrained, turning instead to pick up a mug from the countertop behind him. 'I'm sorry 'bout that. Seems ya got screwed over, hey?'

Screwed over? That was one way of looking at it. Everyone kept telling me how sorry they were for what had happened, yet nobody wanted to *do* anything about it. It wasn't their fault, of course. What *could* they do?

'She can't have just disappeared,' I snapped, irritated by a truth I couldn't accept, frustrated by coffee I didn't want to drink.

'I guess not.' Peter pressed his lips together, something in his tone he wasn't expressing. He looked as if he was hiding something. I didn't dare ask what. 'What's your name?' he added flatly.

'Joshua Raymond,' I shrugged. 'Josh.' What did it *matter?*

'Well, Josh Raymond, if I hear *anythin'* I'll be sure to letcha know. Ya stayin' local? Where can I look if I hear somethin'?' He turned around and headed into his shop, far more pressing matters to attend to than me.

I had no idea. I hadn't thought that far ahead, already expecting to have relocated Georgina by now, my belongings still in the house of a *mad woman*. I assumed we would have left this place and never looked back. It wasn't important where I'd be sleeping tonight. I honestly didn't give a shit.

'Do you know a local woman called Megan?' I followed the man into a space that was thankfully larger and less oppressive than the one I'd just left. I hadn't answered Peter's question. I needed to know more about the stranger who, for reasons now eluding my rational consideration, no longer wanted to help.

'No.'

'Or the Ellis family?' Someone must remember *them*, surely?

There was a pause, a sharp intake of stale breath that seemed to linger in the air. 'No.' Peter had taken too long to answer. I didn't believe him.

'Megan claims the *whole* town knows her? Why would she say that if it isn't true?' I wished I knew her surname. It might have made things easier. Peter *must* have known who she was. He looked as if he'd lived here long enough.

'Is that a fact?'

'Yes. So why don't *you?* Know her, I mean.' I was serious. Megan was beginning to irritate me. Who the *hell* was she?

'Ya sayin' I'm lyin' Josh?' Peter half-turned, motioning a disgruntled head my way with a thick sigh that gave away nothing of his emotions other than to express frustration I'd willingly provoked.

'Well, someone certainly is.' I glanced around the shop, the place half-filled with half-cared-for produce, wilting lettuce heads on the brink of death, potatoes sprouting fresh growth into the dank air.

'Well, it sure *ain't* me.' Peter picked up a box that he carried over to the window, nothing further to say about *that.* He busied himself stacking shelves, his back to me, his day a continued collection of tasks he needed to complete despite seemingly few customers to notice his efforts.

'What *happened* to this town?' Why I needed to know, I had no idea. Maybe I assumed Anna would want closure.

Peter was still stacking shelves, still had his back to me. He didn't reply.

'There's so few people living here.' For the first time since my arrival, I felt sorry for the place, sorry for the residents.

Peter straightened his spine, licking tired lips. 'It's too sad to recall,' he muttered, placing several leeks next to a forgotten jar of dusty pickles that he tossed into a nearby waste bin. 'Too sad, and too damn painful.'

'But this was a thriving town once.' I glanced over my shoulder towards his forgotten collection of farming trophies, recalling Anna's words.

Peter looked up, glaring at me, his eyes narrow. He didn't reply. It wasn't appropriate to share the stories Anna had told me long ago about her beloved hometown, her perception distorted, it seemed.

'I guess. Once upon a time,' Peter breathed, clearing his throat of words he didn't wish to share with me. 'But most of the townsfolk didn't stick around.'

'Why?' I wanted to know the type of people I was dealing with.

'Why d'ya wanna know?' He sounded frustrated, offended. I swallowed.

'Because my daughter is missing and I need to know she's safe.' Even as I spoke, my words caught my throat. *Safe?* It wasn't a notion I could take seriously. I didn't think anywhere here was safe.

Peter sighed, picking up a broom that he wrung tightly in his hands, any attempt to sweep the floor unrewarded by a saddened look that lingered behind his dark eyes. 'There are precisely one hundred and sixty-seven residents left in Darkridge Hollow now, Josh, outta two thousand souls that lived here once. Now that's a real bummer ain't it? Ya can't imagine how that changes a place. Changes those left behind.'

I couldn't imagine, no. I shook my head. 'Why did they leave?'

'It don't matter no more.' Peter's tone had darkened, memories he didn't want in his head surfacing because of *me.* 'And I ain't got time to explain it. I'm a busy man.' He flicked a disinterested wrist towards his shop door as if he no longer wished to continue this conversation, prodding the end of his broom towards my toes. My coffee was taken from my unwitting grasp, the liquid still warm, the cup still full, my company no longer required. I found myself ushered outside, a worn broom sweeping me out of the door along with a pile of debris taken from a perpetually filthy floor. It fitted how I felt, nothing but rubbish that needed discarding before I caused further unwanted issues for the unfortunate people around me.

'Then *who* is the woman who lives at the edge of town?' I called back, irritated that my question remained unanswered. But Peter had already gone back inside and closed the door.

12

I was standing outside Peter's shop in a puddle, my abrupt return to those isolated streets unexpectedly lowering my mood further than I believed possible. It was probably on account of the earlier rainstorm and nothing to do with me, but the lingering silence added to the way I felt, the way I was being treated, disconcerting strangers as unfeeling here as they were in London. I should have been used to it. After all, the way people behave is limited only to the perceptions of the world in which they live. When Anna was in my life, shit like this barely had the ability to touch my mood. Now, nothing could raise it. It wasn't a comforting notion.

Peter had returned to his shop, my problems of no concern to him. He was in his window, meticulously straightening carrots and beetroot, wilted ends lying neatly across wooden crates, no doubt hoping they appeared more appetising than they tasted. It wasn't lost on me that I hadn't seen a single customer. I assumed he was going through the motions, each day as the last, unwanted produce either ending up on his plate or in a bin.

'Hey there!' A voice from behind startled me, bringing me out of a pensive trauma that threatened to put me into the very coma I'd recently invented. I turned around to see an elderly woman leaning against a garden gate, a rake in hand, unconcerned by the weather *or* my presence. Martha,

I presumed. In my depletion, I hadn't noticed she'd been watching me.

'Whatcha doin' out here?' she asked, resting her ageing body against an equally ageing wall.

'I'm not sure, to be honest,' I confirmed, no longer confident I wanted to talk about it. Talking wasn't helping. It was only frustrating my brain, eagerly turning my thoughts to mush along with my child's fragile body. She was still out there somewhere, in *God* knows what state by now.

'You been upsettin' old Peter?' she chided, nodding across the street, the rake in her hands trembling within her weakened grip. I assumed she'd watched him sweep me into the street along with the debris he no longer wanted in his shop. She probably found it amusing.

I glanced over my shoulder, the old man outside again now, shuffling boxes, cracking his spine, mumbling incomprehensible words I didn't care to hear. 'I was *trying* to ask for help,' I muttered, no words leaving my mouth providing any rational logic. *Help?* Were these people capable of such a thing? I was beginning to wonder.

'I'm all ears if you wanna tell me 'bout it.' Martha was keen for my interaction, willing to offer assistance judging by the warm smile she gave me. Rainwater dripped from surfaces drenched by the earlier storm, the pile of leaves at her feet going nowhere. She probably wanted a distraction.

How many people did I need to tell about my missing child before someone *did* something to aid my futile mission? 'My child is missing.' I was sick of saying it, tired of the sickly feeling in the pit of my increasingly churning stomach by the thought of it.

Martha pressed her lips together before leaning her rake against her gate. She looked at me, her silent eyes disguising emotions neither of us wanted to acknowledge. 'I'm real sorry to hear that.' She sounded sorry, sincere, yet I scoffed anyway. I couldn't help it. Most people seemed to *say* all the right things. It was a shame they rarely wanted to *do* the right thing. She tilted her head as if trying to get a better look at me. 'What did Peter have to say for himself this mornin'?'

What kind of question was that? Why was that relevant? I shook my head. 'Not much.'

'Didn't trouble you with tales of the good ol' days then?'

'No.' The guy hardly wanted to speak at all, truth be told.

'Well now that don't sound like Peter. He usually can't stop talkin'.' She laughed. 'I'm Martha,' she offered, stretching a gnarly hand my way. 'Mrs. Harper, to you.'

I nodded and shook her hand, unwilling to confirm that I already knew. I wondered if she stood around watching her neighbours often, dissecting passing strangers with her interfering nose.

'Josh,' I added, assuming she cared, momentarily wondering if she'd noticed my child out here. 'You haven't seen a young girl hanging around have you?' I was desperate for someone to confirm they'd seen her, *somewhere,* the distinct chatter of birds sheltering in nearby trees my only willing allies.

Martha shook her head. 'You'd best not hang around too long either, Josh,' she confirmed, her statement coming from nowhere.

'Why?' I'd answered too quickly. I didn't care. This godforsaken town was growing more cryptic and frustrating with each passing hour I was forced to endure it.

'Cuz shit happens round here, and I'm pretty darn sure you don't wanna find out what. You'd best split while you still can.' The old woman sounded as if she'd escaped from some low budget film set, sent as a warning, a premonition. I anticipated dramatic music to thunder rapturously into the morning air. I shuddered, nothing about this moment ensuring my brain wouldn't create its own demented version, later. *In the dark.*

'I'm not going *anywhere* without my child.'

Martha stepped closer, lowering her chin, grey hair falling momentarily over her eyes. 'Darkridge Hollow is cursed. Better bail before it's too late. This place stinks so bad it'll make your eyes water.'

What? I shook my head, unable to absorb her words. All I needed now was for the woman to raise yielding hands into the air and cast a spell. I half expected her to curse me to hell before disappearing in a cloud of smoke, a demented laugh lingering on the breeze.

'Cursed, how?' *What stinks?* Apart from the drains. I was curious. I didn't believe in stories like that, ghost tales, stupid shit. Yet, I took a couple of steps towards her anyway, my interest piqued, Anna's forgotten taunts of dark myths still rattling around my brain.

'Josh, trust me, you don't wanna know.'

'My child is missing. *Yes.* I do.' I wasn't about to let her say such things without acknowledging my irritation.

Martha looked around as if half-expecting some hooded demon to step out from the trees, grab her by the throat and silence her chattering mouth. She swallowed. 'I guess it began in the 1970s, when a new family moved to the area. A funny bunch they were, though.'

'What family?' *Funny how?*

'The sort that practiced sacrifice, witchcraft. You know the type.' She was whispering as she placed a hand on my shoulder, her garden gate no longer a support, her stale breath too close. Who did she assume would overhear us?

'I don't understand what any of this has to do with my daughter's disappearance.' I honestly didn't know the *type* of people she was referring to. I was just a guy from the UK who lived a simple life. Usually.

'Look around. You must *know* what this place is. You

got eyes, don'tcha?'

'What on earth are you talking about?' I didn't have a clue what my *eyes* were meant to be witnessing or what this place was, other than a total *bloody* nightmare. The only thing I'd experienced so far were a few unfriendly locals, police who couldn't be bothered, and several dead crops in an otherwise decaying town.

Please. For God's sake, someone spare me.

'We were a thrivin' farmin' community once, Josh. But, after *that* family moved here, the livestock died, and nothin' grows no more. Even love left this place long ago. I'm pretty sure you've seen the cornfields. The corn rotted to hell and the rest was left juttin' from dirt that no longer grows a goddamn thing. You may as well light a river on fire and be done with it all.' She was ranting, her eyes wide. I vaguely recalled a story my wife once told me about; The Cuyahoga River which had apparently caught on fire in 1969 due to an oil spillage from industrial pollution. It prompted a major U.S. environmental movement. I had no idea what any of *that* had to do with my missing daughter.

'Most of the locals were farmers back in the day, old Peter included,' Martha continued. 'He was among those of us who chose to stay behind when everyone else moved on. We don't know any other life. We're all just tryin' to get by, best we can.' She nodded towards Peter, the man still straightening vegetables no one was ever going to consume.

'Martha? Where you at?' A deep voice boomed from behind us, the old woman's front door still ajar, potential prying ears now aimed our way. It jolted us out of our private deliberations, my presence no longer a concern, my company no longer important.

'Ope!' Martha exclaimed. She turned away, the rake behind her nothing more than a forgotten task she hadn't yet completed.

'Do you know a woman called Megan?' I needed to ask,

our time almost over. The old woman seemed to understand this town and all its faults.

'Nope. Sorry, afraid not.' Martha had already turned to leave, her story no longer important. She picked up her rake.

'She lives on the edge of town,' I confirmed. Why was everyone claiming to not know her? She wasn't *invisible* for Christ's sake. Yes, her property might have been hidden from the road, hidden from civilization, and, *yes*, she was a bit strange. But she claimed *everyone* knew her. Why were these people lying to me? 'Do you remember a family who used to live here? The Ellis's?' I called out.

'I gotta go.' The old woman scuttled towards the encroaching voice before turning briefly my way. 'Get outta here, Josh. D'ya hear what I'm sayin'? Don't *ever* come back.' She turned around, rake in hand, heading into the house where she closed the door, leaving me standing in the drizzle, alone again and just as confused as ever.

***

I searched for Georgina all afternoon, knocking every door I came to, no luck finding anyone willing to talk to me, Peter included, my depleted energies not helping my cause in the slightest. I hadn't eaten all day, my blood sugar now so low I was becoming weak, dizzy, much of my time spent leaning against hard surfaces for support none could ever provide. I thought about the potential routes Georgina could have taken, my thoughts concluding nothing good, my intelligence overriding logic that she was okay, safe somewhere, healthy.

My streetwise, *very* grown-up child would have found help by now, had she made it this far. It left only one conclusion. A conclusion I didn't want to accept. She was dead and all I was doing was putting off the inevitable. The idea twisted my gut into a knot, my brain unravelling like string that tangled around my throat, making swallowing impossible. What would I do if she *were* dead? I didn't want to think about it.

I watched Peter for a while, hoping Megan would need to come into town to obtain supplies she couldn't live without. I wondered who – if anyone – would acknowledge her, ask after her wellbeing, her health. Would Peter? He seemed the only consistent presence in this place, a resident that, according to Martha, had been here longer than most. Surely he *knew* who Megan was? Maybe he remembered Anna's family? Remembered Anna?

I fully intended on stepping in, should I see the woman, ask why she'd lied to me and demand an explanation. As it was, Megan remained elusive, a long walk to her property unappealing, my body willing only to lurk in the surrounding shadows, launching towards every sporadic passer-by I saw. I had no idea what I assumed I'd find here. Certainly not Georgina. Not alive, anyway, my thoughts in no position to put my mind at ease. *No.* By this time I was ready to accept a truth I couldn't seriously contemplate. I was no longer looking for my child. I was looking for her body.

***

It was getting dark by the time I relented, a lack of sustenance too much. For hours, adrenaline had been the only willing source of energy keeping me going when I literally had nothing left inside. Oxygen depleted blood pulsated violently through my failing organs, metaphorically dragging my screaming soul towards a place I'd often welcomed in the dark. It wasn't comforting. I didn't know how to respond to my surroundings, my trainers continually slapping the tarmac, no variable able to convince me of anything beyond a truth I could scarcely accept. I couldn't stay out here forever, of course. At some point, I needed to accept reality, accept my fate. No one in Darkridge Hollow was willing to acknowledge Megan and neither did they care that I was alone in my desperate search for a child no one even knew existed.

I spotted a sign for a motel located a couple of miles out of town, so I followed a depleted road into the deepening evening, hoping for salvation I feared might never arrive. Once again I kept close to the road's edge, nothing here willing to convince me that I hadn't fallen into a pit of unrelenting vipers in my mind's unfathomed absence. What if none of this was real? What if I was actually in the very hospital bed I'd already invented in my head? I wished Georgina would play some of her terrible music and jolt me awake, yell at me, slap my cheeks. I wasn't sure how much longer I was willing to stay in the darkness alone, unconvinced how much of this private hell I wanted to acknowledge.

The magnitude of this day engulfed my senses, my exposure to nature forcing me to constantly glance skyward, a strange feeling enveloping me. I was out of my depth, seriously concerned I was already out of my mind. Being locked inside a relatively small room had dulled my senses enough so that now, when faced with sounds my ears would typically ignore, I was barely able to abide the volume. Everything irritated me. The constant buzz of crickets. The periodic slapping of rubber soles against warm tarmac. Even my breath was too much for my sensitive constitution to handle.

It was ironic. Confined spaces *never* bothered me. I could sit for hours in my home office, huddled over my desk, frantic, oblivious, no window required for me to connect to my day and any task that needed completion. Yet, now, out in the fresh air and open countryside, I could barely stand the overwhelming suffocation. When the road narrowed by overgrown vegetation no one had deemed important to clear, I thought nothing of it, this place merely another casualty of a forgotten, broken society. I wasn't, however, expecting it to come to an abrupt end, the sudden appearance of a "ROAD CLOSED" sign ahead surprisingly annoying.

A thinly erected beam had been positioned horizontally across the road, preventing unwanted vehicles to venture further. I glanced around, knowing passing drivers would be forced to turn back, take a different route. Many muttered profanities would match muted frustration, no earlier confirmation indicating this road led nowhere. Yet, maybe I'd missed the diversion sign, wasn't looking out for one—didn't care.

The motel was on the other side of this abandoned road, of course, the place no longer obtainable by car. It was another confirmation that Darkridge Hollow was a forgotten entity, a lost cause, no potential guests welcome. I thought of Anna's ghost stories, of the many closed roads that supposedly held haunting secrets she hadn't deemed important to share in detail, instead regaling invented tales of doom before bedtime. She knew I hated anything scary, wallowing in the power she held over my emotions, her stories much source of amusement. I could imagine what she'd say now. Yet, I wasn't about to turn around, give up, *run.* I'd come too far, walked too long, my throbbing legs confirmation of my predicament.

I didn't want to know why the road was closed or what incident had taken place here to warrant such an abrupt obstruction. I stepped gingerly over the wooden bar, my incoming weight ensuring the thing groaned in response. I flinched, confident that, from wherever she was, Anna would be laughing at me. It didn't matter. A light breeze rustled the surrounding plant life, singing to me, a crisp note in a night sky that ensured my wits remained heightened enough to contain my wayward senses. *For now.*

Thickened trees flanked either side of the road, darkening the path and disguising the dead and rotting cornfields beyond. I could have been walking through a forest, the place was so overgrown, depleted tarmac crumbling beneath my feet. I considered running. My only intention was to reach the other side as swiftly as possible, yet I had no genuine idea where I was or what lay ahead, nothing of this place giving me cause for immediate concern beyond a torrid imagination I honestly didn't need.

It didn't take long for me to reach a small clearing, luckily, the road stretching downward towards several tiny lights in the distance. I couldn't stop thinking about Georgina. Was she listening to the same sounds as me, also in the dark, alone? Or was her life already over, nothing remotely reminiscent of the life I'd hoped she'd one day live—what *could* have been no longer viable.

I almost choked on my unwanted thoughts as I trundled along, fear strong in my gut that I might, at some point, run into Megan and those men, their unwanted presence never far from mind, my weakened state no match for anything they might decide to do in the dark. I should have returned to her property, demanded answers and my belongings, my missing wallet only part of the reason I hadn't eaten all day, my churning belly of no consequence to anything.

Yet, how could I enjoy a meal? I hadn't eaten well after Anna died, weeks passing, my weight loss not going unnoticed by those I knew, my ageing dad noticing nothing but my absence from his villa in Spain. Georgina was subsequently left to fend for herself. The fact I wasn't there for her when she needed me wasn't something I wanted to admit. Now, I *couldn't* be, this day a brutal reminder of the one we lost Anna, my heart broken beyond repair, my mind left to deal with the fallout alone. If I lost Georgina too, I wouldn't be responsible for my actions. I probably wouldn't make it out of this place alive.

As it was, the police had given me a fairly straightforward warning. Go home or find myself in a jail cell. Some choice. Of course, I wasn't about to get on a plane and forget everything. Georgina needed me. This was my child's *second* night away from me. Nothing good was ever going to come from that terrifying conclusion. I couldn't overthink the damaged road that now lay behind me, or the one still waiting ahead.

13

In this light, everything looked wrong. My mind had deviated so far from reality it was now creating heinous shapes from my surroundings, every shadow becoming a malignant force I had no strength to fight. I hovered beneath the trees, exhausted, my brain screaming profanities I didn't want to repeat. It wasn't ideal. When I caught sight of what looked like a human form in the middle of a field, I didn't believe it was real, a lack of food altering my perception, my mind creating hallucinations for the hell of it.

Those dying cornfields did nothing for my composure, yet the moonlit sky had now joined the chaos, readily forging an outlandish sight I'd created for effect, the resulting shape pale and distant, seemingly *naked*. I wasn't planning on staying here long, of course, yet it seemed my body was ready to give me up to the incoming night, give me up for dead, sick of dealing with the shit I was continually thrusting upon it. My legs no longer complied, blood flow not forthcoming, hungry wildlife waiting impatiently to claim my miserable carcass for a much-needed meal they no doubt required far more than I did.

I couldn't tell if my imaginary "companion" was male or female, but it danced freely, thin arms flailing, legs skipping and twisting in the darkness. I was deluded, seeing things that weren't there, this country hell-bent on destroying every rational brain cell I had. *Brilliant.* I shrugged, shook my head, shaking off random delusions I didn't need, requiring sleep I wouldn't find, food I couldn't stomach. I assumed it was the location that had altered my perception, nothing more, Anna's ghost tales left to appear when I least expected them, my wife's taunting still strong from beyond the grave.

The figure raised its arms into the air, plunging something to the ground that sent a flock of squawking birds into the night sky. I swallowed, my unhinged brain creating scenes that didn't exist, my legs faltering as I turned to run. I didn't care how stupid I looked. It didn't matter. I couldn't stand being in the dark any longer, my mind creating havoc from a simple, moonlit sky.

I was grateful when the motel loomed into view, my body no more willing to acknowledge my plight than I was—my borrowed trainers developing a flapping sole that dragged mockingly beneath me. I blamed a lack of antidepressants, the things still in my suitcase, unconsumed, forgotten, my bloodstream ready to launch me into a full-blown withdrawal. I was sweating, my rapid heartbeat equated more to Georgina's disappearance than the lack of chemicals I'd become dependent on. It wasn't my fault, my body merely left to the unrelenting devices of this volatile town.

I stumbled into the motel reception, exhausted, out of breath, no funds to pay for a room, no clarity of mind to confirm I hadn't escaped a prison cell or mental hospital. I needed a shower, some rest and, according to my surprised belly, something to eat. Preferably before I passed out. The smell of fake cheese and sausage meat emerging from an opened pizza box was uninviting, yet my stomach growled anyway.

'What the hell, man?' The guy behind the desk sat upright as I practically fell against the countertop. He glared at me, the TV show he'd been watching, rudely interrupted.

He noted my reddened cheeks, shortness of breath and clothing that wasn't mine, the sole of my ugly trainers hanging loose.

What the hell, indeed. Where should I begin? I didn't wish to confirm I'd raced to this location as if I were being chased, potential demons ready to claim me from every field I passed, a closed road ensuring I shouldn't have been out there at all. I was barely upright, my legs a throbbing collection of aching muscles that wouldn't sustain me for much longer.

'I need a room,' I stated, my cheeks flush with desperation, my eyes sore from an impossible hallucination that now saw me continually checking the doorway, just in case. I couldn't help it.

'We got plenty of those,' he confirmed flatly, taking in my unkempt appearance whilst still trying to watch the television behind me.

'If you let me have a room, I'll sort out the payment first thing tomorrow morning.' At that precise moment, all I wanted was a lie down, preferably before I fell down. I couldn't bring myself to tell him I was currently searching for my missing child.

'D'ya get robbed or somethin'?' The guy looked shocked, the state of me easily confirming his theory.

'Something like that,' I nodded, unsure what else to say. I didn't have the strength to explain anything beyond my simple request for a bed. I didn't want him to call the police. They'd frustrated me enough. I just wanted to be left alone to figure this thing out for myself.

'I take it you don't have a dime on ya?' He narrowed his eyes.

He had no reason for concern. Some much earned time out was the only thing I needed right then, my missing child and unstable mindset of no concern to him. He didn't need to know anything other than *when* he was getting paid.

After some coaxing, he reluctantly gave me a room key, my continued protests placated by the promise of prompt payment. I was grateful for his willing hospitality, my missing wallet increasingly frustrating, my explanation somewhat muddled.

Someone in town had my belongings, I told him, along with my money and my *sanity*. I'd be able to retrieve them soon. It was a long story, one I didn't want to go into, and, what's more, I'd had a bad day. I assumed, if nothing else, my travel insurance would deal with it—make arrangements for replacement funds I now urgently needed. They couldn't leave me stranded in a foreign country with nothing more than a police issue t-shirt and an empty head. There were close to three hundred dollars inside my wallet. Along with my credit cards, it should have been more than enough to see Georgina and I through the next couple of days before we headed off to Colorado to complete our planned trip.

I didn't assume I'd be able to stomach food, yet the guy ordered me a pizza anyway. He must have felt sorry for me, my body needing sustenance I was oddly unwilling to provide. I didn't ask his name. I was too exhausted to care. I was unnerved by events I assumed were in my head, my emotional pain matching a psychical one I'd developed from an unrelenting run. I lay on yet another stranger's bed, staring at a ceiling with a broken fan, cold uninviting wallpaper mocking me with its cheap overdone decor. Like Megan's.

The day's events were too much for my brain to process and I fell asleep to a vivid dream about Georgina. She was crying, her emotions raw, pain that only comes from an uncertain future, all too clear in my mind. She had the look of a lost soul and when I woke up, I swear I could see her tear-stained eyes disappearing into the heavily patterned curtains of the room. When my pizza arrived, it tasted like cardboard and most of it remained untouched in the box. It caught against the back of my throat, none of it willing to get past my tongue. I hated that I'd fallen asleep so readily, my body too depleted to deal with anything, my dreams as painful as my waking moments.

I thought about Anna's scented paper, the scribbled location of Darkridge Hollow lost forever now to a damaged car, still in the glove compartment, no longer important. It still smelled of her perfume and the hand cream she used daily, the simple location something that had kept me going when I didn't know how much further I could go. As it was, I was losing more of my wife each day, everything that belonged to her slowly leaving my life for good, Georgina included.

I swung my aching legs over the side of the bed and sighed, rubbing my throbbing head with hands that wouldn't stop trembling. Where the hell were my photographs? It didn't make sense. Printed memories of my wife were all I had left to keep me company in the dark. Anna never confirmed it, but I suspected she was running from Georgina's father, running from a life she no longer wanted. We met under a veil of turmoil, that fateful winter's afternoon laden with heavy rain clouds that ensured our future was sealed before it had even begun. I wished I'd queried more, probed where I'd once felt it was none of my business and asked the questions I was now desperate to understand. I knew very little of Anna's life before we met, our time together the only thing that mattered. How deluded was I, living a life I didn't deserve, disguising a lie I told myself in the dark? I wondered how far she'd gone to escape her old life, this place nothing how she'd described. What else had Anna hidden from me?

I still couldn't understand where Georgina's belongings were, or why her passport wasn't in the glove compartment with mine. It appeared to the outside world as if she didn't exist, no tangible evidence to prove otherwise. No wonder Megan doubted my sanity. Wild animals couldn't have taken it. Yes, they might have dragged our food into the undergrowth and ravaged her suitcase. But removing photographs from wallets, passports from glove compartments and ice cream containers from the side pocket of a car door? *Absolutely not.* I leant forward, resting my elbows on my knees, the mattress beneath me unable to sedate my emotions as a conclusion jumped into my head.

Someone had *taken* her.

It wasn't an idea I'd considered. Yet, I couldn't help deducing that someone was staging this, making me look pathetic and weak in the process. *But why?* Everything mocked me. The car accident, losing Georgina, Megan's help that turned to hindrance, police who wanted no genuine involvement, everything and everyone conspiring to ensure it was *me* who looked unhinged and volatile. Even the locals were more concerned by dead crops than potential dead children. I swallowed, taking a deep breath. I couldn't think like that. Not yet. Georgina couldn't be dead.

The police weren't interested, although why, I couldn't understand. They had taken a statement and logged Georgina as missing, yet I had no photograph to show them, none of them able to pick her out of a crowd if they tried. To them, she was nothing more than a name on a log sheet, a little girl with no face, a tall tale to file away and forget. A sad story. After all, hundreds of children go missing every year. *Thousands.*

I ventured into the bathroom and stared into a cracked mirror that oddly matched the state of my mind. I hadn't shaved since we left England, my stubble now ensuring *I* looked unstable, my hair wild and unruly, a barber and shampoo something I hadn't troubled myself with for a while. No wonder Georgina was so irritated with me. She could vividly see what I wasn't prepared to. Cuts and bruises littered my face, the wound on my forehead scabbing over, wanting to forget what had happened. *So did I.* I undressed and ran the shower, allowing barely warm water to tumble over my body.

I couldn't shave. I had nothing to shave with. So I washed my face and hair as best I could with a bar of sticky soap leftovers discarded by a previous occupant, unconcerned by someone else's hair that clung to it in places. It was a pathetic attempt to clean myself up, to present a better version of Joshua Raymond to a world I hated. I hadn't bothered with such things for a while, hadn't seen the point. I stood in the shower, unconcerned that if I drowned, I probably wouldn't care. If Georgina was already dead, I saw no reason to continue without her. I was beyond saving.

I almost threw up when I heard a knock on the door. I couldn't help wondering if the police had found something, yet I couldn't overthink the fact they didn't even know I was here. I hovered in the middle of the room before forcing my legs towards the door, a towel around my middle, nothing of my persona intact. When I opened it, the motel manager was standing on the landing, my suitcase, mobile phone and wallet in his outstretched hands.

'These yours?' he asked, a look on his face confirming he wasn't impressed that his evening had been interrupted for a second time.

I stared at him, unable to believe what I was seeing. 'Where did you get them?'

'Some guy dropped 'em off. Figured you might be needin' 'em.'

'What guy?' I glanced around, frantic, anxious. The idea that someone had followed me made my skin crawl.

The manager shrugged. 'Y'can pay for your room now, at least.' He handed me my wallet and phone, leaving my suitcase on the threshold before walking away with a blank smile I was glad I couldn't read.

I stood by the open doorway, barefoot, my damp hair adding nothing good to the mood I was in, my appearance an overriding mess. Nobody knew where I was, my decision to come here only made after confirming there was nothing else left to do. Someone was watching me. I glanced around, not convinced I wasn't being watched *now,* momentarily wondering if they were planning to shoot me in the dark. I'd watched plenty of television. I knew how this shit worked. I shook off my ludicrous thoughts and dragged my belongings over the threshold, closing the door, ensuring it was firmly locked and bolted before pressing my back against the frame. I didn't need more nonsense in my head tonight.

I immediately checked my wallet. My money was still inside, not a dollar touched. I opened the flaps. My photos were still missing but my credit cards, unused gym membership, and unwanted items still lay where I'd hastily thrust them, soggy in places where they'd sat on the wet road, slightly bent and out of shape. Why would someone remove my photographs yet leave hundreds of dollars untouched? They meant nothing to anyone but me. It made no sense. I counted the cash, twice, not convinced I *hadn't* been robbed, unsure in my haste I truly appreciated how much money should have been there in the first place. The motel manager was correct. I could pay for my room now. I was grateful. It looked as if I'd be here a while. After all, I wasn't about to go *anywhere* without my child.

I wasn't sure what I anticipated finding when I opened my suitcase. Certainly not my boots wedged firmly along one side, hastily handled, no longer required. I pulled them out, thankful, everything about the last twenty-four hours ridiculous. None of my clothing had been touched, my passport and driver's license thrust inside an unzipped side pocket. I still couldn't find my phone charger. I assumed it was in the rental car somewhere. At least my anti-depressants were left inside the pocket I'd put them. I assumed no one gave a shit about those.

Megan had my suitcase in her possession. It therefore stood to reason she *must* have returned it, *stubble guy* no doubt secretly watching me all day. My disposition was hell-bent on ensuring I saw nothing of value, nothing of what I was searching for existing beyond demonic visions I'd invented for effect. I lay on an uncomfortable bed watching the door instead of the television, sleep finding its way to me sporadically in relentless dreams that ended with Georgina screaming for help. Morning came slowly, my anxiety for the pending day forcing my heart to maintain an uncomfortable rhythm. By the time daylight filtered through the aged curtains, I was exhausted, the entire night unforgiving.

Day Three

14

I hadn't expected to be without my daughter this long. It was illogical, but I was convinced she would have turned up by now, found me before I found her, wondering where the hell *I'd* disappeared to. I lay in that motel room staring at a dusty ceiling fan, my heart in tatters, nothing left to do but encourage my brain to stay strong when the only thing it wanted to do was disintegrate into the bedding and be done with it all.

I managed a shave I didn't feel like enduring, ate a slice of cold pizza that didn't taste any better in the cold light of day, and headed once more into the unknown. I needed to use the motel's landline, yet it was out of order this morning despite the manager using it the previous evening to order pizza. My mobile phone currently sat on a chest of drawers in a locked room, unusable, forgotten.

'Where can I hire a car?' I frustratingly handed over a wad of cash, the room I'd just escaped not worth half the amount being charged. The manager was sitting behind his desk, nothing more than four pieces of wood held together by willpower. He wasn't in a much better mood than the one he'd been in the night before, his only requirement being the money he charged for rooms that barely passed as adequate.

'There's probably somethin' over there that might

help.' He nodded towards a corkboard brimming with cards and memos, some handwritten, others barely legible, each one faded by sun and time. He didn't smile. I wondered if he ever did. His eyes confirmed he didn't sleep well either, strawberry blonde hair swept hastily to one side, stubble left to grow unhindered.

'Can I borrow your cell phone?' Georgina would have been impressed that I didn't say "mobile".

'No.'

'Why not?' I shifted my weight onto my other foot, irritation rising. He didn't have to sound so blunt.

'Cuz if I leant it to *you* I'd have to lend it to everyone and that ain't part of my job description.' The narrow look he gave me told me more than words ever could. I could understand his reasoning. Mine wasn't an isolated incident, my problems not unique.

I thanked him, took the nearest card from the board and left, nothing of my sanity remaining, nothing more to add. I couldn't overthink my miraculously reappearing suitcase, the disconnected phone line something I wasn't convinced hadn't been cut *deliberately*. Visions I didn't need in my head twisted violently along with the chilling concept that someone had followed me here.

As it was, I was forced to venture back into town on foot, no way for me to hire a car directly from the motel now, walking along the closed road with nothing but unfounded thoughts for company. Luckily the place didn't mock me as much in the daylight, didn't seem so menacing. I avoided the cornfield, all the same, my brain still creating devilish shapes from a moonlit evening I no longer wanted to think about. I ignored silent eyes I knew weren't *really* watching me from behind the now silent trees, a new morning and little sleep not enough to place things into perspective.

I scrutinized the streets for signs of life, needing nothing but a telephone and my missing child. It was all I could do to prevent myself from imploding, Megan on my mind, the lies she readily told doing me no favours at all. I needed to speak to her on neutral territory, still unwilling to accept that she hadn't drugged the coffee she'd given me, her unfounded reasons for lying unconvincing. I was clutching at straws, of course, nothing else to do, too many questions rattling around my unsettled head. I'd lost several hours of that first day to sleep I'd never have taken willingly, my missing daughter of no importance to *anyone*. Georgina had now been missing for two days. I couldn't dwell over it, my mind simply left to purge information that didn't belong, nothing I could do able to resolve my problems.

A few locals pondered my hapless intentions as I wandered the streets like a fool. They didn't know me, didn't appreciate my requirements, my desperation kept mostly to myself. All they saw was a stranger loitering where he shouldn't, my face set where it had no business being. When I spotted Megan along the street, I almost didn't believe she was real, my mind rapidly becoming accustomed to impossible visions that twisted reality into turmoil. I didn't assume this moment was any different.

'Hey?' I called out, racing into the road, unconcerned by potential oncoming traffic that would have made this day ten times worse, my intentions anything but good.

She saw me and froze, her eyes widening, uncertain. 'Ope!' The word left her surprised lips as if she was afraid to be alone with me, glancing around for men thankfully nowhere in sight.

'Why did you lie to the police?' I yelled. I didn't care I was making a scene. The woman jolted backwards, scurrying along the pavement, unwilling to continue this unwanted conversation. She hadn't behaved this concerned when she had me in a locked room tied to a bed, her reaction now obviously staged to make me look bad to any unsuspecting bystander.

'We don't like the *pigs* round here, stickin' their business where it ain't wanted.' Megan glanced my way to check I wasn't following, my attention not something she needed.

'But my daughter is *missing*,' I spat, racing ahead and rounding on her to obstruct her escape. I refrained from placing my hands on her arms, shaking some sense into her, demanding answers. I didn't need that kind of attention. How I was able to hold it together, I have no idea.

'Yeah, so you claim.' Megan halted in front of me, her face an expressionless set of features I didn't appreciate. I didn't like what I saw when I looked into her eyes, no concern or remorse for her actions at all.

'What is *that* meant to mean?' I was tired of these games, tired of pointed words aimed where they didn't need to be, my desperation meaning nothing to anyone.

'I can't say this any clearer, Mr. Raymond. You did *not* have a child when you arrived in Darkridge Hollow.' She was no longer calling me Josh. *Mr Raymond* was merely the stranger she didn't want to endure any further.

'Why do you keep saying that? How could you possibly know *who* I was with? She was already missing when I woke up in the car and just because you didn't see her, it doesn't mean she wasn't there.'

'You were *alone*, askin' for directions.' Megan sucked in a sharp breath. 'Now I suggest you get some help for your injuries because, I'm sorry to say, butcha don't seem quite *right* in the head.' She tapped her temple with a trembling index finger.

What the hell? 'Why won't you believe me?' I was practically in tears. It was pathetic.

'I honestly don't know whatcha were doin' out there by yourself.' Megan had no obvious answers to her crazy assumptions, genuinely believing me capable of God knows what. Did she assume me part of a bigger *problem?*

'Did you drug my coffee?' I blurted it out.

'Excuse me?' Megan folded exasperated arms across her chest. She didn't look at me, probably didn't want to expose the lie.

'You heard me.' I needed to ask. I couldn't help it.

'That's pretty darn rude. Now, if you don't mind, I'll be leavin'.' She motioned to walk past me.

'So you *did* drug me?'

'Will you quit sayin' that?'

'Then why tie me up?'

Megan sighed, momentarily wavering, no doubt wondering how she was going to explain herself, needing time to think. 'It was for your own good. You were talkin' in your sleep. Anythin' coulda happened.'

'What was I saying?' It was the first I'd heard of it.

'Somethin' about the car, and draggin' things into the woods.' Megan paused. 'That's why Tommy and Mike went out to check.'

I opened my mouth to speak but thought better of it, nothing I said able to change how Megan saw me now. What the hell was I meant to have dragged into the woods?

'And what did they find?' I almost didn't want to know. I was chewing my lip, irritated beyond reproach.

'Some blood. Nothin' more, I guess.' She stared at me, noticing I was wearing clean clothing and my old boots. 'You gotcha things back then?'

I automatically glanced at my feet. 'I assume *Tommy* or *Mike* followed me out of town.' I didn't need the thought in my head, enough shit in there as it was. I didn't want to assume I'd been followed in the dark, my mind too busy dealing with other uncomfortable images that, for now, I was keeping to myself.

'How should I know? I ain't their keeper,' she sniped. 'Now if you don't mind, I'm busy.' Megan scanned the street, hoping a resident would step in and save her from my unwanted wrath.

I nodded when really I just wanted to scream. 'One last thing,' I stated, trying and failing to keep calm. Megan was already walking away. She stopped, her back to me, hands trembling. 'Why did you *lie* about calling the police?'

Megan turned around and stared at me, nothing in her eyes giving away her emotions, nothing in her tone explaining such a callous act of sabotage.

'I had to calm you *somehow,* didn't I?' She turned and continued along the street, my presence no longer needed, no longer important.

She wasn't about to offer any further assistance. That much was clear.

***

Unable to find a working telephone, I was forced to hitchhike out of town, a curled piece of card clutched in my hand displaying an address I wasn't even sure still existed. Megan's earlier confirmation that no taxi cabs ran directly to or from Darkridge Hollow saw me standing in the street, expecting a stranger to take pity on the crazed English idiot in their path. It was something I'd never done. Didn't think I ever would. I must have looked ridiculous, my head as muddled as my thinking, my hands trembling, thumbs outstretched, my body heading for total catastrophic failure. I would *never* stop to offer a stranger a lift. Why would I now assume someone else would?

'Josh? Whatcha *still* doin' here?' A gruff voice startled me. I turned around to see Peter glaring at me from across the street. He was standing next to an open-tailed truck, the back of his shop no more inviting than the front, his confusion as apparent as mine.

'*Still* trying to find my daughter,' I confirmed, my

sarcasm enveloping the thick morning air. I didn't assume he gave a shit. I was sick of saying it.

'Any luck?'

'Yeah, I found her, but couldn't be bothered to deal with her so I left her where she was.' I didn't mean to sound pissed off or fly off the handle. It was a *stupid* question. I wondered when my anti-depressants would kick in and placate me from thoughts I didn't need. They weren't called 'happy' pills for nothing, my existence hopeless without them.

Peter sighed, wiping perpetually filthy hands on an old rag that looked as if it hadn't been washed in decades. He was unloading his truck, several discarded boxes and corn sacks stacked behind his unhooked tailgate, face flustered with overwork—just another telling confirmation that Darkridge Hollow was a lost cause, the fields beyond dead and forgotten.

'Need help?'

I glanced his way, flawed by the empathy, the tone of his voice unexpectedly concerned for my welfare. 'Do you have a telephone I could use?'

'No.'

Of course he didn't. How did these people *survive?*

I glanced at the card in my hand. 'Then I could use a lift if you're offering?' I scoffed, not expecting him to do so, not expecting much at all from these people now.

'You'd better get in then,' Peter chided, tossing his old rag into the back of his truck. He closed the tailgate, unconcerned by produce now forgotten on the pavement or by my vacuous corpse barely breathing across the street. He opened his passenger door, not anticipating I'd turn down his offer. He had better things to do. Take it, or leave it.

I was growing weary of getting into vehicles with strangers, though there was nothing I could do about that now, nothing of this trip how I assumed it would be. I climbed in, thanking Peter with a grunt, my chosen destination luckily a place the guy knew well. We drove in silence, my lips clamped closed for fear of provoking further unwanted sarcasm, no words I could offer in any way rational. I didn't wish to irritate the guy and be deposited onto the side of the road in a hurry, my declining mood ebbing away with the ticking clock on his dashboard. A strong stench of old socks and cabbage wafted across my nostrils, the passing farmland inducing unwanted vomit for a second time. Those cornfields mocked me, laughing from the roadside, nothing more than a passing blur capable of driving me insane.

I dared allow a brief moment of relief. With transport in my possession, I could scope larger areas, expand my search, *drive* back to Megan's place and demand an explanation. It was the least she owed me, the least I deserved. Her toxic words still lingered in my head and I couldn't understand why she hadn't stolen my money. Those people were well within their right to ignore my existence and claim innocence. I didn't mean to be rude but they looked as if they could use the cash. No one would have been able to prove a damned thing anyway, no one in their right mind begrudging them such an indulgence at my expense. On some level, they must have felt sorry for me, assuming me mentally unwell—probably as bizarre as I now viewed *them.*

I couldn't entirely blame Megan for her actions, of course. I believed her when she told me she hadn't *seen* Georgina. Finding me in the pouring rain the way she had, alone, ranting and raving, covered in blood with a head injury and damaged car in my possession, I'm sure she assumed me misinformed, misunderstanding the situation I'd found myself in. Megan hadn't seen the two of us together, hadn't noticed Georgina with her ice cream and attitude, my unfeigned imagination now left to surmise that she'd innocently reached the wrong conclusion.

As for the police, she probably didn't want to get involved. I *was* a stranger in her town, only *my* word to go by that I hadn't murdered the very child I claimed had disappeared, covering my tracks as I went along and pretending she was missing in order to gain some odd, demented traction with the locals. They didn't know me or appreciate my motives. They were being cautious. I could appreciate that.

It didn't help me now though, nothing about this situation offering anything of importance that might help find my child. I probably should have verified if the police had removed my rental from the roadside, instead of taking Bailey's word for it. I should have queried as to where it was now and what they planned to do next. There may have been vital evidence left inside, something that might, by some impossible miracle, point me towards my child. At the very least, I might have found my phone charger.

I didn't wish to consider the painful idea that lay hidden behind twisted thoughts. It was an unimaginable conclusion left to linger longer than I liked, an idea I couldn't dislodge no matter what I did. A despicable notion that, *maybe,* someone had taken my child, kidnapped her, dragging her into the unknown. Maybe a stranger had happened upon the wreckage, stealing my daughter's belongings, her mobile, suitcase, passport. Or perhaps the very wild animal I'd imagined was, in fact, the reason behind her bewildering disappearance. I didn't know which concept was worse, yet the latter would explain the blood trail.

Yet none of it explained why a supposed opportunist would have stolen my *photographs* instead of my money, leaving *my* belongings behind in the process. I had an expensive camera in my suitcase, worth a few quid, such an item more than capable of making someone's unexpected day. Instead, I was left to the painful conclusion that, for reasons known only to them, someone had staged the entire thing to make it look as if Georgina didn't exist—taking my child along with everything she'd brought on this trip. Either that or I seriously needed urgent medical assistance because something about this did not add up. Darkridge Hollow was rapidly becoming a place I didn't want in my head, its name as disconcerting as its location. I was sick of not having a working mobile phone, my continued complaints to Georgina about using hers too often coming back to haunt me.

'Thank you,' I muttered when I could bare the silence no more, my thoughts too intense, my tone thankfully polite. Peter didn't respond, too busy manoeuvring his bulky vehicle into a car park brimming with rental cars of all shapes and sizes. Brash signs were set in every direction, the bright red, white, and blue of several U.S. flags flapping in the breeze.

'I hope ya find her,' he said as I stepped onto the tarmac, taking a lungful of much-needed fresh air. I attempted a smile, my lips nothing more than twitching muscles pulled forcefully towards flustered cheeks. With every minute that passed, Georgina's chances grew slimmer, every second that ticked by signalling nothing good. Peter didn't need to appreciate my desperation. He had enough of his own problems to care about mine.

15

I collected my new rental with thankfully no issues, grateful to have been reunited with my identity, displaying my driver's license and paying the additional insurance in case of further *unexpected* incidents. I didn't dare tell them I'd left the last one in a ditch. I didn't think such a revelation would have done me any favours. I scanned the area, scoping abandoned buildings, old barns and overgrown shrubbery—putting off the inevitable and going back to the one place I needed to go, the last location I'd seen my child, the very place she might *actually* be.

I couldn't bear the idea of finding my baby savaged and dismembered in some animal's lair, her red trainers and baggy trousers the only items left to identify her. I needed to admit I'd been putting off going back to that stretch of road for fear of what I might find, despite very few places left to look. After all, the longer I could keep her alive in my mind the better. My head was a mess, the assumed protection of my rental car the only thing keeping me functioning, frustration enveloping me like a straitjacket.

I doubted anyone in this town had anything to say I wanted to hear, none of them willing to offer the support I needed. The fact that I'd misplaced my daughter didn't seem to register, a sharp realisation I'd seen *no* kids, a further niggle I couldn't dislodge. Maybe this town didn't *like* children. Maybe they couldn't produce them. Maybe such families had already moved away long ago to live better lives elsewhere. Whatever the reason, I was glad for a vehicle that had unwittingly become a protective layer from an outside world I no longer appreciated, grateful to the fleeting kindness of Peter. Yet that is where my affinity with Darkridge Hollow ended, this town nothing more to me now than a name I no longer wanted to say aloud.

I headed out to the stretch of road that had recently disrupted my entire existence, nowhere left to go, driving past Megan's property and wishing I had the guts to confront her directly. I parked several feet from where I'd last seen the car, Hillborne Avenue no more comforting from this angle, my brand-new rental lingering too close to where I'd unwittingly parted company from my last. Georgina's last words rang loudly in my ears. She was bored, she'd claimed, the continued fiddling with the radio distracting my attention, sealing our fate. I'd snapped at her, hot, irritated, the day too much for me to deal with. Now I wished I could go back in time, wrap my arms around her and tell her how sorry I was—*for everything*.

I closed my aching eyes, not needing those events playing out in my head so violently, frustrated by pain that relentlessly threatened to spiral me out of control. I could still see the rain on the windscreen, if I closed my eyes—the way it raced frantically towards the edges of the glass, taking my increasing temper with it. A stupid tune was playing on the radio, the song forever now lodged in my head. I didn't know the title. I honestly didn't care.

What was the last thing Georgina remembered? I hoped it wasn't my irritated voice or disgruntled features. I wasn't sure I could live with that. I could barely recall my ill-placed words, scarcely able to function rationally since. I climbed out of the car and lingered for several painful moments, the very ditch that had once housed an amalgamation of twisted metal glaring back in disgust. I didn't want to approach the overgrowth, unconvinced I could do this, nothing good coming from what I was surely about to uncover. It was quiet here now, the memory of that fateful day too much for my brain to process.

My boots thudded across the crumbling tarmac, each encumbered step scattering stones and twigs into the verge. I took a breath and clambered down the embankment towards a potential trail of blood I hadn't noticed existed, unappreciative of the horror I assumed awaited my searching eyes. I couldn't overthink what I was about to find, forced to see this through to its bitter conclusion.

I was about to follow a trail of blood that had been brought to my attention by strangers—a misted windowpane unable to hide words uttered assumedly out of earshot. I chastised myself for failing to notice such an obvious thing first-hand, inept fear blinding me to the fact that, had I been less fretful of the situation, I might have noticed directly. I *may* have been able to save her when I had the chance, when time was still on our side. Yet, I could see nothing here now beyond my own stupidity, no trail of red to lead the way, hours of relentless rain covering any residual tracks that may have been left behind.

I didn't know where I was going, my feet doing the thinking for me, my brain unwilling to take responsibility for this moment. The last thing I needed was to come across the body of my dead child lying forgotten and damaged. After all, the police should have taken control of the situation. It should be *them* here, not me, this day potentially producing the last image I'd ever have of her, a painful vision that would forever embed itself onto my retina. I honestly didn't know what I would do if her body was a twisted shape in the grass, limbs I'd barely recognise, her cherished clothing no longer intact. I leant over and vomited. This entire situation felt wrong, my mind left to churn ideas undeserving of attention.

I called her name, hoping if by some miracle she was still out here, still *alive*, she might respond. It was stupid, I know, insane. Yet I scanned every inch of ground for a sign, anything that might tell me I was right to believe such a ludicrous concept. I needed to cling to hope, cling to the possibility she was taking refuge in a hollow tree stump or deep hole. Maybe she'd fallen, unable to crawl to safety, waiting patiently now for rescue, weakened, hungry. I couldn't think of anything else. Nothing else made sense.

The thought of black bears, bobcats, and coyotes devoured my concentration, each capable of devouring a potentially bleeding, unconscious child, taking her into the wilds and leaving her for dead. I didn't want to think about the poisonous snakes and spiders lurking in the shadows around me, the Black Widow spider a deadly, yet common, insect in this area. Georgina had taken great joy in telling me all about it, curled in front of the television, her laptop open and mischief on her mind. She was excited. So was I. Now I wished Anna hadn't told us about this place—ignorance being bliss and all that.

I picked my way through long grass, between dense trees into the woodland beyond, wishing I had a gun. I didn't know what the hell I was doing, every step met with bated, nervous breath. Never in my wildest nightmares did I imagine Darkridge Hollow to be *this* imposing, yet my mind was set now in frantic deliberation, my body along for the ride. Every fallen branch turned into a snake in my mind's eye, every leaf a deadly spider I felt would murder me where I stood, a single bite more than enough to satisfy its insatiable needs.

Glowing eyes glistened in the distance, watching, nothing more, the breeze prodding me for fun. How far could an animal drag a child? Georgina was small for her age, her slim build something an adult bear would have no issues transporting to its lair. I tried to dislodge visions of bloodied corpses, half-consumed bones and body parts potentially scattered amidst the disfigured trees. I closed my eyes. I couldn't think like that. Not yet.

I didn't anticipate the woods to be so tiresome, every step requiring much effort to break through heavy bracken and overgrowth beneath my feet. I understood why most chose to stay away, the locals owning guns, their trucks capable of venturing off-road, their attitudes in a far better place than mine. There were too many things out here that could kill me, too many opportunities for me to find death. It was ironic really.

Several times I was forced to stop, take a breath, my bearings lost to my surroundings, the daylight dimming in and out of focus beneath dense treetops and heavy thoughts. I crossed paths with a few unsuspecting snakes, grateful they were more interested in keeping cool than my demonic appearance. I couldn't overthink the population of spiders around me, insects far outnumbering humanity. I didn't want Georgina's statistics in my head. It wasn't comforting.

I stopped and scanned the immediate area, my bated breath and tightened chest matching the relentless sway of the trees. It was odd my boots seemed the only disturbance the woodland floor had witnessed. If my child *had* been dragged through here by a hungry beast, I was confident I'd have found the trail by now, something to confirm my darkest fears weren't unfounded lies that lived inside my twisted thoughts. Yet, Tommy and Mike had *confirmed* a trail of blood. I'd heard them myself, first hand, Megan offering the same conclusion. They'd already searched this place, apparently, found nothing of interest.

Something wasn't right. Where were *their* tracks? We were talking about two grown men stumbling around the wilderness in search of a trail of blackened blood, a potential dead child at the end of it, the guns in their hands twitching and ready. Where had the trail taken them, and where had it ended? Several times I assumed I'd gone the wrong way, doubling back only to change my mind and keep going, this entire location merging as one, nothing but a maze of shit that kept me spinning on my heels. It was a vendetta now anyway, a paralyzing moment set to keep me walking in circles until I either found my child or my troubled end, whichever came first.

I was lost. *Again.* It was happening a lot, nothing to be done about that other than to keep going. The thought of doing nothing was worse than the powerless emotions engulfing me, the thought of going back to that motel room and waiting, entirely unacceptable. After all, what *exactly* would I be waiting for? Not the police. They'd already made it abundantly clear they could do very little without more to go on, without a visual reference, a *photograph.* A signed report in a filing cabinet was all I could hope to achieve. Whilst I was out here looking, at least I had a chance. It wasn't a good chance, I know, and the longer I stayed, the weaker I became. But the alternative was too much to consider. Georgina couldn't have *vanished.* It was a troubling truth I couldn't dispel.

Now and then a dead animal carcass would catch my attention, guts spilt into the grasslands, flesh and bones torn to pieces, tiny faces set in stone where they'd taken their final breath. I found nothing large, *thank Christ,* nothing human. Just the occasional raccoon, bloodied bird and traces of muskrat that Georgina was obsessed with, a distinct shape in the grass ahead of me identified by a patch of fur and a long tail coated with blood.

I would have given anything to be on the receiving end of her sharp wit and snappy irritation, her metaphoric claws aimed my way. Nothing of my developing child's tantrums meant a thing to me now. It was all irrelevant, all ridiculous in the scheme of things, life passing too swiftly for petty quarrels to ever mean anything again. My complaining. Georgina's grumbling. None of it mattered. I wished she were here to drive me insane and demand attention I'd once assumed unimportant. Nothing else felt real.

Eventually, I was forced to admit defeat and retrace my steps back to the car. My search had equated to nothing more than additional suffering set to keep my brain on a relentless loop of terror, a horror show of my own making. I sat by the roadside, trembling knees tucked beneath my chin, Anna's unremitting memories overshadowed by a drowning sense of doom I couldn't shake. I thought about Martha's warning.

Look around. You must know what this place is. You got eyes don'tcha?

I was looking now, desperately. Yet could see nothing that made sense beyond the fact this place gave me the creeps. Neither the state of the buildings or the people who lived here compared to the imagined abomination lingering in the breeze around me. This entire town was dead, deep within, the people included, as if something terrible had been left to grow unchecked. A creeping decay had crawled its way into every corner of every street, seeping readily into my overworked lungs. I sighed. What the *hell* was I doing out here by myself?

I thought of Anna again, my dead wife as cold as the bracken at my feet, nothing left to confirm our recent crash, nothing to authenticate my chaotic moment of madness. Every trace of Georgina had been removed from this location. By *who* or *what,* I was yet to discover. I took a breath, wishing with everything I had inside me that my wife was here. I wished she would talk to me, help me, tell me what I was supposed to do, what *she* would do in my unfathomed position.

Of course, if Anna were here, I probably wouldn't be. I

wouldn't be sitting ankle-deep in sleeping snakes and spiders that span webs readily into my mind. I wouldn't have got us lost, Anna knowing this place far better than I. Georgina would be safe and well. With me. With *us*. Precisely where she belonged.

***

I drove around for a while, losing track of time, ignoring the fuel light and the dwindling residents of Darkridge Hollow far longer than I should have. I drove past a huge lake, scoping the area twice, yet after finding nothing but dead raccoons and squirrels, I relented and headed back to Abbots View. I saw no other option, and by then, I was practically ready to kill someone, ready to explode.

'You *lost* or somethin'?' Deputy Chief McDonald was behind the front desk, as usual, a sarcastic tone on his lips that didn't become him. The guy was drinking coffee as if there was nothing more important to his day, a caffeine fix all he required to see him through. He glanced my way, a pair of spectacles perched precariously on the end of his ridged nose, uninterested in my presence and what I needed.

'If you must know, I'm *still* looking for my daughter.' My sarcasm hadn't abated. It wasn't ideal.

'Oh? And how's that workin' out for ya?' he muttered, removing glasses he casually placed on the desk. His tone wasn't ideal either. I ignored it all the same.

I narrowed my eyes. I couldn't help it. I was hot, flustered, borderline psychotic. 'I reported her missing yesterday,' I stated, in case such an important declaration had slipped his mind. The guy had practically ignored me then, too, his mannerisms ensuring I was beginning to question his integrity.

He glanced at me as if he didn't care, didn't need me in

his day. 'And, as I told you yesterday, the police'll take care of it.'

'What exactly *are* the police doing to find my child?' I didn't mean to sound so pointed. I hadn't eaten much, hadn't slept, a putrid taste of undigested pizza making repeated unnecessary appearances in the back of my throat every time I swallowed. Why was no one interested in speaking to me? In *helping* me?

Deputy Chief McDonald sighed, a shake of his disinterested head making me want to punch him in the face. 'With no visual reference to go by, I'm afraid there ain't much we can do at this stage.'

I wasn't expecting him to be so blasé, his flat tone hitting me now as if he'd punched me in the face. 'But she's twelve.' My throat began to tighten, something in my eyes threatening to burn a hole directly into my brain. I couldn't ignore the probability that I was about to cry. I blinked. *Jesus Christ, Josh.*

The deputy sighed again, offering a look of feigned sympathy that appeared as false as his attitude. 'I appreciate this must be frustratin'-'

'You have *no* idea,' I cut in, blinking away tears ready to make an appearance. I couldn't look weak. Not in front of these people.

'I'm real sorry for what you're goin' through, but I'm gonna have to ask you to calm down-'

'*You* calm down,' I yelled. 'My child is out there somewhere and nobody in this *fucking* town gives a shit.' I was shouting, everything too much, my bad language emerging from nowhere. I hardly ever swore. I needed to set a good example for Georgina. It was a shame today wasn't one of them.

'Mr. Raymond, please-'

'Is *nobody* out looking for her? She might be in the woods right now.' She wasn't, but *he* didn't know that.

The deputy waved a hand my way. 'I'm *not* gonna ask again.' He was swiftly joined by two further officers, none of them appreciative of the scene I was creating.

'Well, that makes *two* of us,' I screamed. I just needed to find my daughter. I turned around and punched the wall. It was better than punching one of them. It wasn't a clever decision, of course, my unwitting actions ensuring I was grabbed, placed into handcuffs, the outcome seeing me thrown into a cell. I couldn't believe my stupidity, yet my protests remained unheeded as my body was manoeuvred shamelessly into yet another locked room, a heavy door slamming in my face.

'If you've been drinkin', I suggest you sober up.' Deputy Chief McDonald was standing on the other side of cold steel bars. He had no idea how I was feeling or how this was affecting me, although by the looks of him, he didn't give a shit. He was sealing my demented fate without even trying, the look he gave me capable of destroying everything.

'I haven't been drinking!' I yelled, practically spitting into the poor guy's face. He was only doing his job, I know, yet the last thing I was *ever* going to do was get blatantly drunk and avoid achieving the most important thing in the world to me. *Finding Georgina.* What the hell kind of person did these people think I was? I grabbed the bars as if my hands were already around the deputy's throat, nothing I wanted right then as impactful as what was actually happening.

'Then whatever this is, y'can stay in here until you calm down.'

'How the hell can I calm down?' I snorted, projecting a fake laugh his way. Were these people insane?

He grunted, giving me a stern look before turning to leave, his dispersing footsteps leaving me cold.

'Oh God, please. I'm sorry,' I groaned through the closed bars towards an eerily empty corridor. My actions were

making everything worse, my ill-timed responses met only with malice. 'I'm sorry,' I repeated louder, pounding fists against the metal, rattling firmly. '*Please!*' I was trying to calm myself, failing miserably.

A few painful moments passed, my own company as unwanted as this cell, the sound of my stale breath too much. It was probably no more than a few minutes before the deputy returned, yet it could have been a lifetime. He stood in the doorway looking annoyed, a cup of black coffee in his hand, the holstered gun on his hip something I didn't want to think too long about. In the UK, police officers carry pepper spray and taser guns, not life-ending pistols. It reminded me I was out of place here, unwanted, this trip wholly avoidable.

'Drink this,' he instructed sharply. 'You're doin' yourself or your daughter no favors by causin' trouble.'

I didn't *want* to cause trouble. I wanted to find my child and go home. I wished I'd never come here, never booked the plane tickets. Yet, here we were, an unavoidable fate in charge. I took the cup held towards me through the bars and sat down, ensuring I appeared as calm as I could, composed, collected. Inside I was screaming. I couldn't stop my hands from shaking, the hot coffee in my grasp threatening to spill, unable to swallow the liquid without it burning my insides. I had no idea how long they were planning to keep me here, no phone call in the world capable of saving me now.

Thankfully, I wasn't being charged with any crime, merely kept out of the way until I calmed down. They believed I was drunk, despite no tests carried out to confirm it, no need to elaborate on my failing state of mind beyond an assumption made on my behalf. I wasn't *drunk*. Unhinged, yes. Desperate, absolutely. But *drunk?* No way.

An hour must have passed, maybe two. By the time the door was opened and I was allowed to walk free, I could have sprinted out of that cell and never looked back. More time had passed with my child left to endure *Christ* knows what. More pain she might have been subjected to because of me.

'Can I *go* now?'

'Y'can go. But your kind ain't welcome here. Go home. Go back to where you came from.'

I could do nothing but stare at several men in authority, their tone unhelpful, irrational. *My kind?* These people were meant to help law-abiding citizens, yet no one was helping me, it seemed. This was a forgotten, isolated community with small minds attached to even smaller viewpoints. Especially when it came to outsiders. The police were not looking for Georgina, despite their pointed confirmation, their authoritative tone met only with frustration. They were lying to my face. It wasn't a comforting consideration. As it was, I was left alone to deal with whatever this place chose to throw at me next.

16

I drove to Megan's property with too many impossible ideas swarming my brain. I'd tried hard and failed to focus on something other than her last words, nothing she'd said providing any notion of truth. I was no longer concerned for my safety. Our earlier conversation had left me numb and desperate, her continued lies ensuring I was standing on the precipice of hell, waiting to be devoured by demons that came in the form of incomprehensible human beings.

I brought the car to a halt, the engine left running – should I need a swift escape – retaining a safe distance between my vehicle and Megan's domain. Her overgrown driveway was ready to ensnare my wandering feet, should I venture too close, my wondering mind already captured. The entire place was as hidden as my thoughts, her windows dark and imposing—that dilapidated property as threatening in the daylight as it was in the dark. If Megan was trying to make me appear insane, it was working, single-handedly ensuring I was now on the edge, borderline manic, the police having no issues buying her crap.

I'd fully expected police intervention by now, news crews, live interviews, national television coverage promoting a full-scale search for my missing child. I assumed many concerned residents would be ready and willing to help me without hesitation. Yet, as it was, nothing had happened, nothing able to sedate my pulsating brain aside from a few oddly placed comments, a passing gesture of sympathy—death and decay the only things I'd absorbed. That skinny-framed figure I'd imagined in the darkness ensured I was overthinking everything, my mind creating images that didn't exist, my missing child the reason behind it all. "Leave Darkridge Hollow," Martha had told me, her words expressed with volatile force. Why would she say that? What the *hell* was I missing?

The concept made me sick to the pit of my stomach, leaving behind a taste of bile that continually burned my throat. Who could I talk to anyway? Who would *believe* the shit I'd endured? Anna had often joked about places you should never venture alone, many small communities best avoided. Until now, I didn't assume they were *real,* just ridiculous pandering, Anna's imagination running wild, her words designed to poke fun because she *could*.

I loitered beyond the boundaries of Megan's property for well over an hour, my rental car my only willing companion. When someone tapped the window, I wasn't expecting it, my imagination a troubled, tangled mess of shit I'd created from too many impossible scenarios. I turned sharply to see a smiling stranger. It momentarily threw me, such an innocent gesture alien to my senses. I was no longer used to simple acknowledgements, the last couple of days ensuring my mind was permanently set on high alert, antagonistic behaviour the norm. Yet this stranger's smile allowed a brief assumption that I could open the window without provoking immediate chaos. The guy didn't look a threat. I should have been grateful.

'You lost?' He was leaning towards me through the now open window, his eyes cast casually across the interior of a vehicle that smelled of lemons and cleaning products.

I was beginning to detest the sound of that question. *Yes.* Yes, I am lost, if you must know. *Very lost.*

'You could say that,' I muttered, not requiring a response or directions, if that was his objective, my presence here intended, my needs as urgent now as they'd been the day of the crash. I was precisely where I wanted to be, where I *needed* to be, nothing more to add to that equation, nothing this guy could say to change such an ill-considered realisation I was in this alone.

The guy straightened up, allowing me to see his police uniform, his wide-brimmed hat shielding his features from the sun, his badge set neatly on display. I tried not to look at his gun belt or the way his hand rested against his hip, the other tapping the roof of the car. I didn't want to be shot dead where I sat. I still wasn't used to driving on the wrong side of the road, the wrong side of the car ensuring my permanent confusion. Maybe that's why they'd assumed me drunk. Maybe this officer thought I was, too.

'You heading back into town?'

It wasn't something I'd considered, yet I had a distinct feeling this wasn't a passing query. His accent wasn't typical Ohioan and I got the impression he wasn't a local, didn't belong here. Like me.

'I have no idea *where* I'm going,' I replied, my attention firmly on Megan's ramshackle property, a section of damaged roof tiles barely visible through the swaying trees.

'No one lives back there,' the officer confirmed, following my line of sight over his shoulder. He probably assumed my intentions sinister. Did he expect me to break in, or *buy* the place?

I glanced up, my attention caught. 'Sorry? What?' I didn't mean to appear shocked. 'A woman called Megan lives there.' Now I really *did* feel as if I was losing the plot. My earlier fears that none of this was real jumped into my mind again. Maybe I *was* dead, in limbo or a coma, this entire situation staged as a test I was yet to appreciate. I sat upright, unable to comprehend anything of my failing persona.

The officer shook his head. 'Nope. Can't say I've heard of her.' He offered a flat smile that didn't reach his face.

I scoffed. 'I think you might be mistaken.' I didn't want to appear rude, of course, merely stating the facts. 'I was there, yesterday.' And the day before, *unfortunately.* 'Check with your colleagues if you don't believe me.' Surely, even in this godforsaken hellhole, they kept records.

'I'm not trying to make you mad,' he replied calmly. 'But no one's lived in that old place for well over twenty years, so I've heard.' He glanced over his shoulder as if to reaffirm the truth of his statement.

'*Megan?*' I queried forcefully, hoping that by repeating the woman's name, someone in this place might actually know *who* the hell I was talking about. Why was everyone looking at me as if I was an idiot? I wished I'd asked her surname. It would have at least made her *real.*

The officer shook his head, glancing around, looking as if he was trying to locate familiarity and relocate his *own* sanity. 'Nope. Sorry.'

I sighed, wanting to slam my head into the steering wheel and be done with it. 'Why does nobody know who she is?' I didn't expect a response. She was the first person I'd met when I arrived here. Now I *wished* she'd been the last. I wished we'd driven directly to Colorado, avoided this place and the subsequent suffering I was now forced to experience alone. I wanted to question him further but I let it go, nothing for me to do about such an unwanted conclusion right then.

'I'm State Trooper Harrison. Blake, to my friends.' The stranger held an open palm through the open car window, my obvious frustration of no concern to him. I had no choice but to shake his hand, offering a nod I didn't feel like providing. Anything else would have looked rude. He might have assumed me a threat. I might have become one too if left to my own devices, my thoughts anything but rational.

'Josh,' I offered, pleasantries something I didn't care much for right then. He still hadn't answered my question, probably didn't feel he needed to.

'Can I bum a ride into town, Josh?' Blake smiled, tilting his head. Was this some pretentious way of getting me to leave? I narrowed my eyes, giving him a closer inspection, his police uniform suddenly imposing, threatening. Surely he had a vehicle of his own. Why did he need mine?

'Sure.' I reached over and unlocked the passenger door, nothing else to do but agree as my newly found acquaintance climbed in. It was another thing I would never do under normal circumstances, Blake's police authority the only reason I did so now. Georgina would be rolling her eyes at my inappropriate behaviour. *Practice what you preach, Dad.* I didn't want to, but I returned Blake's smile, hoping to look sane, normal. I was acting anything but, of course, my persona borderline unbalanced, skidding violently towards all-out mania.

'I saw you at the station earlier. Couldn't help noticing what was happening back there.' Blake's tone was purposefully light. I didn't like it.

His face gave nothing away of his emotions. Not unlike mine. I didn't wish to acknowledge that I hadn't noticed Blake, the police rapidly becoming an impossible hindrance, the deputy a person I could have gladly throttled. The poor guy could have stood right next to me and I would have missed him, his badge confirming nothing I wanted to see.

'My daughter is missing.' I was sick of saying this aloud to ears that had no interest in listening. No one was doing anything about it. No one cared.

'Yeah, figured,' Blake muttered, swallowing something I wasn't aware he'd eaten. 'I'm sorry.'

'Not nearly as much as I am.'

'You here on vacation?'

Blake was changing the subject. Why, I couldn't tell. The idea of a holiday now seemed so far away it was laughable. We'd been planning this trip for months. Actually, that's not true. We had this thing planned years ago, Anna and I, merely waiting for the right time, the right opportunity. I closed my eyes, visions of my wife's enthusiasm fading rapidly, every word she's confirmed about this place nothing but lies set to create a reality I now realised didn't exist.

'It *should* have been,' I muttered.

Blake leaned back, unconcerned by my throwaway words, my missing child of no consequence to his day. Was he sent here to watch me, to follow my car, ponder my intentions? Did they assume because I was a black man, I was here to cause trouble? The police had requested my removal with a wave of a dismissive hand, and I was no longer confident they weren't all in on this thing together, whatever this *thing* was. My presence here was temporary, my needs something they didn't care about. My paranoia was increasing. It wasn't comforting. Something wasn't right.

I didn't want to but I reluctantly drove away from Megan's property, the place now as empty as Blake's company. Who *was* Megan? Certainly not a figment of my imagination. I'd lost my daughter, not my mind. Tight lips seemed a normal part of Darkridge Hollow, disinterest something I hadn't expected to find so readily.

'What do you *want* from me?' I snapped, biting my tongue. I was tired of all the nonchalance, all the shit.

Blake turned to face me, the seatbelt he hadn't fastened left dangling next to the door rim, the warning alarm annoying me before we'd driven twenty feet. It didn't matter. He was staring at me blankly, unconcerned, his features a collection of solidified muscles that confirmed nothing of value.

'I want to help.' His words were almost a whisper.

'You?' I scoffed. 'Why? *Nobody* else seems bothered.' It wasn't something I'd expected to say aloud. I assumed *everyone* would have wanted to assist me in my desperate hour.

Blake reached down and turned off his radio, taking a breath as if he wasn't convinced he was doing the right thing. 'I'm a good listener.' The seatbelt alarm was still bleeping. I suddenly realised why he hadn't worn it, his words shielded from potential prying ears.

I shook my head, my fists clenched around the steering wheel. 'Did they send you after me?' I needed to know.

'Does it matter?'

'Yes.' I was in no mood for games. Not today. I glanced at his radio, the flashing light no longer flashing. 'Won't you get into trouble for that?'

Blake smirked. 'Probably.'

I didn't want to, but I told him about Georgina, my muted tone matching his, something in his face softening mine. I told him about Megan's hindrance, our missing items, recounting everything that had happened since my arrival, including my frustration for the fact that nothing was being done to help.

'Why do *you* want to help me?' I asked. So far the police had been less than forthcoming.

Blake sighed. 'Because there's things about this town you don't know, Josh.'

'What things?' My heart was beginning to pound, my throat tightening.

Blake took a breath, a moment, the look he gave me confirming I shouldn't interrupt. 'There's talk of a crazy woman in Darkridge Hollow.' He didn't blink. I glared at him but he didn't react, instead turning his attention towards the blurred surroundings, nothing of my reaction required. 'No one sees much of her. Many locals don't even remember her name.'

'Who?' I immediately thought of Megan. No one seemed to know *her* name either. Why was he telling *me?*

Blake shook his head. 'I don't know. I only moved to the area a few months back. I'm not from around these parts.' I believed him. 'But some say she went nuts. They claim her child was snatched during the night, and, according to local legend, she was never the same again.'

I visualised an insane old lady, hair like spider webs, hands like tree stumps, gnarled and bent out of shape, teeth missing, wiry hair growing from protruding moles that stood to attention on her chin. I thought about the family who'd moved to Darkridge Hollow in the 1970s, about the warning Martha had given me, images of *her* gnarled hands not exactly comforting.

'Why won't anyone help me find my child?' I had to ask. I was staring at Blake, my sarcasm unmoving. I should have been focusing on the road.

Blake didn't reply, instead pressed his lips together in concentration.

'Do you think, whoever she is, she might be capable of taking *children?*' I had no idea where the idea had come from, yet it seemed a logical query, an obvious assumption. Her child had been taken. So had mine. Maybe she was on the prowl for a replacement, waiting for justice that would never come? I momentarily considered the idea of a demonic witch-like creature living in the woods, existing off rats, snakes and birds. I thought about the thin-armed figure in the cornfield that, until now, I genuinely believed wasn't real. Bodies of recently ravaged animals popped into my mind, their corpses left where they'd met their savaged end. I still had mud on my boots from today's search. What kind of place was this?

Blake shrugged, unaware of my private musing. 'I

honestly don't know that much about her, Josh.'

'But you *know* the stories?' I didn't mean to snap. Why would he tell me about her if he had nothing important to say? He must have known it would make me panic. Maybe he got a kick out of it. Maybe they all did.

'Everyone knows the stories.' Blake laughed. It was inappropriate and I gave him a sideways look, forcing him to compose himself.

I exhaled slowly, my hands gripping the steering wheel as if it might explode. Firstly, *I* didn't know the stories, nothing Anna *ever* told me painting the very picture that now floated around my head. Secondly, I was sick of being palmed off by strangers, this town housing nothing but demented, racist *freaks* I was tired of dealing with. I didn't mean to reach such a troubling conclusion. It probably wasn't true. I'm sure there were many *nice* people in Darkridge Hollow. I just hadn't met any.

'What if this is all somehow connected to my child's disappearance?' I couldn't help asking. It made sense.

'That's why I want to help.'

'Kids *don't* just disappear.' I was rambling, muttering. It was true. We weren't living in a twilight zone and I couldn't fathom Blake's motives. I wanted to stop the car and get out, pace up and down and give myself some time to think—a time out from relentless carnage I couldn't escape. It was how I dealt with stress. I got up. I walked around. I considered my thoughts, my options. However, I didn't now assume such actions would have been appreciated, so I kept driving.

'In Darkridge Hollow they do, Josh. Believe me, they *do*.' Something in Blake's eyes told me he knew more than he was letting on, more than he was willing to share. He was staring out of the window towards trees I'd willingly created monsters from, no longer wanting to acknowledge the cornfields.

'I *need* to find this woman.' Anything at that moment would have given me *something*, a purpose, a reason to exist. Blake's comment was a potential lead I hadn't expected to be given. What if she had my daughter? What if she'd already murdered her? I took a breath that stuck in my throat, threatening to choke me where I sat. The idea turned rancid in my gut, my blood congealing along with thoughts of random witches and devil worshipers metaphorically slicing my daughter's body to pieces. I thought again about Martha, of witchcraft and strange families and why all the crops were dead. I visualised an unassuming flock of birds that had dispersed into the night sky, the actions of the strange entity I'd seen in the dark something I could no longer assume wasn't real.

'All I know is she's supposed to be real *fucking* crazy.' Blake was still watching the passing scenery, unconcerned by how his words were affecting me. It didn't matter. He'd said enough.

17

'I've only lived in Darkridge a couple months,' Blake confirmed, assuming I was interested.

'Is that so?' I wasn't listening, too busy concentrating on the road. My last rental had ended up in a ditch and I didn't need a repeat performance. I wasn't interested in Blake, didn't want to acknowledge he felt sorry for me and was therefore making small talk, unable to broach the awkward topic of my missing child. I didn't want to read the mind of this stranger or see beneath the false façade of attempted pleasantries, offering fake concern we both knew he couldn't sustain for long. I was past caring.

'Yeah. There weren't too many officers posted out here, so a good friend of mine kinda put in a good word.'

I knew all too well how such things panned out. I'd been in a similar position myself, getting continued work because of Anna's contacts and close friends. I didn't need the reminder. I didn't need to remember how beautiful her paintings were, or how she could escape for hours in a flurry of acrylic and brush strokes that came to life on an otherwise empty canvas. We were both artists, yet Anna had a way with people I didn't, a way of bringing things to life I could never achieve. A part of me died when she did. I didn't assume I'd ever get it back.

I looked at Blake, waiting for a revelation that never came, his police uniform more imposing than it had been a moment earlier. My private suffering was on display, set to ensure I remained in perpetual turmoil, this place violently showcasing a life I didn't want to acknowledge was mine.

'You thirsty?' Blake nodded across the street towards a white-washed building that had, over time, turned a sludgy beige. I hadn't noticed it before, the tavern matching the rest of this town, run-down, forgotten, each building reminiscent of the old wild west, blending seamlessly into a collection of rotting wood and broken roof shingles no one was planning on fixing any time soon. I could imagine what the inside looked like, Peter's dusty shop floor and Megan's crumbling farmhouse still vividly in my mind. I could still see that bloody wallpaper if I closed my eyes.

'No, thank you.' I didn't need any more distractions. Not today.

'Oh, come on, Josh. I thought we could shoot the breeze for a while. You get real bang for your buck in there.'

'No.'

Blake sighed. 'You just look like you could use one, that's all.'

I glanced his way. *Jesus.* Did I look *that* stressed?

He must have noticed my blank expression because he laughed, trying to lighten the mood. It was annoying. I didn't want to speculate his thoughts. I had enough of my own to deal with. I glared at him, not daring to stare too long in case I accidentally saw something I didn't want to see, nothing left to do but bring the car to a halt and turn off the engine.

'I didn't think police officers were allowed to drink on duty?' I stated firmly, unclipping my seat beat, glad for the now silenced alarm of Blake's unhooked passenger belt. Who was I to say what was normal and what wasn't? It was none of my business what the guy did, no other person in

Darkridge Hollow seemingly willing to follow protocol, either.

'Who says I'll be the one drinking?'

I didn't need a drink. I needed my daughter. 'Okay, fine,' I replied, probably too sharply, climbing into the afternoon air, nothing more needed to conclude this rapidly declining conversation. It was obvious Blake wasn't going to take no for an answer. I'd overlooked the fact that he was the *only* person in this place willing to speak to me for longer than a few fragmented minutes. I couldn't risk alienating him too, the idea of having a local police officer on my side potentially holding benefits I was yet to value.

We crossed the street towards a tired-looking dining-style bar, a faded sign above the door barely displaying the words "The Cornfield Eatery" painted in blue. It was an apt name, considering what I'd invented from last night's delusions, my imagination still swimming with impossible ideas. That moonlit cornfield had inadvertently become the perfect location for strange entities, witches and ghouls to devour dead rodents and potential young children. It was only fantasy, of course, ridiculous, yet it didn't help my declining state of mind.

Blake opened the door, stepping into a cool interior where a wooden bar dominated the length of a large room. The space was littered with dusty deer heads, their black eyes and gaping mouths hanging alongside the very guns that had ended their lives. The entire place stank of whiskey and sweat, with stains on the floor that matched the ones on the walls, creased leather barstools that matched the bartender's creased, unsmiling features.

The pub was empty aside from the two of us, a television in the far corner showing an American football game, the volume on low. It instantly caught Blake's attention, his stare now aimed towards a crowded stadium filled with the familiar red, white, and black of the Ohio

State Buckeyes team. People were chanting, today's game not yet begun, their mascot, Brutus Buckeye dancing as usual, the entire crowd on its feet. Anna loved her home state football team, loved Brutus more. I'd have given anything to experience that level of normality again. Just once.

Blake removed his Stetson and placed it on the bar before ordering two craft beers I wasn't confident I had the strength to stomach. I wasn't a big drinker at the best of times and I'd been accused of drunken behaviour today already, despite no breath test or blood sample taken to confirm such unsupported claims. We sat for a while, just two strangers with nothing much to say, this place helping me blend into the stark walls—sludgy stains embedded onto my soul that would never wash off.

'Okay, spill,' Blake muttered eventually, initiating a conversation neither of us wanted. He was swigging his beer, his tone too calm for this moment, too calm for me.

I glanced his way, uncertain what he expected me to say, words I didn't wish to express balanced now on my uncertain lips. 'Spill what? *My drink?'* I returned his throwaway comment with my own, releasing yet more sarcasm into the dry air.

'Whatever it is you're *not* saying?' He didn't acknowledge my tone, didn't react.

I defensively narrowed my eyes. I wasn't confident I could tell him *anything*. I didn't know this guy, didn't know his motives.

'I'm fine,' I muttered, nothing else to add.

'I don't buy that,' Blake confirmed.

I scoffed. No. *Neither did I.*

'Your daughter's been missing for what? Two days now? Must be tough.' He took a swig of beer, a light brew, nothing that would see him fall asleep under the table before the day was done, his duties not yet complete, his time required elsewhere.

Two days. *Jesus Christ.* Had it been that long? Where the hell was she?

'I've been constantly frustrated with her recently, you know.' It wasn't something I wanted to admit openly, yet I blurted it out anyway. You can blame Anna's death for that. Or the beer in my hand. 'Since my wife died, I've been allowing too much time to slip by between us.' I closed my eyes, regretting my recent behaviour, wishing we had another chance, another day. I took a breath and held it. 'My kid is out there somewhere and *nobody* gives a shit. Yes, Blake. It's tough.' I was growing increasingly irritated, the bartender's attention momentarily aimed our way.

'Sorry, Josh. Didn't mean to make you mad. I'm real sorry about your wife.'

I shrugged, nothing more to say on that subject. I no longer cared he was a police officer and could have easily thrown me into another jail cell if he wanted.

Blake sighed. 'We'll talk about something else then. How did you meet your wife?'

I sighed, glad of the distraction. 'We met at a train station.' I closed my eyes, remembering that day, her smile, the way several damp ends of auburn hair protruded from the rim of a soggy woollen hat. 'It was pouring with rain and freezing cold, but somehow she was smiling.' Georgina was asleep, wrapped in several layers of clothing, unconcerned by the weather *or* my existence. I didn't wish to tell a total stranger that unfortunate truth. No one needed to know my child wasn't mine. 'She looked so beautiful,' I managed a laugh, thinking back. 'We grabbed a coffee. She put a smile on *my* face. The rest is history.' I took a long swig of beer, not wanting the reminder, her existence in my life too brief.

Blake offered a nod that I took as a sign to change the subject before I did something stupid and burst into tears.

He glanced around, seemingly wanting to ensure we were alone before saying anything further. Aside from the bartender, who was now busy wiping glasses he stacked neatly onto shelves, busy watching the Buck's game on TV, the place was empty.

'I probably shouldn't be telling you this, but I've seen some real strange things since moving out here. I keep my head down as much as I can, of course, but small-town folk don't like it when outsiders snoop around. You know?'

I gave Blake a sideways glance. I did. 'What things?' I was unable to articulate my thoughts by telling him what *I'd* seen. Blake would assume me insane.

He lowered his voice. 'It's no secret that tourists go missing every year. It's a big world out there, nothing new. Yet this place draws them like a magnet. Once they come, they don't leave. Kids go missing around here more than any place out west. Folk can be just passing through, minding their own business, and before you know it, they're gone, nothing, nada.' That wasn't a confirmation I needed to hear.

'What are you saying?' I wondered if he was confirming what I already knew. That Darkridge Hollow hid uncomfortable secrets I was still trying to ignore. 'What kind of *things* have you seen, Blake?' I was struggling to catch my breath, desperate for confirmation that what *I'd* seen wasn't real.

Blake scoffed. 'You wouldn't believe me if I told you, Josh.'

'Try me.'

The guy licked his lips as if he wanted to say more yet stopped abruptly. 'All I'm saying is there's a place you might find more about that crazy woman I was talking of earlier. Nobody seems interested in telling *me* much, but folk can't help but talk. Nothing stays hidden forever, does it?'

Why was he asking me? I knew nothing. 'Where?'

Blake pointed out of the window across the street to where I'd left the car, the thing parked at an awkward angle on the curb.

'The town hall doubles as a library. Every local record is kept there under strict lock and key.' Blake was beyond whispering now. I had no idea why. I could barely hear him over the ball game, the bartender occasionally shouting out in frustration, the television volume turned up.

'Why under lock and key?' I automatically matched his whispered tone, lowering my head towards my unexpected ally.

'Come on, Josh. You seem a smart man. Darkridge Hollow ain't exactly the *friendliest* place in the world, now is it? The locals don't want anyone snooping around, asking questions.' He emphasised the word "friendliest" with another whisper, glancing towards the disinterested barman as if, at any second, he expected the guy to dive over the bar and grab him, ensuring his permanent silence.

I had noticed that unfortunate reality, yes. This holiday was meant to bring something positive back into our darkened lives, help Georgina and I find closure to a broken past we had nowhere else to place, Darkridge Hollow the one place I wrongly assumed we'd find redemption.

'If that's true, how am *I* meant to gain access?' I was a stranger in town, an outsider. If they didn't like outsiders, I was doomed before I began. I was staring out of the window, curious, anxious.

Blake smiled. 'You're looking at him.' He patted himself on the chest with a nod, his badge proudly pinned to his shirt.

As a law enforcer, Blake held an authority I didn't, the locals holding a legal obligation to allow him entry to any location, should he need it. Any potential secret was hidden only as deeply as Blake's police badge deemed necessary. It gave me a glimmer of hope, yet I had no idea what I assumed we would find. I couldn't presume some insane woman's name and address would be listed freely, her file stamped "NUTCASE" so I could identify her easily. Yet, it was more than I had to go on an hour earlier, and so, thanks to Blake, we finished our drinks in relative solace. The liquid felt cool against my throbbing tongue, almost welcoming, the idea of heading into the afternoon towards answers I never expected to find, ensuring I almost downed the thing in one go.

'Why *are* you helping me?' I couldn't help asking.

Blake sighed. 'Because you're not a bad person, Josh. You deserve better.'

'Better than what?'

'Better than this.' He glanced around. 'I've heard rumours that some of the local police are involved in…' He paused, unable to say more, filling the space with the last dregs of his beer.

'Involved in *what?*' What wasn't he telling me? I thought about Deputy Chief McDonald and his disinterested officers, the glances they gave each other when they assumed I hadn't noticed. Maybe it wasn't just the colour of my skin they didn't like?

'It ain't easy to explain.' Blake placed his empty beer glass on the bar. He didn't ask for another.

'Try me.' I sat upright, my drink no longer wanted. The taste had gone.

I had no idea what I was letting myself in for, no idea what Blake was trying to say. It was getting late, the afternoon passing in a blur of frantic desperation, leaving me clinging to the edge of an existence I wasn't accustomed to. Another day was slipping by with little being done to progress my search, more time passing without Georgina's safe return.

'Let's just see what we find, shall we?' Blake stated,

getting to his feet. This conversation was over. Nothing left to conclude.

***

It was warm outside, although the presence of a police vehicle parked along the street gave me a shudder, the face of a disgruntled officer barely visible through the window. I gave Blake a sideways glance, wanting to believe he was helping me and not hindering.

'Who's that? I asked pointedly, my voice low. I couldn't assume Blake wasn't part of the problem I was trying to avoid. 'Is he the reason you turned off your radio?' I have no idea how I would have reacted had he held any sinister intention I was yet to uncover.

'Yeah. I'll explain later.' Blake smiled as if we were having a light conversation before he turned his radio on again to provide his nearby colleague with a swift confirmation that everything was, in his words, *in the bag*. The guy could *split*. He'd *check in later*. He passed off his malfunctioning radio as unimportant, probably a loose connection, nothing more. I don't know which of us was more relieved when that car drove away, although I'm sure I saw a twitch in Blake's jaw as we headed across the street.

The so-called town hall was little more than an oversized box with a crumbling brick-built bell tower set in stark position above a double-fronted entrance. A bronze bell sat silently at its middle, no longer rang often by the looks of it, no life left in this place to denote such a simple undertaking. The inside smelled of dust and books a hundred years in the making, the reluctance of the solitary receptionist to aid our mission as palpable as the misted windows around us.

I was given a dismissive glance I tried to ignore whilst access to the records vault was granted, reluctantly. I was grateful for Blake and his badge. This was police business, he confirmed, nothing that small-framed receptionist could do other than unlock a solid oak door that segregated the vast, open-spaced hall from several storage rooms and unused offices beyond. We disappeared inside, the atmosphere in here almost as unwelcome as the icy glare I could still feel. A stagnant stench hung in the cold air, old paper, crumbling leather, rotting wood.

'Why was that cop hanging around?' I asked once we were alone, unable to hold it together much longer. I didn't expect my voice to echo so loudly, reverberating around the space before being absorbed by dozens of filing cabinets set against the surrounding walls.

'You gotta understand that I *live* here now, Josh. I'm just doing what I need to survive.' He took a breath. 'It kinda sucks being me sometimes, you know?'

No. I had no idea what he meant. 'Why don't you explain it?' I was trying to keep my voice down but the walls had other plans, my voice rebounding around us. Was Blake's kindness another falsehood of Darkridge Hollow? I genuinely hoped not.

Blake shook his head, shaking off my questions. 'Until I find something concrete, I don't exactly understand what's going on.'

I gave him an unwavering stare. 'But something *is* going on?'

'Just start looking.' He began scanning the walls, dragging out metal trays from forgotten shelving, dumping heavy boxes onto a stone floor that sent shockwaves through the air.

'Remind me what we're looking for?' What on earth was I doing here?

'Anything that might explain the *shit* I've seen around here that no one seems willing to acknowledge.' Blake was pulling folders from old boxes that he scattered across the floor, long-forgotten documents and decades-old incidents, each stored away as a reminder, nothing more.

I glanced his way. Had he also witnessed that *thing* in the cornfields? I couldn't ask outright, of course. What if I'd imagined it? How would that make me look? Blake lived here, worked here, knew most of the people in this town—by now probably even called a few of them friends. He'd unexpectedly told me something unsavoury was going on with the local police. If *he'd* been kept in the dark about such troubling events, no wonder my efforts had gone unrewarded. I couldn't understand why he was claiming not to know Megan though and I still wasn't sure I could trust him. She seemed a large enough character to attract unwanted attention. She'd certainly attracted mine.

I took Blake's lead and began a search for her. If nothing else, I needed to prove she was real. I opened a filing cabinet containing the town's rapidly depleting resident records, pulling out all potential first names beginning with M, no surname to go by, unfortunately. Frustratingly I found nothing of interest. There was an old lady called Mary who'd passed away a few months earlier, someone called Melissa, Martha – who I'd already met – and a guy called Michael. *Mike.* I could still feel his steel grip around my arms as Tommy bound the damned things to that bed, could still feel his eyes on me. Yet, there was nothing to confirm who Megan was. I couldn't even find records for the Ellis family, my thoughts left to question everything about Anna's past.

I sat at a desk that hadn't been sat at for some time, sliding through microfiche on an old machine I was surprised still functioned. I scanned several newspaper articles, projecting Darkridge Hollow's sinister history onto a screen in front of me. I flicked haphazardly, not expecting to find anything of interest, simply searching for something – *anything* – about crazy residents, young or old. I by-passed page after page of missing people reports, faces of adults, children and even dogs flashing up on the screen every few seconds. It made me nervous, the idea that Georgina's face might one day join the rest. It didn't take long before I found an article that caught my attention.

Darkridge Hollow, A dark day for a dark death.
By Thomas Jackdoor. March 9th 1997.

It has today been confirmed that the body of a local black girl was found near Blackhill Lake by Police Deputy Joe Everley while out walking his dog late last night. Eleven-year-old Emily Burns was found on the police officer's property, left for dead, on the edge of the lake that runs adjacent to his summer fishing cabin. Although we do not yet have the full details, her death has been deemed suspicious and a full investigation has begun. We do know she was bludgeoned until barely recognizable, found fully clothed in what is already being deemed as the grisliest case this town has ever seen.

When Darkridge Hollow's supposed *upstanding and well-respected deputy was asked if he'd heard anything out of the ordinary last night, Deputy Everley declined to comment, suspicion increasing around him as to why that young girl was on his land in the first place. It isn't the first time Everley has been in the limelight, the autumn of 1993, seeing him under direct investigation for the disappearance of his brother. He was never charged, and the only thing he has confirmed is that he is determined to get to the bottom of this heinous crime, claiming to know nothing of how Emily came to be there.*

This might be one of the worst murder cases Darkridge Hollow has seen and, although the police do not yet know if the attack is racial, judging by her injuries, it has not yet been ruled out as a motive. No sexual indication has been disclosed, although why the girl was out so late by herself is yet to be determined. Her family have been informed, and we ask they be given their privacy at this difficult time.

As this crime unfolds, it is fully expected to reveal prejudice and abuse in and around the town. Everley is hiding something, something he doesn't assume the good people of Darkridge Hollow should know. There's a hotbed of crime and immorality in the heart of this small town and, if it isn't rooted out, it could destroy us all.

There was an image of a lake, its black and white impression leaving me cold, along with a blurred photograph of a young deputy Joe Everley attempting to avoid the press and failing miserably. There were three further articles by the same journalist written some months later, confirming, in detail, that Everley's career had been ruined by the case, the guy subsequently forced into hiding. No one saw him in public again. It didn't explain why, although I got the distinct impression Jackdoor didn't like Everley.

'Blake?'

'Shoot,' he was sitting on the floor, pulling record after record from boxes that hadn't seen the light of day in decades.

'What do you know anything about a girl called Emily Burns?' The fact she was black had caught my attention.

'Never heard of her.' He didn't look up, busy elsewhere.

'Says here the case ruined the career of some local police deputy.'

Blake turned sharply, scrambling to his feet. 'Who?'

I rechecked the articles. 'Joe Everley.'

'Joe?'

'You *know* him?' I saw the shock on Blake's face. Of course, he did. Everyone knew *everyone,* according to

Megan. Apart from her, it seemed.

'Yeah. I know him.' He sounded sad. 'What did you find?'

I pointed to the screen, allowing Blake to read over my shoulder. 'What do you think the journalist meant? What could destroy them all? What hotbed of crime? What was the guy hiding?'

Blake shrugged, silently scanning the article for further information.

The whole thing sounded like scaremongering, pretentious dribble written to put the fear of God into a community who hadn't expected such brutality on their doorstep. Yet, maybe that was the idea. There was nothing to confirm the young girl's murder was ever solved, no later newspaper articles written. I couldn't help wondering what had happened to Thomas Jackdoor and why he'd stopped reporting on the case.

'Do you think Jackdoor might still be around?' It was a long shot but I didn't have much else to go on. I wondered if he was still writing articles, still *alive.* I wondered about the so-called crazy women I still hadn't found a damned thing about. Could *she* have been responsible for that young girl's death? How old would she have been in 1997? It was twenty-seven years ago. It made sense she would have lived here back then.

'I don't know about that, but Joe lives a few miles out of town.'

'He still lives in the area?' I was oddly enthusiastic. Why, I had no idea. Until a few moments ago, I didn't even know the guy existed.

Blake nodded. 'Still has his cabin out by Blackhill Lake.'

'Can you take me to him?' I'd driven past that lake. Thought nothing of it. I hadn't found anything of value and couldn't bring myself to consider that my child might be floating below the surface.

Blake sighed, gathering files he no longer needed, closing cabinets he no longer wanted. 'Joe's a real salt of the earth guy. He might help shed some light on a few things. Being an ex-cop and all.' He paused, pressing a hand inside his shirt pocket and hesitating for a few uncomfortable moments before handing me a business card that had been hastily folded in half.

'What's this?' I asked, taking the thin card from his grasp. It was single ply, the cheap sort, Blake's name and cell phone number printed in small black ink on one side.

'Just in case you need it,' Blake confirmed, something in his eyes I didn't like.

18

Joe Everley's property matched the downtrodden appearance of the rest of this town. I shouldn't have been surprised. Renovation and DIY were not something people here took much notice of. Set along a weather-beaten track, Joe's cabin was another you'd miss if you didn't know it was there, a fishing hut, nothing more. It was hidden behind dense roadside trees, along a forgotten track, next to the very lake I was now unable to look at without thinking of that poor girl. Its surface was glass-like and still, a shimmering pit of black, the surrounding breeze unable to move its impenetrable stare.

Emily Burns had died at the age of eleven, just a year younger than Georgina. Thinking about her untimely death cut a painful gouge into the back of my brain that gave me a headache. I couldn't help visualising the poor thing lying by the side of this very lake, the still waters ready to claim her for its own. Of all the stories Anna had shared with me, this wasn't one of them. It wasn't comforting.

I was nervous as we pulled up outside Joe's property. I'm not sure why. My interactions with the locals had, so far, been sporadic, unwelcome, often downright unforgiving. We'd arrived uninvited and I could already tell this place didn't see many visitors. The old man was standing on his front porch, his face like stone, stiffened arms pulled across his tightened chest. He reminded me of Peter in some ways, yet he was smaller, rounder, with hardly any hair on his head to stave off the penetrating afternoon heat.

'Joe, my man!' Blake called brightly, unconcerned by the dark look spread across Joe's face and already out of the car before I'd brought the thing to a halt.

'Ope! For the love of God, Blake. You had me wonderin' there for a second if they'd finally come to take me away.' The old man tipped his head back and laughed, relief evident. He was still laughing as the two men embraced, a swift hug confirming their acquaintance. Blake patted Joe's shoulder, guiding him towards the car and my uncomfortably hovering body.

'Joe. I'd like you to meet a good friend of mine. Josh, this is Joe. Joe got me posted here after I qualified from the academy a few months back.' The two men were happily catching up, grins spread wide, palms set in continued acceptance along with an apparent friendship they shared with ease. Blake had introduced me as a *good friend*, yet we'd only just met. I smiled anyway.

'It's real good to meetcha, Josh,' Joe leaned forward and held a large hand towards mine that I automatically took, his handshake firm and solid. 'Any friend of Blake's is always welcome here.'

'Actually, we only just met,' I found myself muttering, momentarily taken aback by the brashness of both men. It seemed people here were either wholly hostile or welcomed you with open arms. Who was I to question it?

'You're English?' Joe queried, his smile spread wide, displaying several missing teeth.

I smiled, offering a wave and a nod. *That's me.*

'So what brings y'all the way out here?'

'Actually Joe, we need your help.' Blake stepped in, his smile slipping, the moment brought sharply back to the tragedy that had become my troubled existence. I took a breath, holding it longer than intended, not wishing to rejoin my struggling brain any time soon.

'Josh lost his daughter recently, and-'

'Jeez, I'm real sorry to hear that,' Joe cut in, turning to face me. The old man's stare was warmer than I'd expected, his brow a furrowed collection of stress lines he aimed my way.

'Oh, she's not *dead*,' Blake confirmed, his embarrassment apparent, his eyes telling a truth his lips couldn't. He glanced towards his feet, unable to add "or, at least, we hope".

'Georgina is missing,' I replied sharply, needing this moment to end before I passed out, no more misunderstandings allowed today.

'*Missin'?*' Joe's brow furrowed deeper, his wrinkles becoming more prominent. He looked as if he wanted to say something. Maybe he still lived with the story I'd read in those old newspaper articles, his own memories too vivid, too painful.

I nodded. There was nothing more I could add to that equation.

'You'd better come on in then.' Joe motioned a hand towards his property, ushering the two of us inside, looking as if he didn't want the wind to hear our private discussions. The surrounding woodlands and cornfields were still giving me nightmarish visions I didn't need, Blackhill Lake now adding its demented form to my struggling mindset. 'How long ago did she…' There was a pause before he added, 'disappear?' Joe closed his cabin door, struggling with that last word as if it wasn't a consideration he needed in his head.

'The day before yesterday.' I couldn't believe it had been *that* long. I felt sick thinking about it. 'But the police don't seem to want to help.' I glanced at Blake, perturbed to be confirming this aloud. It was hardly his fault. We were standing in Joe's cabin, a low ticking clock keeping time with my heartbeat, the entire space nothing more than a single room divided into areas by mismatched furniture. A large pine table sat in the middle, ageing kitchen units beyond, a sofa and armchair to one side, a closed door probably housing a bathroom, fishing equipment piled by the door and a flight of open-tread steps leading to a mezzanine landing. Joe's bedroom, no doubt. Nothing more.

'Blake has been helping me,' I confirmed with a smile I didn't feel like offering. Maybe he felt guilty. Maybe he wanted to correct a damaged system he felt deserved my attention, apologise the only way he could for non-compliant officers he still barely knew. I glanced at my newly acquired *friend,* knowing the poor man could do nothing about the behaviour of his colleagues, my irritation prickling again.

Blake waved a dismissive hand in the air before walking across the room to sit at Joe's table, sliding a heavy chair across the floor with a grunt. Joe followed, the two men giving each other an uncomfortable look. I didn't push it. I certainly didn't want to overthink it, my luck already running short as it was.

'Were you just passin' through, Josh?' Joe picked up a copper kettle from the countertop and gave it a good shake.

'No, it was actually meant to be a holiday.' I almost laughed. *Some holiday.*

The old man stopped shaking his empty kettle and stared at me. 'A vacation? Here?'

I knew what he was thinking. Darkridge Hollow was hardly the ideal place for a break. 'Yes, but I crashed the car.' I couldn't dwell on anything else. It seemed so long ago, so *stupid.* 'When I woke up, Georgina was missing.' The events of the last couple of days were slowly catching up with me. It wasn't pleasant. I blinked back painful emotions, my sinuses tingling violently, my eyes burning with tears demanding freedom I wasn't about to provide. As a grown man, *feelings* were never something I feared. Anna often commented on it. It used to make her laugh. Now I was desperate to hold it all in. I couldn't cry like a motherless baby in front of two strangers who knew nothing about me. I took a breath, holding it longer than was comfortable, hardly daring to exhale. It was pathetic. Both men could see I wasn't dealing well with what had happened. 'I'm sorry,' I spluttered, apologising for an outburst that hadn't yet been allowed to occur.

'No need,' Joe motioned forward, placing his now unwanted kettle on an unlit burner before offering me a chair that I took before my legs buckled beneath me. It wouldn't do for me to embarrass myself. I already looked ridiculous.

'Actually, we got a problem that we kinda need some help with.' Blake looked at me, seemingly disturbed now by my appearance.

'How so?'

'We have no real evidence that Josh was with his child when he arrived in Darkridge.' Blake leant his elbows on the table, cupping his hands together as if he was getting ready to pray.

Joe looked puzzled. 'What d'ya mean?'

'It's okay, Blake, I'll explain,' I cut in, knowing how this must have looked. 'My daughter's belongings were missing from the car when I came round. Some local lady helped me but she claimed she never saw Georgina and swore blind my child wasn't even *in* the car.' I automatically pressed a hand over my back pocket, my wallet of no comfort now. 'Everything belonging to her was gone, including her passport. Even the photographs I keep in my wallet have vanished.' I still couldn't fathom the logic of *that.*

Joe's confusion was apparent. He didn't speak.

'I'm sure the poor woman thought I'd hit my head too

hard or something.' I attempted a laugh that sounded weak. *Poor woman?* Who was I kidding? I couldn't be bothered to ask Joe about Megan. I didn't see the point.

'As you can see Joe, this ain't exactly normal,' Blake pitched in. 'Who takes a child *and* everything belonging to them, including evidence they existed in the first place?'

I was beginning to appreciate why everyone was having a hard time believing my story. Wild animals couldn't do such a thing. They weren't *capable.* Kidnappers wouldn't bother with such a crazy undertaking unless they were planning to rob us, which they *hadn't,* the money in my wallet left to question *everything.* As it were, I had no idea what the hell I was dealing with. Blake swallowed. 'That's why we came to you.'

Joe shook his head, his face set in firm concentration that gave nothing away of his thoughts, his jaw almost as tight as mine. 'Because the police can't help?'

Blake nodded.

'More like, *won't.*' I pitched in.

'I'm not sure what I can do. I haven't been a police officer for well over-'

'I know, I know,' Blake got to his feet, his hands outstretched. 'But I could think of no one else to ask.' He licked his lips. 'I took Josh to the town hall. We found that newspaper article. The one about the young black girl.' Blake looked at Joe as if his embarrassment was too much, hardly able to look at me in case he gave the wrong impression. 'Why didn't you tell me she was the reason you quit your job?'

Joe shook his head, offering the man a sigh of his own, his disgruntled breath more scoff than exhale. 'It was a long time ago. Nothin' to tell.' The old man shook his head again before turning to me, changing the subject. 'You got someplace to stay, Josh?'

I nodded. 'Yes. The motel just out of town.' I hadn't

been back there all day. Didn't want to go back. *Ever.* Yet, there was nothing I could do about that for now.

The old man grunted. I could appreciate the reason. The place was hardly the Ritz.

'That journalist who reported on the murder didn't seem to like you much. Seemed to enjoy talking more about your ruined career in subsequent articles.' Blake was still probing, still querying. Joe ignored him. 'We were hoping to find him. I got some questions I'd like to ask.'

'No point.' Joe had his back to us now. I couldn't see his face. His hand was trembling. I didn't know why.

'Why not?'

'Cuz the guy's dead.' It was a final statement. One Joe obviously didn't wish to elaborate on.

'Shit.' Blake swallowed. 'How?'

'Don't matter.'

Blake looked at me, biting the skin from his top lip. 'Jackdoor spoke about a hotbed of crime, prejudice. Any idea what that was about?'

'Nope.'

Neither of us believed him. I wasn't confident that pushing the old man like this was a good idea.

'But you-'

'It's fine if Joe doesn't want to talk about it,' I cut in. I understood that sometimes you just don't want to drag old stuff up. It's too painful.

Blake gave me a blank look, his police training abruptly interrupted. 'Will you help us?' he asked. I was glad he'd said "us". I no longer wanted to do this thing alone.

'I ain't promisin' nothin'.' Joe was firm about that. However, for the first time since my arrival, I no longer felt so alone in my quest. Without Georgina, everything felt wrong. I kept expecting her to ask a question, annoy me, complain about something and pick at her food. As it was, I'd barely eaten, barely slept, my brain dissolving into a slurry of impossibility. I hadn't heard my child's voice for two days. It wasn't comforting.

'Why do you live out here?' I asked, desperate to change the subject myself now. I was staring out of a window towards a distant void, the lake beyond glistening and oddly threatening in this light.

'Cuz it's quiet.'

It was quiet. I could see that, yet so was the rest of the town. I felt there was more to the story. It wasn't my place to push.

Joe sighed, appreciating I needed clarification, obviously not wishing to appear rude. 'It's true my career *was* ruined after what happened to that poor girl. Jackdoor got that spot on. And you're right, Blake, he didn't like me. Thought I was hiding somethin'.'

I glanced his way. 'What happened? If you don't mind me asking?' He probably *did* mind, yet I'd asked anyway.

Joe took a seat next to Blake, lowering his ageing legs onto equally ageing wood that creaked almost as much as he did. 'I was thirty-five, arrogant, at the peak of my career. Keen to please.' Joe was staring into space, something between him and the air around us keeping a secret he didn't feel the need to share with me. 'It was spring, 1997.' Joe confirmed the date as if it had embedded itself onto his mind, nothing about that year able to leave him. 'The town wanted to hush it up, of course. We were a small community, even then, and folk were far less concerned about a black girl's death than of rufflin' feathers.'

'Ruffling feathers?' I didn't want to dwell on the idea that because Emily was *black,* no one cared about her. The thought made me feel sick.

Joe clenched his jaw tight. 'Her family retaliated, as y'can imagine. Caused a lot of shit for the community, plenty of racist bullshit I won't repeat.' He took a breath, unable to look at me. 'They came here in the 1970s, were never really accepted, but kept their heads down anyway.'

'Because they were *black?*' I felt my fists clench, *my* jaw tighten.

Joe nodded. 'Folk accused them of witchcraft, dark shit. None of it was true, of course, but the older generation couldn't appreciate their culture.' He took a sharp breath. I tried not to notice. 'I was terrified if I kept pushin' for answers about that girl's death the truth would destroy the whole town, and I couldn't uncover what'd happened without exposin'-' Joe cut off, sucking in air as if he was about to say something not fit for our ears.

'Exposing what, Joe?' Blake was sitting upright. So was I.

'Nothin'. It don't matter.'

'Joe?' Blake honestly sounded concerned for the old man.

'I said, it don't *matter*.' Joe got to his feet and walked over to the kitchen sink, his breath a collection of short bursts his chest struggled to maintain. He'd said too much. Blake glanced my way. No one spoke. Nothing about this conversation was comforting.

'If I quit lookin' for answers, I risked abandonin' a lifetime of integrity and destroyin' the town I loved as well as the career I'd worked hard to achieve. But if I kept goin', I'd be sacrificin' too much.' Joe was whispering now, something he'd kept hidden for a long time allowed momentary freedom of this isolated space.

'Too much, how?' I asked.

'Trust me, you don't wanna know.'

'I do.' I was in no mood for games. Not today.

Joe didn't answer.

'What happened to Jackdoor?' I wasn't sure if it was me who'd asked, or Blake. We were probably both thinking it.

'The guy was found on a piece of wasteland at the end of that same year.' He paused. 'Someone had cut his throat.'

Christ. I expected to hear he'd passed away from natural causes. Cancer, or a heart attack. Blake looked at me. The silence was deafening.

'Blake mentioned something about a *crazy* woman.' I didn't mean to blurt it out. I glanced at Blake, needing to move this thing along, thoughts of grown men with slit throats something I didn't want in my head. I still knew nothing about her. I assumed Joe *did.* I assumed he could help if he wanted. There was a lot he wasn't saying.

'A crazy woman, hey?' Joe chuckled, mostly to himself, a low rumble reaching the back of his throat as if the thought of such a person was amusing. He turned around, refamiliarising himself with his empty kettle, glancing briefly towards Blake as if to confirm he should know better than to spread rumours. I assumed he had Jackdoor on his mind now, too. 'Coffee?'

We both shook our heads. 'Do you know of such a woman?' I asked, wishing, hoping.

Joe sighed. 'She's nothin' to go worryin' 'bout.'

Jesus, he *did* know her. 'Who is she, Joe?'

'Stupid stories. Nothin' more.'

'But you *know* her?'

'I didn't say that.'

'But what if she took my child?' I couldn't help asking, my temper rising. I was already on my feet. It was a question that had burned a hole in my thoughts since I'd heard about her. Now I couldn't get her out.

Joe looked at me as if it was the first time he'd seen me. 'Now *why* would she do somethin' like that?'

'You tell me?'

'Nothin' to tell.' Joe turned abruptly and stomped off outside, leaving his cabin door open, my company no longer wanted. Blake glanced my way briefly before rising to his feet in response, heading out to relocate his now disgruntled friend.

19

I found myself alone in Joe's cabin, pondering thoughts I had no space in my head for, a familiar scent in the background making me think of home. It was the smell of paint, a sludgy mix of oil and acrylic that amalgamated with a distinct after-tone of white spirits, our London home perpetually filled with an aroma of wet pigment and damp paintbrushes. Dozens of colourful paintings adorned Joe's walls, different sizes, in differing states of completion, some not yet even framed at all. Several canvases were stacked against the skirting boards, beloved yet forgotten, waiting for something I felt Joe would never find.

'Like art?' Joe's large voice filtered from the open cabin doorway, halting any lingering memories I had of my wife, this moment not appropriate. I hadn't realised how long I'd been staring.

'Do you paint?' I asked, curiously tilting my head sideways towards an image of an awkwardly positioned cat on a rug, the simple artwork obviously done by a child, though I couldn't assume it wasn't Joe's inept artistic talent. I kept the thought to myself.

'Nope, but my daughter does. Or at least, she did. I kept every one she ever did. Can't throw 'em away. Too precious.' He laughed, fond parental adoration something I fully appreciated. I recalled Georgina's artwork, some of it still pinned to our fridge, most of it not altogether passable as artwork at all.

'*You* have a daughter?' I asked, wanting to add, "as well" but refraining. Georgina wasn't mine, no matter how much I wanted to change that unfortunate fact.

Joe's smile slipped. 'Two. A long time ago,' he added solemnly, running a hand over a beautiful painting of a lioness, the intricacy of each brush stroke simply stunning. *This* hadn't been created by a child.

'My wife loved to paint,' I confirmed, needing to change the subject and try, at least, to lift the tense atmosphere that had formed. After all, I'd come here uninvited, already causing the old man much-unwanted discomfort. 'She was a freelancer artist. Sold her work to high-end interior design clients and bespoke craft businesses in London.' I ignored the fact I'd referred to her in the past tense. I still had a hard time thinking of her like that. I didn't tell Joe that Anna's work had also won awards, affording her several places in some of London's most prestigious art galleries. By the looks of it, Joe's daughter was pretty good, too. I didn't want to make him sad.

Joe turned around, offering a nod of disinterest as he began clearing forgotten dishes from his table, thickened rims of crusted food still glued to the edges. He stopped and stared into space, folding his arms across his chest, a tea towel now clutched in his hands. He oddly appeared as if he wanted to strangle me with it. It was my unfettered imagination, of course. Nothing more.

His blank expression and cold eyes gave nothing away of his state of mind, yet it confirmed everything I needed to know. He was missing his daughters. I knew how he felt. I didn't dare ask if they were alive or *dead*. It was none of my business. The old man carelessly discarded his tea towel onto the kitchen countertop, leaving those dirty dishes stacked in the sink. It spoke to me more than any words had over the last few days, the most honesty I'd witnessed from *anyone.*

I took a breath, taking in Joe's environment and the place he called home. In a far corner sat an upright piano piled high with photographs created from an entire lifetime, memories he didn't wish to forget, moments he never wanted to lose. Faded black and white converged with muted amber, sun-bleached images set inside dusty glass rims, smiling faces no longer part of a life Joe had cherished once. His family? I thought about mine again, Anna and Georgina both gone from my life now, too. I didn't want to assume *my* child was dead, not yet, but there was no other feasible option. It had been too long.

Leaving Joe to his dishes and private thoughts, I crossed the room and picked up a dusty frame showing two young girls. They were around the same age, enjoying a summer long passed. It looked familiar. I don't know why. Photographs tend to do that to me these days, triggering something in my own past that doesn't exist. I wished I'd known that Anna's family had already moved away, preferably before I ruined it all by bringing my child to this place and losing *her* in the process. I wondered where Joe's family were now and what had happened to *them.*

'Found somethin' you like?' Joe's voice boomed out from behind me then, almost causing me to drop the delicate frame onto the floor. It would have done me no favours. I was on thin enough ground as it was.

'Sorry. No, I was just-' What exactly *was* I doing? Reminiscing? Wishing for the impossible ability to go back in time?

'It's okay,' Joe muttered solemnly. 'Those are my twins.' He walked up behind me, taking the frame from my grasp, his tone as melancholy as my own. I glanced towards his trembling hand. They weren't identical. Not even close. Joe sighed, sucking in a lungful of air he struggled to release before pressing an index finger over the glass, smudging a thick layer of dust across its surface, momentarily blurring the precious image beyond.

'I'm sorry,' I muttered. I had no idea what I was sorry for, but it fitted the moment. I assumed they were dead. Everything else in this town was.

'Don't be,' Joe concluded. 'It's hardly your fault.' He glanced up at me, an unexpected tear perched in his eye. He sniffed, blinking it away.

'*She* looks familiar,' I said, pointing to a smiling redhead. It was true. It was a stupid thing to say, a stupid thing to think. Anna was on my mind, as always, every woman reminding me of her, every day another painful memento of what I'd lost.

Joe laughed, his affection strong, his eyes still glistening.

'What happened to them?' I really shouldn't have asked such a private question. It was none of my business.

'Oh, it's a sad story, Josh, and not one I wanna share right now if you don't mind.' He placed the frame back onto the piano, repositioning it in the same layer of dust it came from before turning it sharply to face the wall as if the image had burned his hand. He offered a fake smile before walking outside towards the dimming evening light. I wasn't about to push it. It was absolutely none of my business.

***

Neither man had adequately provided details that could have placated my emotions and I was forced to leave Joe's cabin with more questions added to the ones already racing around my head. Despite the promise of an investigation, a handshake, and much-needed validation of support, I couldn't shake the uncomfortable realisation I was still no further forward. Blake would do some digging, he claimed, Joe an ally they both felt I deserved. As pleasant as both men had been, I drove back to the motel with little more in my mind than maggots I couldn't dislodge, vomit that teetered constantly in the back of my throat, and metaphoric ants that crawled freely amongst my unsettled arms and legs.

Blake seemed a decent enough guy, thankfully—Joe, too. Two people who genuinely *wanted* to help. They were also trained police officers. It might be enough for this thing to take a new turn, finally setting cogs in motion to find a missing child most seemed hell-bent on discarding. I was unashamedly ready to give her up for dead, nothing more than a lost cause I could never change. Plenty of people go missing. I haven't been living under a rock. Yet, I didn't want those statistics in my head. Not yet. I wasn't ready.

It was dark again now, another day slipping by without much attention afforded to it, more time added to my incredulous existence. I crept along the black roads, reaching that "road closed" sign before realising my error, my haste ensuring I'd forgotten *everything* other than Georgina. I parked the car to the side of the road, my vision blurring from tears that sprang from nowhere. I could barely bring myself to look beyond the misted car windows, the last couple of days taking me to a place I never imagined existed.

I should have turned around and located a different route, but instead I opened the door and vomited into the road. I was weak, exhausted, in no position to drive *anywhere*. I tipped my head skywards, feeling hot, slightly faint. When a movement behind the trees caught my attention, I assumed it was nothing important, just an animal or the breeze. Plenty of dog walkers must use this space, young couples seeking solace and sedation that only comes from each other's open arms and willing embrace.

Yet, the very cornfield I'd previously imagined a naked *thing* dancing in the moonlight was now inadvertently in my limited line of vision, my failing memory and unstable stomach contents wholly to blame. It was a coincidence, nothing more.

I ventured away from the car, curious, this place unwittingly inventing ideas that didn't exist, my mind once again creating havoc from nothing. I knew almost nothing of the locals, those residents perpetually cold and isolated, often downright strange in their mannerisms and attitude. The ground was still damp, my head still hazy, yet I was surprised by how many footprints were dotted around me. I'm confident they hadn't been there the night before. I would have noticed. I followed a trail that led downhill behind several trees into the cornfields beyond. I was snooping. I couldn't help it, consistent nausea to blame, my heightened emotions permanently alert. I kept low against the tree line, instinctive, secretive. The last thing I needed was to be caught by an unhinged local, this road probably *closed* for a reason.

I wasn't, of course, expecting to emerge from the trees to the sight of a small group of people gathered around a bonfire. They were chanting, Latin I think, something obscure. Whatever it was, it gave me a chill that had nothing to do with the night air or my weakened body. I moved closer, tired of hallucinations, exhausted by the impossible and innocently only wanting to see what was happening.

When I spotted two people, naked and suspended upside down by their ankles from ropes draped around nearby trees, I almost laughed aloud. The campfire illuminated their position, several people scattering what appeared to be corn seeds at their feet. They too were naked, I think, covered in blood, or paint, their skin glistening red in the evening glow. I almost screamed, glad I didn't, instead cupped a sweaty hand across my mouth, the taste of bile still lingering.

I couldn't look away. Of all the stupid, satiric visions my mind had invented, this was the most ridiculous. I assumed I'd fallen asleep, recent vomit and lack of clarity the reason for my apparent exhaustion. I've heard how the human mind sees only what it wants when stressed, believing wholeheartedly everything happening in dreams as if it was real, the brain fully capable of inducing heart failure and death in extreme circumstances. I knew I was dreaming, of course, and I wanted to wake up, but I was unable to coax myself into consciousness. Instead, I kept out of sight, along for a strange ride, bizarre logic ensuring I remained crouched behind a discarded farm trailer, just in case. It wasn't real, so it didn't matter, my apparent dream nothing but fantasy I'd laugh about later.

It was odd. This entire thing smacked of some kind of ritual, my mind once again inventing *shit* for the hell of it. I was unable to prevent it, unable to wake up, yet despite knowing it was all in my head, the rustling trees kept pace with my heartbeat, forcing a stampede of protesting blood that pulsated through my body. In my dream, I recognised the couple hanging by their twisted ankles as Mac and Morag, their Scottish accent adding to the ridiculous pandering of my brain, lies easily forged from what my closed eyes envisioned. Although I'd met them only once, my mind obviously hadn't forgotten them, their Glaswegian accent strong, the newlywed couple from the petrol station now firmly in my mind. It wasn't ideal, I know, stupid even, my brain finding it all too easy to create carnage from the chaos of the last few days. I'd been unable to think straight and now my sanity had finally dissolved along with Georgina's belongings. *Well done, Josh.* Just what I needed.

Morag was crying, her upturned body lunging wildly towards the encroaching darkness, her terrifying world upended. She was at the mercy of strangers, the unforgettable bulk of her husband unable to help as he screamed in desperate protest beside her. None of it was real, but I took a sharp breath anyway, shocked at the level of realism I was able to bring forth, strong body odour and fresh blood mingling with rotting vegetation at my feet.

The chanting continued, low at first, becoming louder as several naked forms surrounded the couple—odd, demonic words allowed uncensored freedom of this dying cornfield. When a female stepped forward, a large kitchen knife in her hand, I assumed I was imagining *her* face too, randomized features of strangers allowed full access to my torrid imagination. I didn't want to think of that Scottish couple being subjected to an unfounded attack, my mind wholly unhinged, the concept of their forthcoming murder *ludicrous.* Yet my eyes were choosing to incorrectly witness Megan's distorted features looming from the moonlight now as well. *Jesus Christ.* As much as the woman had unnerved me, I could never – in my waking moments, at least – assume her capable of *this*.

Megan – or at least the version my brain had invented – raised blood-streaked hands above her head, the chanting increasing, excitement gathering. Without hesitation she plunged the knife into young Morag's belly, slicing it wide, allowing her entrails to tumble to the dust-ridden ground below. Mac screamed. I think I might have done too. I could do nothing but watch in horror as that poor woman convulsed and died thirty feet from my unwitting eyes. I hate horror films, always have, despised Anna's taunting more. How the *hell* I'd created this, I had no idea, but my wife would have been impressed.

I vomited again. It wasn't pleasant, this moment surreal. My dreams aren't usually so vivid, so intense, and I don't have *psychical* sensory perception. Most of my dreams barely have colour, barely any logic. I *always* know I'm dreaming. Yet, the heat of the fire encroached over my skin, the dampness of the ground cool against the thin soles of my boots, too intense, too real.

Still unable to wake up, I was forced to watch helplessly as Morag dangled on the end of a thrashing rope, warm blood spitting violently onto the ground below. The group then unhooked her body, holding it above their heads, still chanting, still dancing, her corpse nothing more than a sacrificial goat they tossed into a now raging fire. I caught a strong whiff of burning skin, like pork crackling—succulent flesh left to cook in the wild evening air. *I might never eat meat again.* Once satisfied, they turned their attention to Mac, that same blood-soaked knife plunged for a second time into *his* body. The poor man screamed again, his dying breath forcing me to pinch myself hard. I punched my legs, desperate to wake up, everything about this moment too much.

With no choice other than to clamber to my failing feet, I raced from the scene back to my awaiting car, away from Mac and Morag towards much-needed reality. I needed something to jolt me out of this lunacy, my painful real-world oddly better than *here.* I turned sharply, my mind a thickened slurry of shit, the darkness closing in. I didn't anticipate running straight into the outstretched fist of Tommy's right hand, barely catching the words, "you should've stayed away" before everything went black, nothing of this day ending how I'd imagined.

***

When I woke up, the first thing I noticed was the silence. I was on my back, glad my ordeal was over, grateful for the cool air of the lingering evening. I took a breath, glad to be awake, no dream I'd experienced *ever* this vivid. I couldn't recall falling asleep, this day taking a rather unfortunate toll. My heart was pumping and a nasty taste of iron sat on my tongue from fresh blood coating my lips. I had bitten my tongue during my nightmare, it seemed, my waking reality now ready to pick up where my dream had left off. My head was throbbing, too. I tried to sit upright, assuming I was back in the car, yet I couldn't confirm I hadn't been sleepwalking, inadvertently hitting my head on a low-lying branch. I wasn't anticipating a cold stone floor beneath me, solid brick walls looming on all sides.

I had no idea where I was, but it wasn't anywhere good, a basement, by the looks of it, although I couldn't fathom how I'd got there, my body a convulsing wreck I couldn't sedate. I patted myself down, ensuring I still had all my limbs, my insides intact. I couldn't vouch for my mind. I had no idea what was happening, alone in a darkened room, once again pathetically attempting to relocate my bearings. I couldn't get those images of Mac and Morag out of my head.

Moonlight flooded the space thanks to a narrow window overhead, my mind triggering yet more drama it didn't need. I could no longer assume tonight's vision wasn't real, my dream not a dream at all, in the end. I couldn't presume that I hadn't, in fact, witnessed that Scottish couple's brutal murder, Megan on the end of an unfeeling knife, Tommy a major part of it all. It wasn't something I'd anticipated, Tommy's fist suddenly feeling *very* real. Why the hell were they keeping me alive? If I'd witnessed them kill someone, surely that now sealed my own deranged fate?

A sliver of soft light emanated from an open doorway some feet away. I took a moment, confused, concerned. Why was the door open? *What the hell was going on?* Someone was either playing a seriously messed up game or I'd finally lost the plot. At that stage, it hardly mattered which. I crept on tiptoes towards the door, my only aim to get out of there while I had breath in my body, preferably before I provoked more chaos and ended up dead. I tugged the handle, not expecting it to swing open so easily, my trembling fingertips nothing more than an extension of a wayward mind that no longer expected reality. I didn't want to know who or *what* was on the other side.

I tilted my head around the doorframe cautiously, the space beyond housing a narrow staircase that led towards a panel of light above. Someone had left a sandwich on the bottom step, along with a bottle of half-consumed fizzy pop, a penknife and a key. It was odd. I couldn't assume I wasn't hallucinating, my injured head and prevailing panic to blame. After all, I hadn't eaten for hours, my lips bloodied and sore, my mind already tainted with ideas it didn't need. I grabbed the knife and key, leaving the food where it was. I couldn't assume it wasn't poisoned and I had no time to consider any other option.

Was this a game or was someone *helping* me, and if it was the latter, then *who?* Aside from Tommy, whose fist I was becoming uncomfortably familiar with, and Megan, who surely *couldn't* have done what I saw her do, no one knew I was here. Nobody was aware of the vomit I'd left next to a car now unattended by yet another roadside, the vehicle the only thing ensuring my sanity. I swallowed hard, momentarily wondering about Joe and Blake, contemplating if they were involved in this, or innocent in events I never saw coming.

I crept upwards, my back against the wall, glad there were no uneven floorboards here to give away my unwitting position. I didn't know where I was, the idea of causing irreparable harm to someone else, not a consideration I wanted. Unsurprisingly the door at the top of the stairs was locked, the very key in my possession potentially able to aid my escape. I couldn't overthink why. I pressed the metal into the lock, not anticipating much, not assuming the door would unlock. Yet, unlock it did, easier than expected, the key turning without incident, my permanently held breath threatening to suffocate me where I stood.

I took a shallow breath before unhooking the handle, emerging into a brightly lit kitchen, a familiar scent of *lavender and honey* and a dirty orange and cream décor I *never* anticipated seeing again. Megan's kitchen. *Jesus.* I glanced around, taking in my surroundings. The very chair I'd sat and drank coffee on only days earlier was still in the position I'd left it, my jacket still where I'd draped it.

I glanced behind me, Megan's basement demonically laughing at my back, mocking the terrible sight I'd witnessed tonight. I didn't want to believe it. It had to have been a dream. Nothing else made sense. Megan was many things but I couldn't assume her a cold-blooded killer, no matter how infuriating she was. Yet, all I could see now was her blood-soaked skin glistening in the darkness, that bloody knife.

I tiptoed across the kitchen, wanting to retrieve my jacket and get away from this property once and for all, my second escape from this location not lost on me. The back door was thankfully unlocked, although I could no longer tell what was luck and what wasn't, the illuminated glow of the kitchen silhouetting my fleeing body as I sprinted into the night.

20

It took a moment for my eyes to adjust, the darkness imposing, choking my thoughts as shadows encroached on me from every angle. I fully expected to run into Tommy, or *Mike,* both men capable of far more than I'd initially imagined, Megan potentially an unwitting adversary to it all. My unsteady feet pointed me towards the road, my eyes set in firm concentration as I rounded the side of the property.

I didn't intend what happened next. I was in a hurry, trying to get away. Yet I ran straight into a piece of spiked wood propped against the house and almost impaled my foot on a rusted nail. Thankfully my misplaced boot missed its unintended target, my outstretched hands taking most of the impact. Dozens of large nails were driven into the wood, each one protruding in incremental positions along every side, rusted, dangerous. My jacket had innocently protected my palms, though only just, several tears along a sleeve ensuring it too now needed a dustbin. *Great.* The offending item was around four inches in diameter and eight to ten feet long, maybe longer, discarded recently by the looks of it, left amidst overgrowth unable to disguise its shame. *What the hell was it?*

I moved closer, needing a better inspection. It was crudely made and used many times judging by the gnarled protrusions and damaged sections, yet it wasn't until I noticed several pieces of shredded rubber attached to the out-turned nails that I realised its intended purpose. My brain took a painful moment to absorb what I was seeing, slowly appreciating my blown tyres were no accident. I wouldn't have seen this lying in the road, the fog too dense, that fateful day a perfect opportunity to provoke an *accident.*

I didn't want to overthink my discovery and I didn't want to know *why* such a monstrosity existed. I certainly didn't want to think too long about Mac, Morag, *or* Megan, this night damaging my mind in ways it would never recover. I tossed my jacket into one of Megan's dustbins before sprinting across her gravelled driveway, nothing left to do but run. I was tired of these games, continued nausea something I was now profoundly used to. I couldn't get those images of Mac and Morag out of my mind. That *poor* couple, the two of them joined in the afterlife instead of wedded bliss. I wished I'd helped, *could* have at least tried, but I thought I was *dreaming*, for Christ's sake, nothing for me to do. My brain was overthinking, over-elaborating, everything that had happened coming down to some irrational logic I held in my twisted belief that I should have at least *tried* to prevent the outcome.

For the second time in as many days, I found myself racing away from Megan's property. I couldn't understand what I'd witnessed, the woman allowed to roam this area unattended, no one in this town willing to acknowledge her existence. Maybe they knew who she was, *what* she was and what she was capable of, their silence maintained purely from misplaced loyalty I was yet to understand. The whole thing was beyond ridiculous. Surely the police knew about her? *She was a killer.* It was an impossible consideration, a stupid conclusion, yet I knew now I hadn't imagined *that.* I considered going to the police and explaining what I'd witnessed. Would they arrest her? No. With my luck, they'd probably arrest *me.*

The thought of being disbelieved matched the unwanted idea that Megan was capable of doing something like that to *Georgina.* The concept sat disproportionately uncomfortable in my gut as I crept through the trees, losing my bearings several times and fully expecting to be found dead before this night was done. It was a relief when I reached Joe's property, drumming trembling fists against his front door, no concept of the time, nothing on my mind other than to find the help the police would never provide.

'For the love of God, Josh. Whatcha doin' out here by yourself at this hour?' Joe appeared barefoot on his porch, his ruffled bathrobe matching the dishevelled look of his disbelieving face, exhausted eyes I knew all too well. If the guy had hair, it would have shared the same exasperated look as his cheeks, his slumber interrupted abruptly, annoyingly—by me.

'You have to help me, *please!*' I was out of breath, out of my mind, at odds with everything that had become my recent existence.

'What the *hell* happened? You look like shit.'

I honestly didn't know where to begin, Joe's place the one location I assumed might, by some impossible miracle, save my rapidly failing mind from its increasingly disturbed devices. I was no longer concerned by wildlife. I'd happily take my chances with *them* over everything else.

'I think I witnessed something tonight, Joe. Something that can't have happened.' I closed my eyes, half expecting Megan to appear from the darkness wielding the very knife I now couldn't get out of my head, gut me where I stood, poor Joe an unexpected witness to her actions. I could still see the horrified look on Mac's face.

Joe stepped aside, ushering me into his cabin, no further words required. The only light in the space was a small lamp in a corner that illuminated several cobweb-ridden beams in the ceiling, throwing demonic shadows overhead.

'You'd better start from the beginnin' then,' the old man muttered, busying himself with the kettle on his stove, lighting a gas burner, his back to me. There was nothing in his tone that displayed shock at my sudden appearance aside from the inconvenience of having been woken up, my words hitting nothing but his cold, hardened features. 'What *exactly* d'ya think you witnessed?'

I sat down, my legs no longer able to hold me in place, willing myself with every breath I could muster to explain what I'd seen. Where on earth would I begin? The field? Mac and Morag? Tommy? Megan? Or finding myself in a basement? It was the second time I'd been held against my will in that hellish place and I still didn't know why. This week had turned into a goddamned nightmare.

'I think I saw someone being murdered.' *Two people, actually.* I couldn't believe I was saying such things aloud. I closed my eyes, images of blades and blood something I'd be stuck with forever.

Joe turned, glaring at me, his eyes blank and unseeing.

'I know it sounds stupid,' I continued, not needing more disbelief aimed my way. 'I don't *want* to believe it.' I was still trying to convince myself I'd dreamt it all. The old man was staring at me as if I'd lost my mind. I could still feel the impact of Tommy's fist, the look in Megan's eyes. Why the hell didn't he *kill* me when he had the chance and save himself from further trouble? Why risk my escape? *Again?*

'Who d'ya think you saw bein' murdered, Josh?' Joe asked. He was far too calm. I didn't like it. It was almost as if he wasn't surprised, *murder* merely a word he used daily.

'A couple of backpackers, I think, in a cornfield on the outskirts of town. Behind that old, closed road.' Even as I spoke, my words sounded impossible. Murdered backpackers in a cornfield? *Who would ever take that seriously?* 'I wish I'd never come to this god-awful place,' I muttered, my face already in my hands. It was true. I didn't mean to dislodge Joe's fondness for a town he called home.

Joe sighed, pulling his robe around his frame as if to stave off my unwanted words. It wasn't cold out. 'Then why *did* you come?' He was standing by his kitchen table, the thing crammed with all kinds, sketchpads, coffee mugs, a half-eaten meal. He'd hardly acknowledged my words, a declaration of murder something he oddly deemed unimportant. I didn't want to know why.

'Did you not hear what I said, Joe?' I questioned nervously, wondering if I'd done the right thing by coming here. Maybe I should have called Blake? I still had his number in my pocket. Would that have helped?

'Oh, I heard you,' Joe replied flatly. 'But I'm more interested in why *you* came to Darkridge Hollow. This place ain't for the likes of you.'

'The likes of me?'

'Yeah, Josh. You look normal to me. *Sane.*'

I narrowed my eyes, swallowing a lump that wouldn't get past my throat. Joe knew something. I almost didn't want to know what. I automatically glanced around, half-expecting to require the penknife now tucked in my pocket, anticipating having to defend myself against another unfounded attack.

'Why d'ya come here?' the old man repeated. He was pacing, thinking, something in his mind I was glad I couldn't see.

'To find *family.*' I blurted out, almost laughing at the concept, the very idea ridiculous. 'Well, to find my *daughter's* family, more to the point.' It had slipped way down my list of priorities. I wasn't sure why Joe cared.

'Your *daughter's* family?' Joe stopped pacing and glared at me.

With everything that had happened since our arrival, I

had given very little time to ponder the reason we had come to this place. Beyond an earlier conversation with Megan that now seemed so long ago, it was irrelevant. She'd confirmed all I needed to know, my visit ending in ultimate disaster. The Ellis family were *gone*. As was Georgina.

'Georgie's mother was born here.' I confirmed solemnly. I didn't want Anna on my mind right then and wasn't grateful to Joe for putting her there.

He was boiling his kettle again, the darkness of the evening keeping a much-needed distance. This was not the conversation I expected to be having, Anna's family *not* important, nothing of the last couple of days viable. I didn't assume I'd ever be able to track them anyway and to be honest, I was no longer sure I wanted to. I glanced towards the old man, realising he might have known them, might remember if I asked. He may even recall where they'd gone.

'There was only ever one black family in Darkridge Hollow, Josh, and their little girl died, as you well know.' Joe was looking at me as if he didn't believe a word I was saying.

'I married a white girl,' I confirmed. 'Georgina isn't my biological child.' I despised having to confirm *that*.

'I see.'

I'm not sure he did.

'And where's the child's mother now?' It was the first time anyone had asked. I took a moment, staring at Joe's back. Why wasn't he interested in discussing the *murder* I'd witnessed? I was still shaking.

'Dead.' It was the first time I'd said the word aloud. I don't think I'd even yet admitted it to myself. It was too painful, too final.

'I'm sorry, Josh.' Joe was in the middle of setting two mugs on the tabletop, the objects hovering in his hands. I wished I knew what he was thinking.

I shook my head, my wife on my mind now, nothing I

could do about her missing child or my missing sanity. I thumped my fists against my thighs, feeling nothing. Joe sighed, still looking at me, no doubt wondering what to do with the mugs dangling in his grip and the strange oddity in his home.

'How'd she die?' he asked. It was an innocent question.

'Why do you want to know, Joe?' I was on my feet, ready to run. I didn't like his tone.

'Indulge an old man, will ya?'

'A drunk driver,' I confirmed, not wanting to remember, merely going along with Joe's lunacy. 'I was at home, cooking dinner, just a normal day. Georgina was busy with her homework, driving me insane as usual.' I tried to smile but failed, my turbulent relationship with my daughter something I felt embarrassed by. 'The guy mounted the pavement, according to the police, pinning her to a bus shelter. She died immediately. Never saw it coming. None of us did.' I sucked in a mouthful of painful air, hoping Joe wouldn't see the raw agony I'd been forced to live with every day since. 'Jesus Christ,' I scoffed loudly, more to myself than him. 'Anna would be so *pissed off* with me if she could see what I've done.' I couldn't help confirming it, couldn't help but swear. Everything was too much. Even this cabin was closing in on me. I hadn't yet accepted Anna's death and could barely process the idea of losing Georgina. Now I had Mac and Morag's deaths on my conscience, too.

'Anna?'

'My wife.'

'Your wife's name was *Anna?*'

I nodded, glancing skyward, nothing of Joe's query hitting its mark. The old man was still hovering with those mugs in his hands, yet he was staring at me now as if he didn't know how to respond. I couldn't read his features. I assumed he must have remembered the family and didn't expect to be told that the little girl he might have known well was *dead.*

'Were you together long?' He asked. For a moment, something sour lingered in the air, something bitter.

'Why?' *What did it matter?*

'Tell me.'

'Why?' My turn now for the questions.

'Just tell me!' I'm sure Joe was holding his breath.

'Ten years. I asked *why?*' I was almost yelling at him.

'Because, Josh, my daughter's name is Anna, and she was born here, too.' Joe laughed, yet his laugh wasn't convincing and we glared at each other, neither of us ready to acknowledge what we were thinking. Joe blankly turned a mug around in his failing grip. It had a name printed on it. ANNA.

'But your surname's Everley,' I stated, merely hoping we had our wires crossed. I was trying not to look at the mug in his hand. 'Anna's maiden name was *Ellis.*' It was printed on our marriage certificate. The thing was still in a drawer somewhere, an unwilling momentum of my pathetic life.

Joe released a breath, carbon dioxide leaving his lungs too quickly. He'd gone pale. 'Ellis?' he muttered. I could tell he was clinging to hope that, somehow, I'd created a false reality.

I nodded. 'Yes. Anna Victoria Ellis,' I stated innocently, confirming my wife's full name.

Joe sucked in a lungful of air, closing his eyes, nothing in his mannerisms able to calm my rapidly failing composure.

'Joe?'

'That was my mom's name.' Joe had pronounced the word as *mahm*, exactly how Anna used to.

Unforgiving tears sprang from the old man's eyes as he took a further breath I felt might take the air out of the entire room. He manoeuvred his ageing legs around the table, dropping both mugs to the floor with a crash, his body no longer a willing assistant. I hovered on my own, the thump I'd earlier inflicted creating a dull ache I tried to ignore, the one Tommy had given me, far worse. Joe didn't offer any further words as he climbed his staircase, clinging to the banister as if it was the only thing keeping him alive.

'*Joe?*' I repeated, terrified of the silence, wanting to know what was on the old man's mind, frustrated I'd placed unwanted thoughts in his head, already having interrupted his sleep.

As it were, I was forced to stand in his cabin for several uncomfortable minutes, wondering if I should check on him or leave. Yet, the idea of heading into the darkness again wasn't something I wanted to consider, so instead I hovered like a wasp next to the old man's faded armchair. When he reappeared something was clutched in his outstretched hand. He began descending the steps, his frame hunched over, things on his mind no doubt matching my own.

'We named Anna after my mother,' he confirmed, handing me the item he was holding. 'Before we discovered she was a twin and subsequently had to come up with *two* names.' I could tell he wanted to laugh, glad he didn't.

I motioned forward and took it from him. A photograph.

'D'ya know this woman?' he asked, his voice a broken collection of strained syllables I could barely absorb. I glanced down, dreading what I was about to see and willing this simple piece of paper to confirm the image of a stranger I could discard easily. I wanted to put Joe's mind at ease if nothing else. I couldn't consider my own. Tears lingered in his eyes. I couldn't help the ones that fell to my cheeks in grotesque acknowledgement of the image smiling back.

'*Please,* tell me you don't recognise her, Josh?' Joe discarded his thoughts with a wave of an outstretched hand.

I could barely bring myself to look down. The photograph must have been taken a short time before Anna moved to England judging by the familiar face that met my desperate gaze, her long auburn hair set in the style I loved, her bright green eyes penetrating my soul. I wasn't sure what hurt the most—the fact I was looking at my wife's face again, or the idea tht I was about to devastate her unwitting father. I glanced towards the poor man, my father-in-law, standing in front of me, waiting, a jumbled collection of nerves and no doubt terrified of what I was about to tell him. His daughter was dead and the granddaughter he hadn't seen for over a decade was missing. How the hell could I confirm *that?* I pressed my lips together, trying and failing to prevent the tears that fell, unforgiving, unrelenting. I couldn't speak, even if I wanted to.

'No. No. For the love of God, no!' Joe breathed, sucking enough oxygen from the room to kill us both, the truth too painful to accept.

I wanted to comfort him and tell him everything was going to be okay, yet *nothing* about this was okay. Nothing rational had happened since I arrived in this awful place, this moment just another in a long list of crap I'd been forced to endure. I thought about Megan again and the lies that spilt readily from her twisted mouth. I shouldn't have been surprised. She was a nutcase, a lunatic who killed tourists for fun. It was a ridiculous idea that danced in my head.

'I'm so sorry, Joe,' I found myself offering instead. It was all I could do. I'd had six months to process this. Joe hadn't yet had six minutes. I wished I'd handled this better, done things differently. I wished I'd *known* who he was beforehand. This was not the way I'd expected to do this.

I couldn't read my father-in-law's emotions, yet his legs faltered anyway, something in his mannerisms crumbling. He was hunched forward, struggling to stay upright, a few insufferable minutes passing before the old man stiffened, taking the photograph from my grip. He crumpled it tightly as if he didn't want to acknowledge the words I hadn't yet uttered. I wondered how much of this was sinking in, how much he was able to process. Until twenty minutes ago, the poor sod was in bed, asleep, his daughter alive and well in the world somewhere—this kind of shock not something anyone could take lying down, so to speak. Why didn't Anna tell me she had a *twin* sister? I momentarily wondered if she was dead, too.

I needed to refamiliarise myself with Joe's armchair before I ended up on the floor. I bypassed the idea Anna had given me a false surname, the reasons she'd fled this place far more worrying than I'd initially considered. I thought about Georgina's biological father, wondering how dangerous the guy must have been for my wife to flee with their young child in her protective arms, her surname something she needed to throw off, throwing away potential secrets of her unwanted life.

Why had Anna changed her name, and why hadn't she told me? Had she been married before? I briefly wondered if *our* marriage was legal, the idea she'd used a false name throwing our entire wedding into question—the last ten years potentially *fake.* How many more lies could I stomach? I looked at Joe, wishing I could read his mind. Should I hug him? I wasn't sure which of us needed it the most. As it was, all I could do was watch and wait, hoping he'd shed light on the painful subject of my dead wife, my missing child something that, by now, he must be desperately pondering over.

'Did she suffer?' Joe asked. He was leaning against the banister, his back to me, nothing else for him to do.

'Apparently not. It happened too fast, they said.' There was nothing else for me to confirm. It wasn't a comfort.

Joe nodded, his understanding not yet accepted, not

appreciated. When he turned around sharply, his brow was furrowed, eyes wide, something jumping vividly into his mind I was yet to acknowledge.

'Megan!' he whispered sharply, his features distorting as he glared across the room, a tiny light bulb going off in his head.

'What about her?' *What was I missing now?* It was the first time another person had acknowledged the woman. I wasn't expecting it.

'Come with me,' he commanded, a strong voice emerging from nowhere.

'Where are we going?'

'There's somethin' you need to know.'

'What?' The word caught against my tongue. *What the hell was happening?*

Joe grabbed his keys and his trousers, heading out to his truck, the darkness threatening to drown us both in a lake that, in this light, was no match for my emotions. I had no idea where he was going or what he was talking about. Despite my relentless questions, Joe was unwilling to speak, the poor man unable to confirm our shared suffering with words that wouldn't have meant a damned thing anyway.

I wasn't anticipating he would drive directly to Megan's property. If I had, I might not have been so willing to go with him. I'd literally just left the place—in a hurry. *Again.* Surely Joe wasn't a part of this, too? I glared at him, unsure what was happening, forced to watch as Joe's old truck came to a shaky halt along the street. He was gripping the steering wheel, the engine still running, his vehicle a collection of jolting springs and mechanics that had seen better days. For a moment I wondered about his motives, his emotions. Yet he still didn't say a word. Probably couldn't. Instead, he turned off the engine and climbed into the night, reluctantly forcing me to do the same, purely out of painful curiosity, nothing more. I had no idea what was happening, merely hoping he'd left the keys in the ignition, convinced I'd need yet another swift escape before this night was done.

We walked together along the road's edge, towards the very driveway I was genuinely sick of seeing, my mind unwilling to acknowledge logic as I headed back to a location hell-bent on destroying every brain cell I possessed. I tried not to notice that Joe was now holding a loaded shotgun.

'Why are we here, Joe?' I questioned, nothing forthcoming as to his motives, nothing telling me I wasn't about to make yet another *stupid* mistake. My voice had developed a wobble. I was in my very own horror film, the pathetic actor who kept returning to the scene of the crime, the haunted house the very place he should have been running from, screaming for his life.

'Melissa?' Joe yelled, still walking, his pace increasing. We were already outside Megan's property. He tightened his fists around the barrel of his gun. *'Melissa?'*

Who the hell was Melissa?

No answer.

'What's going on?' I asked, increasingly nervous now. I stopped, hovering some feet behind, wholly unsure what to do. 'Joe?'

Joe didn't respond. It was as if he could no longer see me, no longer capable of hearing my words, my presence no longer permitted.

'Melissa?' He screamed again. 'Where the *hell* are ya?' The old man was frantic, banging windows, tugging a firmly locked door, this place an unpleasant memory I didn't want in my head. Joe was frantic, frustrated, nothing I said able to calm him down. That oddly spiked wooden "thing" still sat in the darkness somewhere, mocking me, laughing at my increased stupidity, the back door no doubt still open.

I hovered for longer than was comfortable, nothing to do but watch Joe closely, my breath heavy, Megan's kitchen light shining mockingly through those filthy windows. I didn't want to refamiliarise myself with her cold basement floor, *ever*, her bedroom wallpaper just as terrifying. I didn't know what I should do. Run? Stay? When a set of headlights lit up the driveway behind me, the decision was taken out of my hands, a distinct blast of a police siren adding further chaos to this night. I wasn't sure whether to be relieved or *terrified*. I turned around to speak, but Joe was gone.

Day Four

21

The police always turned up when I least expected them—not to help, but to hinder, acting as if everything happening around me was my fault, my problem. I didn't assume their actions constituted typical police procedure, my existence to blame for their non-compliant attitude. Darkridge Hollow didn't like outsiders, they couldn't have expressed it more firmly and I knew that included black people, yet I wasn't about to leave Georgina to her fate. How many residents knew of the strange rituals taking place in the dark, the edge of normality something most here seemed happy to ignore, the edge of town unfathomable.

'Jeez, not *you* again?' The now familiar features of a police uniform loomed from the darkness as unappreciated torchlight was shone in my face. I had no idea what I'd done to warrant such attention, only here *now* because of Joe, the old man part of a family I was unfamiliar with until half an hour ago. I glanced around, searching the darkness that was annoyingly capable of concealing everything but *me*. I was still wondering who Melissa was, nothing about this town surprising.

'I'm not sure what's happening,' I muttered. I genuinely didn't. I was standing in the middle of Megan's depleting driveway, hands aloft, hoping I wouldn't be shot dead where I stood, my life ending before it was able to reach an unsatisfactory conclusion. I couldn't fathom who'd called the police at this hour. Megan, I assumed.

One of the officers stepped forward, tilting his head as if assessing my motives, my next move. I recognised him. Bob Bailey.

'We received a call. Seems someone's been prowlin' around out here. The owner has gotten herself all spooked like. It's lucky we were in the area.' Bailey had his hand on his gun. He nodded towards the house, the place far too silent, its thin walls looming aggressively at my back.

Prowling? Up until a few moments ago, Joe was banging on the door, yelling, Megan no more willing to welcome us into her space than I wanted to be anywhere near it. There was no danger *anyone* could have accused him of prowling. I didn't vocalise my thoughts, of course. I didn't assume it would have done me any favours.

'I was told yesterday that *nobody* lived here,' I scoffed sarcastically, Blake's earlier confirmation still in my head.

'Is that whatcha doin' out here? Tryin' to enter the place *illegally?*'

'*No*. Of course not.'

'Then what *are* you doin'?'

'Just trying to find my daughter,' I confirmed flatly, my words tiresome now, boring, relentless desperation teetering on trembling lips that hadn't yet verified a thing.

'Well, you won't find her in there.' Bailey's tone was as flat as mine, leaving me in no doubt about who was in charge.

'You *know* that do you?' I muttered under my breath, not wanting him to hear, wishing Joe would step in and save me. From what, I had no clue—probably myself.

'So you figured you'd *terrorise* the young woman who lives out here?'

'No,' I stated firmly, shaking my head in a manner I wasn't confident was healthy for either of us. There was only one person who'd been terrorised tonight, and that was *me*. I was still searching the darkness for Joe, my search for Georgina wholly futile.

I thought of Mac and Morag again, their suffering far worse than anything I'd experienced at Megan's unrelenting hands, Georgina's disappearance hardly *her* fault. Or, at least, I hoped. I swallowed several unwanted thoughts, wondering who would miss Mac and Morag now, their absence not yet realised, their honeymoon over. There would be no excited phone calls to entrusted family, no confirmation of their safety. It wasn't comforting.

'We don't appreciate strangers frightenin' our women, makin' unsubstantiated claims to stories no one needs to hear.' Bailey's hand was still resting against his gun belt.

Stories? Is that how they saw this? Stories I'd invented for light entertainment? I didn't want to drop Joe in the shit, obviously, but they needed to know I hadn't come here by choice, hadn't come of my own volition. I'd rather be *anywhere* right now than here.

'I didn't come here alone,' I confirmed, still searching, still hoping. I didn't *want* to be here, my stupidity to blame for everything.

'You got an accomplice?' Bailey shone his torch behind me, expecting some crazed gunmen to be hiding in the shadows, poised, ready. He lifted his gun, his training triggering a jerk reaction to his twitching trigger finger. Was I about to get caught in an unfettered crossfire that would leave me dead on this hellish ground, bullet wounds through my already lifeless chest?

'Not exactly. Just-' *Just what?* What the hell was I trying to say? That a deranged old man had driven me here, his intentions unknown, our connection barely acknowledged by a family truth I never expected to uncover?

Where was Megan? And more to the point, where was *Joe?* A vision jumped into my mind of him in the darkness behind the house, held captive by Tommy or Mike, a gag over his mouth, grappling hands around his torso. I glanced behind me. The kitchen light had been turned off. When that happened, I couldn't say. I hadn't exactly been watching, too busy trying not to get *shot.*

Maybe Megan was behind a curtain, her bloodstained hands providing an uncensored view of my discomposing corpse. Maybe she was laughing at me. Maybe they both were. She must have heard Joe's demands, choosing to ignore him, this unfolding situation bizarre. Maybe *she* knew who Melissa was. How the police had arrived here so quickly was beyond logic. Something smelled off. I didn't like it.

'D'ya *enjoy* hangin' round stranger's properties?' Bailey narrowed his eyes, wanting a clearer look at me.

What kind of question was *that?* I didn't like his pointed tone, the glare he gave me in the darkness, blinding torchlight ensuring I saw little beyond the glisten of his loaded gun. I shook my head.

'We warned you to leave Darkridge Hollow. Folk in this town are *good* people. They don't appreciate the likes of you, wanderin' around, talkin' shit.'

The likes of me? I was sick of hearing that phrase. There may have been many good people in the world, but I doubted Darkridge Hollow housed many. I opened my mouth but closed it, nothing I could say that would have helped. I wasn't even convinced the *police* were good people. They certainly didn't like me. They couldn't have made that clearer if they'd tried.

'So, what am I supposed to do now?' I had no idea why I was asking such a stupid question, nothing about the last couple of days proportionate. I didn't for one second assume that telling them about the murder of two innocent tourists would have gone down well. They might assume *I* was the killer.

'It's becomin' mighty clear you're not intendin' on leavin' of your own volition, so you've given us no choice but to escort you directly outta town. We just wanna ensure you make your connectin' flight home, sir.' Bailey gave me a firm nod as if I was an alien who needed dealing with immediately or suffer the consequences, the addition of the word "sir" merely confirmation he was just doing his job. Was this guy *serious?* 'Get in the car please, Mr. Raymond.' It wasn't a request.

I hovered for a few unfounded seconds, unsure what the hell I should do next. Should I run, stay, admit defeat and accept a fate I didn't want whilst leaving my child to the demented hands of Darkridge Hollow and its deranged residents? When Bailey raised his gun, the safety-catch now off, the decision was made for me. With a heavy breath that threatened to choke me, I reluctantly climbed into the awaiting vehicle, my hands still held high. All I needed was honest consideration and a little compassion. I wasn't the bad guy. I wasn't in the wrong. We headed onto Hillborne Avenue, nothing more to be done, Joe's old truck no longer parked along the street. Where the hell was he?

***

I couldn't believe it. Without so much as an explanation, I was escorted to the police station, any attempt to vindicate myself unheard, my emotions unravelling. I tried to explain about Mac and Morag, although my words were discarded, continued blank looks aimed my way. I found myself once again standing in the police station, dawn creeping around the edges of windows that saw very few truths.

'I figured after our last conversation, you'd be leavin' Darkridge Hollow, Mr. Raymond,' Deputy Chief McDonald grunted. 'So I'm givin' you a choice. Leave quietly, *today*, or find yourself at the mercy of this great nation's police justice.' He glared at me, something in his eyes I didn't like, his tone beyond arrogant.

'Today? Are you serious?' What did they assume they could charge me with? *Telling the truth?*

The deputy glared at me from the rim of his lowered glasses. 'Bet your sweet *ass* I am.' He licked his lips. 'But I gotta warn you, we got our own way of dealin' with things round here.'

I swallowed. I didn't doubt that for a second. I didn't know much, but I knew none of the officers behind that desk were prepared to let me walk out of this place a free man without confirmation they were getting rid of me. *Today.*

'Why won't you believe I saw something in the cornfields?' I'd tried several times to explain what I'd witnessed, yet none of these men were taking me seriously.

'We don't need more stories. We got better things to do.'

'They're not stories. *For God's sake.*' What the hell was wrong with these people?

The deputy stood straight, stiffening his spine, smoothing his uniform. Thankfully he ignored my comment. He didn't speak.

'Please,' I pleaded. 'You need to check the cornfields.' They needed to check Megan's property too, but I didn't dare tell them why.

The deputy shifted his weight uncomfortably, as did several other officers, their reaction nondescript, mine met only with blank faces. They didn't respond, didn't flinch. *They didn't believe me.*

'Can I speak to Blake?' He never seemed to be around when I needed him.

'State Trooper Harrison was called away on important police business.'

How convenient.

'There are rumours you've been snoopin' around the

town hall, Mr. Raymond.' The way the deputy was glaring at me now, he didn't need validation. He already knew. *Rumours?* Why would checking old files be a problem? I assumed he knew Blake had helped me. Was that why he was called out of town so suddenly? *Important police business, my arse.* It was obvious they didn't want him getting too close to truths I wasn't yet even aware existed.

'Joe Everley can confirm everything. He can tell you why I was at that house tonight.' I desperately needed Joe to explain what had happened, what I'd already told *him*, confirm the reason we were standing outside Megan's property at one o'clock in the morning, because I literally had no clue. He'd been a deputy too, once. Surely his authority counted for something.

'Old Joe Everley ain't lived round these parts for years,' the deputy confirmed, looking at me now as if I had a serious mental health issue he hadn't been made aware of. 'We used to go huntin' together, back when our kids were small. I think I'd know if he was still livin' in that old house.'

'What old house?'

The deputy looked at me as if I was stupid. 'The one you can't seem to stay away from.'

Was Megan's house *Joe's* house? If so, it meant that Megan's dilapidated property was once my wife's *childhood* home. I glared at the deputy, visions jumping into my head of this man with Anna when she was small, laughing and joking, offering her sweets, patting her hair. I didn't dare tell him who *I* was. 'Joe lives in his cabin now, next to Blackhill Lake,' I confirmed, almost choking on my words. I appreciated the old man sought a solitary lifestyle, but I was concerned as to why Deputy Chief McDonald didn't already know this, if they were *indeed* old friends.

The deputy glared at me, his eyes as cold as his words. 'That old fishin' cabin ain't been used for years. But you'd know that already if you read the newspapers.'

I swallowed. Why the hell would Joe want to remain hidden? I hope I hadn't said something I'd later regret. Had I missed something vital in those old articles? These people weren't prepared to believe a word I said, no matter how forcefully I pleaded my case. Nothing I could confirm about Mac, Morag, or Georgina reached ears that were probably never listening in the first place. There was no evidence Georgina was *real,* nothing to confirm Mac and Morag's presence, no checks made to confirm my wayward ramblings.

I had no idea who I could trust, convinced their bodies would never be recovered, even had I driven them to the cornfield myself. The police were tired of my chattering mouth, bored of the lies they assumed I was telling. My throbbing head was left to deal with a situation beyond my control, an impossible mission made all the more troubling by the ignorance this place seemingly had in spades.

22

Time doesn't matter when you're dead. A minute can go by, or a decade. The ticking clock pays no attention to your ghostly existence, the rest of the world obliviously continuing without you. Right at that moment, I felt dead, nothing existing beyond sharp air my lungs struggled to absorb. Today was another confirmation of my volatile reality, my painful life teetering on completion. I'd tried to care for Georgina the best I could, watching with a swelling heart the young woman she was becoming. Yet I'd failed as a father, failed as a protector. They may as well do what they wanted now. I was done with it all.

I was escorted to the motel to collect my things, another day dawning, another impossible moment in time passing. I'd been given a police escort out of town, the officers whose consistent presence was steadily suffocating me, both standing unmoving outside my motel room door whilst I gathered my belongings, the motel manager in shock as to what was happening. I was bundled into the back of their car like a criminal, everything unravelling too fast for my brain to keep up.

I sat in stunned silence as we drove onto the highway, every mile a greater distance than I could handle, additional time added to a life sentence away from Georgina. I wanted to scream, smash the windows, run for my life. Instead, I sat stone-faced in the back of a stranger's vehicle looking to the world as if I'd lost my mind. The silence was deafening, the handcuffs behind my back a source of irritation, no words spoken that meant a damned thing to anyone.

It's odd what goes through your mind when the world is rushing past at speed. Everything blurs into obscurity, sending you into a spin from which you can never recover. I was leaving Georgina behind, somewhere out there, alone, lost in a country neither of us understood. How was this possible? I leant forward, perpetually nauseous, tilting my head towards the roof of the car in protest of my churning gut. Bailey and Montgomery were chatting amongst themselves, oblivious, their job merely to accompany me out of town, my presence of no real relevance, my emotions left to decline. I endured their nonsense until I could take no more, my brain metaphorically rolling backwards in my skull. I was almost sick when Cleveland Airport loomed into view, no traveller aware of the breakdown I was about to have in public.

'Outcha get.' The car came to a halt and the door swung open, the voice issuing the instruction clipped, sharp. It matched my mood. I was beginning to detest State Trooper Bailey, the look he gave as he uncuffed my wrists saying more than words ever could. This wasn't the first time I'd found myself in the back of a police car, of course, not the first accusations aimed my way. I was used to being treated like dirt, nothing ever changing about people's attitudes, no matter how much protesting we did. I reluctantly climbed into the morning sun, my legs no stronger than an unset jelly, my gut twisting putrid sludge around my panicked internal organs. I couldn't feel my tongue.

'I can't just leave her,' I protested, my words failing to reach ears that would ever acknowledge my desperation.

'Well, you ain't stayin,' came a dry response. Bailey had no expression. I wondered if he was a father, yet it was doubtful. If he were, he'd understand.

'But my daughter is out there somewhere.' I couldn't have said that any clearer.

'Yeah. So you *claim.*'

Why the hell were these people acting like this? What had I *ever* done to warrant such continued aggression? I could think of nothing beyond a rapidly increasing body count, missing tourists lodged forever in my head. How many people did Blake claim went missing each year? I swallowed. *Georgina was now one of them.* I was handed my power-depleted mobile phone, my wallet and passport, my suitcase already heading for a luggage compartment, no further words offered that could have confirmed more than that simple, pitiful gesture.

I held my lifeless phone for several seconds before placing it inside my shirt pocket, frustrated I couldn't use it, the possibility there might be a message from Georgina on it, too much to consider. I hadn't showered since yesterday, my clothing still bearing the marks of last night's trauma, last night's *terror.* It didn't matter. The departure lounge loomed at my back, aircraft coming and going. This wasn't how things were meant to be.

Exuberant holidaymakers with excited children ambled around, boarding passes clutched in frantic hands, gates awaiting keen adventures. None of them were aware of my existence, or the fact I was becoming steadily neurotic with each passing moment. Air came towards me in painful, sporadic jolts, each inhale suffocating my every breath. No one noticed. I would shortly be forced to board a plane, take my seat, keep quiet. I wasn't confident I could do that.

I pressed trembling fingertips against my wallet, contemplating how I could make a retreat and avoid this impossible situation. I was close to vomiting, *again,* the anticipation of my impending journey unprecedented. Both officers remained by my side as I was checked in at the front desk, loitering like poison in the unbreathable air. My lungs filled with toxic gas instead of oxygen, my brain brimming with toxic thoughts instead of helpful ideas. How the hell was I getting out of this?

I thought about a plane journey I'd taken only days earlier. Georgina's time had been spent watching in-flight movies, distracted by her mobile, ignoring her dad. I'd slept for most of it, ignoring my *daughter*. What the hell was wrong with me? We should have been making the most of our time together—looking out of the window, watching passing birds below and laughing at clouds that looked like marshmallows and funny faces. I wasn't convinced I could endure such agony again, forced to stare out of the window for the duration of the entire flight, ignoring *everyone*, my absence of mind the only thing willing to make the journey pass faster. I was desperately trying to keep my overactive brain in check and my last meal in my belly. I didn't need more trouble. I just wanted this thing over and done with.

I lost track of how long I endured the painful agony of the seat beneath me, my legs trembling, my gut ready to explode on cue. I couldn't sit here and do nothing, fingernails bitten to oblivion, bored police officers obliged to babysit my forthcoming departure. They didn't deem it important to *talk* to me, more interested in the passing world, their phones, scantily clad women. I couldn't get Blake's comment out of my head that the police were involved in something. What that was, I couldn't fathom, though it would explain all the undesired attention.

'Excuse me? I need to use the toilet,' I stated suddenly, getting to my feet in a panic. I didn't. I needed a plan, a distraction, time to think of something before I spontaneously combusted.

Both men turned and stared at me as if they'd forgotten I was in the room. 'Now?' Bailey grunted, unimpressed.

'Yep. Unless you want me to cause a scene?' *Piss all over*

the floor. The way I was feeling right then, I'd gladly oblige.

Bailey sighed, placing his mobile inside his bulky trouser pocket. 'You wanna take him, or shall I?' His disinterested colleague was busy elsewhere, social media far more important than *me.*

Montgomery glared at me as if I'd asked him to jump from a tower block roof without a parachute. 'You got two minutes. Hurry up,' he snapped, knowing we were close enough to the entrance for them to notice if I tried anything stupid, enough security around to prevent any unexpected departures.

I was barely able to contain myself as I offered a swift nod, glancing around for facilities that might see me evade the attention of these men, a few moments all I needed to make my escape. I tried not to grin. My feet stepped away, unsteady, uncertain, both men already re-engaged in their previous discussions, females and doughnuts more important to their day than me. My legs didn't want to cooperate but I kept walking, my pace automatically increasing with each miscalculated step I took. I wanted to break into a run, race from this place, my suitcase already on a plane somewhere without me.

Instead, I headed towards the toilets, no idea how I maintained a steady pace, the bustle of the airport disguising any potential wrongdoing. I had no idea what I was thinking, no plan in place. I just needed to get away, locate space I assumed I'd never experience again. I stood in front of a dirty sink, my head dangling in front of a smudged mirror, my hands resting on either side of a ceramic tiled unit. I looked as if I was about to be sick, no one around me willing or able to ease my suffering, sideways glances unnecessary. *Now what?* What the hell was I doing?

I was fully aware those police officers wouldn't wait long, my time in this room limited to the number of minutes they assumed I would need to carry out my ablutions, bodily functions annoyingly necessary, this windowless box of no genuine help. I glanced in the mirror, my reflection unrecognisable; three days seemingly all that was needed to succumb to the last six months of my wretched life. My eyes were a sunken grey mess, my beard growing out, unkempt, unattractive, the spirit that Anna had loved so much, finally broken.

The bathroom door opened periodically, strangers coming and going, chatting, unconcerned, no doubt pondering my unknown intentions, my ill-considered actions. I didn't care. I washed my hands, twice, not needing to draw unwanted attention, needing to appear *normal* to any passing stranger. I was one of them, just passing through—nothing to see here, thank you very much. From my current position, I had no clear vision of Bailey or Montgomery, out there, waiting. It didn't help. I hovered next to an open door for several painful moments, peering into the void and hoping my next move wouldn't be my last. I couldn't think about the consequences. This moment was too important.

When a group of chattering men in suits walked out of the restroom, I took my chance and stepped out behind them, just part of their group, nothing more, my single intention to slip away undetected and *disappear*. I glanced around, ensuring I kept out of sight, my head held low. My chaperones were still on their mobile phones, laughing with a couple of women – luckily for me – neither aware of what was happening behind them.

I didn't dare look back, fully expecting a heavy hand to grab my shoulder, my moment of madness over. Yet I kept walking, nothing preventing my impossible mission, nothing behind me but air. I didn't have long. Their attention would be alerted soon enough, irritated by my absence, my bathroom trip firmly over. It wouldn't take much for them to realise what I'd done.

I spotted an open service door some feet ahead, scarcely imagining it might be a potential escape route. I had no idea where it led. I honestly didn't care. All I knew was I needed to move fast. That door wasn't meant for visitors, of course, opened briefly by a maintenance staff member, my opportunity short-lived. I picked up pace, my legs barely cooperating. I almost dared believe I'd make it until radio chatter filled the space behind me, a distinct boom of Bailey's voice catching my attention.

With no time to lose, I raced through the open door, slamming the thing behind me, no connotations of where I was heading or who I might run into. My only thought was to disappear from the ever-watchful eyes of those who would have liked nothing more than to see me rotting inside a jail cell. It didn't matter how long I had. *Anything* would be better than this. I needed to disappear whilst I thought of a better plan, keep going until I could go no further, nothing else left to aid my impossible mission.

A blast of air caught my senses, forcing me to lean against a railing, this area intended for maintenance teams only, the "no entry" sign I'd ignored testimony to my failing sanity. By this point, I was certain Georgina was dead. She'd been missing too long and I couldn't go back to my old life without her. She was the *only* person keeping me alive. Without my child I'd have been dead months earlier, joining my wife on the other side of this godforsaken existence that everyone else calls life.

I took a breath, a nagging thought tugging reality. What if she *was* alive? The idea seemed almost ridiculous, yet it was enough to ensure I couldn't give up on her just yet. I'd spent the last three days hoping beyond logic she was safe, praying beyond rational thinking that nothing bad had happened. I owed it to my child to, at least, find out—owed it to Anna. If by some unfathomable reasoning, anything bad *had* happened and I never found out what, I wasn't confident I'd be able to live with that knowledge. It would be just another thing pointing me towards my doom.

I lurched forward, my legs unstable, mindful to retain a firm grip on railings that dug relentlessly into my clammy palms for fear of losing my footing and falling. I no longer trusted my ability to remain upright, apprehension that I might unwittingly throw myself into the path of an oncoming aircraft, lodged firmly in my head. After all, the idea of suicide was never far from my mind. It wasn't comforting. I didn't assume such imbalance would prevent the premature death I'd recently welcomed the idea of.

Bailey's police car ambled around as I headed across the tarmac, its flashing lights too bright for my eyes. It exasperated the already painful dazzle of the morning sunlight, hurting my head, adding more shit to my failing state of mind and persistent queasiness. I hesitated. Radios chattered frantically, as did the officers who spoke urgently into them. Not unlike their thoughts, my mind was wreaking havoc – not for the first time – my existence readily bringing about this impossible situation.

23

I didn't know what to do. If I remained where I was, my whereabouts would be uncovered, yet if I ran, I wasn't sure I'd have the strength to evade capture for long. With no chance to think or change my mind, I darted around the side of the building, no time to assess my surroundings, my only requirement being to head into the city and disappear. I'd honestly never witnessed so much police activity in a single location. It was as if a riot had ensued. Surely my whereabouts was not of such great importance? I'd reported a missing child, for God's sake, not committed the murders I'd been unfortunate enough to witness.

I leaned over and vomited. It was a mess. Body fluids and remnants of something I couldn't recall eating spilt into the morning air along with putrid, congealed bile that angrily swamped the tarmac. It threatened to expose my position, my weakness, my head already spinning out of control. Should my presence be uncovered, the police would undoubtedly shoot me dead, my appearance no better than the alien beings they were metaphorically trained to dispose of on sight. I could barely breathe, my body incapable of functioning, my legs nothing but slabs of dead meat that pulsated in the dabbled shadows. I strained to understand the insurgence, wishing Anna was here. She'd know what to do. I sat sandwiched between two service vehicles as Bailey and Montgomery circled the perimeter, their frustrated faces unseeing, unaware. I held my breath, barely acknowledging the distorted voices that added to my already confused mind.

'I'll meetcha out front,' Bailey grunted, his flushed head aimed blindly in my direction. 'That son of a bitch can't have gotten far.'

I held my breath. *Was this it?* Was this the pivotal moment of my entire life? The complete sum of everything I'd so far failed to achieve? To die in an airport, far from a life I once assumed I knew? I held my breath, hoping he wouldn't notice me crushed between metal and mechanics, hidden from the very officer whose job was to ensure my imminent departure.

'I can't see shit back here,' Bailey growled into his radio.

He rounded the building, leaving me alone with thoughts that came in the form of desperation, my lungs screaming with each painful breath I took. I sighed, waiting until the coast was clear, terrified I had nowhere else to go but directly to my ultimate end.

My escape had created the very panic I'd anticipated yet I couldn't understand why they were behaving so aggressively. I'd done nothing to warrant their venom, a failed endeavour to find my child something those people assumed unimportant. I couldn't imagine why. Surely even forgotten towns like Darkridge Hollow weren't so ignorant that missing children were of no relevance; that isolated town no stranger to wanton acts of repulsion. I raced towards a nearby taxi rank, diving into the back seat of the nearest cab and almost knocking some woman to the ground in the process. I didn't apologise.

'How far away is the city?' I practically screamed into the driver's face, my words deranged, my mind damaged. Several suitcases were still scattered on the side of the road, waiting to be loaded, the poor woman trying to work out what had happened.

'What are you doing, dumb ass?' the taxi driver yelled through his open rear window, the guy ready to punch me in the face. He gave his would-be passenger an apologetic glance before turning his aggression onto me. He was still holding some of her luggage.

'I don't have time to explain, but I *need* your help,' I spluttered, no time for niceties either, it seemed. I dug a trembling hand into my pocket, yanking out my wallet, ready to hand him everything I had.

Seeing the cash in my outstretched hand, the taxi driver left the disgruntled female standing in the road, offering her a few well-placed words of apology before climbing in. Despite my unexpected appearance, he was happy to engage in conversation, no doubt glad for the overpayment he was about to receive. I kept my head low, ensuring I remained invisible, my struggling lungs unhelpful. Airport security staff had now joined Bailey and Montgomery, each scratching frustrated heads. Did they believe I was an immigrant? A terrorist? I didn't dare think about it.

Cleveland wasn't far from the airport, luckily, yet by the time I climbed out of the taxi, I was just glad to be alive, my trembling muscles scrunched tightly like discarded newspaper, my legs barely keeping me in place. I was failing to calm a racing heart in a chest that no longer knew how to breathe properly. I was nothing more than an intruder, lost in a sea of invisibility, oblivion not quite the bliss I'd have hoped for.

I thanked the driver, paying heavily for the privilege of his company before scurrying along a busy street, rejoining a crazy world I'd recently left behind. It was surreal. Before Anna's death, places like these hardly bothered me. I lived in the middle of London, England's capital city always alive and bustling. Now, everything was too much for my overworked mind to cope with. What the hell had happened to me? Even my house had become nothing more than a roof that kept the rain off our heads—four walls, a front door, a broken fence, windows that needed cleaning. I couldn't call it home. Not anymore.

The first thing I did was head in pursuit of a replacement phone charger, unwilling to rest until I could check my messages. The fact my suitcase was already heading to England without me was irrelevant. The shop assistant tried to sell me a new mobile phone, something a little more up-to-date, he said. I didn't want a new phone. I wanted to check the messages on the one I owned.

'This model would suit your needs just fine.'

'No. Thank you.'

'But it has the latest technology.'

'Not interested.'

'But the camera on this model is far superior to anything else we do here.'

'Look. I've just told you. I need a charger for *this* one.'

I was holding my phone towards the guy's face. It was a Samsung, and I liked my Samsung. Yes, it was an older style, one of the earlier ones, and Georgina was impressed it still worked, but it *worked* and that's all that mattered. Surely they had a charger I could *borrow* if selling me one was an issue.

Begrudgingly, the guy reached beneath his counter, pulling out a thin white cable he reluctantly handed to me. It cost me ten dollars. *Hallelujah.*

I asked if I could use his power outlet, just for a moment, just long enough so I could turn the thing on. I think I might have begged. I was desperate, helpless. It was pathetic. After taking pity on me and not wishing to cause an unrequired scene in front of customers who *were* spending money, my silent mobile phone was afforded a brief surge of energy, my failed composure something the shop assistant did not want in his day.

The only thing I needed was to confirm a text or call from Georgina, for her to explain that something silly and innocent had happened, validate she was okay. We'd laugh about it tomorrow. Yet the thing in my possession failed to sedate my nerves or ease my pain, almost forcing me to scream aloud when the only notification it confirmed was a missed call from my dad and a message from my phone provider offering me an upgrade. There was nothing from Georgina.

I thanked the shop assistant with a panicked grunt, stuffing my phone and newly acquired charger into my jeans pocket for fear of losing either again. I needed to get back to Darkridge Hollow. Nothing else mattered and despite being warned what would happen if I was seen in that town again, I didn't care. Going back was the only thing I could think of that made sense, the only thing that kept me going when I barely had any energy left to function.

I found myself once again flagging passing cars, searching for anyone willing to take me to that incomprehensible destination, hitchhiking now an essential part of my day. I had exactly sixty dollars in my possession. If I needed to hand it all over to a passing driver, I would, a cashpoint something I knew would draw immediate unwanted attention, inbuilt CCTV flagging the nearest police unit. I kept low, out of sight, watching and waiting for any opportunity that might arise, the police seemingly on every street, ironically. I couldn't assume they were *all* looking for me, of course, criminal activity rife in *any* city, their time better spent dealing with dangerous drug dealers, gunmen, gangs. Nevertheless, I assumed my description had been circulated by now, the officers I'd left at the airport already in deep trouble with Deputy Chief McDonald.

I wasn't exactly blending in. My overgrown beard and English accent stood out like a sore thumb, my entire appearance ensnaring my fate. When I spotted a truck stop,

I wasn't convinced I was doing the right thing. Large vehicles rolled in and out of the city, their day crammed with busy schedules, my needs of no concern. Do I just walk up to someone and ask for a lift? I hesitated, legs unsteady, uncertain of my next move, my next *thought,* staring randomly at several vehicles as if I was visiting from another planet.

'You lost?' A deep voice startled me. I turned, unsure if I was about to be caught or shot dead. A large male stood staring at me, a baseball cap pulled over a fattened head, rosy cheeks telling me he needed a better diet.

'I need to get somewhere,' I stated, trying to sound as casual and calm as I could. I'm not convinced I pulled it off.

'Somewhere?'

'Darkridge Hollow.' Why did that name now sound so demonic?

'You never heard of the bus?' he was chewing, looking at me as if I was an idiot. Maybe I was.

I smiled, knowing how I must have looked, this guy knowing nothing of what I'd been through. 'I just need to keep my head down for a while.' I didn't want to flag myself as an escaped criminal although I certainly felt like one. It wasn't ideal. Taking the bus was too public, too exposed.

The guy glared at me, nothing else to do. 'I'm heading out that way in ten minutes if you wanna ride?'

'Yes please,' I stammered, unsure what the hell I was letting myself in for. This guy could be a mass murderer for all I knew, a shotgun or machete waiting in his cab.

'The name's Garret,' he confirmed, assuming I'd want to know.

'I'm Jo-'

'I don't wanna know your name,' Garret cut in, glaring at me as if I was about to tell him a deadly secret. 'The less I know about you, the better.' What the hell did he think I'd done? *Did I look that bad?* I needed to explain my actions, my position, yet I could think of nothing of value to say.

'Thank you.' I reached for my wallet. 'I can pay you.'

Garret shook his head. 'Keep your money. Just don't let me regret it.' He walked passed me without glancing back. I followed. I wasn't about to cause him any trouble. I'd created enough of that today.

'Thank you, I won't,' I called after him, unsure what else to say.

***

Garret's truck was large, the type I'd only ever seen in movies. A huge front grille was inset with a chrome emblem of some description, thick tyres towering over me. I hauled myself into the passenger seat, the inside of the cab larger than my spare bedroom. I wanted strike up a conversation and ask if I could pull the cord on his air horn, press buttons, climb into his sleeping quarters. Instead, I sat in silence as the thing sprang to life, sliding into my seat as we drove out of the city. Garret noticed. I tried not to overthink it. I felt like a child in awe of my surroundings yet terrified of asking questions in case I was told to shut up, sit still, this truck *not* a toy.

Every police vehicle that drove past saw me shrink further into the seat. It was pathetic. None of them were looking our way, no one cared, yet my heart threatened to jump from my chest and sit mockingly in my lap anyway.

'You a wanted man or something?' Garret's large voice filled the space, his radio alive with unfamiliar banter only truckers understood.

'It's a long story,' I was staring out of the window, glad to be heading in the right direction at least, a little closer to Georgina. I couldn't overthink what condition I might eventually find her in. I couldn't think about that. Mac popped into my mind again, Morag's insides sliced open in front of the poor guy whose face would haunt me now forever. How could I begin to explain *that* to Garret?

It was strange. Darkridge Hollow was seemingly further away on the drive back than it had felt on the way out. I had no possessions on me other than my passport, my wallet now containing just sixty dollars, and a mobile phone I was too terrified to use in case it ran out of power again. I must have looked nervous. When Garret pulled into the very service station where Georgina and I had stopped for ice cream, I almost screamed, déja vu not something I anticipated experiencing today.

'Are you sure I can't pay you?' I asked again as Garret's air brakes brought the huge bulk to a halt.

'Nope. I'm good,' he replied, more concerned by his own requirements than mine. 'I'm heading south, but Darkridge Hollow is a few miles-'

'I know,' I replied, remembering the way more than I ever thought I would.

'Well, alrighty then,' Garret confirmed, a nod of his large head telling me it was high time we parted company.

'Thank you, Garret,' I attempted a smile that didn't look convincing, climbing out onto the roadside with a nod that didn't look stable. I was standing in the very car park I'd spent an afternoon with my daughter, talking about ice cream and fondly remembering her mum. It felt like a lifetime ago. Garret returned my thanks with a disinterested shrug as I closed his truck door, driving away without a single glance back. It was almost as if he couldn't get away from me fast enough. I couldn't blame him.

I tried not to dwell on my previous visit, those kinds of visions not required today. Instead, I allowed an idea to form in my head. It was a simple idea, an idea I should have thought of long before now. I headed inside the petrol station, hoping to locate the same guy who'd previously given me directions and irritated grunts. I think his name was Troy. He might remember me, might have remembered Mac, if I asked. After all, we were both Brits, Mac's colossal personality something I'm sure even *he* wouldn't have missed.

I was relieved to see the young man sitting behind his counter, several CCTV monitors set behind his head, unwatched, unrequired, not even when someone behind me placed something inside a jacket pocket they assumed hadn't been captured on file. Troy didn't notice and I wasn't about to tell him. It was none of my business. I had more important matters to address. If I could gain access to the surveillance footage from three days ago, it would be all the proof I needed that Georgina existed, proof of what she looked like, the very ice cream I'd bought for her pivotal to my mission. I could point Mac and Morag out too, their disappearance finally out in the open.

Compared to the outside, it was quiet in here, only two customers inside aside from myself, one of which hovered with a bottle of cheap booze wedged inside the pocket of an oversized coat. I hung back, waiting for them to leave, nodding politely to each as I opened the door as they passed by. I was careful not to stare at the bulge inside a pocket that barely hid a thing, careful not to meet the guy's vacant features. It didn't matter. The thief nodded a thank you as the door sprang shut, leaving me to my pending mission, his reddened cheeks and perspiration peppered hairline confirming he wasn't a regular lawbreaker.

'D'ya need help back there?' Troy called my way, a look of suspicion on his face. He probably assumed *I* was the shoplifter he'd already failed to notice, loitering, waiting for my chance.

'I seriously hope so Troy,' I called his name as if we were old friends, heading towards him between a row of chocolate bars and canned drinks. 'I'm hoping you remember me.'

I smiled, knowing I hadn't changed *that* much in three days, despite everything that had happened since then ensuring it now felt as if the world had stopped turning. I glanced at his nametag, glad to be reacquainted with young Troy, his reluctant help the only thing I needed. He stared at me, absolutely no idea who I was. He probably didn't care. I smiled. I could relate to that, yet Troy was going to help me, whether he wanted to or not.

24

I should have stopped and considered my actions, preventing an unprecedented moment in time I never saw coming. Yet, this air-conditioned space dislodged my thoughts, the outside world of no relevance. My next move should have been a means to an end, nothing more, a way for me to deal with a situation afforded to me the moment I stepped out of Garret's truck.

'Do you remember me?' I queried again. I was standing in front of a young man I'd only days earlier rolled my eyes towards in frustration.

'Can't say I do,' Troy muttered, more interested in video games than my presence, no change in the young man's persona today.

'Three days ago.' Had it really been that long? I'd almost forgotten what sleep felt like. 'I was here with my kid. She's twelve.' I had no idea why her age was relevant. Troy hadn't seen her standing out by the car. He barely saw *me*. Why did I assume he'd care?

'Yeah, that's great man,' he sighed, consistent bleeping and agitating music echoing into the otherwise silent space, the purr of a refrigerator unit doing nothing for my failing sense of composure.

'I *need* your help, Troy.' I couldn't help it when I slammed my palms onto the countertop, in no mood for games, jolting the poor kid's phone from his hand. It landed with a thud in his lap, causing him to look at me with a contrived attitude. I didn't mean to behave so badly. I was desperate.

Troy stared at me. 'Dude, what's your fuckin' problem?'

'*Look* at me when I'm talking to you,' I spat, my thoughts twisting, the outside world keeping a painful distance.

'I *don't* remember,' he confirmed flatly, picking up his mobile phone and cursing that he had to restart his level, rolling irritated eyes into the air. I didn't give a shit about his gamer score. I almost snatched the thing from his grip.

'You *must* remember me. How many English people do you see coming through here?'

'Plenty.' Troy was no longer looking at me, no longer bothered by the raging look my face had developed, veins bulging at the side of temples he assumed of no consequence to his day.

I took a breath, a moment. 'Forgive me,' I offered tritely, knowing I didn't need to get on his wrong side. That wouldn't help anyone. 'I was hoping you could show me the CCTV footage from three afternoons ago.' I hoped to *God* these people didn't delete the footage each night.

Troy glared at me. 'Now why would I wanna do that?'

I sucked in a lungful of air. 'Because my child is missing and I'm steadily going out of my mind.'

It was true. It wasn't a comfort. I needed something to take to the police, prove I wasn't inventing all this, *show* them what my goddamned child looked like. I needed them to start looking for her and take me seriously. I couldn't overthink the fact I also wanted footage of Mac and Morag. The police needed to understand their last known movements, trace them to their final destination. I didn't want to think about what might happen once I walked back into that police station, already having meant to be on a plane by now, the officers in my company having unexpectedly lost their wayward traveller to the bustle of a busy airport.

Troy glanced my way as if to confirm I wasn't joking, winding him up for the hell of it. It was hardly a rational declaration. I could see how it sounded. 'I can't go showin' you the CCTV. How do I know you're tellin' the truth?'

'Of course I'm telling the truth,' I yelled. 'Why the hell would I make that kind of thing up?' How stupid did this kid think I was?

'Don't know, don't care,' Troy shrugged, still not grasping the magnitude of this moment or the maleficence of my desperation. He turned his attention to his phone again, his game more important than my needs.

'Please, Troy. I just need to see the footage from three days ago.' He was beginning to annoy me now.

'I already told you man. I can't go showin' strangers the company CCTV. My boss would go nuts.' He narrowed his eyes. 'And quit callin' me, Troy. We don't know each other.'

I was about to "go nuts" in a minute if he wasn't careful, and I'd call him something far worse if he didn't change his attitude.

'Then get him, or *her*, on the phone!'

'Can't.'

'Why not?'

'He's outta town.'

I bit my lip, my tongue, trying to form rational thoughts. *Seriously?* I took a slow intake of air, holding it longer than intended, longer than was healthy, only wanting to reason with this lanky-haired idiot. I tried hard not to swear. 'I don't think you understand my urgency. My child is *missing*.' I was tired of saying it.

Troy's mobile phone was beginning to irritate me, thumbs perpetually pressing keys that clicked mockingly. He was unconcerned by me *or* this conversation. 'And, as

I've already explained, I can't help.'

I have no idea why, but something inside snapped and I lunged forward, grabbing the kid by his shirt collar. I shouldn't have done it, I know. He wasn't that old, and I'd been raised better. Yet, his shitty attitude was more than I could stand. Georgina was missing and with every passing minute, her chances of being found alive grew slimmer. I couldn't dare think about the idea of recovering her body. It was too terrible to imagine.

'What the hell are you doin', man?' Troy yelled, pulling away from my grasp, his face set in a tight knot that matched his gnarled gamer thumbs. His mobile phone dropped from his hands and hit the floor, unavoidably breaking into sections, dislodging the battery and cracking the screen. At least it was silent now. He clambered to his feet, his shirt still creased where I'd grabbed him.

'For God's sake, I just *need* to see your CCTV footage,' I spat, my words increasingly frustrated with every laboured breath I was forced to take, this kid unappreciative of my disposition. *'Now.'* I was no longer asking nicely, no longer calm, my features steadily developing an urgency I didn't want to consider.

'Fuck you,' he spat, his words slurred, slow, totally misjudging this moment and my mood.

A split second was all I needed to compose myself. I didn't need to lose my shit. Not today. I turned around, forcing my aching legs to walk the length of the shop, stopping next to the entrance, hovering. Troy assumed I was leaving, already taunting me from behind, a slurry of insults only winding me up further.

'Yeah, you'd better go, motherfucker. Goddamn, crazy fuckin' asshole. Cock suckin' son-of-a-bitch.'

I probably would have left that shop, had his attitude been different, yet even I didn't anticipate just how Troy's taunts were provoking an enraged reaction. *He* didn't realise what was coming. If he did, he would have shut up, calmed down, the power to calm *me* down entirely in his hands. I clicked the latch over the lock, ensuring we wouldn't be disturbed, nothing on my mind aside from extracting what I needed. I didn't care how I had to do it, or how long it took. There was no way I was leaving this building empty-handed. I'd had enough shit aimed my way to last a lifetime. I'd reached my limits.

'Whatcha doin'?' Troy yelled, stepping out from behind the counter, still trying to collect pieces of his damaged phone from the floor.

'You are going to get me that CCTV, Troy,' I confirmed, probably too forcefully, no other request made that might have made me sound less insane if I'd tried. I was merely stating facts. I was done being nice.

'The hell I am,' Troy scoffed in defiance, attempting and failing to press his battery back into its broken slot. He deliberately spat on the floor.

I wasn't expecting it, his complacent attitude something I wasn't about to take well. In the three days I'd forcedly endured infuriating people, treated like I didn't matter and left to deal with things no sane human should, being spoken to so abruptly by a young man barely out of his teens wasn't something I was willing to take lightly. I stormed up to him, fists closed, teeth clamped so tight it gave me a headache. I didn't *want* any of this, didn't expect what happened next. I just wanted to find my daughter, leave this place and go *home*. Instead, I punched him hard, his jaw exploding with the magnitude of my clenched knuckles. I was angry.

Troy grunted and staggered backwards, his young face exploding in a torrent of fresh blood and shock. When he reached below the counter for a rifle, I wasn't expecting *that* either. I wasn't used to how things worked in the states, American gun law something I didn't anticipate being on the wrong end of. I would never get used to how people here found it so acceptable to carry guns—owning a gun their apparent *God-given right*. What the hell was he going to do? Shoot me?

I couldn't allow that to happen, of course, nothing about this moment logical. I lunged forward, shoving him backwards, just hard enough to force the firearm from his grip, and for the kid to *get a grip*. However, the gun went off, bringing down a section of suspended ceiling, his body jolting towards a fully stacked shelf of processed goods. The rifle landed hard, skidding across the floor, the thing still smoking, still hot. I was grateful it hadn't killed me, sending me directly into Anna's outstretched arms.

Stupid *stupid* kid!

I didn't intend for Troy to trip and lose his footing, his unexpected fall something I didn't initially notice. I was angry, frustrated, shocked by the sound of gunfire in my ears, a practical *child* on the end of a deadly weapon. I needed to deal with this escalating situation before it got out of hand, before there was no going back for either of us. I wasn't expecting to look down and notice that he was no longer moving, an expanding pool of blood forming beneath his unconscious head, a sharp corner of a metal shelving unit coated in red.

I raced to his side, unconcerned I was kneeling in blood, merely needing to bring this ridiculous situation back on track. All I wanted was to check the CCTV footage. Now, look what had happened.

'Hey?' I yelled, hoping to force a groan from the kid, wake him up.

I no longer cared how many names he called me. I was the adult. I could take it. I leant towards his lagging mouth to check his breath, unable to hear anything other than my own. Amidst everything that had happened since my arrival, this was up there with the worst of it, my brain unwilling to acknowledge I might have killed the bloody kid. I nudged him. He didn't move. There was nothing beyond the pounding of my heart, no warm air against my open palm to sedate my nerves. I pressed my fingertips against his neck, trying to locate a pulse. *Nothing.* I lifted his wrist, yet it simply flopped to the floor the moment I released it. Oh my God. *What the hell had I done?*

I clambered to my feet, staggering backwards, unwilling to accept reality, unable to think beyond my own stupidity. Things were getting out of control, my thoughts only on waking this kid up. I'd kick him if I had to—anything to change an impossible outcome that couldn't possibly be real. I stared for too long at his lifeless body, unwilling to accept he was anything other than unconscious, knocked out, still *breathing.* He'd be okay in a few minutes. He *had* to be. Nothing else made sense. Why the hell didn't he *help* me and hand over the goddamned recordings? Why did he have to be such an *idiot?*

There was a movement outside, a passer-by, just someone wanting to pay for gas and finding themselves unable to get through the now locked door. I crouched down, out of sight, my brain a collection of screaming contradictions that danced in frantic desperation. I hoped no one had witnessed what had happened. I pulled my mobile from my pocket along with Blake's folded card, grateful for the limited power I'd reserved and for the foresight of a friend I never expected to make. I dialled his number, my hands barely cooperating, hoping beyond disbelief he might actually help me.

'Yo!' Blake was too calm. I didn't like it.

'Blake?' I could barely speak.

'Hey Josh, how's it goin' my man?' Blake's relaxed tone echoed around the desolate space, yet I couldn't respond, nothing of what I was about to tell him rational. 'Dude, I'm real sorry for what happened,' he continued, seemingly glad I'd called him, grateful to have been given a chance to speak to me before I left. He probably assumed I was heading back to England, already on a plane. 'I didn't know they were sending you home.'

I couldn't speak. I honestly didn't know what to say.

'Josh? You there?'

I was sitting next to a pool of blood, barely able to look down, let alone speak, a sticky smell of iron tickling my nostrils.

'I'm here,' I stuttered, unconcerned by anything he had to say and unsure my voice was my own. 'I need your help. I think I might have done something really *fucking* stupid.'

25

I was staring at the body of a young man, the kid scarcely a few years older than Georgina, his entire life ahead. Yet now, if I wasn't mistaken, he was *dead.* What the hell was I meant to do with that kind of information? Blake was on the end of an unassuming telephone, barely any power in it to maintain this insane conversation, the man I hardly knew forced to listen to words that made no sense. I couldn't hear his voice, unsurprisingly not yet ready to listen, my ears ringing violently with so much noise in my head.

'Talk to me, Josh,' Blake's words were distant, almost cold. 'What happened?'

'I think I *killed* someone.' It was crazy, ludicrous. The very thought stung my eyes, narrowing my throat, my world falling apart.

'*What?* Where are you?'

I had no idea how to answer. Everything had escalated too fast, no time for me to register the pace at which things were taking place. Blake was still talking, yet I was shutting down—something deep inside long dead, already festered and rotted away.

'Josh?' Blake repeated, frustration apparent. 'Where *are* you?' he was beyond anxious, his concern too late.

'The petrol station along route seventy-one, *I think,*' I muttered. 'A few miles outside Darkridge Hollow.' I glanced around, no longer convinced of anything. Whoever had been trying to get into the store was no longer in sight. Maybe they'd given up, oblivious, no indication they'd noticed the deranged madman beyond glass I couldn't now assume would protect me. I dared not look at my feet, Troy's mop of dirty blond hair heavily coated in sludgy red liquid seeping slowly into the cracks of several broken floor tiles.

'What the hell are you doing out *there?* Weren't you meant to be on a plane?'

He was right. I was. I didn't know which was worse, Georgina's disappearance or *this?* 'I killed him,' I repeated, my throat ready to strangle me for such a suggestion. I had blood on my hands, literally, spots of red that peppered my skin, my jeans, my hair. I'd seriously messed up this time.

'Stay *exactly* where you are. I'm on my way.' The phone went dead, leaving me abandoned, nothing of what had happened registering. I was unable to look at the lifeless body next to my foot, the continued purr of the refrigerator units making me want to scream. What was I meant to do? Call the police? No. I was in enough shit as it was.

I lost track of time after that, nothing about this moment willing to appease my whirring thoughts. By the time Blake arrived, I'd twice hidden from people who would have discovered my grisly secret had they looked closer, uncovering the scene behind an unassuming locked door. Someone yelled the young lad's name, a local who knew him, knew his family. I closed my eyes. I couldn't sit here forever. There would be repercussions, a jail sentence. Surely this couldn't be happening?

***

I almost missed Blake's frantic yells as he drummed frustrated fists against the doorframe, shouting through several large windows towards a face I wasn't convinced was mine. I was sitting blankly between upturned trays of confectionery, glancing beyond the madness strewn across the floor.

'Open the door, Josh,' my friend repeated, his tone concerned, his cheeks red.

I was on the floor, unmoving, unknowing, forced to claw my way towards the door, clinging to my sanity, struggling to unlock it with one hand whilst trying to steady the other. Blake rushed inside, his face a collection of features I didn't know how to appease, slamming the thing shut and locking it against a world I no longer wanted to acknowledge.

'What the hell happened?' Blake was only asking a simple question. It should have resulted in a simple answer. Yet I couldn't find the words to articulate events that couldn't be real. I couldn't even look at him. I pointed to a pair of upended trainers covered in blood, the body they belonged to lying unmoving some feet away, this impossible moment alien to everything I knew. I still hadn't gained access to the CCTV footage I needed, instead adding my own demented crime to the cameras overhead.

'*Motherfucker!*' Blake yelled, following my trembling index finger. He raced forward, kneeling down, lifting the kid's lagging hand whilst checking his pulse. 'What in God's name did you do?'

Nothing of his desperate words hit their mark. I couldn't reply, could hardly remember what *had* happened. I shook my head. 'I needed to see the CCTV footage from the day Georgina and I arrived. But he refused to show me.' I could barely swallow. It was a simple request. How had it resulted in such a complex result?

'So you *killed* him?'

I shook my head, still unable to look at Blake, not wanting to know what I'd find if I did. 'Not intentionally.'

Of course, not intentionally. 'I don't know what to do, Blake.' It was true. I had no idea.

'Okay.' I could tell Blake was trying to remain calm. 'Tell me *exactly* what happened.' He got to his feet, double-checking he'd relocked the shop door, peering beyond the windows to confirm there were no witnesses to this impossible situation. Everything felt hazy.

'He fell and hit his head.' It was true. Surely they couldn't blame me for *that.* I tried not to look at the bruise already formed on the poor kid's cheek, blood inside his mouth, his shirt still wrinkled where I'd clung to it, struggling to recount an event I could never now change.

'He just fell?' Blake didn't sound convinced.

Part of the ceiling was lying across the tiled floor, Troy's discharged rifle still where it had landed. Bags of sweets, chocolate bars and cans of pop were littered around us, my face and clothing still showered with bloodstains about to become my final downfall. My fist was still red, my teeth still clenched.

I nodded. I didn't need the contradiction, didn't need to see his disappointment.

Blake glanced towards the cameras, tiny flashing green lights proof of my deadly deed. 'I'll check the CCTV before someone else does.' The guy was ever the professional, ever the police officer. It was lucky the cameras had no sound that could link *him* to any potential help he might now offer me. Help? After what I'd done, did I have the nerve to ask for such a thing?

'What do I do Blake?' I couldn't keep my voice steady, nothing about this moment logical, desperate for answers I was never going to get. I was hoping the young lad was still breathing, of course, that I'd merely knocked him unconscious with my impromptu shove. I wanted to believe I was overthinking everything and that this *was* going to be okay.

'Gimme a second.' Blake was assessing the situation, going back several times to check poor Troy's corpse as if hoping he could change the outcome.

I wanted to thank him but didn't know how, wholly unable to reverse what I'd done. Joe popped into my mind, I don't know why, the last time I saw my father-in-law still weighing heavily on my mind. It was hardly the time, hardly appropriate. 'Have you seen Joe?' I hardly recognised my strained voice.

'No. Why?' Blake was busy removing CCTV footage from the in-store computer system, wiping conclusive recordings from existence, removing vital evidence and basically covering my arse. I hoped the system didn't automatically produce backups, or we were *both* screwed.

'He's Anna's father.' I was shaking, unnerved by too many tragic events.

'Your *wife?*'

I nodded. 'I think he might be out looking for Megan.'

'The woman who helped you?'

Helped was a debatable concept. 'Do you know who she is, Blake?'

'No, I'm sorry, Josh I don't. But I do know that Joe has a daughter called Melissa.'

I glared at him, my heart in my throat. 'Sorry…what?'

'He doesn't talk much about her and I've never personally met her. Joe's a private man. Keeps to himself.' He swallowed. 'I honestly thought he only had one kid. I had *no* idea you and he were related.'

There was no way Blake could fathom the shock on my face, nothing of what he was saying hitting its mark. I thought back to last night, to Joe's frantic yells to a woman called Melissa who I'd mistakenly assumed was Megan.

'She and Anna were twins, apparently.' My legs almost faltered and Blake was forced to steady me. 'You have to help me. *Please.*' I couldn't stand to look at that blood-drenched body a moment longer, nothing I could do about the state of poor Troy now. I was a fugitive, a desperate search for my missing child the least of my problems. I'd already evaded the police, nothing for me to do now but run, do whatever I needed to find my daughter and disappear. I needed Blake's help. I didn't know who else to ask.

'I will, Josh, but I can't just cover this up.' Blake did not look impressed, overlooking the fact he'd removed the CCTV footage and therefore already had. I hoped he appreciated my desperation. I wasn't a bad person, not really, everything happening out of my control.

'I know. But I *need* to find Georgina. She's all that matters.' I glanced at poor Troy. Did I not assume he mattered, too? He had a family who loved him, a family who would now need to bury their boy because of *me.* If my child was – by some horrific travesty – found dead, I'd gladly hand myself in to the police and spend however many years I had left of my pathetic life behind whatever bars they deemed suitable. Did this state impose the death penalty? I couldn't remember. Wasn't sure I wanted to know.

Our unspoken plan was rudely interrupted by a yell outside, the sight of a second officer jolting us back into reality. It was Bailey, his gun cocked ready.

'Police!' Bailey yelled, his angered voice confirming things were about to get a whole lot worse. 'Come out with your hands in the air, and don't try anythin' stupid.' I panicked, glancing at Blake whose face displayed a similar expression as mine. *What the hell?*

I couldn't imagine how the police already knew what was happening, Bailey ready to shoot whoever was causing trouble without hesitation. I was once again left wondering about the people I'd placed my trust in. I could barely look at Blake as he raised an unsteady index finger towards his lips, a simple gesture requesting I remain silent, for now, that he would deal with this. It failed, of course, fear growing in me that my friend wasn't a friend at all.

'It's okay Bob,' Blake called out. 'I have everything under control.'

'That you, Blake?'

'Yeah.'

'What the hell, man? We got a call 'bout a disturbance out here. Some guy beatin' on a kid.' I could see through the window that Bailey had his gun ready, his finger hovering over the trigger. Montgomery was behind him, elusive as always, keeping a distance that made him appear sly.

Someone *had* seen what happened. At least it wasn't Blake's fault. I should have found it comforting. I didn't.

'Yeah, I know. That's why I'm here,' Blake yelled, stepping carefully towards the locked door, an unsteady hand held towards me. 'Go with me on this Josh, and it'll be okay, I promise,' he whispered. What the hell was he going to do? I felt sick.

There was no further time to think as Blake led me by the arm towards the front of the shop. He unlocked the door, opening it wide, allowing sunlight to flood the doomed space. 'Don't say anything. Just raise your hands where Bob can see them.' He was still whispering, guiding me outside. 'Don't worry.'

'Blake, what the hell's happenin' back there?' Bailey queried, lowering his gun at the sight of his colleague heading into the sunlight with me in supposed custody, my raised hands trembling, my jelly legs unstable. 'How'd you get out here so fast?'

'I was heading back into town when the call came in.' Wow, Blake was good at lying. It wasn't a comfort. 'You?'

'Same. Just had a few loose ends to tie up first.' Bailey was glaring at me, my unexpected disappearance the very loose ends he was confirming. 'Why didn'tcha radio for backup?'

'I didn't know what I was dealing with until I got here,' Blake was attempting to remain neutral, something in his tone telling me I wasn't going to like this next part. 'I found this guy held up inside. Needed to talk him down.' *Talk me down?* What the hell? I glared at Blake. He ignored me.

'Where's Troy?'

Blake sighed. 'Dead.'

Bailey took a deep breath, lifting his gun again and pointing it directly towards my head. 'Getcha hands above your head, *now,*' he screamed, unsure how else to react, tears already perched in his unseeing eyes. It was obvious he knew Troy, the kid's family no doubt good family friends. I hadn't meant to hurt him, hadn't intended to *kill* him. It was an accident. I instinctively raised my hands higher, the idea of being shot dead something I hadn't considered.

'Goddamn it, Bob.' Blake's curt tone sliced through the sharp tension. He marched unceremoniously up to his colleague, the gun in his hand no more dangerous than a water pistol aimed towards a half-starved cat. 'What the hell are you doing?' He placed irritated hands on unmoving hips as if telling off a two-year-old. All he needed now was to tap a waiting foot. Had the situation been different, it might have been funny. I'd done the same thing to Georgina. Many times.

'Blake, keep outta this. I'm takin' it from here. This guy's dangerous. He's given me the goddamn runaround all mornin' and I'm gettin' real tired of his bullshit.' Bailey glanced briefly at Blake but didn't lower his gun or express any change in attitude, glaring at me as if I was a dangerous criminal he needed to silence. He'd shoot me dead if he deemed it necessary.

'Seriously, Bob?' Blake was unconcerned that he was standing next to a loaded gun pointing directly at my head.

'I guess you're planning on shooting him then, huh?' He glanced over his shoulder. I couldn't move, not even if I wanted to, my legs set in place by invisible glue. 'He's not even armed. Just look at him.' My newly acquired accomplice waved a casual hand my way as I held ice-white hands in front of me, trembling, weak. I probably looked a pathetic sight. I certainly felt one.

'I've known Troy's family my whole goddamn life. He's a good kid. What am I supposed to tell his folks?' Bailey was staring at me as if fully expecting me to do something to warrant his impending attack.

'I know. And we'll get justice for Troy, I promise. But this ain't the way to do it.'

'The guy's *dangerous,* Blake. Lemme deal with him.' Bailey raised his gun higher.

'This dude ain't worth shit. Don't add to the madness.'

I wasn't expecting such an abrupt conclusion, but Blake's words must have hit their mark somehow because Bailey reluctantly lowered his gun, allowing me to step back a couple of well-needed paces. He and Montgomery looked at me briefly before racing inside shop to assess Troy's irreparable condition. Blake nodded, no more words offered that might aid my failing desperation.

'What the *hell* are you doing?' I asked, desperately hoping they were out of earshot.

'Bob would've shot you, Josh. I did you a favour.'

A favour? Christ. I'd hate to see what would have happened if the guy wasn't on my side.

A few moments later, Bailey reappeared, his face as white as ash. He looked at me as if it was taking everything he had inside not to strangle me. I think Montgomery threw up.

'What the hell did you do?' he spat. I was leaning against Blake's vehicle, the fact that I'd escaped a possible shooting not yet evident on my face. I may as well have been as pale as Troy, no colour in my cheeks to keep my brain functioning or my lips moving.

I shook my head. I remembered punching him, shoving him backwards. Nothing more. He'd fallen. *I think.* It was an accident. I hadn't meant for any of *this* to happen. I would never intentionally hurt anyone, especially a kid.

'What d'he ever do to *you*?' Bailey continued, unwavering, still clutching his gun, a bead of sweat trickling along his cheek. Bailey was right. Troy did nothing to warrant dying, yet he was dead anyway.

'I only shoved him,' I stated, desperate for them to understand I hadn't meant for any of this to happen. It didn't absolve me. I refrained from confirming that I'd punched him first, in the middle of demanding CCTV footage he was never going to give. I didn't need further drama adding to his already complicated day. 'It was an accident, I swear.'

'Tell it to the judge.' Bailey holstered his gun and grabbed my arms, clicking handcuffs over my trembling wrists.

I glanced at Blake, his expression giving nothing away of his thoughts, yet I thought I heard him say, 'I'm sorry Josh,' as my head was pressed into the back of Bailey's awaiting police car, medics already on the way to deal with the poor dead boy behind us. It didn't matter. It was too late now anyway.

26

I was tossed into an empty cell, no shoes, no sanity—left for hours to stare at grey walls and graffiti, far too much time to think. I watched a mug of milky coffee go cold and form a skin, enduring thoughts I couldn't abide, wishing I was anywhere else but here. *I'd murdered someone.* The thought made the lining of my stomach wrench violently, my toes numbing with confusion. I hadn't done it on purpose, of course, but the result was the same. I'd ended someone's life. I couldn't believe it. The kid was *dead* because of me. I closed my eyes, thinking of Georgina, as always, worried she too was dead, that everything I was doing was for *nothing.* What the hell would she think of me now? What would Anna?

I wasn't sure how long I stared at a piece of crumbling plaster, silently making friends with a spider too busy wrapping a dead fly in silk to notice me. When Blake burst into my cell, his face was distorted, both hands raised in the air, his brow tight, jaw twitching. I clambered to my feet, unsure how else to respond. No one had yet confirmed what would happen to me, every officer I'd met since my arrest unconcerned for my declining welfare.

'I know you didn't mean to hurt that boy, Josh,' Blake stated flatly, no time to check I was okay. I opened my mouth but he stopped me, a single shake of his head all that was needed to placate my swimming emotions. 'And I *know* something hasn't been right in Darkridge Hollow for quite some time.' His face was blank. I got the impression he'd known for a while, unable to find anyone who would listen until now.

'Did you find Joe?' I was desperate, hopeful, a heavy stench of Troy's blood still strong, most of it unfortunately still on me.

'No. I looked everywhere. I even went back to that old house where you say Megan lives. But the place was empty.'

I gave Blake a blank look. I wasn't expecting anything else.

'I *did* find out who that crazy woman is, though.' Blake took in a sharp breath, something he didn't look convinced by teetering on trembling lips.

'Who?' I felt my body tense.

'They call her *Melissa*.' Blake stared at me, his features beyond pale.

'Joe's daughter?' My words emerged as a whisper. I got to my feet. That couldn't be possible.

Blake nodded, embarrassed he hadn't joined the dots a while ago.

It took a moment for me to absorb the declaration, thoughts of my wife I suddenly didn't want. Did she know this uncomfortable truth about her sister? Her *twin* sister. Was it the reason she left Darkridge Hollow all those years ago? Why the hell hadn't she told me? I couldn't now assume that everything happening since then wasn't connected. Somehow.

'How did you find out?'

'Martha.'

Of course. We probably should have asked the old woman in the first place. It would have saved time.

'She was asking about you, Josh.'

'Me?'

Blake nodded. 'Said she'd warned you to stay away.'

She had. I hadn't listened. And now I'd made things ten times worse.

'According to her, back in the nineties, a local family were accused of contaminating the water,' Blake continued, not needing a response from me. We both knew who he was talking about. 'Blackhill Lake forms part of the town's main water supply, and after their daughter was killed there, Edward and Shanice Burns supposedly poisoned it as revenge, putting a curse on the entire area. The crops and cattle died and most of the residents were subsequently forced to leave. The Burns family had moved away by then, of course, but the story of the curse stuck around.'

'Emily Burns' parents? The young girl whose murder Joe investigated?' Surely these people didn't believe in shit like that? Curses! *Seriously?*

'Yeah.'

'Why wasn't it documented? If that's the reason most of the town moved away?'

Blake shrugged.

I thought about Jackdoor again, his obsession with Darkridge Hollow and Joe in particular. Surely such a story would have been newsworthy? Did he know something about Melissa?

'You knew, didn't you?' I had to ask.

'Knew what?'

'That I'd need to call you at some point. It's why you gave me your card. How did you know I'd need it, Blake?' It was now with the rest of my meagre belongings, confiscated at the front desk when I was brought here. Probably still had Troy's dried blood on it. It didn't bear thinking about.

Blake gave me a look that made me feel sick. 'I wasn't sure you'd believe me if I told you, but a few months back, I was out on patrol. It was late, my first night on the job. I thought I was imagining a figure coming out of one of those cornfields. A woman. She was covered in blood and carrying a young child in her arms. It looked dead.' He didn't look comforted by his recollection, visions of Mac and Morag still strong in mine. I recalled a different evening, a flock of birds scattering into the night sky, a slim figure dancing in the moonlight. Maybe someone was being murdered that night, too, and I didn't know? Was it Georgina? *Oh my God!*

'I watched as two people were brutally murdered in front of my eyes,' I confessed then, nothing else to say.

'When?'

'Last night.'

'Jesus Christ, Josh. Why didn't you say something?'

'Who would believe me?'

Blake stared at me, knowing no one would have.

I closed my eyes. 'Why didn't *you* investigate what you saw, confront the woman in the cornfield directly?' It seemed the most logical cause of action. He was a police officer, for Christ's sake. The idea that Blake had witnessed something so brutal yet chose to ignore it made my blood boil. Yet I'd been confronted with a similar situation. I ran away.

'Joe warned me to keep my head down. Told me this place needed a someone like me to bring things back on track.'

'Someone like you?'

'Yeah, you know. *Decent.* Law-abiding. He told me there are things about Darkridge Hollow that just ain't right. Said he was sick of it all. Told me I should watch the place for a while. Gather evidence. Stay low.'

'Evidence?'

'Yeah. Anything I could find out about missing kids and tourists.'

'And how much have you found?'

'Enough.'

Shit.

'Are you telling me that Joe already knows what's happening?' Megan's face shot into my mind again. It wasn't pleasant.

'I guess. As soon as I heard your daughter was missing, Josh, I tried looking into it for you, I swear, but for some reason, the case had already been closed.'

'What?' I almost threw up. *Christ.* I wasn't expecting that.

'I'm sorry I didn't tell you. But I needed to check out a few things first. I didn't want anything coming back on me.' Blake looked dejected. For the first time since we met, I saw something I wasn't expecting. Fear.

'What things?'

Blake glanced behind him. 'There are apparently several police officers involved.'

'And *are* there?'

'Oh yeah.'

I thought about Bailey, Montgomery, and McDonald, their displaced attitude now making perfect sense. 'Does Joe know?'

'I think so. I think that's what he was warning me about. Why he needed an insider.'

'He put you at risk.'

'Yeah.'

'Why?'

'That's what I've been trying to find out.' I believed him.

'If this place is so bad, why the hell did Joe get you mixed up in it?' I couldn't imagine Anna's father being that kind of person. Yet, to be honest, I didn't have *any* idea of the type of person he was until today.

'He said it was high time Darkridge Hollow got cleaned up. That it had been left to go to shit for too long. I'm sure he knows more than he's saying. When I told him what I saw that night, he didn't look surprised.'

I thought back to Joe's reaction, the blankness of his expression as I told him about Mac and Morag. *He already knew.*

'I need to get out of here,' I spat. It was true. I couldn't do a damned thing from behind these bars. If Georgina was dead, I needed to know why.

'That's why I'm here.' Blake licked his lips. 'I'll help you, but this can *never* link back to me.'

'Absolutely.'

Blake probably wanted to tell me all this before, our friendly *chat* at The Cornfield Eatery merely a way to explain what he knew. Yet, like me, he assumed I'd think him mad, so he chose to stay silent. I'd thought the same thing. It didn't matter now. I was desperate for my friend to do whatever it took to get me out of this place. I had no idea how this was going to work or what he was planning but I was willing to go along with whatever he deemed necessary.

'We gotta make it look like you escaped,' Blake confirmed. I nodded, Blake's words music to my ears.

'Anything.' At that point, I would have done anything. *Already had.*

'There's a car out back and the keys are on the front desk.'

'How do I-'

'Piece of cake. You overpowered me. Punched me in the face. I didn't see it coming. I was just bringing you a drink, my guard down.' Blake was serious. It didn't matter I would look the very monster they all believed me to be. I nodded, grateful he was willing to get me out of here whilst I still had breath in my body to do so. 'Take the keys from my belt. I'll pretend you knocked me out. I'll sit here disoriented. That should give you enough time.' He smashed a brimming mug of coffee against a greying wall, making me flinch.

'Won't they expect you to have a bruise?'

'Yeah. Punch me.'

'No.' Why did I ask?

'Punch me. Come on, Josh, just do it.'

'Blake-'

'Just *do* it.'

I didn't want to but I punched him. Not as hard as I probably should have and it may have connected a bit feebly. But Blake was an ally. I didn't want to hurt him. He was a friend I never expected to make.

'How do I get past the other officers?'

Blake smiled, rubbing his jaw where my fist had barely touched him. He didn't say anything about that, thankfully. 'Josh, this town ain't much bigger than Darkridge Hollow. There are never more than two or three cops on duty at any one time, and I've already sent Bob and Will out to buy donuts.'

I looked confused. 'Will?'

'Deputy Chief McDonald.'

Of course. I had the distinct impression the deputy lived for nothing else, his protruding belly proof of that, comfort food a welcome intrusion to his day.

'We gotta act fast,' Blake added, glancing behind him.

I swallowed, this moment unexpected. 'Okay, fine.'

'Ready?'

'As I'll ever be.' I'd never felt so sick in my life.

I was unprepared for what happened next, the entire moment surreal. Blake turned around, facing me, our plan about to unfold, our eyes set in firm concentration. I was focused on my own requirements, unaware that he'd stopped abruptly in the doorway, motionless, an obtuse, confused stare aimed my way. I opened my mouth to speak, convinced that Bailey and the deputy had returned, our plan ruined, this merely another in a long line of impossible moments hell-bent on destroying me.

Blake started choking, something clawing the back of his throat as blood erupted from his shocked mouth. His eyes were blank, unseeing. I staggered backwards, appalled to see spikes of cold steel protruding from Blake's stomach, fresh blood erupting from his body. My friend glanced down briefly before lunging forward, falling to his knees, blood spitting from his lips as he spluttered and gagged. He opened his mouth in shock, unavoidably projecting angry red liquid my way. *Fucking hell!*

I glanced up, traumatised, not expecting to find Megan a couple of feet behind, emerging from the shadows like a demon possessed. She had a pitchfork in her hands, the bloodied thing aimed now where Blake had only seconds earlier been standing.

'Goddamn it, Josh,' she muttered, looking from me to Blake as if I should have heeded her warnings, known better. 'You were *expressly* told to leave this place. Now look whatcha've made me do.' Megan had an unhinged look on her face, eyes that saw nothing but fury, a cold demonic stare I couldn't acknowledge.

What the hell?

I glanced down. Blake was on the floor, bleeding out, dying in front of my eyes, like Troy, his last breath ready to leave his body, yet another corpse brought about because of my immeasurable actions. I dropped to my knees, needing to check him, to *help* him, but Megan raised her bloodied pitchfork towards my face, pressing it against my jugular, tutting loudly. I was forced to lift my chin along with my hands, slowly rising to my feet as cold steel was pressed against my clammy neck, the smell of blood overwhelming. I was in no position to do anything other than what I was told.

'I just want to check he's okay,' I found myself saying, knowing, of course, she didn't care. Blake wasn't okay. We both knew it.

Megan scoffed, rolling unfeeling eyes skyward before plunging the pitchfork into Blake's spine for a second time, leaving me in no doubt as to her intentions. Blake grunted, falling silent.

'There now. No need to go worrin' 'bout *him* anymore,' she laughed, licking her lips, clinging firmly to the blood-soaked weapon in her grasp. There was something seriously wrong with this woman, the way she was grinning, the coldness in her eyes. 'They'll say you broke free, attacked *poor* Blake and left him for dead, just like you did with Troy.'

Where did she assume I would get a pitchfork from inside a cell? How did she think she could pin this on me?

'I didn't mean to kill Troy. It was an accident.' Never in my life did I ever expect to utter such a ridiculous sentence. 'But *you* just killed a police officer.' It was true. I'm sure she didn't care.

'I killed plenty, Josh.' Her confirmation wasn't comforting.

'Why Blake?' I couldn't believe what she'd done to the poor man.

'He was getting too close.'

'Too close to what?'

'You'll find out.' She grinned then, enjoying herself. I rued the day I ever met the stupid bitch.

'What the hell do you *want* with me?' I could barely speak, barely able to acknowledge my now-dead friend. What had I *ever* done to her? I thought about my recent escape, cold warnings from unhinged strangers, an unwanted desperation to get me on a plane, everything pointing towards a much bigger problem. 'The police will be back any moment,' I concluded. I was desperate, yet it wasn't a comfort. I still didn't know for sure *how* the police were involved.

Megan rolled her eyes again then as if she was finding

my company excruciating. 'Joshua, Joshua, you don't seem to appreciate my influence with the local police.' She jabbed Blake's leg with her pitchfork, confirming what we both already knew. He wasn't getting up any time soon. Blake was dead. 'Jeez, Josh, looks like you developed a taste for killin' folk.' She tilted her head, a smile on her face I didn't appreciate. 'It's a real shame Bob and Will got held up in town with Tommy ain't it? They probably would've enjoyed this.'

'What do you want with me?' I repeated, unable to stop myself from yelling. She obviously wanted something. I'd be dead otherwise.

'Patience, Josh. It's all part of my plan.'

'What plan?' I didn't know what she was talking about, didn't want to know what she had to say. I couldn't stop staring at Blake's body, more blood soaking into my boots, more memories I'd never forget.

'All in good time. Now move it.' Megan jabbed the end of her bloodied fork towards me. I did as I was told, unable to do much else. Mike was behind her in the corridor, handcuffs in his grip and a grin on his face. He was wearing a police uniform. I couldn't assume he wasn't a real officer, wasn't part of a much bigger problem I didn't want to address. If I had any ideas about grabbing her weapon, they were short-lived, the sight of Mike ensuring I thought twice. I didn't want to end up like Blake. Instead, I was forced to leave him on the floor of that police cell, the door open, his keys now in Megan's unhinged possession. Could this day get any worse?

27

I had no idea where they were taking me, although it was obvious I wasn't getting out of this easily. Not this time. Megan was unwilling to relinquish the grip on her weapon as Mike bundled me into the back of her truck, Blake's blood still dripping along the handle, coating her fingers. I wouldn't have been surprised if she'd licked them, one by one, relishing the moment, enjoying herself. It was quite sickening, actually. I could do nothing but go along with this ridiculous charade, hoping beyond logic I'd somehow find the help I knew wasn't coming. They collected Tommy a few streets away, both men chatting, ignoring me, Bob Bailey and Deputy Chief *William* McDonald left to consume doughnuts alone. They'd shortly venture unwittingly back to the station, another scene awaiting them I could never change. Was this a setup? Did they already *know* what was going to happen?

We ended up miles from Abbotts View, Darkridge Hollow a distant unwanted memory, both locations oddly more welcoming than here. I wondered where Joe was, the idea of finding him growing slimmer by the second, the idea of finding help, damned near impossible. I was handcuffed, gagged, *and* blindfolded, just to add more shit to the equation, my hands inaccessible, material stuffed in my mouth that tasted like cow dung and sweat. I could barely breathe, a disgusting combination of filth and animal faeces overwhelming every sense I had. Terror had embedded itself into my chest, leaving me to choke my last breath in the back of Megan's truck.

It seemed to take forever but when the vehicle eventually stopped I was ushered outside, my covered eyes unable to see, my gagged mouth unable to scream. Our route little more than a dirt track that slopped downward, my ankles twisting from constant stumbling, my boots offering no protection, my bound hands unable to steady me if I fell. Megan taunted me, her throwaway words confusing, that late afternoon sun burning into my memories, forever haunting my emotions.

'I have a big surprise for you Josh,' she called out, laughing now, her tone telling me it wouldn't be anything good.

I took a breath that caught the back of my throat as my boots scraped the rocky ground, forced to hold back muffled gasps of pain for fear of further repercussions. Although I couldn't see, I could tell she was still clinging onto that pitchfork, prodding the ground every few steps. Her laugh was demonic, her face no doubt awash with excitement that only added to my growing sense of turmoil. Tommy's grip was unmoving. Stiffened by authority and dictation, he played his part well, his identity held in higher regard than he should have possessed. With each inescapable sound I made, he tightened his grasp on my shoulder, stripping every molecule of dignity from my already failed existence.

'Shut your mouth or *I* will,' he spat, deep-rooted acrimony for human life something I'd *never* appreciate.

I hadn't spoken a word, couldn't, the gag too tight, my restraints threatening to cut off my circulation. Tommy raised his hand, yet I was unable to register what was happening until my cheekbone felt the brunt of his gloved fist. I fell sideways, the ground coming up to meet me. I coughed, choking back blood that ran down my throat, nowhere else to go, more grunts of frustration erupting from my wilfully silenced lips. I could do nothing as Tommy stood overhead, his arms tense with a weight of authority he had no business holding, the significance of this situation taking hold like a bomb exploding in my head.

He grabbed me as if I was a rag doll, pulling the blindfold from my eyes and yanking me into a sitting position. If I wasn't gagged and handcuffed, I'd have instigated a fight I'm not sure which of us would have emerged alive. He glared into my eyes, seeing nothing there but contempt. I'd honestly never hated anyone so much in my life. A droplet of sweat ran along the ridge of my nose, my fists clenched tightly behind my back, my legs sprawled unceremoniously across the filthy ground. I was at his whim, nothing I could do, my body hovering between thoughts of my daughter and my dead wife—poor Georgina, Mac, Morag, Troy, and now Blake, unfounded casualties of this entire goddamned thing.

Surely these people *must* have known the value of family and love, yet they were torn apart now by hatred and intolerance—humanity at its worst. I dug my fingernails into my cuffed hands, not daring to breathe in case I provoked something more permanent. Why didn't they just kill me? Why were they prolonging the agony? Tommy dragged me to my feet, pulling me roughly along the overgrowth into a disused barn, my eyes still adjusting to the pale light around us, his soulless face nothing but a grotesque display of oppression.

A hand touched mine and I turned to see Megan staring at me, a woman that, until a couple of days ago, I'd wrongly assumed normal. My cheek was swollen and bruised, my mouth a bloodied mess, eyes burning with an unyielding fear for the reality of this impossible situation. She peeled the gag from my mouth, a strong taste of shit now on my tongue along with words I could never say in front of a lady.

'You'd better choose fast, Josh?' Megan spat, a broad smile on her face that made her eyes glisten and mine narrow.

'Choose what?' I choked, unable to speak without dust tickling my throat.

'Why, how you're gonna die, of course. It'll be quick, and if you're lucky I'll show mercy.' Her dispassionate words echoed around the barn, a glorified notion she was capable of such a thing, completely undeserved. It made me want to vomit. Was *this* her surprise? To choose how I die?

'Seriously?' I asked. I didn't want the answer. '*This* is your surprise? Why drag me out here when you left Blake in a police cell?' I swallowed. Is this where she'd brought Georgina? It didn't bear thinking about.

Megan grinned, something in her tone unseeing, blank, already dead. I'd never met anyone like her, nor did I want to again. 'No, Josh, of course not. This is just a little bonus, for me. *Your* surprise comes later,' she joked mockingly in my ear.

I was forced to my knees, enduring mud that reeked of stale urine and odours too foul to describe, a sense of despair overwhelming all who'd inhabited this hellhole before me. Was this where she brought her *victims?* No living creature would choose this despicable place. Even the rats had the good sense to stay away. I clenched my fists, cowering on crippled knees, forced to stay silent and unable to prevent the tears already falling across my reddened cheeks.

A sound—a shrill, explosive reverberation that rooted me to the spot, taking the very breath from my body, jolting electricity from my head to my toes. A gunshot. Clean. Quick. It was over in an instant, making me question if it had happened at all. Had she shot me? Had Tommy?

Silence, followed by a faint flutter of bird's wings overhead. I couldn't tell if it was my heartbeat pounding or Megan's.

I bit into my bottom lip, an automatic response, this location imprinted forever in my mind. A drop of blood landed on my jeans, soaking the fabric, a taste of iron in my mouth. I thought about Anna and how annoyed she would be at my carelessness. I wanted to laugh at the irony. Everything in my life suddenly felt fake, superficial, pathetic. I blinked hard, struggling to breathe, the feelings running through my body so strong, the pain so real. I didn't know how to handle this. All I could think about was Anna—my beautiful Anna. *Was I dying?* Was this how it felt?

There was a commotion around me, someone shouting, but I was too focused on my pain to notice. We were miles from anywhere, miles from civilisation, the rational world a place I now questioned existed. No one would find my body here. Maybe that was the point. Megan shifted her attention to Tommy, cursing his carelessness, the guy still holding the smoking shotgun he'd used on me, still hot, my body rapidly succumbing to the reality of what had happened. I slumped to the ground, my hands still cuffed behind my back, my jaw taking the brunt of the incoming dirt.

'Melissa? You out here?' A voice outside sounded like Joe, yet I couldn't take it in. He was yelling, unaware of what was unfolding inside this barn, yet he must have heard the gunshot, no doubt already heading in our direction. I couldn't turn my head, couldn't yell back. I tried to speak but my mouth wouldn't cooperate. 'Mel! Where in darnation are you?' Joe's desperate voice continued, his lungs struggling, his quivering tone imposing.

'For the love of-' Megan sucked in a mouthful of air, frustrated to have been so rudely interrupted, her eyes rolling back in her head. She nodded towards Tommy who headed outside, the smoking gun still in his hands. I couldn't allow him to shoot Joe, too. I still wasn't sure *who* Melissa was, the thought of meeting Anna's sister too much for my brain to contend with. 'Sweet dreams, Josh,' Megan whispered before placing the gag back over my mouth. I was dragged backwards, my right leg and hip exploding with pain as Mike shoved me carelessly against a post. Thick ropes were wrapped around my shoulders and neck, the same type they'd used at the house. *Fitting.* I was once again left alone, ready to pass out, the world already tilted sideways. Is this how my life ends? In a barn? In the middle of nowhere? No way of *ever* finding my child then.

I needed to speak to Joe, visions of Blake's lifeless body still fresh in my mind, Troy's corpse set to haunt me forever. I needed to explain. I lunged out wildly, hoping to make as much noise as I could, alert him to my presence and *warn* him. I kicked blindly into the void, connecting with a bucket, the thing clattering loudly around the dank space. When Joe raced through the open barn door, I almost didn't believe he was real.

'Josh, what the hell happened?' Joe knelt by my side, pulling the gag from my mouth.

'Help me,' I spluttered. The pain was so intense I could barely function. I'd been shot and I was losing blood. It was all I knew. I had so many questions, so many emotions, my body already turning cold. 'He shot me.' I expected Tommy to shoot Joe in the back, sending the poor sod to meet Blake and the daughter he hadn't seen in a decade. I couldn't let that happen.

Joe tilted his head towards the rafters, tears I wasn't expecting to see rolling freely down both cheeks. 'Goddamn it, Josh, I'm so sorry. I had *no* idea who you were.'

I had questions of my own, plenty of them. My confusion was evident, my body in agony, and I was losing blood. I didn't respond.

'I gotta make this right,' Joe was muttering, removing

his jacket, tearing his shirtsleeve, pressing firm hands across my right side to stem bleeding from a wound I didn't yet know the extent of. I couldn't move.

'You *knew* all this time what Megan was doing, yet you chose to stay quiet?' I was angry, needing answers I didn't expect to get, senseless words leaving my desperate mouth.

'You gotta understand that when Anna left, her sister wasn't actin' right. She hadn't been right since the night Emily Burns died.'

'What the *hell* does Emily Burns have to do with *any* of this?' *Or Anna's twin?* I wasn't interested in a history lesson. I was too cold, Blake's earlier confirmation about that family, too vivid.

Joe sighed. 'Melissa killed that black girl, Josh.' His confession barely registered with me.

'What are you talking about?'

'Anna found them out by the lake. The child was already dead, of course, nothin' we could do 'bout that.' Joe was looking at me but he didn't see me, not really. His expression didn't change, remaining stone-faced, tears falling onto his reddened cheeks, memories forged in iron that he would never forget.

'Are you *serious?*'

Joe nodded.

'Your daughter *killed* someone?' A bigger picture was emerging and I was becoming uncomfortably aware of who we were talking about. Joe couldn't look at me, no emotion, no response. It was all old news to him, nothing he could do to change it now.

'Who is *Megan,* Joe?' I still didn't want to grasp this thing, still wasn't willing to put two and two together. I *knew* who she was. I just didn't want to hear it.

Joe sighed. 'She's Melissa, of course.'

I glanced at the old man, wishing things were different, wishing I hadn't asked. Nothing made sense. Why would she assume someone else's name? I couldn't think of her by any other now. She would always be *Megan* to me. I finally appreciated why no one in town *knew* who she was. They only knew Joe's daughter. No wonder I'd received so many blank looks and disinterested dismissals. No wonder they thought I was insane. I thought back to the photographs in Joe's cabin, grateful my wife was not a mirror image of her twisted twin. I'm not sure I'd have coped well with coming face to face with Anna's double on that misty, isolated road. I wished to Christ I'd known who she was. I thought of my missing photographs, the denial, Megan's lies—that goddamned spiked piece of wood still housing sections of shredded tyre. *It was Anna's sister the whole time.* Panic began to rise in my gut. I no longer cared I was bleeding to death and probably wouldn't make it out of here alive.

'Why would she lie about her identity?' I couldn't move, couldn't think. I was expecting her to return any second and silence my thoughts *permanently.*

'I guess she wanted to get to you, Josh.'

'Me?' *What the hell had I done?*

'Yeah.'

'Why?'

'Revenge maybe? I don't know.'

'Revenge for *what?*' I'm not sure whether blood loss was playing a part, but I was now on the verge of passing out.

Joe shook his head. 'Melissa couldn't have known who you were when she found you out on that road. I guess she saw your photos, realised who you both were. It must've come as a shock.' Joe wasn't answering my question, just throwing out random comments that made no sense. 'I should have realised, but how could I?'

'I don't understand.' I was getting stressed now.

'Josh-' Joe paused. 'Melissa is Georgina's *mom.*'

28

I could do nothing but stare at Joe, unable to absorb what he was saying. He was wrapping a sleeve of his now torn shirt around my leg, stemming the blood flow, soothing my suffering, yet his words had already left a hole that would never truly heal. He was talking to me, but I struggled to understand a word he said.

'If I'd known who you were, Josh, I'd have done more, I swear.' He didn't confirm the colour of my skin discarded the possible idea that I could have married his daughter. Probably didn't think me worthy.

I scoffed. 'So, you're saying you didn't offer more help because you assumed I was a *stranger?* Nobody important. Nothing special. Just some foreign idiot passing through, a black man you could discard like trash?'

'It ain't like that.'

'Then explain it to me please, because none of this makes sense.' *Anna* was Georgina's mum. Until three days ago I didn't even know Melissa existed.

'Melissa was always promiscuous. She'd gotten herself pregnant several times before she carried a child full term, had affairs with most of the men in town, caused a lotta shit for everyone. She believed she might *never* have a child. Saw it as a punishment from God for Emily and the others. I can't tell you how many doctors tried to help. How much money we threw away.'

'Others?'

Joe nodded. He didn't look at me, instead chose to grind his teeth in frustration. 'Of course, when Megan was born, it didn't take us long to question how far she might take things.'

'Megan?'

Joe glanced towards the floor. 'Jeez, Josh, Megan is Georgina's real name.'

'What?' I tried to sit up but pain shot through my spine, my brain rapidly succumbing to more shit.

'It's why I didn't realise the significance of who you were.' Joe was talking as if he was innocent in all this, unaffected by events he was proclaiming an unfeigned ignorance of. 'How was *I* to know my goddamn granddaughter was in trouble?' He hung his head, his shame obvious. 'I didn't know anyone called Georgina. Anna must have changed the kid's name to protect her identity.'

I thought about Melissa, the woman I'd only ever known as Megan, and Megan, the child I'd only ever known as Georgina. My wedding photo would have come as quite a shock, the little girl in the passenger seat, the woman's long-lost *daughter*.

'Why would Anna take her sister's child?' And why had she never told me?

'We were worried Melissa might kill her own baby. She'd already killed several others by then.'

I swallowed, my missing child part of a much bigger problem than I realised. I didn't know if I'd ever see her again.

Joe continued talking to himself, my presence of no concern, trying to process years of torment I'm not sure he'd ever accept. 'Mel was convinced *God* was talkin' to her, tellin' her to save Darkridge Hollow and reverse a curse she'd started. She only wanted to save the dyin' crops and bring back the dwindling residents.' He almost sounded as if he was making excuses, making her actions sound acceptable under the circumstances. 'After a few months, we figured Melissa was plannin' somethin'. Her behaviour was erratic, wrong. So, late one night, Anna took her niece to protect the child from her sister's twisted mind, leavin' Darkridge Hollow to begin a new life someplace else. I didn't know where she was goin', only that she'd taken her passport and wasn't plannin' on comin' back. We couldn't take the risk that Melissa wouldn't sacrifice her own child.' Joe didn't look at me. Probably couldn't.

Georgina wasn't mine, not my real flesh and blood, but I'd raised her, loved her with all my heart. The idea that her mother wasn't even Anna but some twisted, murdering *freak,* totally freaked me out. No wonder Anna ran. I thought about that handkerchief, the one *Megan* had offered me on the day of the crash, the letters M.E. printed in a corner. *Melissa Everley.* Or was it *Megan* Everley? I felt sick again. Anna had one just like it. It was probably from the same collection, a pair no doubt—*twins,* a reminder of a life unfulfilled. I couldn't assume Tommy wasn't, in fact, Georgina's real dad. The idea made me cringe.

'Where's Georgina, Joe?' I almost vomited, unwilling to acknowledge what I now knew to be true, terrified the old man already knew her fate. Was *that* Melissa's surprise? That she had my child this whole time? *Was Joe in on this?*

Joe shrugged. 'I don't know.'

'Joe?'

'I don't know!' He sighed deeply, taking too long to look at me, tears cascading over pale cheeks. I didn't know how much more shit could I take.

'Does Melissa have *Georgina,* Joe?' I felt sick. It didn't bear thinking about. If she could sacrifice other kids, why not her *own?* I didn't dare ask. I still couldn't call my child

Megan. *Megan* was the woman who'd locked me up, whose twisted partner had punched me, *shot* me. Georgina was an innocent in all this, her other family merely strangers Anna rarely talked about. For the first time ever, I understood why. Had Melissa killed her daughter? Did she even appreciate who the twelve-year-old was?

Joe shrugged. 'I figured she must have her held up somewhere. I don't know for sure, of course, but I was out all night lookin'.

'Why did you leave me to deal with the police by myself?' I needed to know why he'd disappeared. I'd been through hell since then.

'Thought it would be easier if you didn't get mixed up in my problems.'

'Georgina *is* my problem.'

'I figured if the cops took you back to the motel, I might have a better chance of finding Melissa and Megan.' He paused before muttering 'Georgina,' closing his eyes at the thought of the only name the poor girl had ever known. 'I searched our old house. Thought she might've taken her there. The place has been empty for years.' I know. I couldn't get it out of my head. 'Melissa goes back there sometimes, rememberin' when she and Anna were little. Likes to pretend everythin' is still the same. Better times.' Joe smiled, hardly able to look at me, attempting to remember those *better times* himself, failing miserably.

'She doesn't *live* there now?' I wasn't relieved to hear it.

'Hell, no. That place ain't fit for shit.' Joe attempted a laugh that didn't reach either of us. He glared at me, his hands red with my drying blood, veins that stood out against his clenched fists. 'She lives with me in my cabin when she ain't runnin' around with Tommy and the others.' Joe didn't seem comfortable sharing that knowledge, knowing what he knew. Knowing he was an accomplice.

I opened my mouth to speak but thought better of it.

Joe sighed, slumping to the ground beside me. 'You gotta appreciate that Melissa ain't right.' He tapped the side of his head. 'She ain't been right for a while.'

'What's *wrong* with her?' I didn't want to sound rude but there was obviously something seriously wrong with her.

'The doctor called it "Paranoid Delusional Disorder". Melissa believed Emily Burns was trying to kill her. Had nightmares 'bout it for weeks. Said God was talkin' to her, showing her the light.'

'And *was* Emily trying to kill her?' I doubted it, but I needed to ask.

Joe shook his head. 'Course not. But it tipped somethin' in her mind. Something bad. She's been killin' for the last twenty-seven years. Got a real taste for it, too. Even those local folk who got too close to the truth.'

Joe's words were a kick to the gut. Why did he have to sound so blasé? *Twenty-seven years?* Surely I was hearing him wrong? I was still trying to come to terms with the idea that Megan was actually Melissa, that Georgina was Megan, and the woman I believed was her mum, was, in fact, her *aunt.* The idea that killing an innocent eleven-year-old child had triggered a lifetime's worth of murder wasn't exactly up there with the shit I needed in my head, the concept of a subsequently increased death toll unimaginable. I thought of Blake, a good man, dead and gone, because of that woman. I'm sure Joe was only telling me this because he assumed I'd be dead before nightfall and therefore it wouldn't matter.

'You *knew* all this and said nothing?' I attempted to back away, the man by my side a potential madman, the ropes around my body preventing any shift in trajectory that might have saved me. *Was I next?* Joe reached trembling hands towards me, his body shaking wildly.

'Try to understand. I needed to protect my family. I had

no choice but to cover up what happened all those years ago.' Joe was talking but I couldn't hear him, his words insane. He was untying my ropes, my body aching with the effort.

'And what about last night?' I'd stood in his cabin, sick to my stomach by the shit I'd witnessed, two more deaths that could have been prevented.

'She's my daughter, Josh. I'll always protect my girls, you gotta know that.'

'But why the *fuck* would she kill so many people?' I could still see her blood-soaked face, a grimace I believed I'd imagined.

'Because she wholly *believed* the curse that family put on this town, watched several of our animals die in agony, stood by while all her friends moved away. It took a toll.'

'You do know that so-called *curse* was nothing but poison put into the water supply because the poor Burns family were too devastated to think straight? Anyone can see that. How stupid must you be to believe anything else? It wouldn't create a *killer*.' It was true.

Joe shrugged.

A thought popped into my head that wasn't pleasant. 'Did *Anna* have a hand in killing Emily, too?'

'She played a part in it, yeah.' Joe glared at me as if I was an idiot, that I of all people should appreciate the bond between twins. Until today, I didn't even know my wife had a *sister*, let alone a twin. 'She saw the two of them arguing that night. She was only tryin' to help. Twins can be close, Josh, very close. Melissa stabbed Emily five times in front of Anna. Thought nothin' of it. But Anna knew if the girl lived, her sister's life would be over. Anna and Melissa were inseparable back then, Josh. You should've seen 'em.' He laughed, remembering better times I honestly couldn't picture. 'They made sure that girl was dead before dragging her body to the lakes edge. That's when I found them, covered in blood, tryin' to cover their tracks.'

I couldn't take it in. I couldn't think. 'Any other revelations you want to share with me?' It was a joke. I didn't expect an answer, was still expecting *Melissa* to storm back through the barn door any second.

'When I found the girls' mom dead at the bottom of our basement steps a few months later, I thought she'd slipped and hit her head. That was until I saw the knife wound in her leg.'

'What?' I jolted my head around to look at Joe, his own hanging low. 'Someone stabbed your *wife?*'

'Yeah. I found a knife under Melissa's bed. I confronted her, of course. Mel broke down. Told me Clare had discovered what had happened to Emily and Jackdoor.'

'Jackdoor? Please don't tell me Melissa killed him, too?' I almost laughed. This was ridiculous.

Joe could barely look at me. 'My girls acted cagey for two weeks after his body was discovered, but we *couldn't* have known they were involved.' He was wringing his hands frantically.

'*They*?' Surely not Anna?

'Melissa didn't mean to kill her mom, of course. She just panicked. But she'd caught the femoral artery and bled out fast, her fall ensuring she never got up. Mel later confessed she'd only lashed out because Clare had uncovered the truth about that journalist, too, the poor kid still traumatised over Emily. She just wanted it to go away.'

Traumatised? *Seriously?* 'Did *Melissa* kill Jackdoor?' I repeated, firmly. She was a serial killer. A freak. Why *wouldn't* she?

'No.' Joe paused. 'Anna did. She didn't want the guy snooping around, digging up shit about her sister and Emily Burns. Told me she couldn't let that happen. I *had* to cover it all up to protect my children.'

Bloody hell. I wasn't expecting that. Anna had played a

major role in the murder of an eleven-year-old child *and* she had killed a grown man. *My* Anna. *My* wife. The woman I thought I knew better than anyone else in the world. I leaned forward and threw up, nowhere else to aim my bodily fluids other than into my lap. It wasn't pleasant. The idea my wife was a killer, too, honestly hadn't entered my head.

'She's still in Blackhill Lake.' Joe was whispering, remembering.

'Who?' He certainly wasn't talking about Anna.

'My wife, Clare.' *Who else?*

Jesus Christ. What the hell was I listening to? I thought about Anna again, the secrets she'd kept from me, the entire family crazy, it seemed.

'I had to protect my girls.' Joe swallowed, unsure what else to say. 'But my shame became too much and we had no choice but to move outta town, away from our family home. That secret cost me everythin' I had, Josh.'

'But you were a *police officer!*' He was supposed to be the deputy. Someone to trust.

Joe laughed. 'How could I uncover the truth without exposin' what my girls had done and sacrificin' my entire family in the process? They were fourteen years old. What else could I do?' He glared at me. '*You've* got a daughter, Josh. You'd never do that to Megan, would you?'

I still couldn't think of Georgina as Megan, confusion swamping this day, blood loss no doubt the culprit. 'Do you *know* what your daughter does to innocent tourists, Joe?' I couldn't believe I was asking. I'd wrongly assumed he would be as shocked as me to discover what I'd witnessed, painful visions of Mac and Morag looming whenever I closed my eyes. No wonder the old man wasn't overly surprised when I'd explained about those backpackers. He'd seen it all before.

Joe nodded. 'I've tried to get her help. You gotta believe

me.'

'*Help?* Are you kidding me?' I was yelling. I was in pain and it hurt. I didn't dare ask what she did with the bodies and it wasn't a comfort to know Joe was in this thing up to his neck. I thought about Blackhill Lake, that unassuming location filled with far more than I'd ever imagined.

29

I wasn't ready for Melissa's return, her strained vocals jolting me violently back to this impossible moment, no time to contemplate my current position. I didn't want to look at her, knowing what she'd done, Joe and I nothing but two unhinged people with only each other to express immovable irrational thinking.

'Oh my goodness, what do we have here?' She stopped in the doorway, unnerving me, her entire persona a contradiction to her immeasurable actions. 'I guess I should've known you'd show up here, Pa.' Melissa laughed, seemingly unsurprised to see the old man kneeling beside me, covered in blood, preventing me from bleeding to death where I sat.

Joe got to his feet. 'What the hell are you doin' Mel?' There was a wobble in his tone, something in his eyes I was glad I couldn't see.

'What I always do, Daddy,' she confirmed, hands on her hips, head to one side. It was uncomfortable, hearing her refer to Joe like that. Tommy was hovering behind her, the recently discharged shotgun still in his clenched fist. I couldn't assume he hadn't reloaded it, ready now for round two.

'This ain't right. You gotta stop.' Joe looked pale.

Melissa scoffed, staring at her father as if *he* was the

crazy one. 'Why should I stop? You never helped me. You never loved me.' She was whimpering like a child, her full lips pouting.

'That's all I've *ever* done,' Joe spluttered, unsure how he was going to resolve this thing, too late now to redeem himself.

'You made me believe someone had snatched my baby girl, when all this time she was alive and well.' I thought I saw a tear in Melissa's eyes. I couldn't look at her, instead glanced at Joe, wondering what was going through his mind. I still couldn't think of her by any other name than *Megan.*

Melissa laughed, noticing the pained expression on my face. 'It's okay, I know who *you* are, Josh. I've known since I picked your pathetic corpse off the roadside. *Megan* and I have been gettin' re-acquainted.'

She spoke my daughter's real name as if I had no right to question anything. I shot upright, the pain raced through my body almost causing me to pass out, the shock on my face obvious. Was Georgina a*live?*

'Surprise!' she laughed, the reason she'd brought me out here suddenly painfully obvious.

'What the *fuck* have you done to her?' I screamed, unable to stop myself from swearing. I couldn't stand up, several ropes still cutting into my body, Joe still very much concerned by the continued blood loss that was making me weak. He'd given up trying to untie me. I wasn't now convinced those ropes weren't keeping me *alive.*

'Oh, *please.* Spare me the theatrics.' Melissa rolled impatient eyes, pacing the barn. 'She's *fine.*' She paused, hovering above me. 'Did you think I targeted you because you're *black,* Josh?'

The thought had indeed crossed my mind. I shrugged. Melissa laughed. It wasn't a comfort. I already *knew* why she'd targeted me. Because I had her *kid.* I didn't confirm it.

She turned to her father, his fists and jaw clenched tightly, crimson blood mocking us both. 'You put me through *hell,* Pa,' she spat, walking directly up to the old man and pushing him in the chest. She was in his face, the pitchfork still in her grip, her clenched fist something I assumed might become our downfall before this day was out. I expected her to plunge it into him as she had with Blake. She didn't seem to mind killing people on a whim.

'I only wanted to help.' Joe was trembling.

'You knew all these years that *Anna* had taken my baby butcha said nothin'!' Melissa was yelling, her face a mixture of snot and tears. I couldn't stand to hear my dead wife's name muttered so readily from her poisonous tongue.

'You *needed* help.'

'I needed *you!*'

'You were sick, Melissa. What else could we do?'

'I needed support, not persecution.' Melissa was sobbing, the fork in her hands trembling. She turned to me, her eyes dancing with personal suffering I didn't need to witness. 'Do you know that God spoke to me in my hour of need, Josh?' Was she asking, or telling?

I shrugged. I honestly didn't know what else to do. I didn't *care.*

'You should've seen the look on your face that day out on the road,' she scoffed. *Jesus,* was she laughing at me? 'It was priceless.' Melissa was pacing again, chuckling now. 'Butcha gotta understand that when I found you, I didn't know who you were. How could I? You just showed up, more *stupid* tourists lookin' to get what they deserved.' I thought about Mac and Morag, forced to swallow a painful lump that caught in my throat.

'Why did you tell me your name was Megan?'

Melissa grinned. 'Call it karma, if you like. But it just seemed kinda fun to give myself the name I gave my baby all those years ago.'

'*Crazy, fucking bitch!*' Did I say that aloud?

'Maybe.' Melissa closed her eyes. 'Do you believe in fate, Josh?'

I didn't answer. I wasn't interested in playing any more of her games.

'Human blood is key to my rituals. The sacrifice of strangers is the most satisfyin' achievement.' She was breathing deeply, her so-called accomplishments nothing but brutal murder she didn't see was wrong. It was unnerving. 'We all must sacrifice ourselves in the end, anyway, each and every one of us a part of God's bigger plan.' Melissa's feature's darkened. 'But when you sacrifice children,' she tilted her head skyward, her eyes closed against a world she could never be a part of, 'it holds the power to produce *wonderful* crops. They're pure, Josh. Innocent. Not like the rest of 'em. Not like *you.*'

Melissa opened her eyes, glaring at me. 'One day I'll break that curse, I swear. I'll set everythin' right in this old town, I will.' The woman was sucking in air as if breathing pure, clean oxygen, her words her gospel, her emotions strong, genuinely believing every word she uttered. She lowered herself to the ground next to my rapidly failing body so I wouldn't miss her next declaration. 'I didn't mean to start this thing, you gotta believe that.' I didn't believe a word she was saying. 'I was plannin' on takin' your money, your child, your *life*. Imagine my surprise when I checked your wallet and saw my sister's smilin' face lookin' up at me from a goddamn weddin' photo?'

I couldn't look at her, didn't want her to see my reaction.

'I was confused, at first, why a picture of my sister would be in *your* possession. Then it all slotted into place. How Megan's disappearance just happened to coincide with my sister's sudden desire to travel.' She stared at Joe who now had Tommy's reloaded gun pointed towards his head.

'I couldn't believe that the child in the passenger seat was *my* child until I checked the birthmark on her shoulder and date of birth on her passport. How could this tiny thing in front of me be the very baby I believed had been brutally snatched away by God as punishment for what I did to Emily Burns all those years ago? You see, Josh. Megan was born with the very birthmark on her left shoulder you told me your *daughter* had.' She emphasised the word "daughter" as if it was a laughable concept. 'I once believed it was a sign of the devil. Thought she was sent to destroy me. Funny, don'tcha think?'

I scoffed. Nothing about this was funny. I wasn't thinking of anything beyond getting away from this mad woman, getting my child from wherever she was and running like hell. I still wasn't convinced she was alive. Joe glanced towards his daughter, the two momentarily exchanging glances that made me nervous.

'Where is she?' Joe queried shakily, reading my mind, asking the question we were both desperate to know. 'Where's Megan?'

Melissa took a breath. 'I just wanted you to feel how I felt, Josh, when Megan was taken from *me* all those years ago. I wanted you to understand how it felt, losin' a child and havin' everyone tell you it was in God's hands, God's will.' Melissa was grinding her teeth, her knuckles pure white where she was holding the pitchfork too tightly, her cheeks grey. She was ignoring her father entirely now. 'Why didn't ya tell me you were married to my *sister*? Did none of y'all think to invite me?' Melissa had closed her eyes as if questioning my existence. I didn't answer.

'Where *is* she?' I spat, repeating Joe's question. 'If you've done anything to her, I swear-'

'Oh, please,' Melissa laughed. 'As *if* I'd hurt my own child.' She turned her attention to Joe again, the old man unmoving, the gun in his face ensuring his continued silence. She laughed, a memory popping into her thoughts she hadn't yet shared with us. 'It was *all* so easy, leavin' a trail of blood from your car to the woods. A stroke of genius. I only needed a tiny bit of Megan's blood.'

'What the *hell* did you do?' I was panicking, the idea of Georgina being cut open, something I wasn't ready to hear.

Melissa's glare darkened. 'I cut her hand. Smeared some onto your clothes, extractin' just enough to leave a trail that would point waggin' fingers your way, should the authorities come lookin'.' I had a hard time acknowledging the idea of Georgina being cut into. 'Megan was fine. I told her she'd cut her hand durin' the crash. Gave her some pop. Cleaned the wound. You know how good I am at cleanin' wounds, Josh.' She took a breath, sucking in a lungful of air. 'I was gonna kill you, of course, make it look as if you'd crashed and died as a result. I couldn't have my baby girl thinkin' I'd done somethin' awful to her daddy now could I?'

I swallowed. *Jesus.*

'But it's been fun watchin' you squirm.'

'What have you done with Georgina?'

'Her name is *Megan,* and she's fine. You don't need to go worryin' 'bout her. We've been gettin' to know each other real well.' She rolled her eyes and grinned. It wasn't pleasant. I desperately needed to know where my child was.

'If I can just see her-' I began. Just one last time would be all I could hope for. I needed peace of mind that Melissa was telling the truth. I wasn't anticipating getting out of here alive. Not today.

'You're ruinin' my story, Josh,' Melissa spat, stamping her foot, kicking mine, causing pain to spike through my leg. 'Tommy helped me carry Megan to my truck. Once I knew who she was, I couldn't see anythin' bad happen to her now, could I? I'm not a *psychopath.* I knew you'd come round at some point and I couldn't have someone else findin' you. The first thing you'd ask about was the child. So I took everythin' belongin' to Megan outta the vehicle, includin' anythin' that could link directly back to her.' That explained her missing passport and empty ice cream packaging. Christ, this woman really *was* deranged.

'I setcha car on fire and we drove into the afternoon. It would've been perfect if it hadn't rained, threatenin' to put the damn thing out. Of course, my curiosity got the better of me and I drove back to check you were dead. Imagine my surprise when I saw you staggerin' around, covered in Megan's blood and rantin' about ya missin' child.' Melissa glared at me. 'Tut, tut, Joshua.'

'You *lied* to me.'

'I *helped* you. Where would you be now if it wasn't for me?'

'In a hotel room somewhere. Safe. With my *daughter*.' I wouldn't have a gunshot wound, either. I couldn't dwell on that.

'She's *my* daughter. Let's not forget that.'

'Why did you tell the police I was ranting about ghosts? What were you trying to achieve?' It was a ridiculous thing to recall, more important things I should have been focusing on, too many ghosts already in my head.

Melissa laughed, loudly, remembering her early morning conversation with Bailey outside her old family home. 'Oh my goodness, we've had a real blast over the last few days making you suffer. I betcha now believe that cops around here are all nuts?'

I did. It wasn't ideal. 'So why ghosts?'

'Josh, don'tcha get it? It was *me* who'd seen the ghost. *My child.* I couldn't allow you to keep her. *She's mine!*'

She turned and ran out of the barn, on the verge of tears, obviously not wishing to showcase her savage emotions so openly. Tommy lunged forward, cracking Joe in the jaw with the butt of his gun, knocking him out, leaving me to ponder his next move. Joe fell with a thud beside me. He wasn't moving.

I didn't know if Georgina was okay, what she'd been subjected to, or what *Melissa* had told her. She would have been as upset by the news that this stranger was her mother as I was. I still couldn't believe Anna never told me. I couldn't believe my wife was a *killer*. Such a truth was too painful to acknowledge. I honestly didn't want to think about any of it.

***

A few moments passed before Melissa returned, holding Tommy's shotgun, finding me trying to free myself whilst nudging Joe awake with my foot. It was a pathetic attempt not to die alone in the middle of nowhere, forgotten, discarded. I was done with the woman, tired of relentless games that got us nowhere, anticipating more shit she was incapable of avoiding. I glanced up, not expecting to see Georgina standing next to her. What the *hell?*

'Georgie?' I called out, not convinced she was real. Maybe I was hallucinating, my injuries too traumatic. Maybe I was dead.

'Dad?' my child returned my greeting. She looked pale, thin. She'd been crying.

I turned to Melissa. 'If you've hurt her-'

'You'll do *what*, Josh? You're in no position to call the shots.'

'Are you okay?' I was desperate to know that my trembling twelve-year-old had come out of this in unscathed.

She nodded, seemingly unsure what else to do. I was blinking wildly, unable to accept the impossible vision in front of me was *real*.

Melissa pointed Tommy's gun towards Georgina.

'Should I kill her now, Josh? Bang!' She laughed. The bitch actually laughed. Georgina didn't flinch. Not once.

'No! Please.' *Dear God, not now.* Not after everything I'd been through. I was trembling. I couldn't tell if it was from blood loss or fear. Probably both.

'I've been dyin' to know where is Anna, by the way? Where's my dear sister at?' Melissa was looking around as if suddenly expected her twin to come bursting through the door and give her a hug.

'She's dead.'

'I don't believe you.' She looked confused, her strained brow furrowing, a trembling gun still aimed in the wrong direction.

'I don't care what you believe Meg... *Melissa.*' I didn't want this woman to speak about my wife, this moment neither the time nor the place. My ropes were cutting into me, my body ready to welcome death I ironically no longer wanted.

Joe moved, pulling me painfully back to reality. He was stirring, groaning in pain, his bloodied head matching whatever damaged part of me I was still unable to acknowledge. We both needed medical assistance, my daughter now standing a few feet away, trembling, needing her dad. I wanted to run to her, hold her, tell her she was safe. As it was, she had the same gun pointed to her head that had caused much trouble today already. I wasn't about to make things worse.

Melissa shifted her attention from Georgina to Joe. It was a fleeting action, yet long enough for my intelligent, beautifully *brave* girl to take her chance and race out of the barn, no time to look back or change her mind. Melissa swore loudly, pursing stressed lips together as she turned towards my fleeing girl.

'Run!' I couldn't help yelling. I wanted her to get as far away as she could and never look back. It didn't matter what happened to me.

'She won't get far,' Melissa chided, a laugh escaping her lips that I wanted to slap clean off her smug face. She was still looking at Joe, no doubt wondering why he had an injured head, nothing of Tommy's recent actions registering.

I wondered if she was going to shoot my child and end this thing, but thankfully she allowed Georgina to run into the awaiting fresh air outside. I assumed Tommy would catch up with her soon enough, bringing her back kicking and screaming if necessary. It wasn't a pleasant thought. Joe was coughing, spitting blood across the filthy ground from a split lip and bloodied cheek. He tilted his head, glaring into the face of his demented daughter, his expression unmovable. There were no words exchanged, no look of love or appreciation.

Melissa smiled, turning the gun towards me. I sucked in a lungful of air, the anticipation of being shot dead where I sat. Melissa was grinning, something in her eyes telling me she wasn't living in the same world as the rest of us, a piece of her already broken deep inside, an extremely troubled young woman emerging.

'I expect you're wonderin' 'bout Megan's pa?' Melissa was laughing, her features a contorted collection of purple veins that popped violently from flushed cheeks, eyes that danced with unfounded excitement. I'd wondered about Georgina's dad for several years. It had kept me awake at night. Anna never knew. Seems we'd both kept secrets.

'He was a tourist, Josh. Like *you*.' Melissa took a breath, offering me a wink I didn't appreciate.

'Was he *black?*' I shouldn't have asked, my sarcasm inappropriate.

Melissa grinned. 'He was *attractive.*'

The idea that Melissa found me attractive didn't help. I narrowed my eyes at the wink she offered. Either that, or she'd developed a twitch.

'The guy was just passin' through, nobody special. But when our brief summer fling left me pregnant, that asshole wanted me to abort my baby. Can you imagine?' Melissa was pacing, ignoring me, impatiently recalling a time long passed. 'I tried to reason with him, but he didn't care. Stupid motherfucker. So I killed him.' Melissa closed her eyes, recalling a memory I wished she'd refrained from sharing with me. She was so matter of fact, so cold. 'It wasn't the first time I'd killed someone, wasn't my last, although I'll be the first to admit Emily's death upset me for a long time. She was my *friend*. We grew up together and I loved her.' I swallowed, not daring to interrupt. I already knew how she treated those she *didn't* love.

Joe was fully awake now, muttering, calling his daughter's name, attempting to diffuse an unexploded bomb with dry, ineffective words. Melissa gave her father a blank stare before becoming serious, licking her lips, stroking a pale hand across her sweat-induced hairline. She cocked the gun, forcing me to take a breath and screw my eyes shut in response.

'I only kept you alive so you'd suffer. So you could see what ya did to my family. Now I'm done. Goodbye, Joshua Raymond.' Melissa breathed out slowly. She was *enjoying* this moment.

The silence was deafening. I could never imagine the end of my life looking like this. The gun fired, a blast of smoke filling the air, gunshot pellets peppering the surrounding gloom. I took in a sharp breath, assuming it was my last. I felt nothing. I believed I was dead. A few seconds passed, yet I felt no different, my surroundings unchanged. I was still breathing, still absorbing the hell around me. I opened my eyes to the sight of Melissa drawing a sharp breath of her own. Her hands fell to her sides, the gun falling from her failing grip, its wide tip still smouldering from the shot she'd aimed in the wrong direction. I glanced towards Joe, his shock matching my own, neither of us yet appreciative of what the hell had just happened.

30

Melissa was glaring at me, yet she didn't see me, something in her eyes expressing the pain she'd inflicted onto others. When she opened her mouth, I assumed she wanted to speak, but all that emerged was inky blood that poured from her slackened jaw, shock on her face I wasn't expecting. A thin line of red appeared around her neck, like a choker chain, faint at first then thick, fresh blood pumping violently from several severed arteries. I shuffled backwards, getting nowhere, Joe equally recoiling in dismay. *What the hell?*

She took a short breath and dropped to her knees, her face blank and expressionless. I wasn't convinced what I was seeing as her entire head slid from her neck, bouncing aggressively, rolling towards my feet, her body slumping to the dirt in response. I glanced up. Georgina was standing behind her in the darkness, a glistening farm scythe in her hands, a calculated look on her face. I could see nothing in my child's eyes to tell me she was disturbed by this event, nothing to confirm she wasn't now as troubled as me.

I wavered, this moment surreal. I could no longer see my innocent twelve-year-old girl standing in front of me. Something had changed. I couldn't understand what. Yet her features had taken on a new façade, and she now looked – if I wasn't mistaken – like Melissa. I always believed I could see Anna in my daughter. Now I saw only a killer. In the brief moment it had taken my child to murder the biological mother she didn't know she had, I witnessed what Anna probably feared her entire young life. The *real* reason she fled, the reason she'd kept her own terrible secrets for so long. She was terrified Georgina would turn out just like *them*—that the apple never really falls far from the tree.

Georgina lowered her gaze, her breathing calm, almost demonic. I wanted to assume it was because the poor kid had been subjected to God knows what kind of hell over the last few days, yet something in her face told me this was much more. I glanced towards Joe, unable to bring myself to look at the severed head on the ground, its bloodied mouth agape, swollen tongue lolling to one side, eyes wide with surprise. I have no idea how long Georgina stood in the middle of that barn, staring into space, her vacant expression matching the unexpected corpse of her dead mother at our feet. The only consolation I took from this was that Melissa would never hurt another soul again. It was all I had left to cling to.

'Georgie?' I called out, hoping to reach my seriously damaged kid, hoping to finally end this impossible moment and bring our lives back to a much-needed reality. Today wasn't something we'd get over quickly, if ever. Georgina blinked, offering a thin smile I couldn't read. I had no idea where Tommy or Mike had gone. I wasn't sure I wanted to know. Joe was still disorientated, and I was still bleeding. To make matters worse, I was a wanted man, my child now subjected to a murderous deed of her own. This was not over. Not even close.

'Are you okay?' she asked. Her voice was calm. Too calm.

I swallowed, unsure how to respond. *God no.* I would never be okay again. I nodded, nothing else to do. 'You?'

Georgina lowered her head into a terse nod, pressing a steady index finger over her mouth to shush me. I couldn't get up, couldn't move, my body still bound to a wooden post, my mind in more pain than any physical injury could inflict. Georgina knelt at my side, calmly cutting my limbs free from unforgiving shackles with the penknife I once had in my possession, uncuffing my wrists with the key Mike had earlier placed in his trouser pocket. I wasn't convinced I wanted to know why she was covered in so much blood. She glanced at me impassively, nothing of my twelve-year-old remaining.

'I'm sorry I wasn't able to get you out of the basement, Dad.' Georgina was speaking, yet the poor kid no longer sounded like my sulky pre-teen. Something had changed. I couldn't tell what.

'The basement?' How did she know about that? Joe was sitting upright, staring at his granddaughter as if he couldn't believe she was here, in the flesh, alive.

She removed my ropes and handcuffs, my wrists all the better for it, my leg painfully sore. At least the bleeding had slowed to an irritating trickle, stemmed thankfully by Joe's quick thinking.

'I only had enough time to unlock the door and leave you some food and a key to the kitchen,' she confirmed.

'*You* helped me?' I couldn't believe what I was hearing. It couldn't be true. Why didn't she wake me up and confirm she was okay? Put me out of my misery? How had *she* escaped? I had a horrible realisation Georgina hadn't been held prisoner at all, merely a guest in her mother's house, remaining there under misinformed obligation. It wasn't ideal. Had she been there the whole time? Was she there when I was sitting drinking coffee in the kitchen, tied to a bed in a spare room and jumping from an upstairs window? Was she in the room with the ticking clock?

There was nothing on Georgina's face that expressed

how she was feeling, her eyes blank, inscrutable. 'Why *wouldn't* I help you? You're my dad.'

'But why didn't you wake me up and show yourself?' Surely she would have known how desperate I was.

'I tried. But you were unconscious and *they* were never far away. I did what I could.'

I thought about my child's failed attempts to shake me awake, the very metaphor I'd recently created now wholly coming back to laugh at me.

'Why didn't you run?'

'They told me they'd *kill* you.'

For the first time, I understood the change in my child. She'd feared for her life, feared for mine. I glanced at Joe, the last few days taking a toll I never expected to experience. 'Did they treat you okay?' I was terrified of the answer.

Georgina shrugged, nothing she wanted to tell me about that. 'Is it true she's my…?' She was staring at Melissa's severed head, unable to finish her sentence. I hated the thought of what that woman might have told her. More lies, more pain.

'There's probably plenty you wanna know,' Joe pitched in then, a trickle of glossy blood lining his cheekbone. He probably had a headache. 'But there'll be time for that later.' He gave his granddaughter a warm smile, his ageing eyes crinkling with a sincere love I hadn't seen for a while. Not since Anna…

I stared at my child, so much blood splattered across her young features, her eyes so cold. An icy conclusion hit me. *She wasn't sorry.* It seemed overnight Melissa had created a monster. Or maybe the monster was always there, waiting to be discovered, hiding in the shadows. Was *that* why Anna never spoke of her family? Was she afraid Georgina would become just like her mother, setting the whole sorry saga in motion again? After all, do we become our parents, in the end? I took a breath. Georgina was a killer too, as was I, both of us becoming the very people we assumed impossible, this place taking everything from us in a few terrifying days.

***

We emerged from the barn to a starlit sky and an uncertain future, this location matching my mood with shadowy outbuildings dotting an overgrown void. My wounds weren't life-threatening, thankfully, the shotgun pellets penetrating my upper thigh, most of the cuts superficial. No organs were injured and no major blood vessels had been damaged. I was glad Tommy was a terrible shot, my blood loss mostly due to adrenaline and stress.

He was lying on a patch of grass, his body cut clean in half, the last remaining flies of the day hovering over his corpse. Some feet away lay the dismembered torso of Mike, his police uniform the only identifiable marker, his head no longer attached. I didn't dare look at Georgina, didn't want to ask what she'd done with it. There was no expression on her face, nothing of value spoken about the carnage she'd created, struggling to relinquish the grip on the scythe she was holding until Joe prised the thing from her grasp. Shock, he said. Nothing more.

Two vehicles lay discarded to the side of the barn, covered with branches and leaves in a bumbled attempt to disguise their existence. It was difficult to discern in the gloom, but I knew they were my rental cars. Melissa had planned everything in detail, at my ultimate expense, everything occurring *now* remaining forever out of my hands.

'I never thought today would turn out like this,' Joe coughed, attempting a joke none of us thought funny. His murderous daughters were dead, twins I never knew existed, his granddaughter now catching up where they'd left off. Georgina was wiping his head with her sleeve, her grandfather a confirmed part of her life and the only real family she had left. She would want to get to know him, of course, to better understand her past. He looked into her eyes, the hazy moonlight allowing much-needed reflection. 'My God, you look just like your mother,' he concluded.

I wasn't sure what hurt the most. The fact a serial killer was my child's biological mother, or that Anna had lied to me for so long. The very thought left me cold. I didn't want to be reminded of Melissa, yet here I was, Georgina a direct connection to her—a child I'd raised for over ten years, called her mine, assumed she was Anna's. To now discover she didn't belong to my wife at all wasn't something I could process easily. It didn't matter. I loved this girl with every breath I had. I would always protect her. Exactly how Joe had continued to do to this very day.

'What about *them?*' I motioned my throbbing head towards the carnage behind us. Too many bodies littered this place.

Joe stared towards a barn that contained what was left of his child. I didn't want to know what he was thinking. 'This place has been abandoned for years, Josh. Nobody's gonna find 'em out here. Why don't you head back to my truck? I'll take care of it.' Joe glanced behind briefly before handing me a set of keys, nothing on his face expressing his pain, his plan. I didn't dare ask how many bodies might still be here, Mac and Morag's bones left to decompose alone.

Unable to conclude anything good about that, Georgina and I headed to Joe's truck, arm in arm, nothing of this trip intact. Although I couldn't believe she was here, alive and well, she was guilty of murder. It wasn't an accident, wasn't self-defence, and she couldn't claim momentary madness. I wasn't worried about two dead men who probably had families of their own to grieve them, my child merely doing what was needed to protect us. Yet, Blake was still dead,

Troy too, the police assuming I was to blame for both. All this was on *me.* I'd unwittingly caused the death of a young boy, my guilt just as strong.

When Joe returned, his hands were shaking, his face set in stone. It matched my child's unreachable features. He didn't look at me, today's actions changing us all in some way.

'Have you seen Blake?' he asked, glancing around as if remembering his friend's absence, assuming he'd be hot on our trail by now. 'I can't get him mixed up in this. He's a good man, Josh. Deserves better. When I see him, I'll explain everythin'.'

How could I confirm where Blake was, his crumpled body no doubt still on a police cell floor?

'Melissa killed him, Joe. I'm sorry.' I couldn't bring myself to look at him now either, yet I absorbed the deep intake of breath. He didn't ask what had happened and I didn't tell him.

'I should never have gotten him posted here.' Joe was crying.

'No. You shouldn't.' Yet, if he hadn't helped me, I'd still be in jail. I'd probably be dead. As it was, I was now the number one suspect in *two* deaths, Melissa's secrets retained. As far as the police were concerned, I'd committed a second murder, nothing but a dangerous escapee with an unhinged mind, my airport escapades ensuring this impossible situation was allowed to happen in the first place. I didn't need that image in my head. It wasn't comforting, wasn't helpful. I half-closed my eyes, trying not to remember what I'd done to poor Troy. Was I any better than Melissa? My *wife?*

'What happened to your brother, Joe?' I didn't even know the guy's name, Anna's uncle yet another elusive character in a life I would never know.

'How did you-'

'One of Jackdoor's articles.'

Joe sighed. 'I don't know.'

'Joe?'

'I honestly don't!' He looked over his shoulder. 'And I never dared question Mel 'bout it. I guess I didn't wanna admit she might've been involved. Ben was an astute man. He'd raised some unwanted questions 'bout his nieces mental health, probed where he shouldn't.'

'Was he ever found?'

Joe shook his head. He still held many secrets he hadn't shared with me. Probably never would. I could understand that. I had one, too. He genuinely looked broken. He stared into space, tears forming. 'Melissa was part of a circle I never wanted to acknowledge. I hid away in my old fishin' cabin, tried to forget, tried to ignore what I didn't wanna see.' He sighed. 'Deputy William McDonald either turns a blind eye or a profit from the secrets this place hides. We were friends once, you know.' Joe attempted a smile that missed its mark. I understood why the two men no longer saw each other and why Joe didn't tell him he now lived so isolated out in his cabin. 'Some of his officers are directly involved, folk like Mike and Bob Bailey. Others get paid well to keep their mouths *shut*.' I thought about Mike's dead body, Bailey's obvious hatred and the continued silence of James Montgomery.

'Why?' I was unsure I wanted the answer. Of all the things I'd heard today, this was the most disturbing, the non-compliant actions of Deputy Chief McDonald and his team wholly terrifying.

'Because Josh, there are places on earth that just don't make any goddamn sense and some folk are best steerin' clear of.' He sighed. 'I guess, in the end, it got Blake killed, too.' For all Joe's faults, he wasn't responsible for any deaths, innocent in every murder committed since 1993, his brother included. I'm sure that is how he slept at night, no other option available, no other thoughts to contemplate an otherwise impossible situation.

We drove back to his cabin in silence, nothing more to say. Aside from a few corrupt police officers, no one knew his daughter was responsible for killing dozens of tourists and children, the last twenty-seven years set to haunt us *all* now forever. Joe patched my wounds whilst chatting with Georgina, just happy to be a grandpa again. Despite everything, Anna would have been happy about that, the secrets we must now keep, designed to ensure our continued freedom. None of us spoke of what happened in the barn. We probably never would.

Joe packed as much as he could into an old rucksack, making sure we had warm clothes and food, our aim to head north into Canada. He placed a photograph on top of an old blanket, ready to pack that, too. I picked it up, scanning its contents. The image was of four people. Two young girls, a small man, and a woman who looked like Anna – only older. They were standing at the edge of a long narrow driveway. Behind them was a freshly whitewashed sign pinned to an oak tree, the words "Everley Residence" painted onto its surface. It was the house Anna had once called home, her family home, many childhood stories overshadowing the very place that would haunt me now forever. I would never look back on our life together with fondness—most of it lies anyway, it seemed.

I considered calling my dad but thought better of it. I wouldn't be going back to my old life any time soon and he'd find out about my crimes and hate me all that more. He'd believe every word. I didn't want his persecution. We barely knew Joe, yet he was ready to drive us into the night, ready to do far more for us than my own father ever had. Georgina climbed into Joe's back seat, staring out of the truck window, her mobile phone already in her hands, distracting her damaged mind from *everything*.

She glanced my way, offering a smile showing no real emotion before leaning forward and handing me something. I never expected to see my photographs again, yet here they were, reunited with an owner I was no longer convinced worthy. My wedding photo. Anna and Georgina at the park. Georgina as a baby. I'd missed them so much. Now they just seemed like lies. I swallowed, unable to ask how my daughter had retrieved them. I'm not sure I wanted to know.

'Georgie-' I motioned to speak, yet changed my mind, too much left unspoken between us. I wondered if we could ever go back to how things were.

Georgina shook her head, her face a cold, unreadable stare. 'It's okay,' she muttered. 'From now on, Pa, y'can call me Megan.' She had adopted Melissa's twang. It gave me a shudder.

I couldn't respond, nothing I could have said right then able to gauge such a statement. Instead, I stared out of the window too, ready it seemed, to say goodbye to far more than six months of hell. We had a new secret we must now keep, Joe's past coming back to haunt him, Georgina's only just beginning. It taunted every choice they ever made, new choices we would make together.

We couldn't stay in Darkridge Hollow, of course. I was a wanted man, a fugitive, no one left alive who could prove I hadn't killed poor Blake Harrison, young Troy's death the result of nothing more than a tragic accident, a fall gone wrong. The police were heavily involved with Melissa's demonic rituals, one of which was now also dead. I couldn't assume she wouldn't have slept with them all, if she could, offering favours they couldn't refuse, religion and desperation an overriding factor in the terrible choices they made. They would lynch me to keep their secrets, making me the scapegoat of their unthinkable crimes.

I took a breath. I was lost again, forever and always the

perpetual outsider. I didn't know where that left us, yet with Melissa gone, maybe Darkridge Hollow could rebuild a lost reputation and find closure to a suffering it had endured for so long. We passed those cornfields, old pain leaving a mark no one could change. It didn't matter. Darkridge Hollow could finally heal now. It deserved it.

Acknowledgements

This novel was made possible because of the support from Twitter and all those Ohioans who helped bring reality into these pages. Thank you for your feedback regarding what it's like to live in Ohio, USA, including local dialect and phrases that have ensure my characters feel authentic.

Thank you, as always, to my incredible husband for his unwavering support, and to SRL Publishing, who see beyond traditional story telling methods, searching for stories that delve deep into the human psyche and beyond.

SRL Publishing don't just publish books, we also do our best in keeping this world sustainable. In the UK alone, over 77 million books are destroyed each year, unsold and unread, due to overproduction and bigger profit margins.

Our business model is inherently sustainable by only printing what we sell. While this means our cost price is much higher, it means we have minimum waste and zero returns. We made a public promise in 2020 to never overprint our books for the sake of profit.

We give back to our planet by calculating the number of trees used for our products so we can then replace them. We also calculate our carbon emissions and support projects which reduce C02. These same projects also support the United Nations Sustainable Development Goals.

The way we operate means we knowingly waive our profit margins for the sake of the environment. Every book sold via the SRL website plants at least one tree.

To find out more, please visit
www.srlpublishing.co.uk/responsibility